PETERMAN

Edward Barham

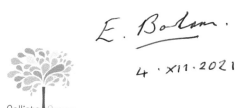

To Ernie.

May new horizons ever beckon.

E. Barham.

4 · XII · 2021

Callisto Green

Peterman
A Callisto Green Book

ISBN 978-1-909985-31-5

First published in 2018 by
Callisto Green Ltd.
4 Caprice Close
Swindon
SN5 5TB

www.callistogreen.com

Callisto Green

A copy of the CIP entry for this book is available
from the British Library.

For Ursula

Chapter 1

The dark, still, lonely things that disturb in nature need only a little courage to understand them. An old man in Africa told me this when I was five years old, and because I believed him I grew into a child who could walk by himself in woods that were trackless, lonely and still. It was his parting gift to me before I was sent away, and he added something else: that whenever I found myself alone in the mild English woods I would rule over them whether I knew it or not. All I had to remember was that every tree and creature saw us as hunters, and had done since the flight out of Eden.

In the ten years that followed, through my unbroken exile, I wandered when I could in the solitary, silent places until I felt more at home there, with their faint echo of the savannah, than I do here in this isolated school with its taint of old tile polish and disinfectant.

Now I'm lying awake, still emerging from a dream, and having a bit of a job drifting back into sleep. I sleep pretty well normally, so it takes a dream of the troubling kind to find me like this. When it happens I just get up, go to the landing and sit by the window for a while until I feel right again. We're not supposed to do it; there's no rule or anything, but they don't get on with too much waking in the dark reaches of the night.

The window's open a crack. I ease it up and cold air spills in around me along with some moonlight. Outside it's dead calm so all I can hear are the little snufflings and squeaks of a roomful of dreamers. You can see the woods from here, a ragged band of dark whose every path and hollow I can navigate blindfold.

When I first came here and needed to be on my own I would disappear in my free time and roam the sun-dappled paths until I knew they were mine. As I got older it was the dark of the forest that called me to evade my keepers and venture where it seemed that no one else dared.

In summer after Lights Out, in the drier spells, I'd be off, out of the window, through the wicket gates, walking where I wouldn't leave tracks in the dew, ranging alone under the moon, coming back smelling of the night well before sunrise. The few who knew about it kept my secret safe. In winter the going and coming needed more thought, more nodding at risk like an old friend.

Until tonight. Tonight I feel the friendship isn't what it was. There's a hint of warning in that wall of shadow beyond the fields. You thought you knew us, it whispers; but in truth no one does. We can always turn you back into a stranger, leave you to discover the difference between unreasoning fear and reasoning fear, and see which you prefer.

And that's why, this time, sitting out my worries by the window hasn't done the trick. Those words, that choice, just came into my head, and it's not the way I think or speak. I know it's because of the dream. But dreams are just night nonsense.

There's a mist forming in the woods, white and silent, rising up from its own bed in the ditches and streams and drifting across the meadow. Good; good because it's real and I need some reality right now. I lean out and feel it turning to dew on my warm back.

In my sleep I saw the old black servant again. He came towards me in a moonlit forest clearing where everything was flat silver and his face was without expression. What I told you when you were very small — he said to me in a voice that wasn't his — was perfectly true. It just isn't the whole story. There are things beyond nature, and familiar courage won't be enough; nor will the desire to understand; nor will you need to look for them. That's all.

And I was left there, looking around me, calling out: then show yourselves! Bravado comes easily in dreams, but my voice was choked and my muscles cold and stiff. I'm not happy when I leave the window at last and climb back into bed.

When dawn breaks the mist encloses everything. All day and through the following night it holds the countryside in a clean embrace.

But far away in the big city it finds bad company and hangs around. Sulphur and soot and still air; a million chimneys and acres of railways and factories. It deadens sound and confounds people as they shuffle in slow motion along the bottom of an acid sea. They slip under buses that are feeling their way; they fall into canals and wander like orphans in the open spaces. The smog seeps into front parlours and kitchens and hospital wards, gripping babies in their cots and coughing old people to death. Theatres and music halls close because you can't see the stage. The lights in shop windows merge into colours that are sickly and make passers-by grotesque. A couple of days of this in these years just after the war can kill you. A bad one leaves more dead and dying than an air raid.

Out here in the Oxfordshire countryside I'm part of another world. On the next night, the one after my dream, I've decided – after mustering some not very convincing excuses – to decline the invitation of the cold, velvety whiteness that envelops our remote community. Before long it'll be Lights Out and, I hope, some undisturbed rest. Only three weeks now to the Christmas vac.

Meanwhile in London the smog just gets worse and worse; and a strange, unseen transformation begins. In the dark corners men start to twitch with villainy. Their little red eyes shine in the gloom. On their forest a different dusk begins to fall.

Through these streets walks a figure who seems to know his way with the assurance of a blind man; with the air of someone who took note of his surroundings in better times. He wears a raincoat and a bowler hat and he moves empty-handed against the hushed crowd, going towards his work instead of feeling for the Underground and home. Hayden McFee is a sergeant of detectives and he keeps the hours, and more than the hours, that criminals keep. He disappears down a side alley, enters the door of a nondescript building left intact but empty since the war, and begins to climb a staircase. Halfway up, his brisk pace slows to a stop.

Something has made him glance back, to where the indistinct light falls on a tongue of smog that has edged in behind him and spread over the floor. The first few steps vanish into it and an eddy of draught gives it the viscous look of a grey, dirty river on a falling tide. And just for a second, a parody of a hand spirals slowly out of the flood, like the stumpy, rotted fist of a long-drowned man. McFee stares at it; waits for the apparition to resolve once more into the smog filling the tiny hallway. He knows that his mind has seen more than his eyes have, and an old familiar weariness comes over him. More slowly, he continues up the stairs.

Behind a warped, peeling door is a grubby room in which another man sits at a trestle table with a telephone and some papers neatly squared up to the corners.

Big Ben, a long way off, booms out the hour. The sound struggles through the fog and swells through the missing pane of a sash window.

"All set?" says McFee.

Almost as though his presence has caused it, the leaden murmur from outside is replaced by the ticking of a clock and the hiss of a gas fire.

Detective-Constable John Davies can tell it's going to be a night of few words.

"Yes, ready," he says. "Fancy a brew?"

"Why not?" McFee takes off his hat and coat.

Davies fires up the Primus stove. The room is running on car batteries and bottled gas and there's a blackout blind at the window because this building is supposed to be empty. With its peeling wallpaper and constant reek of damp it's become a squatter's bivouac where the squatters are the Law; the forward HQ for a routine stunt that's just one more sign of the times.

A bunch of amateurs – deserters, most likely – have been emptying lorries and flogging the stuff on the black market. They haven't been adopted yet by one of the serious gangster operators because McFee has done that himself. This overweight, messy plain-clothes copper has infiltrated their ranks and is now their shadowy, unseen Mister Big; and tonight it's all going to wind up here, downstairs. Davies, whose posh Welsh accent hasn't given him away in this end of London, was the driver who got talking carelessly to the wide boys, parked up to get a cup of tea and came back to a cleaned-out truck and a fiver on the seat. It's the kind of undercover stuff he doesn't really like.

"One day," he says, just to make conversation, "we'll crack cases using electronic brains, and send robots in helicopters to nick villains using X-ray telescopes."

"You reckon?" from behind a cloud of blue pipesmoke. "Well, till then we'll keep running 'em down with dirty tricks and sending the boys in blue to feel their collars." McFee closes his eyes and muses a bit. "Of course the villains'll have robots too by then; might even be robots. Then we can all sit back and let 'em just get on with it." He opens his eyes suddenly. "You've heard of the Black Widow spider?"

"Yes. Never seen one."

"Well, no; you'd have to go abroad. How do they nab their prey?"

"A web, I suppose."

"Spot on. Ugliest web you ever saw; a mess filled with dead rubbish and leaves and whatnot. Just like the rest of the world, then. And that's why her victims just walk right in. Mess, my lad. Blend in. If you want shining armour try another shop."

John Davies puts on a weak smile and places a mug of tea among the layers of papers on McFee's table. The mug is badly chipped. It seems it got that way when it fell off his filing cabinet at the Yard. That was eight years ago but it still goes everywhere with him. It's one of three things Davies knows about his boss; the other two being that he made a name in the big manhunts of the Thirties and the even bigger spyhunts during the War, and that he's still only a Sergeant, although he can't get a word of sense out of anyone about why that is. He often wonders himself about McFee; sometimes even toying with the idea that he's an imposter, like one of those men who put on a white coat and wander round hospitals pretending to be doctors. Anyway, he's back now after making the Big Call to the wide boys from a phone box, because the phone on Davies's table is only wired for receiving. He's waiting for two more calls here: one to say the force are on their way to lie in wait; the second to report that the toerags are on their way too, to stash the stuff downstairs like Mister Big told them. And it's all got to work first time, before the real underworld gets involved. It's all about getting a few spivs off the street, not starting a turf war.

For now, just the clock ticking and the hiss of the gas fire. That and the air of complete unconcern that McFee seems to be showing about the whole business.

There's a thump, thump on the stairs and in barges D.C. Hartington. Third leg on the team and loud and late as usual. He's dressed like his own idea of a wrong'un, almost comical given he usually dresses like a spiv anyway. His job is to guide the villains and their van around to the back and into the arms of the law.

Nobody likes him much. "Well, well! Here we sit like bloody crows in the wilderness!" he says, scraping a chair round and sitting astride it like a G-man. Matey familiarity, which he hasn't earned.

"Get him a tea," says McFee, and closes his eyes, teeth still clamped round his pipe.

John Davies has to clean out the vent on the Primus before he can get it going again, and as he fiddles they hear yet more footsteps on the stairs. This time it's Phil Waterman, Detective Sergeant and probably McFee's closest colleague. His trenchcoat and hat are filmed with smog. He's obviously been hurrying.

Davies turns and can't hold back a frown. What's Waterman doing here? He's not on this case and it's a bit risky having too much going on in what's supposed to be a derelict neck of the woods. Has something gone wrong? He's got a leather pouch under his arm. And he looks worried.

"What's the game, Phil?" says McFee, pretty calmly considering this is a bit of an intrusion. Waterman, still breathing hard, takes out a folder and places it on the raftering chaos of McFee's table. He shoots a look at the other two and John Davies suddenly realises that he and

Hartington aren't wanted. But it's too late now. Anyway, in a team nothing ought to be that private.

"For your eyes, Hay. Had to foot it here smartish. Quickest way in this. Couldn't use your line, obviously." He hesitates for a second.

"It's the prints from Sowerby's. The safe."

McFee doesn't glance at the papers, but at Waterman. "Take a breather, Phil. It's a bad night."

"Could be I know that," says Waterman. "Look, I'm meant to be on a bloody train in twenty minutes; and I'm not sending you this in the post. You'll see why." His voice takes on an impatient edge. "Hay, you need to look at these prints."

"Mm. Sowerby's. You needn't have. I only expressed a mild interest. Nothing taken, was there?" McFee's eyes wander over the enlargements. "Very clear, these. Your real peterman doesn't leave prints, never mind this. This bloke's an amateur."

Phil Waterman's voice has turned a little dry. "Afraid not, Hay. They don't belong to anyone."

"So it's a new boy? Hard luck. This many, this clear; bloody Christmas."

McFee is peering intently at the prints now, as if trying to divine something in them. Waterman darts another look at Davies and Hartington. He clears his throat.

"I had a feeling – don't ask me what – so I did a bit of digging. Not in the current records. I looked where no one in their right mind would look. Luckily it was me who did." He waits for McFee to say something, but he doesn't.

"It's Smallwood, Hay."

McFee takes the pipe from his mouth; looks up.

"That's ridiculous."

But he looks suddenly tired.

"Ridiculous," he says again. Waterman's expression is saying: there is no mistake.

John Davies sees that his boss's hands are gripping the prints and trembling. McFee stares at him. "Sit down, will you?" he says.

He puts his pipe on the desk. It has gone out. The room has gone quiet once more; gas fire hissing and clock ticking in the silence. That and McFee's breathing as he begins to speak, slowly, like a country bobby giving evidence in court.

"These prints that Phil just brought in are clearly those of Albert Gordon Smallwood. They were found fresh this morning all over a botched job at Sowerby's fur warehouse in Mitre Street, down in Whitechapel."

He pauses.

"Albert Smallwood was the finest peterman I ever met. An artist. He died of consumption in Pentonville prison hospital on today's date, November 27th."

A catch; an atom of time.

"Nineteen thirty-three. Exactly fourteen years ago."

Chapter 2

The train's slowing and I'm alive and floating. Everything fills me with the freedom of a first morning; delivered from the past; each moment filled only with time to come. Five minutes to one, Day One. I pull my head in out of the cold and smoke and stand beneath the luggage rack alone in my compartment. A backwards jolt, suitcase down and on the seat, steam hissing, no sound of doors thumping shut. Just me, but I'm in no hurry. Each time you do this you make it new by tasting everything. I'm in slow motion.

This branch line journey in a single carriage pulled by an old saddle-tank is my Orient Express. I've seen everything before but I still want to see out of both sides at once. The train strolls along the embankments, taking little bridges by surprise, then plunges into dark cuttings where you wait for the track to end in undergrowth. We pass lonely houses and stop at country halts with odd names where I lean out of the window and – every time I do it – breathe the air of a strange new country.

And all too soon we pull into Inglefield and the restrained excitement grows with the slowing of the train.

Inglefield. Two platforms, crossing, signal box. I'd give a lot to be the signal man for just one evening; to light my lamps, pull those levers and turn that great wheel to swing open the gates; the ding-ding of the telegraph, the thunk of the signal arm and the world beyond framed in the latticed footbridge; the track growing smaller until it's swallowed up, flanked by great gloomy trees as old as churches.

A few steps to say thanks to the driver and fireman. The locomotive subsides in a cloud of steam as I turn away. Here and there frost still coats the platform. I say hallo to the porter, pick up my case and walk through the ticket office to the yard. This is always where it really starts. Adventure, freedom. Refuge.

There's no one to meet me. Maybe they're late. My eyes roam round the gravelled space that is the centre of Inglefield where, in total silence, six cottages make a ring with Morpeth's General Store and the Laughing Angler Hotel. This winter high noon the whitewashed inn sits quiet as ever; under its creepered verandah the same delivery bike and ginger cat. The place is deserted. My breath clouds round me. Far off, rooks begin cawing in the high trees. The engine gives a quick toot and steams out of the station. I listen as it shuffles away down the line and sniff the coal smoke as it descends on everything. When the sound has died I turn to go and sit by the fire in the waiting room.

"Master Clement?" A voice – not English – comes out of nowhere. I stop. There's a short, portly man in a duffel coat and felt hat. I've never seen him before.

"Yes?" I'm on my guard. "My uncle will have sent someone. He's expecting me."

"He has sent me. This way, please?"

"My uncle has a car," I say. There's no car that I can see.

The man walks towards the coal yard and wheels out a rough-looking motorbike and sidecar. "Please sit in and hold case before you," he says, and kicks the pile of machinery into life. The rest is noise. We charge out of Inglefield in a cloud of exhaust. Out on the open road he lets her go. My nose and ears begin to burn with cold and my eyes water.

The portly man hunches over the handlebars, face hidden behind scarf and goggles. His hat brim flaps up as he goes faster and faster, and I get colder and colder. At last I see the final straight coming, close my eyes and only open them as he crashes down through the gears and slews left. The gate pillars and lodge house of Inglefield Place rush by at a strange angle, and he's puttering innocently down the long dark drive with deep plantations and abandoned glasshouses on either side.

I'm on the edge of frostbite. This isn't the usual welcome but here I am; home. Or as near to home as I've had for the last nine years. Our machine makes a half-circuit of the box tree and shudders to a halt. We wait while the engine bangs, spasms, tries to start again by itself and finally dies. Its place is taken by a huge stillness. Not a twig moves. Only the rooks clattering, a county away.

"Thank you," I try to say, but my lips are numb. The engine pings in the cold.

"I show you in. Your uncle is here." He takes the case and we pass into the hall.

My uncle is Doctor Jackson Armitage. Not really an uncle but he's family and he's a real doctor who stopped practising when he inherited Inglefield Place. I've never asked how he makes his money; never been curious. Rumour has it he writes on medical subjects in obscure publications. Possibly; I just don't know. When I was small I saw his name on the wash basins and cisterns round the house along with a Mr Shanks. So I called him Shanks. It was easier and sounded better because he was tall and spindly. Adults' nicknames are the satire of children. With him it's as far as I dare and there's no glory in going further. I risk everything by offending him.

"Had lunch?"

The man himself ducks out under the study door. "No sir," I say. "Hallo, Uncle."

He hasn't seen me for over four months, but that's the standard welcome.

"Good. Alphonse here will fix you up. See you later, Clement."

In the kitchen my ears and nose and lips rejoin my face. This reunion is celebrated with a plate of stew prepared by Ludmilla, who is Mrs Alphonse. The stew's fine but I'm not. Since I started coming to Inglefield, Shanks's manservant and cook have been a couple called Raymond and Victoria. They looked after me like the child they never had and now they're obviously not here. And I've known nothing about it.

It's a big thing, really big; and it's thrown me almost before I've set foot in the place. Alphonse and Ludmilla sit down, not exactly watching me.

"Are you filling in for Ray and Vicky?"

They look at each other. Ludmilla says, "Your uncle, he not tell you?"

"Tell me what?" It's a bit early in our acquaintance to inform them that he hardly ever tells me anything, or that it doesn't bother me; usually.

"They not here anymore. We here now."

"So they're not on holiday?"

Alphonse looks as puzzled as I feel. "They give notice. Soon after you go in summer. So we come. Is not to worry."

Really? Not even a letter. I'll have to ask Shanks, but I'll need to pick my moment because there's an odd feel to this.

"Are you French?"

Ludmilla leans back and slaps the air. "No! We are Lithuanian!"

"Right." Lithuania. Russia. The Baltic. She goes on, more quietly. "Russians come to our country nineteen-forty. We decided, must go away. My husband was dispatch rider in army." She grasps imaginary handlebars and swivels her wrists. "Voom! Voom! You know, eh? He became deserter and we come to England after many, many troubles."

I'm ready to be impressed, but Ludmilla falls silent. They both get up and she starts to prepare a tray. Alphonse puts on a white jacket and takes the tray out. It's laid for two.

Ludmilla looks at me. She has a round face like I used to see under headscarves in Eastern Front newsreels. "Doctor has visitor," she whispers. "No, two visitors. One old man, one girl, same age like you."

"Did they come together?"

"No. Girl arrive early today in taxi. Old man, one hour, in taxi. Not to disturb."

"Do you think they are together, though?"

"All we know is not to disturb."

Right. Got that. I'll stay here where it's warm.

A girl my age. If I'm lucky I might get to meet her. Sounds like good news but it doesn't cure the growing sense of oddness.

Everything's different. Not completely different, just skewed a bit, like pictures hanging crooked; enough to make you have to line up your thoughts.

"Do you like it here, Ludmilla?"

"Yes. Very nice. Very peaceful." She doesn't look up as she stirs something on the range.

Warm smells mingle with the aroma of scrubbed woodwork and creamery bowls. She starts humming a discordant tune that sounds like something from deep forests where wolves roam. Suddenly she says, still not looking, "My husband, he takes your bag to your room. Not to worry. Not worry, eh?" Then the humming again. I look through the diamond panes at the still branches outside. Other visitors. Shanks hasn't mentioned anyone in his telegrams, but then he wouldn't, not if he can neglect bigger stuff like this. Maybe he's started practising again. None of my business then. I stay at the kitchen table and read a copy of *North Oxfordshire Archaeological Notes: Summer 1938*, that's lying around. It uses up an hour or more before I let myself back into the present.

So much going on beneath our feet.

Time hangs heavy and my thoughts have holes right through them.

I get up and go out into the cold. A walk round the grounds might make me feel less strange, less of a stranger. The world's changed since I stepped off the train.

Chapter 3

The air has grown colder, more still. The overcast sky has gone from white to grey and suggests the short day's closure. Behind it the sun is sinking into the branches of the birch spinney opposite the house. My jacket and scarf keep me comfortable but the cold penetrates my shoes and makes me need to walk. I turn left, left again and pass under an archway of ivy into the long, terraced sunken garden, which looks south and east across the water meadows. A flagged path runs the length of this garden, dodges round a fountain halfway along and ends at a summerhouse. The fountain is silent. On the north side looms the house with its twisty Tudor chimneys that make it look taller than it really is.

The terraces are without colour. Harshly pruned shrubs stick out of drifts of dead leaves. The distant cawing of rooks is crackly and incessant. The countryside's a graveyard without burial, the ground strewn with the skeletons and desiccated corpses of warmer days. Nothing moves or feeds or drinks in this pit of the year; there are only things that skulk and suck and scavenge. Doctor Armitage rarely talked to me much when I was younger, but he would try to reassure me when he caught me looking around at scenes like this. There's a beauty of apprehension in this dead time, he'd say: a call to optimism, of better things coming. I generally had no idea what he was talking about because to him the few children he met were just another audience. But I get it now. Except that right at this moment I don't feel it. That dream I had a month ago taps me on the shoulder and points to all this and says: there's more here. Much more.

Hands in pockets, I walk a few steps, then slow. There's a shape ahead, midway between the fountain and the summerhouse. As I approach, the details separate.

A girl. A girl in a black coat with the collar up, a white beret on the back of her head, white stockings and little boots. She sits slouched, legs straight out, on the garden seat. I become soundless and stand behind the fountain. The girl's blonde hair is short and fringed, her eyes half-shut. I step forward.

"Hallo."

There's warmth in my voice and a cloud of breath swirls slowly over my shoulder. She looks up. It's a cool look, and she sweeps her fringe off her brow with a gloveless hand. Her eyes narrow slightly and I smile not because she's pretty but because she isn't plain or ugly. An alert, intelligent face; and Ludmilla seems to have been right about her age.

"Hallo," she says.

"I guess you're Uncle's visitor. I'm Clement. Pleased to meet you. I say that with feeling. Welcome to Inglefield."

"Do you live here?"

"Sort of. I spend all my holidays here. It's like home."

"Did you say Clement?"

"I'm sorry. Garner, Clement Garner." I pull my glove off and hold out my hand. She eyes me for a second and takes it. Well-mannered, no pressure. I smile again.

"Is your name really Clement?"

"Afraid so."

"Then we share a problem. Mine's Berenice."

"That's quite a reasonable name. It's part of a constellation. May I sit down?"

I ease myself onto the seat, keeping strictly to one end.

"What do your friends call you?" she says. Only she pronounces it *frinds.*

"They call me Garner. What else would they call me?"

"Even your best friends?"

15

"Well, yes."

"That kind of school, is it?"

"Afraid so. What about you?"

"Don't go to school."

She isn't too old to be like me, doing privileged extra time. She just doesn't go to school. I shake my head in admiration.

"How long have you been sitting here?"

"About a half hour longer than you." She isn't looking at me anymore and her voice has an edge. I sit forward to get more than her profile and study her grey eyes. Her cheeks have a few freckles and her hair is so blonde it's nearly white. Her lips are pale too and it gives her a serious, waif-like look I haven't seen among the Hollywood actresses I'm having affairs with at the moment. But she's here and they're not.

"I've spent most of the time so far in my room or in the kitchen," she mutters. "Then that bloke showed up. So I took a stroll."

"What bloke? I thought you were with him somehow, or I'd have looked for you."

"The one Uncle seems so interested in. Bustling around all morning even before he got here. If I'd dropped dead he'd have stepped over me. Are you my cousin? I've never heard of you."

"I've never heard of you either. Have you been here before?"

"No, never. My first time abroad. I'm from New Zealand."

"Wow! And you're alone?"

"Of course not. I've got a governess. Actually I prefer the word companion. Where we live there's no one for miles. I'm home educated. So now we're travelling to broaden my mind. And lose my accent. We spent the summer in Switzerland and the rest of the time stuck in Scotland. And now I'm here." She looks around and shivers. "And I have to tell you, it's bloody grim."

I'm all sympathy. "It is a bit nippy. But it could be rain, or sleet or snow. Or hail."

Her stare dismisses me. "It's not the cold. Are you my cousin or not?"

"No. Shanks isn't my uncle, he's distant family."

"How distant?"

"Out of sight. I don't ask. My parents are in Kenya. That's where I was born." I go for the human-interest angle. "It was on a steamer crossing Lake Rudolf because I was premature. They should have had me in England. There was a storm going on at the time. We both came on a bit sudden."

She blows down her nose. "Clement means calm, doesn't it?" She doesn't believe me and it isn't true anyway. I made it up for some daft reason once. Change the subject.

"So where's your, er, companion?"

"With friends in London. She might be here for Christmas, might not. We're easy."

"Didn't Shanks ever tell you about me? In his letters or anything?"

"No. Surprised? You know what he's like."

I stand up and stamp my feet. "Let me give you a guided tour of the place and swindle some tea out of Ludmilla. I think she's on our side."

Berenice gets up. She's slight, about three inches shorter than me and her movements lack enthusiasm. "Why do you call him Shanks?" she says suddenly.

"It's on all the basins and, um, conveniences," and I wish myself back five seconds. "Don't bother," she sighs, but I have little to lose.

"Will you take my arm?"

Before she can brush me off we hear Alphonse calling.

Back indoors he says, "Doctor is seeing you soon." Berenice looks at him. "That's lucky. I didn't have an appointment." Alphonse is probably a stranger to sarcasm, at least in English. "Please wait in library. I show you."

17

The garden tour's off but the house tour can still run, and I need success. "It's okay," I say, "I know the way."

He gives a small bow and withdraws.

The hall is a small flagstoned space, not a grand entrance with stairs, and four doors lead from it. They're low, dark and pointy. "That's the kitchen, that's the billiard room, that's Uncle's study – strictly private – and this one. Please to follow me, yes?"

I'm tempted to babble on about every room and turning I show her, but I resist it.

The smells of woodsmoke, old polish and generations of leisurely ownership cling to everything. Clocks that clunk away time in centuries stand and watch us pass, then, from far off, strike hours and half-hours that flow down the passages like crystal. This doesn't need me to tell it. But it's an effort for all that. Inglefield Place is the home of a single man and his servants and it's short on family amusements or warmth. I feel like an estate agent showing someone round who's already decided against it. We come to a door that isn't going to change a thing.

The room is large, the largest in the house. It smells of ancient wood and it echoes because the floor is bare and the ceiling and walls all panelled oak. It also echoes because it isn't used. White dustsheets cover a few armchairs and the huge fireplace contains ashes of fires long dead. There's a large painting hanging over the mantelpiece. Berenice stops under it. The room with its dry echoes demands hushed voices. "What's it called?" she whispers.

"Don't know. Sorry."

I'm not sure it has a name. It's always hung there as far as I know. If you stand back a little you see this great mountain face, a vertical wall of rock with buttresses, ledges and gullies filled with snow. You can't see the summit and that makes the precipice seem terrible, unclimb-able. But when you look closer there's an eagle, in mid-air, wings outstretched against that backdrop, beak wide, about to plummet on unseen prey. It looks alive; you can almost feel the mountain wind and believe it lives; ruling among remote peaks, a kingdom still untrodden. Berenice shivers.

"I don't like it," she says quietly.

Till now the picture's never bothered me. Now in the failing light in this room I start to wonder if that's really true. Did I avoid it when I was younger? Did it appear in my infant dreams as I slept in this house? Have I imagined myself lost among mountains, pursued by eagles? I'd remember if I did, and yet... Suddenly I feel less comfortable. I stand next to her so our arms touch and she doesn't move.

"Would Jackson mind if we just turned it round or covered it up or something?" she says.

"I think he probably would. Do you dislike it that much?"

"Yes. I hate it. Look, get that sheet off that chair and hang it over it, will you?"

My unease contends with the desire to please her, and loses. "That's better," she says softly. Then she smiles. "Lead on, Clement."

We walk down a narrow, panelled gallery that flanks the stable block and is always cool in summer. Any other season, the draughts moan through it like they do in the kitchen range on quiet evenings. Today the cold hangs about inside it like a fine mist. It's a no-man's-land between the refuge of rooms, and high leaded windows only bring the outside closer. Berenice stands by one and gazes out. A lawn that's been frost-covered all day gives onto bare ploughland scattered with elms and poplars. "Where's the fence?" she asks.

"There's a ha-ha. You can't see it from here. That's the whole point. It's a..."

She nods. "I know what they are."

The earth looks hard as iron. Rusty iron, because in its last hour the sun has appeared in time to cast a red glow over the landscape. A rook or two flaps homewards. Berenice hugs herself. "It makes you glad to be indoors. What's in those trees over there?"

A group stands like an island in a lake of furrows.

"That's the church. You can't see it because they're yew trees. We'll go there tomorrow. It's further than it looks."

The shadows of the gallery are suddenly touched by the red glow and it gives a sad softness to everything. Berenice tilts back her head and closes her eyes.

"This big empty house. How do you stand it?"

"It had its moments. During the war." Truth is, I like it here. There are many reasons.

Her eyes close more tightly. "I'm a long way from home, cousin. Uncle Jackson seems very preoccupied. Mother says when he gets like that the rest of the world can take a walk. I'm glad you're here. I'd hate to be here on my own."

My eyes never leave her face as she says this. I see her riding over the fields in her distant home; warm, free. And now stuck here in this lonely place. I've never been so close to a girl of my own age; never heard a girl say she wanted me around. Along with my unease, all my sense that nothing is in its right place, there's this young face to make strangeness something I can share. She turns and smiles into my eyes and I'm slightly, pleasantly afraid.

Chapter 4

Berenice browses along the books and I poke the fire and things are looking up, when in strides the Doctor followed by Mystery Man, a baggy middle-aged character smoking a pipe.

"Ah! Berenice and Clement. Been getting acquainted? Good! Berenice, this is Mr McFee who is also our guest for a few days. Mr McFee, this is Berenice, my sister's girl from New Zealand, and Clement, about whom I've told you. He's on school holiday but my niece has a governess, so her breaks are planned with more imagination."

The library's the only room in the house with carpet wall to wall, like how I imagine a bank-manager's office. It mellows sounds like a good wireless cabinet. We all shake hands and I say, "Good evening, sir." The napkin comes off the tea tray and it's muffins and silence for about a minute.

I try not to glance at Mr McFee. Being foolishly happy just then, I want to call him Mister Magoo and have to stare intently into my teacup till I get over it. He's nothing remarkable. Bit dumpy. Bit uncared for. Looks like he lives alone, but without Shanks's advantages. Balding fast, and the lines in his face are deep. He's looking at me.

"You like observing people, young man?"

"Er, no, sir." The muffin breaks apart in my hand and lands mostly in my lap. Berenice gets up, takes the napkin from me and throws the crumbs in the fire. Shanks laughs. "Well, well, eat up! We've plenty of time to talk." We eat, and I watch my honorary cousin instead.

Pitch dark fills the world outside and the talk is entirely between Berenice and Mr McFee, and I take note because it's her and an adult and she's witty and self-assured.

"You eat like a horse and there's nothing of you," he says.

"Oh, it would take a lot of these to annoy me." She smiles; the girl from across the world. A girl who kicks around with cattle, sheep, horses and rough men used to rough ways. 'Good vac, Garner?' they'll say when I get back. "Oh, yes, sir. Something new out of Inglefield."

When Shanks tugs a bell-pull to summon Alphonse I watch him too. He clears things away without a word and without meeting anyone's eye. It's a skill I'm beginning to appreciate. He returns with a polished wooden box and sets it down between us.

"We shall leave our two colonials to their amusements," says the Doctor. "Mr McFee and I have much to discuss. Clement, teach Berenice how to play chess." He winks at her. "He's very good. Plays for his school. See you at dinner."

I start to lay out the pieces. "Don't bother," she says, "I'd rather read."

"I can beat him, you know."

"That's nice."

"There was this hot day last year. I wanted to swim in the pond and he said okay, if you can beat me even with my queen, because he'd always not played it to give me a chance. So I did. Mate in twenty-four moves."

"That was kind of him."

"Pardon?"

One of my chestful of medals unpins itself and falls with evil slowness to the floor.

She flicks a page. "I can play chess. But in his world girls don't. So I'd rather read." She settles down with *Mansfield Park* and I settle down to *Muskeg Pete and the Athabaska Patrol*. She'd be at home with either of them; me with just the one. It makes me think and I'm supposed to be taking a break from thinking. I need to get back to a comfortable spot, regain a little composure.

I enjoy it here because I can roam the woods and fields and Jackson Armitage hardly knows or cares – except for the lake – as long as I turn up for meals. Until the gardener's kids left school and went to work we were out together all day in all weathers. When we weren't doing odd jobs I was a backwoodsman, a voyageur, a *coureur du bois* in the endless forests of the north. So maybe Berenice does those things for real where she comes from. Never mind. She gets moody sometimes. Never mind. This is my forest and I'll be her guide. The fire crackles and the minutes pass by in silence.

Far away the gong sounds. Without a word we go to our rooms and reappear for dinner. There is serious social constipation throughout this event. McFee is morose, Shanks lost in his thoughts. There are long silences. We return alone to the library and thankfully take up our books, but after ten seconds lower them and look at each other.

"Wait there," I tell her.

I walk along the gallery to the big panelled room. It's in darkness but moonlight has turned the furniture covers to shrouds. The eagle picture is there and the sheet has been removed. I turn and bump into Berenice. Our faces are close, so I don't need to do more than whisper.

"I think you'll have to get used to it."

At nine-thirty Alphonse brings us cocoa and a biscuit. He senses we aren't having a good time.

"I tell you this story. When we come to England I was manservant. Strange country! First I work in big house for old diamond merchant, very rich. But very sick, all year in bed. Good health is better, huh? One day I bring him tea, but Mrs Stankeivitch and me not really knew how tea cosy to use so she put it next to pot, on tray. Old man says, put cosy on; is cold in here! So I put cosy on head. He had on nightcap and I look like Cossack! He thinks I am lunatic, no?"

We laugh, then Alphonse grows serious. "Doctor and Mr McFee very busy. Very heavy matter. Very big problem, I think. You must retire at ten o'clock. Master Clement, I prepare your things. Young lady, my wife will attend you. Good night, Miss."

My own room. In all the world.

Inglefield Place has an octagonal turret that overlooks the sunk garden and the water meadows and this is its first floor. Most of the eight walls have shelves and alcoves and they all harbour shadows. A bedside lamp throws golden-brown light into these spaces but the shadows swallow it. I remember how Victoria would lead me by the hand to this room and I could never explain what frightened me about it. Things are different now, after years of sleeping in beds that aren't home.

Alphonse has put the stone footwarmer in and my pyjamas are laid out. There's a smell of old linen, an odour of decades. In ten minutes I'm kneeling on the counterpane and opening the casement to catch a sound like a finger tapping quickly on a wall. Far away the last train through Inglefield chugs across the night. And the wind's risen, bringing a whisper from the weir over the meadows, like the sea heard in a shell. The ragged twin poplars in the near field are sighing too and I kneel in the cold air trying to breath in familiarity and peace.

But sleep is hard to come by. A hundred things have shifted in a landscape that stays the same. I pull down a book; the *Wonder Book of Wonders*, ten years old and still describing the world as I think I know it. In the dim, incomplete light the pictures disturb me the way they disturbed me when I was a little boy, alone and anxious in a far end of a dark house. Even the paper has an unfriendly, unnatural smell. I put it down.

The eagle picture comes back to me. Just a picture that hangs there. And strange visitors. What does he want with a doctor? What exactly does Jackson Armitage cure? Then this foreign couple appearing out of somewhere unknown to drive others so easily from my memory. I'm sitting alone in a familiar theatre now dark, and a new cast steps out of the shadows: Berenice, sitting forgotten amidst the dead of winter, a pale exile; her face, eyes closed, tinged by an end-of-the-world sunset; bothered by a picture. The eagle in its home. Eyrie. Eerie. Not quite right. Totally wrong you can confront; with not quite right you have to wait and see. It's the fixed smile that unnerves you, not the frown. The more I try to shake it all off the more it insists.

Wishing for sleep is replaced by wishing for the light of day. I no longer want to sink into that dark and meet these thoughts alone, my mind weighed down, my courage mislaid.

Chapter 5

What raises me from a cavernous sleep is the blundering of a moth against the window. I peer but there's no moth, just the sound. Still dark. Mice in the rafters?

It's a knocking, on my door.

"Are you decent?"

"What?" Must be Berenice. "I'm pretty fair-minded. What is it?"

"Idiot! Are you in bed?"

"Of course I'm in bed. Why aren't you?"

I'm rubbing my face awake as she swirls in, sky-blue silk pyjamas and no dressing-gown.

"What is it?"

"Clement! You have to come! Now!"

"Why?"

"Because I can hear things! Move yourself!"

She grabs my wrist and half-drags me into the corridor. We stop outside a partly open door next to her own room. Then she goes calm. "You must be quiet. Promise me."

"Whatever you say. I showed you this room earlier. It's empty."

She steals in, stops halfway in the semi-dark and whispers in my ear. "Couldn't sleep, so I went for a wander. See that fireguard? I just wanted to look at it. And I heard voices coming up the chimney."

I'm not prepared to whisper. "Look…"

She puts a hand over my mouth. It smells nice. So I shrug and put my mouth to her ear. That smells nice too.

"Look, this is directly above the billiard room. Uncle and the man with uncle are having a game. He always stays up late. They haven't got a fire lit because there are radiators in that room. So you can hear them. That's all."

She sounds impatient. "I don't care about that. It's what they're saying."

"Okay. What are they saying?"

"It's McFee. He's being haunted."

"So he's a nutcase. What's that got to do with us?"

She stops whispering. As she speaks she nods to emphasise the words. "Look, he hasn't actually said he's haunted; you can tell from how they're going on. He wants Jackson's help. They've obviously been yackering on about it ever since he got here."

"I thought he looked worried. But so what? Aren't you tired?"

She steps carefully to the firescreen and lifts it to one side. Even from where I stand I can hear them: snatches of murmuring; the faint click of billiard balls.

Berenice beckons me over. "It's hard to follow. They keep moving round the table." I put my head right into the chimney. She's right. I listen, lose them, listen. But their talk's moved on: nothing about ghosts or haunting. "Okay," I whisper, "I think the show's over. Let's go. He wouldn't appreciate it, believe me."

I pick up the firescreen. It's old, heavy iron and it's had about enough. As I lower it to the hearth its handle comes off. Whoever made it designed the handle to be its linchpin, so the thing separates into many parts and in its fall it involves a set of fire-irons and the noise goes on and on. Berenice, more guilty and more quick-witted than me, dives out of the room. Tidy-minded and conscience-stricken, I waste precious moments trying to reassemble the screen, then give it up and run too. Halfway back to my room I collide with Shanks. He must have moved like lightning. He turns a light switch and looks at me.

"Everything all right? I heard a terrible din up here. Why are you up?"

I'm spared the lying. A sense of remorse runs through some of my generation like letters through seaside rock, and our little world isn't ready yet for the self-destructing firescreen. Shanks remembers his niece and turns back along the corridor. Her first mistake is not shutting her door properly so it's still swinging slowly open; her second is being too convincingly asleep.

We get into our dressing-gowns, lead him to the scene and Berenice tells all. The fullness of her confession astonishes me. Whole chunks of their conversation, word for word, like a record machine. She knows more than we can possibly be asked to forget.

Alphonse stumps along the corridor in his nightshirt and overcoat and waits until Berenice has finished. "Is everything in order, sir?"

"Perfectly, thank you, Alphonse. You may leave it with me. Good-night." And when he's slowly and doubtfully retreated, "Outside the study in five minutes. God help you both."

Like a stunned man I go back to the firescreen and fumble with it but there's no resolution left in me. Berenice looks out of the window and runs her hands repeatedly through her hair.

My hands sink to my sides. "I haven't been allowed in his study since I was seven years old. I've never tried to look in there, not even through the window. I believed—" – a little acid drips into my voice – "I believed it was probably none of my business."

"I'm sorry," she says. "Sorry for getting you into a mess. You won't be stopped from coming here again, will you? Where would you go?"

"I don't know and that's the truth. He said 'God help you both' and he didn't sound mad. That's a bad sign. You didn't need to sing the whole bloody song, did you?"

McFee is standing with his back to the study window. Shanks is poking the fire. Berenice curls up in an armchair and looks very small. I let my eyes take in a place that I haven't been in for a long time, then sit down as if I've never tried a chair before. Jackson Armitage rises to his full height and, silhouetted against the leaping flames, begins to speak. Wherever he is and whatever he does he always sounds like he's dictating a letter. Right now I'm glad of it. I need to catch every word.

"I realise that I have not been the perfect host, but it has been a long day for some of us. Mr McFee and I have been discussing a matter of great interest to me and of great importance to him. Something quite out of the ordinary. Had you, Berenice, heard less than you did I would not hesitate to keep this entire business from both of you. Your unwarranted curiosity and abuse of hospitality has brought us to this position."

I steal a glance at her, knees drawn up in Shanks's leather armchair. Her hair is tousled and her eyes are tired. And I'm right there with her, because whatever happens this is my ground, even this forbidden corner, and I'm going to stand between her and all harm. For her, I will face the grizzly in his lair.

"I have just spoken with Mr McFee. We're going to pay you a greater compliment than your conduct deserves, by having him give you a brief summary of the case he has brought me. You owe this to our belief that to overhear half a thing opens the door to fabrication, speculation, gossip." His voice quickens. "Embellishment. Rumour. And rumour is the messenger of confusion." He pauses, controls his breathing, swallows. An Adam's apple worthy of Don Quixote. "You will hear what Mr McFee has to say, then put it aside. I will learn soon enough from Miss Maybury – and your housemaster – if you utter a syllable to anyone else. Is that clear?"

Why don't I feel like a complete idiot? Easy. For the first time in my life Jackson Armitage is about to share a secret with me. It's like the Old Bailey in the films: members of the jury, you are charged not to discuss what you have heard outside this court. This isn't chess. I'm not being strung along. Even if McFee is off his head it's about to become my business. I straighten up in my chair and rest my arms. Quite a day. This is me shedding an old skin grown too tight, one I started to cast off when I looked at Berenice in the sunset gallery. Here I am getting comfortable in the new skin. Clement Garner, of the world of adult secrets.

The curtain undulates in the rising wind. It reminds me how close the night outside is. This room turns its back on the outside. It's wary, equipped; ready to meet the darkness as an explorer, not a native.

For a second I have to stop myself. I hear an echo of a doubt. Why did I just think that?

"Clement?"

"Sir?"

"I said, do I have your word?"

"Er, yes, sir."

Having to do this takes off some of the shine. Maybe this isn't going to be a free show after all.

I hardly know that evening how ill-equipped I am to understand the times I'm about to live through; thrust blindfold into the drama, hearing and touching only confusion; forgetting the observant wisdom of my childhood.

Chapter 6

The man in the baggy pullover moves to the fire and relights his pipe with a spill that he holds a long time in the flames. He does not pay us any attention. He's used to being in control. He has to be a lawyer or something. When he speaks, he looks at all of us at once.

"You know my name. I'm a policeman, a detective. Not Flying Squad; just plain CID. I run down villains and solve crimes, or what pass for crimes in these days. One case at present occupies my mind: it concerns a man I know well, a unique villain. A man totally unlike any other.

"About a month ago I was shown a set of photos: fingerprints taken at a routine safe job in the East End of London. The safe was blown skilfully. That means there was little damage, yet nothing had been taken.

"And prints all over the place. We thought at first the peterman had been disturbed at his work – or thought he had been – and made himself scarce."

I frown. He stops.

"Peterman. A safebreaker, often one who uses explosives."

He stops again because I've still got that no-clue-what-you're-on-about look.

"A peter's a safe."

I nod and smile.

"We treated it as another bungled job until the prints were examined. They turned out to belong to a dead man."

At first this too doesn't sink in. Dead man? Maybe they're old prints, not the criminal's at all. I'm trying to concentrate too hard, lose some of McFee's words; have to catch up.

"Died in prison before the war. It was me who arrested him and had him put away for the last time. His name was Smallwood. Albert Gordon Smallwood. We had the evidence; we had the villain. Case closed."

Pause. "Only not closed."

He puts his pipe back in his mouth and it rattles faintly between his teeth. Shanks fills the silence.

"Sergeant McFee's superiors have allowed him time to look into this occurrence. He has approached me in my capacity as Secretary of the LSI."

Berenice and I wait.

"The League of Supernatural Investigators of England and Wales."

I fail to hide my surprise. For my whole life this side of him has been unknown to me. None of the people around him have ever revealed a clue about these activities. None of his visitors, holding their meetings in this house; chattering on the lawns while I was the moccasined runner of the woods, the trapper hiding and seeking with the Indians through the reedbeds. Not one book on ghosts in the library. They're all here, all around us in this room. A closed world, closed enough not to have reached the eyes and ears of my school, itself a world of its own. Close enough to avoid the knowledge or praise of relatives – or maybe not respectable enough to seek it. Under my nose, secure in my indifference.

McFee speaking: "Plain truth is the whole business has affected my health, makes it impossible to do my job. I'm being haunted. Haunted, dammit. I as good as did for him. He was never a well man. He was sinking when he went down for his last job. No, not his last job, was it?"

He's agitated; looks at the doctor, looks around him as if casting about for the scent of his meaning; an old tired hound. I look at the fire. Shanks is on the point of rising from his seat, his hand upheld to say, enough; you've heard enough. But Berenice, curled up in her armchair, her voice not sleepy like her eyes, says:

"What was Mr Smallwood like?"

Shanks signals that McFee need not answer, but the sergeant of detectives looks at her as if she has freed him to do that very thing. He manages a wry smile. "Would you like to know?" She raises her eyebrows familiarly.

"Please."

"Right. It's not your average life story. Albert Smallwood was born in 1885 in Deptford, near the docks. His middle name was Gordon because of General Gordon in the Sudan. You know about that. Well, he kept out of trouble when he was a kid, unlike most villains, who start young. But his father found him a disappointment. He was too delicate to get work as a docker so he ended up working in a shop. In 1914 he tried to volunteer for the Army but failed on medical grounds. Don't forget he was twenty-nine by then and he'd led a pretty dull life behind a counter. He kept on trying to join up and finally they took him and put him in the Pioneer Corps, in one of those units who followed up after a battle and cleared all the debris: scrap and barbed wire to melt down or use again. That was his military career until the summer of 1918, when we began our final push. Now Albert was a bit of a dark horse; he had a streak of adventure in him. One day he turned up a live shell and defused it while his mates cowered in an old trench. He enjoyed that, and from then on he messed about with all sorts of dangerous relics until ordered to leave off. He graduated from that to using abandoned explosives – anything really, to blow up obstacles, do little demolition jobs. The more he got away with it, the more they left him alone. He was saving people work, after all.

"One day he and another chap were poking around a ruined building when they fell through the floor. Turned out to be a bank and they were looking at the vault. The armies had passed through but the locals hadn't returned and the whole area was infested with deserters and bad characters. So Albert crept back later with some guncotton and blew his way in. Nothing in it, of course; he should have realised the Germans would have seen to that even if the deserters hadn't. Still, it whetted his appetite, and in the last weeks of the war he did a little job or two that paid his way. The speed and confusion of our advance kept him out of trouble, see? So when he came back after the Armistice he struck out as a fully-fledged peterman."

Shanks has left the study and I haven't noticed. It feels like a good time to join in.

"Was he in a gang?"

He relights his pipe. "Didn't operate like that. He wasn't a desperate character; too weedy to be violent. And he never kept a penny that he stole."

We both look perplexed. I try again. "Does that make him an honest villain, then – like in the movies?"

McFee snorts. "Honest villain? Bollocks. Pardon me, Miss, but you should be used to it where you come from. There is no such thing, laddie. Villains are villains. Are you asking if he was Robin Hood? All stuff. Look, Albert was no fool. He knew the big money was in strong safes that only a few pros could crack. So he worked for other villains. They set up the job and laid on the transport. Do you know how heavy bags of coins are? And they organised the share out; only he wouldn't stay around for that because he insisted on being paid in advance. D'you know why?"

No, we don't. He gives me a steely look. "That's because they teach you every damn thing in those posh schools except how to think. Anyway. One: if a gang's rich enough to stump up your fee then they've probably got a good track record, if you get me. Two: well, try this. He always charged the same. He always made them pay his expenses and he always left the minute the job was done. "Good evening, gentlemen," he'd say, and leave them to clean it out, start mistrusting each other, splash out and finally get caught. But they never shopped him."

Berenice listens, but I need to repair damage. "Honour among thieves?"

"Honour among bollocks. Where d'you find all this? There is very little honour anywhere, my son, never mind among thieves. They

34

needed him, that's all. He was a specialist. He had no enemies, no axe to grind. If he could carry on his trade outside, then chances were that those inside, and their families, might get some benefit in roundabout ways. He was always clean. No prints, very little mess, made himself scarce. He lived simply, banked his money carefully, gave to the Seamen's Mission, got married and bought a respectable house in Wapping. Don't look surprised, little Lord Fauntleroy. It can be done."

I accept the pleasantries with good grace. Shanks reappears with a tray. Tea, and hot milk for the colonials. Another surprise on a night of surprises. I've seen Jackson Armitage serve drinks of his own making less often than King Saud of Arabia has watched his women eat. His action warms me more than the contents of my mug. I smile with slow delight at Berenice and want to say something smart like 'out of the strong cameth forth sweetness' because it fits, because I want her to think it applies to me smiling and because I've seen it on tins of Golden Syrup. "I think," says Shanks, "that we might call it a day."

But Berenice asks if Sergeant McFee could finish the story.

We sip slowly to make it happen.

"His luck ran out in 'twenty-six. He went up to Birmingham to do a job in the middle of the General Strike, which the Villains' Union did not support. For once he had to go up by car. He hated cars, can't remember why, and he could have put it off; he had that kind of authority. Anyway, it was a big factory and no one would have been surprised to see the odd bobby on guard, because the owners thought the Revolution was on its way. So the gang were dressed up as police; even Albert was togged up in blue, helmet and all. He must have looked a sight: stooped shoulders, droopy moustache. Keystone Kops third eleven. They had a van done up like a Black Maria ready for the getaway.

"The safe went off nicely. Huge payroll – and the boardroom silver. The only problem was down in the machine shop, where a hundred and twenty specials were bedding down for the night.

"They were billeted there in case of strike trouble. Before the gang and Albert could turn round they were face to face with the law in overwhelming strength. You have to picture it. Six men in uniform collared by a crowd of the real thing in long johns. Smallwood went down for a long time but he got early release because he was pretty ill by now. We kept an eye on him all the same."

McFee pauses. I will Shanks not to call it a day again. He's probably heard this already and we won't be able to argue for more without sounding like insistent children. The silence lasts a long time while a man swimming through memories treads water.

"I was a detective constable; knew my way around. March 1932 this was. We got a tip-off. A voice on the phone said Smallwood, time and place. I'd got to know him and his little ways and I was sent with a uniformed man to pick him up. We knew he wouldn't make trouble. Still I was intrigued; a small job and him acting alone. So we got to this pawnbroker's down by the river. It was a damn good year for the uncles, 'thirty-two, and this one didn't trust banks. Why should he? Anyway, there was a filthy smog that night. I told the man to stay put and crept up this outside staircase. It was wood, creaked a bit. Then I opened the door.

"He was working by a dark lantern, crouched down in his cloth cap and long overcoat. Just his face was lit up and he looked like death. 'Hallo, Albert,' I said. He didn't show any emotion, just looked a bit dazed. 'Good evening, Mr McFee,' he said. 'Come on,' I said, 'You should know better, with Alice so bad. What will she do now?' His wife was dying. She wasn't all that old. I tell you, if I'd been on my own I'd have let him go. I surely would. 'Too late,' he said, 'Too late to worry now.'"

He closes his eyes. We sit like statues.

"I took him down the steps. The bobby was still with the car a little way off. Just round the corner there was a night-watchman guarding piles of wood paving blocks. They were mending the road, see? Albert started coughing and asked if he could sit by the brazier while I had the car brought round.

"He couldn't have run for it in his state and the watchman was a big bloke. He gave his word and that was good enough for me. I walked slowly to get the car because I was trying to make sense of the whole thing. I was asking: why try a job now, with Alice so near dying? Why here? And who could have shopped him? If we'd been left to run him down he'd have been with her at the last before we got to him. Bastard. Honour among thieves?

"Alice died a month later and he went down for six years. I was in court when the judge passed sentence. Albert just stood there in the dock and said, "Thank you, sir." That was all. "Thank you, sir." He'd stopped fighting, see?"

What I see is a sad, downtrodden little man. Charlie Chaplin without the laughs. It's hard to meet McFee's eye but all at once he sounds more distant. He's talking half to himself.

"There were more strange aspects to that case. The pawnbroker he'd been trying to rob had two shops and the other one had been done about six weeks before. Loose floorboard under the counter. Hundred and fifty pounds in notes. We never cracked that one. The really strange thing was when we got the uncle round to check that his safe was all right. It was a little one and Albert wasn't using explosive. He was such a pro that a simple double-lock armoured door was child's play to him. Anyway Rosenblum, the uncle, said the safe was empty anyway. Albert was wasting his time. At first I thought that with Alice dying he'd lost his touch and got his facts wrong. Rosenblum always kept his real money in the other shop. I reckoned Albert had been set up. The squeak knew Albert was probably desperate and just...set him up. I believed it then and I believe it now. I'd love to have got that bastard. Then Albert died in the prison hospital at Pentonville. TB. He'd had it for years. And fourteen years later to the day he comes back. He does one more job. A dead man. And then..."

Shanks's voice at last. "And then three days ago the same prints appeared on another safe in another part of the East End. At which point Mr McFee contacted me."

"Two jobs," I say. "That puts it beyond coincidence." It sounds right. I feel appropriate.

"He's a ghost, isn't he?" says Berenice. "A revenant; someone who comes again. Do you think he's after you?"

Her tone is direct, like her look.

"That will be the thrust of our investigations. You have the full story. Now go to bed."

The fire is embers and the study has grown cold. Berenice and I are empty. We only glance at each other as we go upstairs.

She touches my arm lightly to say goodnight.

"Well, now we know."

"Yes. Sleep well."

This time thoughts cannot prevent sleep. But my dreams, when they come, find me alone in a derelict city lit by a moon the colour of blood. The tops of the buildings are torn and eroded like ancient mud and their dwellers cower in dark spaces. I float among black-water wharves wreathed in fog, listening for a sound: a cough that echoes through the streets. Something draws me onto those streets where no one will go, draws me towards the only other thing at large in all the ways of that city; a half-being, a husk of lungs, that sends his whisper through cracks and windows to clutch screams from children in the stricken silence of the night.

Chapter 7

Y ou wake. Can't remember where you are. It doesn't matter
though, because this is one of those moments when youth is one
with the glory of the morning. And the words fit because *everything* feels
right. Your body is weightless; the sheets comfort you without touching; nothing sends signals of distress. Perfect ease, balance, wellbeing.
And it lasts for a long instant until your brain blunders in to share it,
with all its debris from dreams, its reminder of physical needs, of the
body's imperfection.

My eyes dart all over the little room. I listen to every suspicion of a
sound and breathe in familiar smells like a man snatched from suffoca-
tion. But it takes a long time before the sense and taste of the terrible
ruined city leaves me. Even before it does I step from the bed onto a
strip of sunlit floor and let the warmth wash my feet because that's real.
It must be pretty late. Slowly the glow fades. Greyness comes over and
you know it'll hang over everything for the rest of the day.

Less than twenty-four hours ago I was standing on a branch line
platform at Oxford Station. Where am I now? Looking back when
I should be looking forward. Looking back on a life of freedom, an
existence more golden than I've had the sense to recognise. This house
and its grounds, its servants, its woods and waters, with a guardian who
leaves me at liberty because it suits him; this has been the great refuge
from a school that manages to ignore you and oppress you at the same
time. No wonder McFee isn't struck on schools like mine. They turn
out people like me, who don't know we're born. The unquestioning
life is over. I've walked into an ambiguous world just by hearing a tale,
not from the radio but from a man who's probably half crackers. I don't
remember a single nightmare about the war; though I heard the bombs
dropping on Oxford and saw newsreels I wished I hadn't. But an hour

listening to a stranger who's not even sure what's happening to him has got me off balance. That and the rest. From now on I'll be seeing less of the blue untroubled sky while I mind where to put my feet.

It begins well enough. All smiles at breakfast. Berenice asks nicely if Mr McFee can't stay on through Christmas and it takes me a minute to see she's putting us on. She makes tiny signals to me with her eyes: it's okay, I don't want him here either. Nice man, but creepy. Then Shanks drops hints about getting presents for unexpected guests. He's doing pretty well. Maybe he's found the answer to Mr McFee's problem while we slept.

Under a cold overcast Berenice and I get into the car for a trip to Stoveleigh and last-minute Christmas shopping.

Alphonse on four wheels is a hearse driver. We drift quietly down the grey-brown lanes expecting anyone on foot to doff their hats and bow. But the countryside is innocent of people until we reach Stoveleigh itself, the nearest place whose shops don't offer to post your letters as well. Alphonse pulls up by the war memorial and unfolds a newspaper. "Half hour only. Very cold to sit here in car."

"Why don't you go in the tea shop? It's really cosy in there."

He snaps the paper irritably. "Woman in there thinks I am German."

"Well tell her you're not."

"Na. No use. East of Rhine, is all deutsch. Inyorant. Hurry, uh?"

We split up, being still fond of seasonal surprises, and countermarch between the four shops that are any use to us. Meeting once, we take stock:

"Where are the kids in this place? There's only old ladies."

"Disposed of by order of the parish council. Any joy?"

My second visit to the newsagent. Quick look back to check I'm not being followed. Deep breath, hand on *Girls' Companion Annual 1948*. One of Stoveleigh's army of old women purses her lips behind the counter and slaps the change into my hand.

I tap on the car's misted window. "Over here," comes Alphonse's voice from the bench by the war memorial. We sit together in silence and I show him the book while glancing around wildly for Berenice. He flicks through it and grunts.

For the trip back in the hearse he throws in the funeral as well, and she joins him. It gets so bad I ask him to drop us off at the church track.

The car stops as if by itself. I meet his resigned look in the mirror and say, "We'll be in time for lunch, scout's honour."

"Ya, scout. I know." The car glides away and I breathe a silence that at least is mine. "He's strange. What's eating him?"

She looks at me. "I thought you knew him?"

"No. They're new. I'll, er, I'll tell you about it sometime."

My little hesitation there is because as I speak I'm wondering why I haven't mentioned it to her before. Yesterday it seemed important. For a while, anyway.

"The church is along this track. I said I'd show you. Okay?" It's a half-mile of flinty frozen mud flanked by naked trees and undergrowth. Berenice eyes it with distaste. More English winter. The rooks make their ancient racket, perched in the high trees.

"You met him first," I say, "when you arrived before me."

"Are they Polish? He didn't like being taken for a German."

"Lithuanian. I thought he was French – Alphonse – no, he's had a hard life. It's made him grumpy. Looks like Bela Lugosi, don't you think? Maybe I heard him wrong. Maybe he's Transylvanian."

Then I do a party piece. Eyes hooded, I lower my voice:

"I am Count Draculaaah, and I bid you...velcome!"

Berenice lets out a sudden cry and leaps back, her hand spread on her chest. "For God's sake don't do that! That was horrible!"

"Hey, I'm sorry. Didn't mean to – was it that good?"

She shouts. "It was just awful! Don't ever do it again!"

41

Shivers run across the top of my shoulders and meet to shoot up my neck. Stupid, stupid. I hold her hands and we look at each other, both shocked, while she takes deep breaths. Her fear frightens me.

"All right now?"

She nods, eyes closed.

We walk on, scuffing skeletons of leaves.

Try talking. "See? The villagers had to walk two miles nearly, and the squires of Inglefield Place came across by carriage. There used to be a track over the field. We'll go back that way."

Berenice doesn't respond and I keep glancing sideways. She has her hands deep in her pockets, beret pulled down to the ears, collar up, chin hidden in her scarf, eyes on the ground. She's the girl alone in the sunken garden. Maybe she's missing her parents; edgy, a long way from home, like she said. But I'm here. She's not alone now.

"What about last night? What about Mr McFee and his ghost? Haven't thought about him."

And we're not going to mention him now, either. She's going to hate her present. Wish I knew what was wrong. I have done nothing to offend anyone this morning. Apart from a little miscalculation back then. But she was like it already.

We come to a gap in the brambles. "There's the house over there. See those two poplars? I can see them from my bedroom window. They used to scare me. Everything used to scare me till I got used to it."

Contact. "Did you really not know about Jackson? About his ghost-hunting society?"

"No. Honestly. There were always odd people coming and going, mostly during the war, but I didn't take any notice. I played or worked with the gardener's kids – till they left home – or just explored by myself. When he had company I ate in the kitchen. It's interesting I suppose, bit spooky. McFee's interesting in his way. No, his story is. But it wouldn't break my heart if I'd never heard it."

"Nor mine. Clement?"

"Mm?"

"Have you got a middle name?"

"Mackinnon."

"That's better. Family name?"

"No. Remember I said I was born on a Lake Rudolf steamer? Not true. I made that up in a panic once; can't remember why. Actually it was a railway station between Nairobi and Mombasa called Mackinnon Road. It was my father's idea, the name, I mean. The bit about me being early is true. So there it is."

"Sounds just as weird if you ask me."

"No. Honest. Maybe it's why I like trains. Honest."

"Ya. Scout's honour. I know."

"Sleep well after all the drama last night?" We're walking again.

"Not really. I had this dream."

"Want to tell me?" Hearing other people's dreams doesn't make top of my list but it's conversation and I need to keep it going. She thinks a bit and then:

"I was alone in this dreadful ruined city at night. It was like it had been bombed and never rebuilt, and there were a few thin, hungry-looking people around who just kept out of the way. Then I was floating round this horrible dark waterfront but I didn't feel wet. What did we have for dinner last night?"

But I'm walking more and more slowly. My answer isn't about dinner.

"And next thing you were walking down these empty streets as if you were looking for something you didn't want to find. And there was this coughing that you could hear from somewhere, and you imagined some kind of – I don't know – like a...a tracery of a mummy or something. How you thought that Smallwood bloke would look."

We've stopped walking. We just stand there. She doesn't need to speak.

The cold begins to steal into my clothes.

After a while of just looking at each other I say, "Maybe it's because we shared a strong experience or something."

There's no one around and we're almost whispering. In the frosty still air our voices sound flat, imprisoned. Berenice tries to smile. "Or maybe we're twins in spirit; you know, born on the same day. Perhaps."

"I'm sixteen in March," I say.

"I'm sixteen in August."

Then she says, "That would be March of 1932."

"That's right.'

"McFee arrested Smallwood in March '32. He told us."

"Life's full of coincidences, I guess." But it troubles me more than it should.

We move off slowly, Berenice stepping an invisible tightrope on the track. Neither of us looks up. The path ends round the next bend; and suddenly I'm not happy about it. I know that old church.

"We don't have to go in."

But we do. It's small; stone and dark flint with a stump of a tower, a scattering of headstones foundering in the brown grass and shadowed by yew trees through which the sun never shines. Even from the outside it smells of damp and gloom and decay. Surely people don't get baptised or married here. Buried, I can believe. They don't come to worship. They come to huddle, hiding from sin.

The smell inside is strong. That fragrance of years of polish and fading flowers is long gone, but in here it isn't even rotting stone; here it's the earth itself in your nostrils; the earth just beneath the floor. This church is being slowly swallowed up. It's afloat in the soil but the pumps aren't gaining. There should never have been a church here. The consecration hasn't worked as it should.

It feels like a place of the dead; and all the little strangenesses of the day are somehow solidifying. I want to tread softly, to disturb nothing.

Berenice is walking in front of me, gazing around with wary interest at a piece of the past that forms no part of her pioneer world. She reads the tablet with the names of Inglefield's war dead. *Their Name Liveth for Evermore.* What if more than just their name? I smell the last sweat of the unwilling departed, of the Black Death deliriums, of the murdered in terror, all in the damp stains of these walls.

It's no good. I turn to go.

"Have you seen this?" Her voice stops me.

It's a notice stuck to the scaffolding that's always propped up a part of this hope-abandoned place: *Members of the public are forbidden access to the chancel and apse. Visitors with a special interest in the tower are asked to contact the sexton (address in porch).*

There's a separate note in faded type: *The masonry in many parts of this church is in a poor state. Contributions towards preserving the fabric of the building may be left in the collection box by the entrance. Thank you.*

Thanks. You can't save us then; we're supposed to save you. Berenice can see the look on my face. At one go I harden myself against my fears. Let her know the disdain you feel for all this; this mouldy, leaky refuge from the fear of sin and death. When she beckons me over to the monument that dominates half the church I shoulder my way through a crowd of craven superstitions to join her.

The last resting place of Sir John Holland, Lady Holland and six of their children. Jacobean gentry, doublets and ruffs. They lay side by side, hands together in prayer, long fingers pointing upwards to the roof of their canopy; he bareheaded, she in a widow's peak, their eyes dead marble. Sir John's nose is broken off and two of her fingers are missing. The whole thing with its paraphernalia of saintly rest is carved from dull, porridge-coloured stone that smells and feels unwholesome, unnatural. It lords over the quieter, lesser plaques on the wall and of all the panoply in this church this is the bit I like least. When I was a little child Victoria would bring me here while she lit a candle for someone, and if I displeased her she'd tell me solemnly that the couple sleeping there would take me away if I didn't behave. Thank goodness Shanks isn't a churchy type. He never attends services and I've never seen the place with more than two people in it and that suits me fine.

Berenice runs her hand over a pillar of the canopy and kneels to look at the carving on the sarcophagus. Four girls dressed as miniature adults kneel in prayer in order of age facing two miniature males in short capes.

"Signifies they all died in infancy," I say. This place listens to you, but not like the woods.

"All her children?" says Berenice. "That's tough." She reads out the eulogy in stone to Lady Anne:

All Her Waking Momentſ Were But ſtepſ to Heaven.

"Bit of a saint to bear a loss like that," she whispers, and moves away.

I linger. Then run my finger down the head of the smallest kneeling boy.

Something warms the skin of my back.

The warmth begins to move in waves up to my neck and onto my scalp.

I turn to stare at Berenice, her face hidden from me. My eyes narrow and prickle but the rest of me feels very good. My muscles seem to tense by themselves.

She's got a nice neck. Nice throat.

Take that scarf off; I'd like to see your neck; all of it.

Now.

And I'm breathing fast. Rasping. Panic. What is this? I sink down but my eyes still fix on her and I'm snarling, teeth bared.

Her calm glance finds me, on all fours as though looking for something, but gasping, choking. She runs across the echoing stones.

"I couldn't let go of it," my mind says, but the mouth only moans, hanging open. Her eyes widen. I stagger upright while she holds my arms to my sides, and as I look at her I know what she sees: red, wild eyes, unbearably prickling.

She begins to shake her head slowly, then, never letting her look leave my face, steers me towards a pew. I sit with my head in my hands and feel her handkerchief on my brow before I realise that cold sweat is standing on every inch of my skin.

"Are you all right now?" she whispers.

No, I'm not.

"Just give me a minute. I had a funny turn."

And it might have stood at that if she hadn't looked so full of concern. Swallowing a taste of sick I say:

"For just a second – after touching those carvings – I had this feeling of power. I looked at you and wondered how it would feel to have my hands round your neck. Then I realised what I was thinking and ended up on the floor. I had no control over it."

Halfway back across the broad field the old short cut once used by the squires of Inglefield simply runs out. The farmer's got tired of respecting it and put his plough across it. We stumble over furrows that are frozen hard and all the way I have to lean heavily on Berenice.

After a few yards I stop, look back at the church, then towards Inglefield Place.

Nothing is the same. The perspectives are wrong. The sky is wrong.

The house emits a growl of brass, but I know only I hear it.

I've collapsed into cowardice, piling fear on fear. Panic again. I'm on my hands and knees a second time.

"Am I ill?"

"Yes. Yes, I think you are."

"Don't tell them, please. Just say I had a giddy spell. Say you'll keep an eye on me or something. I don't want to be sent away. Put away. Tell them anything."

On again, the chimneys swaying, feet plunging in surprise into deep furrows.

Chapter 8

For the second time I wake feeling good. A girl's voice is crooning in my ear:

Lazybones, sleepin' in the sun / How you goin' to get your day's work done?

"Do they know?" I ask her. She's ruffling my hair in a way that makes me careless of whether they know or not.

"No. It could only happen in a place like this. Jackson and McFee were walking in the woods and Alphonse and Ludmilla aren't speaking. I made you an omelette and brought it to you here."

I'm in a library armchair and there's a blanket over my knees. "I don't remember eating," I say.

"You slept like the dead."

The dead. "What's happening, Berenice? What went on back there? I felt like I wanted to strangle you or something. It only lasted a second."

"I think you're overwrought, that's all. Things have built up on you and you just snapped. Maybe you're a bit snaky at school and you'd like to wring someone's neck."

This is true, but not convincing. I'm fit, active, fifteen and not highly strung.

"We've got two crowds at school; the Long-hairs and the Cavemen. The Long-hairs are brainy, weedy and nervous. So guess which I am. I shouldn't be feeling like this."

"I thought you played chess?"

"It's worse than that. I'm school vice-captain." I look up at her. All this attention is great, warming me in my cold anxiety.

"I play rough, though."

She smiles a smile that's becoming familiar and I lean my head back and close my eyes. I like Berenice. Strange how much better I'm feeling already, below the neck.

She stands up. "Well, tough guy; enough of me playing Matron. You need to get out of yourself. Anyone for tennis?"

"Tennis? It's the middle of winter."

"It's the middle of summer back home. You do play, don't you? Caveman?"

"Oh, yes, I play. But you're not serious."

"I wandered round while you were asleep. The tennis court is free at this moment."

"Berenice, that tennis court is hardly ever used. The gardener's kids and I were almost the only ones. The rackets are God knows where. This isn't a good idea."

Next to the orchard stands the rusty wire-netted enclosure. I work at the gate catch. *En Tout Cas*. What kind of a trademark is that? What am I doing here? All the way along the overgrown gravel paths I've moved like a sleepwalker, reaching out to touch branches to remind me of something I know should be important. There was a good untroubled time once but it's far away. The gate scrapes open and we enter like children happening on a forbidden place.

There's something odd about this spot and the further I venture in, the more the feeling grows.

Right. I've never been in here in the winter; ever. Places are out of bounds because out of season; places in terrace-house gardens, places in our lives that we forever walk past. There's nothing to stop you; a step out of your usual way brings you there, but habit orders you: eyes front! So as I stand there I see a different quality of sky, of almost-shadow in the diffuse light. The dry leaves piled into corners are crackly with the cold that sits still on the wide flat surface of the court. My senses roam in the discovered winter space. A welcome, correct strangeness, as if I'm standing in a temple enclosure in some remote Korea; some Land of the Morning Calm.

Maybe this won't be too bad after all. I whack the sagging net with my racket and go to crank it up. Berenice is stepping along the tram-lines like you do in ballet. She found the kit in the boot room and now she's humming some classical tune or other.

The brass handle won't budge.

"You do ballet, then?"

"Mm."

"What, at school?"

"Don't go to school, remember?"

Stiff, this handle. She'll notice in a minute.

"No, right. What about tennis? Do you play much?"

"A bit. Having trouble?"

I step back. "Just a bit stiff, that's all. I play for the school."

"Right. Can I try?"

She grunts, and the handle begins to squeak round. Slowly the net rises. I almost have a problem with what I'm seeing, but then I'm not as well as I could be. We both know that.

She stands at one end of the court; skirt, jumper, white stockings, no beret. Her fair hair barely covers her ears and she looks wispy. She shouldn't have been able to turn that handle.

Three or four years ago a few opponents faced me across that net on summer afternoons. Nothing serious; Shanks's friends during the war were a languid bunch. I picture them now as fellow-members of his ghost society. They haven't been around much since.

"Good for a game? Say one set?" I call into the silence. From far off she replies, "Suits me. Three times over for serve?" Her voice barely reaches the net. My ears have to meet it there.

"Okay." I lob a ball across. Berenice stands like a statue, legs slightly apart, racket swinging idly, till the last split-second; then springs and arches it back. A sitter. I smash it; then relax. My feet sink into wet concrete as it comes whirring past. Several bounces later I pick it up and toss it to her, and an uncomfortable feeling is on me.

She serves. Four aces.

It doesn't go the distance and few words are exchanged. Leaving the tennis court is like leaving a churchyard after an unknown relative's funeral; you've understood nothing and now you feel nothing.

She leads me back into the house and sits at the old upright piano in the cubby hole next to the kitchen. A little Chopin or Rachmaninov to cheer me up. Ludmilla leaves her chores to lean against the door and smile and sigh and say to me, "Why you no play like this girl, huh?" I smile a lying half-smile and mutter, "I no play at all."

She tells me about her horseriding, over to neighbours back home, working on the farm, plus a bit of competitive stuff. A cabinet with a few trophies. Do I ride? No, actually. Not all that struck on horses, to tell the truth.

She does gymnastics on the pergola between the kitchen garden and the orchard. It creaks and sags but she doesn't give a damn. Upside-down her skirt falls around her. We pass through a wicket-gate onto a meadow where she throws stones further than me. I'm not well. What's all this about?

My face shows how I feel. She looks at me and lingers there long enough to catch my mood, but each time she turns away to show me something else. Her actions have a way of robbing my anger of any strength or importance. She cared and now she doesn't care. It goes way beyond anything I can understand.

It's the apple tree she climbs while banging on about her mountaineering that gets enough of me together to fight back.

"You enjoy kicking people when they're down? Big thrill?"

"Don't be boring," she calls back. The smaller branches thrash around as she heaves herself higher. Small withered things clump to the ground.

"Okay then. What about a three-mile race, right now? Better still, down to the station and back? More like four miles. What do you say?" From someone not in the best of health this sounds plain stupid. A nun in full regalia could beat me.

She jumps down and stands there, hands on hips. "Don't tell me, you run cross-country for your school."

"Yeah. Worried?"

"You also play tennis for your school, I believe." Her grey eyes are full on me. Several of my muscles leave the ranks and skulk away. Before I can say anything she holds her hand up.

"If it's more than a mile you'd beat me. Satisfied?"

Thank goodness for that. "What's this about? Just tell me."

"You think girls are all Long-hairs; am I right? Weak and nervous?"

"Actually I had you down as tougher than that. I was beginning to like you till you started your three-ring circus.'"

"Cavalcade," she says, then turns. "Climb this tree."

"No."

"Got the jimmies?"

I'm tired and defeated; weary patience is all that's left. "Try to grow up," I say. "I'm not frightened by old apple trees. I have climbed all these trees many times. I explored the woods and plantations on my own, in the dark, when I was half your age. I box...I box for my school, but I can hardly challenge you to a match. I've swum in Hob's Pond...."

She spins round and points to a pair of small, dank old carp ponds beside the orchard. "Like those? Let's go!" She starts running towards them. Dark, freezing, unwholesome water.

I know she'll do it. She knows I won't. Shanks will come down on me for letting her. Game, set, match.

"Don't!"

I watch her stop at the edge, then turn and head back for the house. My limbs are like lead; the leaden sky is once more closing out the day. A bad day. Worries that have no name afflict me. Strangers have appeared to turn life strange and people my dreams. And it's all things you somehow can't push against. I'm losing my balance; losing my grip. Just now a little bit of normality would go a long way.

I slump into the armchair in the library. The patterns and smells of this familiar place have retreated from me. Normality isn't going to be possible. She comes in and looks at me and I avoid her gaze.

"How are you feeling?" she says.

Oh, please.

"How the bloody hell do you think I'm feeling? You know better than I do."

"Fancy a game of chess?"

"Let me guess. You play – a bit."

"Mm."

"Please excuse me." I get up; not an easy thing at that moment. "I'm going for a walk. On my own."

She puts her face a little closer to mine than necessary and it's impossible to tell anything from her steady grey eyes. Any other time, with a different history, this would look like a very promising moment. Now her nearness offends me.

"You'd like to wring my neck, wouldn't you?" she murmurs, in a way that puts it beyond doubt.

I narrow my eyes and nod. It feels at last like being on equal terms.

She nods too, but more subtly.

"It wouldn't be the first time today."

For a second there's no heartbeat and a ripple of cold runs through me. I step to the door, hook my foot round it for a look-no-hands slam. It clacks feebly behind me and I stop, nod to myself, get my coat and walk from the house.

Gestures are for fools. Everyone else is in comparative comfort getting ready for tea while I exile myself. The conventions of empty gestures oblige you to continue till you've saved face or everyone's forgotten about it, and that means staying out of the way for at least an hour. Now I'm angry with myself. Fists clenched in pockets, eyes blazing like James Cagney, I set off on a Long Angry Walk. After three fields I'm approaching the weir and my eyes ache.

Dark has descended. At the weir the water foams spectrally.

In its depths lay silent cold-eyed fish who have no worries.

I think about things.

My introduction to the world of adult secrets. You no longer watch at your ease. You are now in the film. But of course you are only fifteen.

Fifteen. It seemed all right at first. There's a price of course. You still have to run after sticks the big people throw, but you don't have to be so panting, tail-waggingly eager about it; and anyway sixteen's just over the hill. But really it's a bastard. It makes your legs all different lengths. Spots, boils and gross mis-timing pepper anything more sophisticated than the usual monkey-tricks of the sports field. The Age of Blame. The Era of Embarrassment. Assailed by feelings you can't control. But someone the same age swans in and without breaking into a sweat makes you feel ridiculous. She throws sticks that you scamper after, only you find you can't lift them. And all this on top of a lot else that isn't going right.

I think of McFee, but I don't want to think of him bringing his taint of crime into the house. Plus he's probably crazy. And Shanks giving him house room for how long? Till Christmas?

And multi-talented, exotic Berenice now the apple of everyone's eye. Absolutely spot on that she should shift that antique firescreen for no good reason and it should fall apart in my hands.

I lean on the rail of the weir for a long time and slowly my anger dissipates, flaking away with the curdled torrent.

Bad move. What replaces the anger is reminders: reminders of the nightmare, reminders of the Holland tomb. Worse still, something is advising me from somewhere well back in my memory. Remember what used to scare you as a tiny child? The visible things. The gnarled trees of the woods, the shapes and shadows in the house. All that is nothing. That was you. And you got over them. Full marks; not that anyone cares. But that dream a month ago was right. There are things outside all that.

The things of place: the things under the earth.

The power of adults is at least comforting. This power is different. It has touched the sergeant of detectives – Whatshisname McFee. And now it has touched all the people in the house you think of as home. Better start worrying about that and forget the rest.

Doctor Jackson Armitage has the weapons of his calling.

Alphonse and Ludmilla are armed with the stoic indifference of servants.

Berenice can be frightened, but she has the assurance of physical prowess; the girl on horseback.

You have – what? Think about it as you make your way back, past the trees and shadows.

Fifteen; when you blindly contend, and suffer without dignity.

You can keep it.

Chapter 9

The heavy oak door swings shut behind me. Has it closed? Doesn't matter. A cataract of cold air sweeps down off my coat as I hang it on the hallstand, and I'm moving with stiff deliberation towards the library, where the remains of tea will be waiting; or maybe not.

She's there, alone, fencing with the lamp standard, an umbrella stabbing and twirling in her hand. Fencing too, and her opponent disarmed. I know how it feels.

The idea of just turning away before she notices is very strong. In my mind shelves of trophies jeer at me with the voices of grand pianos as I hold my one certificate and shield before me like a fig leaf. It hasn't been a vintage year for personal achievement. In the old homestead back in New Zealand with your own tutor the years don't matter and the prizes just come along. Well, it's cold tea here or cold room upstairs. I decide to stay.

In the middle of the second muffin a crumb takes the high road. Berenice looks up from her book as I cough, choke, recover. This is rock bottom and it feels…

Good.

Surprisingly good.

Peace through complete acceptance of your fate. Stop struggling. There is nowhere to go.

I smile serenely at Berenice. No, I bestow a serene smile on her. Her brow furrows slightly and she pretends to carry on reading. For a little while my mind feels the same ease as my body did first thing in the morning.

Enter the Doctor.

"So there you are, at last! I hear Berenice has been showing you a thing or two, eh? Well, well!"

I smile at him. Well, well.

"Shouldn't we put up some trimmings?" I say. "They've been up by now, other years."

"Good thought," he answers, and pulls a tasselled cord.

"Alphonse, find a six-footer in the plantation and take an axe to it. We'll have it over there in the corner."

The Lithuanian ex-dispatch rider stands puzzled, unmoving, to attention. "Sir?"

A couple of minutes later we hear his boots crunching along the gravel. I imagine him in his duffel coat and felt hat, axe on his shoulder and hurricane lamp in his hand, striding into those dark pine woods.

"Must remind him of home."

"What's that, Clement?"

"Alphonse."

"I think," says Berenice, "that he's not struck on our Christmas. They do it differently, don't they?" She pauses. "Can we have the tree in the big panelled room? Cheer it up a bit?"

Boxes are taken down from lofts and we begin to put together a Christmas that I hope will live up to earlier times in this house. There were sometimes lively gatherings here, apparently. The gardener's family, the Moffats; Raymond and Victoria's relatives and their children; the odd academic type dropping by. Although Shanks is in the place once occupied by the squires of Inglefield, he sold off the family's local interests and retreated from village life. The gentry round about still make their social calls, but Jackson Armitage leaves them wondering, on the edge of speculation; curious with not enough to fasten onto.

One thing he never had here was evacuees. Sometimes I wonder about that.

But it's going to be uphill this year. One way and another the prospects have dimmed in the last thirty-six hours. One preoccupied host, one haunted policeman, a pair of lukewarm house servants, a girl who's going to win every party game; and they all get along. I'm barely getting along with myself. That serene feeling didn't last long.

And the invisible guest that McFee has brought with him.

More and more I sense him loitering.

About half past six, up on the library steps with a handful of drawing-pins and a joggling snake of trimmings, I hear Berenice say, "We're throwing a farewell for himself after dinner."

"What's that?"

"He's going, in the morning. Jackson thought we'd do something festive in this season of good cheer."

"Thank God for that. What's the deal?"

"Hey, talking Hollywood. Parlour games, drongo! Come on, it's a price worth paying, isn't it?"

"Now he's going I suddenly feel uncharitable. What kind of Christmas is he in for?"

I open out filigree paper bells and prick myself on holly.

What's happened to excitement? It's children's privilege to be unstintingly selfish at Christmas, to lose themselves in the daftness of it. Worrying about why I'm more worried than happy just makes me more worried. I'm back in my first Christmas here, an age ago: a few trimmings in a few rooms; the rest of the house in gloom, made emptier by these islands of faded colour.

After dinner it's card games. McFee doesn't approve of poker and its cousins so we stick to snap, beggar-my-neighbour and finally what Shanks called Pelmanism. The whole pack is shuffled and spread out randomnly face-down. You have to try and pick up pairs first by guesswork then, as you see wrong cards turned up and replaced, from memory. Remembering where pairs might be gets easier as the pack dwindles, but my mind isn't on it. Nor, I think, is McFee's. If he's leaving, is it because Shanks hasn't been able to help him?

Still, with his memory for facts and clues he takes the first two games easily. Then Berenice and Shanks warm to it. Laughter and concentration. Four people as different as the points of the compass, in a lighted room in a dark house in a dark world in the austerity time.

At last Shanks gathers in the pack and pulls a large red spotted cravat from his jacket pocket.

"Something more interesting to end on," he announces. "Berenice, come round."

He blindfolds her. "Lady and gentlemen, you have made child's play of this game so far, so we shall raise the, ah, level of difficulty. I shall lay out the shuffled cards as before, but this time face-up. All except Berenice can see them. She must try to pick up pairs nonetheless. Got that? If she is particularly proficient she is allowed to astound us by stating the number and suit as she picks up. Our job is to tell her whether she is correct or not. Three minutes to amass as many pairs as you can."

It's a laugh; the best yet. The others all have their turns. Their hands wave uncertainly over the table, confident pronouncements are uttered and pitifully few pairs captured. My moment comes round. Blindfolded, I'm rotated three times while the cards are spread out afresh.

It's then I realise that just for once I can put one over on Berenice.

In one second all my reasonableness in the matter of winning and losing evaporates.

I'm not handsome. Not conventionally, anyhow. Bone structure has not brought me favour or raised my prospects in any way. Till now.

I can see below the blindfold.

If I keep my head up and swivel my eyeballs downwards it's possible to focus on a narrow strip of vision under my nose. It makes the eyes ache but in the pleasure of this discovery I don't register that this is the third time in a strange day that they've hurt. I lean forward and tilt my head back as though searching the unseen heaven for inspiration.

It works. I can see every card on the table.

Mustn't arouse suspicion. Go canny.

My first three tries are deliberately hopeless. Loud chuckles.

Then two fours. Murmurs of 'Oh, well done.'

Jack and ace followed by two nines. 'Well done again!'

Laughter gives way to silent anticipation.

Circling the table, I hear chairs moved backwards. Time to play the audience a little. This is much better. Wish I could see their faces. Wish I could see her face.

"I shall now pick up two kings, a red and a black. Thank you." Sceptical chuckle from Shanks.

I reach out, let my hand rest on the king of spades. Intake of breath from someone. My hand leaves it to hover over the jack of clubs next to it. Then back again, fingers flexing, uncertain.

The tension.

Better be careful; you're among experts here. I lift the jack and a sigh wafts into the circle.

The performance is repeated, and I hold up the king of hearts.

A slight gasp from Berenice. Yes, honorary cousin; eat your little heart out.

Time's moving on. Now for the *coup de grace*.

I pick up fives and nines, get one wrong on purpose – but narrowly – and finish with red eights from opposite ends of the table. "Three minutes," says McFee in a subdued voice, and the blindfold comes off. I can see her face now. Worth every penny.

I'm the Comeback Kid.

"How did I do?" I ask, just out of interest.

"Remarkably well," says Shanks, carefully. He's not sure.

McFee whistles softly. "Five pairs and a couple of near-misses. What's the chances of that, Doctor?" His tone is wary too. There's an atmosphere of doubt that deflates the moment. Berenice remains silent. Shanks holds the cravat up to the lights, those mock-candle things on brackets with little shades, and mutters, "Impossible to see through. Well, Clement, let's see you do it again."

I oblige, this time putting in a bit of nervous finger-twining and licking of dry lips. Complete attention follows me as I find pairs and speak my predictions in a serious voice that says: this is no longer a party game. Out in the birch spinney a fox barks where nothing is ever a game.

Seven pairs.

"Sit down, will you?"

Not even doubting now; Jackson Armitage is plain suspicious. I realise I'm in deep. So we come to one of those knife-edges that fate strews along the way; the old fork in the road. And as far as that goes I might as well still have the blindfold on.

"You aren't cheating in any way, are you? There isn't some way that you can see the cards?"

The first step. "Well, sir, no. And yes." I try to sound a little mystified.

The dread inside me is still no bigger than a man's hand. There is time to pull out while we can still share a joke that's this side of tasteless; but that would hand the whole bag of tricks to Berenice. So now I'm licking my lips for real and my heart is hammering.

She whispers something to him and without a word Shanks once more ties the cravat around the back of my head. Frankly the juice has gone out of this thing but I no longer have control. Three times I turn, then approach the table.

The cards are there, in frozen Brownian array.

Face down.

A shaft of pure cold opens through the length of my body. The future stands out hideously clear and it holds the image of Clement Mackinnon Garner, an honorary cousin I once met, a schoolboy staying at a house I once visited, a boy whose guardian I was; a cheat, a wretch without modesty or courage.

Concentration swallowed up in preparing to explain the fiasco that's coming, I swivel my eyes towards the unhelpful little rectangles on the table. My hands are sticky with sweat.

Oh God. I wish that could be the six of clubs.

Gingerly I turn it over.

Six of clubs.

Sometimes at school you're next in line for rendering a sentence into Latin or solving a quadratic equation out loud and you know you can't do it, and just as the beak intones, "And what about question five, Garner? Hmm?" the bell rings. Do you collapse inwardly with relief? Yes. Do you promise to learn enough to cope next time? No. A seductive, calm little voice says, this was meant to happen. You deserve your luck. Don't make a song and dance or Fate will feel tempted. So with the six of clubs.

Mystified, yet calm as a stone, I wish again.

Please be the six of diamonds.

Turn over.

Six of hearts.

A chorus of surprise.

I wish this were the ten of diamonds. Turn over. Ten of diamonds.

Be the ten of spades. Ten of spades.

It goes on, and a symphony breaks out in my head: the relief section, the fear section, the triumph section all piling on the volume; and it stops working, the tricks stop coming, until I restore calm to all this mental noise. The pairs are wished, hoped, commanded into being until the table is clear and I collapse, shaking, while hands support me to a chair. Sight regained shows me three faces. The two men look puzzled and Berenice's eyes are wide with surprise, even horror. Her distress should move my heart but I don't have it in me right now. I'm fifteen and I've suffered wrong at her hands and though nothing is making any sense I parade in victory in front her. This is skill and she gazes at me like an infant gazing at a conjuror. Doctor Armitage finally speaks:

"Remarkable. Remarkable. Completely abnormal, even for a first-class psychic."

It takes a while for these words to sink in.

I was told once that in the triumphs of ancient Rome the victorious general would have a slave in his chariot, standing at his shoulder and holding a wreath of laurels over his head, and whose task it was to whisper repeatedly in his ear, *remember you are a mortal man*. More tactful than Doc Shanks would have been: remember you are a psychotic megalomaniac with acute delusions of grandeur. Abnormal?

Abnormal means crackers.

Suddenly he's all bedside manner. "Just relax, Clement. Good man. That was quite a display. I've met people with the gift, but not nearly to such an extent. Remarkable. Quite remarkable. Would you care for some hot milk and a biscuit?"

I surely would. And something for this headache. Alphonse is summoned, given his orders and while we wait Shanks takes my pulse and pulls up my eyelids as if I'm ill or something. When Alphonse returns it's obvious he thinks something's up.

"Is everything in order, sir?"

"Perfectly. That will be all for tonight."

On the other side of the door Alphonse crosses himself. I just know he does.

"When we have finished our refreshment," says Shanks, "we shall adjourn to the study." To McFee he half-whispers, "We have to be careful. They are utterly reliable but this is beyond their scope. It's even more important now that none of this gets out."

I'm shivering now. Berenice is kneeling by my side with her warm hand round mine and I don't feel powerful anymore. I'm naked. I feel like a frog pinned out for dissection.

I wish for a pair of cards: one to say, this hasn't happened, and one to say, return to normal.

But the little wishes are for you to play with. The big ones are out of your control.

Chapter 10

In the study, for the second time in two nights, I stand on some kind of threshold.

"What's a psychic?"

I know damn well what a psychic is.

It's a fat woman in a long baggy black dress. It's an unattractive old fraud sitting round a table with a bunch of unattractive dupes.

And I appear – apart from one or two details – to be one.

But surely Doctor Armitage isn't mixed up in taking the bored rich for a ride? Instead of a lecture, he tells us a little story.

"Last year a woman came to see me, to try to enlist the help of our society. She was wealthy, well educated and in some distress. Just before the war, she told me, she, her husband and young baby were holidaying on the French Riviera. They found themselves in the path of a sudden forest fire and became separated in the smoke and confusion. Each believed the other was with the child. It was the nanny's afternoon off. When they were reunited they discovered to their horror that the baby had been left behind. It was never found. The parents' grief and recrimination led eventually to the dissolution of their marriage. A very sad business altogether.

"After the war the lady remarried and she and her new husband honeymooned in Portugal, by the sea. One afternoon as she lay in the sun a group of beggars came along the beach. They were importuning for money and to get sympathy they paraded a child of seven or so, hideously disfigured. An old and despicable trick, one which I warn you against whenever you are abroad. The woman, on seeing the child, was overcome by the feeling that this was her lost son. She became agitated and began calling out his name, at once overwhelmed by the certainty of his identity and yet repelled by his appearance. The beggars scuttled away, leaving the woman in no position to follow.

"All attempts to trace the vagabonds came to nothing, so finally she came to me. I examined her for indications of second sight. They were very strong. Of course I made certain enquiries to establish a background, to eliminate possible trickery. This woman satisfied me that she could see or sense things beyond the normal range of human perception. In other words, she is psychic. Unfortunately it may prove impossible – because of her mental state – to apply her powers to her own problem. I am still working on the case and am ready to admit that in this instance Mr McFee's expertise may ultimately prove more fruitful."

"How?" asks Berenice. "Are you going to investigate it?"

He takes the pipe from his mouth. "No. The police forces of France, Spain and Portugal might, though."

So psychics are ordinary people. Still, something needs clearing up.

"What about all those clairvoyants? All those seances and ouija boards?"

Shanks cuts me off. "I do not associate with rogues and confidence tricksters. Neither do I associate with those worthless characters who use some psychic power to delude the public. You can have no idea of the damage they do. After the Great War bereaved relatives applied in their thousands to so-called mediums to be put in touch with those killed or missing in action. What happened? They were fobbed off with sordid pantomimes! Parlour tricks! It was the activities of these charlatans that led me to apply serious methods to psychic research."

He subsides, and no one speaks. Except the voice in the back of my head.

"Why didn't I realise before that I'm psychic? I never had a clue."

If I've got second sight, I'm thinking, how come I knew nothing about what really went on in this house?

Shanks lets out a sigh. "So much is uncertain in this world. All I can say is that the power is latent in most of us. Sometimes it appears with the onset of adolescence and is triggered by a single event; sometimes it reaches its peak at that time, and sometimes it dwindles away. I have no satisfactory answer to your question."

All of us can see as he speaks that the doctor, the upright, solitary, four-square man of science and letters, is caught in a cross-tide of contradictory emotions. His voice quivers with excitement as he utters matter-of-fact statements. He's obviously never remotely had the gift of second sight. His entire journey through his researches has been step by step, plodding along as if studying the free flight of birds while chained to the earth.

Why am I thinking like this? I'm starting to go on like a Long-hair. I'm putting things into words that I never use. I hardly recognise myself. And it's totally daft that the kind of person he's been searching for was under his nose all the time, waiting to pop up because I wanted to get back at some girl who'd... It's crazy, all of it.

The headache's getting worse. My body finds no comfort. The room is swirling with more things than I can handle. What I want is something to hold fast to, an anchor; anything.

Berenice is trembling too. McFee looks intently into the fire. Come on, Berenice, say something. You're the only one here on firm ground, above the clutches of the whirlpool. It can scare you, but only from looking. Just say something.

"Uncle?"

"Yes?"

"Tell us about the Holland monument. We saw it this morning. There's nothing like it in South Island. Obviously."

"Strange thing to ask at this time."

So she speaks softly, as if telling a child that, despite its wishes, it is time for bed.

"I'd like us to change the subject for a bit."

He and McFee exchange glances. I squint at Berenice. Her look says, it's all right; I'm not splitting on you, but I need to know things too.

Shanks clears his throat. "Well, that's odd. There is a great deal of psychic influence around the Holland tomb as it happens. I can tell you this:

"In the summer of '38 – the year before you first came to stay, Clement – signs of subsidence were noticed under the north wall and work was started to strengthen the foundations. No doubt you saw the scaffolding. The whole place has been under repair ever since.

"It meant disturbing the Holland remains, so the two large and six small coffins were removed to a corner of the churchyard and covered with a tarpaulin. The weather was fine and I had a colleague – a rather weak psychic – staying here, so we went over to watch work in progress. While standing near the coffins he began to register alarm. I pulled back the cover to reassure him that they were only the coffins of an old family of good repute. He trembled – I remember this clearly – and said, "You're a doctor, Armitage; I beg you to arrange to examine their necks." Believe me, in this branch of science you take every hint. I undertook the examination myself, in what I admit were unorthodox circumstances."

Shanks pauses, then lowers his voice to a deep murmur.

"Every one of the children's necks showed unmistakeable signs of having been twisted and broken."

Berenice screams.

The three of us are round her in a second. Now it's me holding her hand as she breathes quickly, trying not to cry. "You all right?" I ask. She swallows a couple of times. "Please finish the story," she says. Her smile emerges like a swimmer from lightless depths but the tears are running.

Without any of us moving away Shanks goes on. The bedside manner again.

"All the evidence points to Lady Anne. She developed a pathological hatred for each child as it grew, and strangled them all to death." He shakes his head. "An atrocious crime. Yet each death was passed off as natural. The complicity of servants and the forensic ignorance of the time. She got clean away with it, and everyone thought she was an angel of piety and forbearance."

"Yes," Berenice whispers, "Every Waking Moment was but a Step to Heaven."

"Every lucid moment perhaps. She was stark mad of course. Does that satisfy you?" He gazes at her tearstained face. "I don't think you are very satisfied, my love."

My love. It's the first endearment I've heard him utter in about a thousand years.

"I wrote a short piece about it in the *Glass*. The journal of our Society. Without, of course, revealing too much. More as a piece of historical enquiry. In any case the psychic fraternity were full of Harris and Borley Rectory that year."

"What was that?" I say, and I yawn. Shanks puts his impatient voice on.

"Borley was supposed to be the most haunted house in England; had been for nearly a century if you cared to believe it. And Mr Harris was supposed to be a psychic investigator. I wish I'd had a tenth of his resources. It was all nonsense. Harris manufactured most of the sightings and noises himself. Everyone involved came clean at some time or another. Wretched, wretched business."

He looks around at each of us in turn. "I cannot tell you how much it has threatened all our reputations; every society investigating the paranormal, everyone like me. That's why I choose carefully, why I rarely go out of my way on so-called ghost hunts. What we are dealing with here – Mr McFee's problem – must be handled with the seriousness it deserves." With that, he seems to subside into his own thoughts.

Something happens in the silence that follows. It's about silence.

We've had no music in this house. Apart, that is, from Berenice on the piano for five minutes and some tuneless humming from Ludmilla of the Far North. The wireless hasn't been on once. It's been like a deserted monastery. "Can we put on a record?" I say. "Anything. I've had a trying day." I sound different to myself; I'm talking more... I don't know. It's been a trying day.

McFee chooses, winds up the gramophone and for a few minutes we rest back while solemn, soaring music washes over us. If the pillars of cathedrals could walk they would march in slow step to this. "Beethoven," says Shanks. "Beethoven. My God. He was stone deaf when he wrote that glorious, majestic music. Imagine his agony. Do you know what his last words were? This genius?"

No.

He said, "I shall hear in heaven."

His voice drops away to nothing. "I shall hear in heaven."

"It's what psychics do," he adds, "and saints, I daresay. The rest of us can hear only earthly sounds."

And I begin to cry until my whole body shakes, crying like a lost child reunited after a disaster. I hear a few words: 'overwrought', 'something to help them sleep', because Berenice is crying again too. I don't know about her, but I think I'm letting it all out for Jackson Armitage and for me. His search is over. He's come home. And I'm setting out for somewhere I know I don't want to be.

When we calm down, Shanks tries to reassure me. Tomorrow we shall conduct tests, do important research. I shall be at the forefront of discoveries. Practical science to draw these things into the fold of the known, the knowable. Perhaps be able to assist Mr McFee.

And so on. I decline the something to help me sleep. The late hour will perform that office.

I've never thought in words like this before. And I don't like the new Clement Garner, who might just be a nutcase after all.

Afterwards, alone, I make swirly patterns in the dentifrice before brushing my teeth, remember lists of facts, recite tables in my head, listen to the gurgling of water down the basin, the fox barking in the spinney. All normal stuff. The hunt will be after you on Boxing Day, Mr Fox. Normal thought. The mosquito-like whine of country silence. Real; real.

But on your back in bed you lose that old primate superiority.

Normal people are protected from the things, whatever they are.

Normal people can crawl all over the Holland tomb and feel nothing. With them the past stays where it is, the future remains a mystery; the present walks discreetly alongside.

A tapping on the door makes me leap with fright. It's Berenice, in her sky-blue pyjamas. She sits on the bed and gazes at me with her direct grey eyes still rimmed with red.

"Are we friends again, Clement?"

"Yes, of course. Why doesn't this power of mine work on you?"

"You mean knowing what I'm thinking? Like X-ray eyes?"

"Something like that."

"Well, don't take this as gospel, but I think emotion gets in the way."

"Emotion. There's a lot of it about."

"And anyway, it can't be all apples. Being invisible sounds cushy till you start getting knocked over because nobody sees you."

"I suppose so. How's Shanks?"

"Like a dog with two tails. I guess it means you'll be asked to help out with old McFee."

"Berenice, I'm scared. I'm glad you're here."

She smiles. "That's what I said to you yesterday."

We look at each other for a long time, but not long enough. I really like her.

"I seem to be thinking more clearly just now. I mean, more than in my whole life. So I can say something I wouldn't have thought of once. You reckon my psychic powers can help Shanks. Well, your earthbound, no-bloody-nonsense powers can help me. To stay sane. Right?"

"I get scared too, you know. You saw that tonight; me and spooky stuff."

"That's what I mean. You're normal."

"Okay, it's a deal. Seriously, stick with the real life, the physical things. I'm sure half this second-sight business is only clear thinking anyway. I reckon our so-called sixth sense is just what our early ancestors' normal five senses added up to. We just don't use them properly anymore. I bet cavemen had it as standard kit because their heads weren't full of...well, horseshit. Now get some sleep."

"Yes, Matron."

She laughs, bends towards me and kisses me lightly on the forehead. I smell warm silk and the kind of talcum powder I don't use.

It beats all the second sight in the world.

Chapter 11

The first thing he does is make me an honorary member of the League of Supernatural Investigators of England and Wales. It's in his gift and I'm to keep it to myself. Then we get to work.

Berenice takes notes, McFee goes for long country walks and Alphonse comes in and out with a look that gets more old-fashioned as the day wears on.

And it feels all right, at first.

Shanks pulls out boxes of equipment from the cupboards that line the study and sets them up till the place looks like a mad professor's laboratory. Which it is, sort of. He even takes off his jacket.

I have to sit on the far side of a screen rigged up across his desk, facing away from him and blindfolded. He doesn't tell me he's pointing to cards or pictures; he just asks me to think of images in my own time, but I sense they're picture cards anyway. I close my eyes to intensify the mind's solitude.

I wish that to be a…not a number…not even a playing card. An egg.

"An egg?"

"Go on."

"Um, a rocket. A V2. No, a pagoda."

"Carry on. Take your time."

"Er, a list of questions." These among many. Sometimes, often, I shake my head.

Afterwards he shows me. An oval, the Eiffel Tower and a crossword grid. Not bad.

We press on and I get tired, but Shanks is in his element. Despite the stuff about taking my time he drives the tests on. Pictures, inkblots, wires taped to my skin, thermometers dangling on strings. A break for lunch, then more. Questions this time, probing my dreams, fears, weird moments, incidents of *déjà vu*. I don't mention the business at the church because it still smacks of madness and I want it to disappear.

At last he calls a halt. Berenice has a pile of sheets of paper beside her, and writer's cramp. I have mental cramp and the feeling that I've been wrung out like a sponge. But it could have been worse. Shanks explains that tests with cards usually go into hundreds if not thousands before percentages begin to look significant. The results of a single morning have convinced him of my powers.

Because I wasn't guessing. I knew. And like everyone who knows, I sometimes get it wrong. Just as well, he says. Or it might get worrying.

"I shall put it in simple layman's terms. ESP falls into three main categories. I tested you for all three. In the first I could see the cards myself. That was telepathy."

"I could read your thoughts."

"Just so. In the second I did not see the symbol until after you had spoken. That was clairvoyance. And the third; the third is a strange business. I neither shuffled the pack nor dealt them."

"Yes?"

"Precognition. Your scores were high in all three; highest in telepathy. The highest I have ever recorded."

"And telepathy is the most useful one – for us, I mean?" says Berenice.

"Because?"

"Because," she goes on carefully; "because people's thoughts contain the truth that their words hide."

I have to know. "Did you do this a lot with people when I was younger? Here, I mean?"

"Occasionally, my boy. Of course I always drew the curtains – to avoid distractions – and to ensure privacy. Believe me, promising subjects were few and far between."

It's Christmas the day after tomorrow. McFee isn't going away; I know that now.

Nor is Albert Smallwood. He lurks around through the day and upsets my concentration, reminding me that he's no longer none of my business. But the Doctor seems satisfied with our day's work and piles us into the car to take tea in Stoveleigh. When we get there the tea room's shut, so he simply drives back, still happy, still babbling on about what a great find I am, how I'll impress the society and all those who disdain to believe. The motion of the car has its effect on me and we have to stop so I can take a leak.

It's a relief to be out of the misted-up atmosphere but I have to walk a fair way to be private. And the feeling grows stronger that this is the farthest I've been from Berenice all day. As I stand with my back to a copse of beeches I feel the darkness of its shadow in the growing gloom of evening. It's weighted with the cawing of rooks and the insistent whisper of the wind. The kind of thing that doesn't bother me at all.

Yet there's no wind. Not a breath.

The tingling begins, up and down my spine.

I button my flies and walk quickly, scrunching through the undergrowth back to the road.

The car's gone.

My eyes search both ways. Surely this was right? They were right here. What kind of a stunt is this, after all that's happened? Is this a joke? Anger explodes in my head. "Not funny! Not bloody funny! At all!" But my voice is muffled and robbed of strength. Silence lays an unfriendly hand on me. I step out onto the road. The trees overhang it, forming a tunnel, but the surface glints with the dead white of bones and tombstones and I'm alone.

Panic fear is the old, nameless dread that Pan lays on those who walk in his woods. Whole regiments of soldiers have famously fled from nothing at all in sunlit glades filled with birdsong. It strikes me now in the dusk. Me, who's spent years ridding himself of natural terrors. It isn't the forest-fire of sunset glowing through the tracery of branches: nothing visible. Just complete, unreasoning fear. I run down the empty road under the tunnel of trees, moaning as though trying to call out in a nightmare.

It's the same moaning that escaped from me, slack-mouthed, at the Holland tomb, and it forces itself at last into the shape of a cry. I'm bellowing meaningless things into the gloom, trying to push away the dark with waves of nonsense as though idiocy might make me dangerous to whatever's there.

When the headlights catch me I'm running from one side of the road to the other as if trapped in flames.

I'd gone off hundreds of yards away in the wrong direction. They only heard me when they became impatient and got out of the car.

The journey to Inglefield Place finishes in a huddle of cold sweat in the back seat and numb shaking of the head in answer to every question. I spend the rest of the evening in a series of disturbed snatches of sleep, of waking, acid-mouthed, in unknown places that take ages to make sense of, of swallowing things to help me over it, of overhearing bits of conversation. It's my version of delirium, but the fever is of a rare kind. Four times in the night I start up, crying out. Two of those times Berenice is there. The last two I'm alone in my room. The lamp's been left on, and everything's exactly in its place, exactly the same.

If there'd been an earthquake or a bomb had fallen and reduced my surroundings to rubble I would be all muscles and hands, a combatant rising above disaster. Bruised, covered in dust, naked, dispossessed, but still there, clearing, levelling, re-arranging. Redoubled by physical challenge. A builder of pyramids.

But the rubble is me.

It won't be put together again. This is the pattern. From here on, unbidden horrors will stalk the ruins like dogs under the moon. The awful city where Smallwood's presence roams is what remains of my normal past; its thoroughfares are now my psychic powers.

Powers. Really?

Outside the control of any other power I have. Even this new clear thinking only makes me see my defencelessness for what it is, like paralysed prey watching itself being eaten alive.

After the real earthquake stops you can pick up the smallest stone and place it, to say: look, I can change the landscape too.

In the deep silence the shelves, alcoves and cornices regard me.

Chapter 12

"Good morning, Master Clement! Here is cup of tea. Others are eating breakfast and after will visit you. You have slept long time. Do not look out of window for you will see nothing. Heavy fogging out there. Much mist!"

"Morning, Alphonse."

Things seem strangely reasonable. Another fair start to an uncertain day.

"Alphonse?"

"Yes, Master Clement."

"You've had an interesting life, yes?"

He tilts the teapot back so the flow stops, and looks past me.

"Mrs Stankeivitch and I still alive, still free. That is interesting enough for us, I think."

I take the cup and saucer. Here is Alphonse Stankeivitch, in his white jacket, with his foreign English and those comfortable manners of old Europe; of whose past sufferings I know nothing and would barely understand if I did. And he's normal, courteous, sane. There are millions like him in the world, pushed around by the struggles of a century that isn't half over yet; maybe dreaming of home, maybe stripped of family and inheritance, pursued day and night by evil memories. As I drink my tea I feel more than just its invigorating warmth. I feel better about everything.

"Alphonse?"

"Master Clement?"

"I've never properly introduced myself. May I shake your hand? Excuse me for not getting up."

He extends his hand, gives a little bow and says, "Stankeivitch!"

"Garner! And I have a lot to thank you for. Is Ludmilla around?"

He goes to the door and calls out something. She's in Berenice's room and comes along the corridor. More words, a questioning look, and she too comes in and shakes my hand without saying anything. "Madame, I'm honoured," I say. "Thank you."

She gives a little smile and a shrug. "For what?"

Before I can answer there's movement by the door and everyone else crowds into the tiny octagonal room. The two servants make themselves invisible.

For a couple of minutes I'm a celebrity. Am I feeling better? Is there anything I want? Am I ready to face the day?

Oh, yes. Just give me a moment to get ready and I'll be with you all.

When they've gone I count backwards from a hundred and get up. The room's chilly but it helps me feel normal, unremarkable. Everyone, great and small, has to get up, sit on something, brush their teeth and socialise their armpits before taking their place in the ranks. The necessaries are good reminders.

Walking out in the mist an hour later, the four of us retrace my steps of the Angry Walk across the fields. "The overcast's breaking," says Berenice, "sun'll soon be out."

Jackson Armitage and McFee are strolling ahead. "Makes you smile," she goes on.

"What does?"

"Uncle wears a coat and fishing hat and he's tall and thin and brainy."

"Yes?"

"And McFee is short and stocky and wears a bowler hat."

"So?"

"Hey, you're pretty dense for a psychic. So Jackson looks like Sherlock Holmes and McFee looks more like Doctor Watson."

"You have me," I say, "at a disadvantage. What the hell are you talking about?"

She sighs. "Jesus wept. Well that's it! Jackson is actually the doctor and McFee is the detective!"

"Oh, right. Yes. Very good."

After a while she adds, "Uncle's very keen to use you in cracking this Smallwood business. Just be careful. Mother's told me about how obsessive he gets about things. She says how he goes after the truth, whatever – or whoever – it costs. Do you get me?"

"I'll be careful. Didn't your mother know anything about this ghost society racket?"

"Mm? Oh, yes, but she thought it was just a hobby of his. He actually started out as a country doctor and got interested in psychiatry. He told me something while you were asleep yesterday."

"Do tell."

"He was at medical school during the First War and felt he'd been lucky to be out of it. Do you remember him feeling pretty ripped about those fake mediums gypping people? Making out they could get in touch with the dead?"

"Or missing."

"Yes, well; he treated some of the relatives for nerves while they were actually in the clutches of those flaming ratbags. He couldn't do much for them, he said. Some shocking cases, apparently. So that's why he feels like he does. If there's really anything in it he wants it to be straight, honest, scientific. I warn you, Clem, he's mad keen."

"Thanks."

I stay quiet for a bit. The sun begins to poke through the mist.

"I don't want to keep calling you Clement," she says, "or Clem. Makes you sound like your Prime Minister."

"Old Attlee? He's okay, I think. Most of the masters at school reckon he's the Antichrist; but there you are."

"What's it called again?"

"Haven't I told you? It's called Monk's Hill. You wouldn't want to know about it. You're really lucky not to go to school. Must be beautiful."

"Just tell me one thing about it – anything – and I'll leave off asking. Deal?"

"Deal. I'll tell you two things and then you never mention it again while you live. Okay?"

"Okay."

"Right. There've never been any monks and it's not on a hill."

"A very full and fair description, Mister Not-Clement. I'd like to call you Mackinnon if that's okay. Has a ring about it. Mackinnon. Sort of Randolph Scott; riding out of town after sorting out the bad hombres."

"Sounds just like me. You're not taking the piss, are you?"

She gives me one of her serious looks. "No, I'm not. Before long, if I've read this right, you'll be riding into the big town to sort out a problem those two can't solve on their own. And if I'm further not mistaken the briefing'll start any minute, out here under the wide open sky. Just remember to be careful. See you back at the house." She squeezes my arm. "I'm not far away. Good luck."

Next thing, I'm leaning on the field gate by the weir with only McFee for company. We stare at the foaming water for a long time before he speaks.

"What do you know about detective work?" he says suddenly, not looking at me.

"Er, not a great deal, sir."

"Well, try the little that you do know."

"Um, it's all to do with um, motive…means…and opportunity, I think."

He's silent again for a long time. The sun's out now but the cold's creeping down my neck. I want to move about, but we're two men leaning on a gate, so I don't.

"Agatha Christie."

"Excuse me, sir?"

"Pure Agatha bloody Christie. And stop saying Sir. And try to bloody relax. You're having a conversation, not helping me with my enquiries."

"Sorry."

"Right. Now, how many murders do you think I've investigated in my time?"

"I really can't say, sir. Er, sorry."

"Very few. It's mostly been sordid, humdrum little crimes committed by rancid little misfits. And of the few murders I've solved how many have taken place in lonely country houses where the guests can't leave and I'm knocking around with nothing else to do?"

"I'll say, none?"

"Right first time. If I'd done someone in at Nob Hall during a bloody shooting weekend I'd get out, fast, before a passing Boy Scout showed up and cracked the case in five minutes. It isn't like that, son. Not for me, not for Fabian of the Yard or anyone."

"I suppose not. Do you know Inspector Fabian?"

"You'd be surprised who I know."

He starts to fill his pipe. He still hasn't actually looked at anything but the troubled tumbling water at the foot of the weir. I've spent many happy hours doing the same thing, but that was way back in my childhood.

"Still, let's try out your crime novel methods. Motive, means, opportunity. It passes the time. Let's say there's a body lying on the canal towpath in Little Venice – that's in London, Maida Vale, near where I live. Young woman, head bashed in with a lump of concrete. The victim's been dead an hour. Who did it? Start with opportunity. No rush."

There isn't much choice about taking my time. At last I say, "Assuming that's where she was attacked, anyone within an hour's travel of the scene of the crime?"

McFee exhales a large cloud of blue smoke. "Mmm. So we pull in most of London. King, Queen, Archbishop of Canterbury, the Government, eight million assorted people excluding the obvious, and anyone getting off trains at Brighton, Reading, wherever. We also put up roadblocks on every route out of the capital. Fair enough?"

"I didn't mean absolutely anyone...no, not very practical, really."

"So go on to means."

"Well, we know the means; a piece of concrete. A blunt instrument."

"Don't get clever, laddie. Lumps of concrete have sharp edges. And they don't murder people by themselves. Come on, think. Use some of your expensive education."

I'm not enjoying this, but I need to keep my head above water.

"Right, it could only be someone strong enough to lift it above head height. That's if it wasn't dropped from above."

"Good. Does that narrow it down?"

"No. Not nearly enough. That leaves us with motive. Doesn't it?"

For the first time he looks at me.

"How did I crack most of my cases, d'you suppose?"

I shake my head, slowly. It's rude to shrug.

"Somebody told me who did it."

"Oh."

"As you say, oh. If you're going to get murdered it'll usually be by someone you know and that someone must have a reason. You look around among the victim's circle and sooner or later it comes out. Bit of gossip, a grudge, affair of the heart. Motive. Unless it's a madman."

He's spent his little speech and become silent once more. But as I gaze intently into the water and hope he'll leave off now, I know what he's said is too simple. I read the papers and listen to the news and I'm sure one or two recent big murders have been solved by amassing lots of small clues, and by bringing in big-time forensic experts like Bernard Spilsbury.

Is motive really the thing? If Toady Hopwood got bumped off at school there'd be several hundred past and present Monksonians with excellent reasons for doing him in. I'd be a prime suspect myself. Not that I dislike French; it's the singer, not the song.

"Your silence is eloquent," McFee says suddenly. "You'll be thinking: hang on, this isn't right. You can't arrest a person just for wishing somebody dead. Am I close?"

"Yes. It wouldn't stand up in court, would it?"

"Wouldn't get to court. The jilted lover you pull in has to have no alibi, traces of concrete dust on his furniture and in his turnups and the right blood spots on his clothes. A confession helps."

This time he looks straight at me for several seconds, as though examining me. His voice falls quiet but in a strange way it still blocks out the noise of the weir.

"I know what he did and when he did it. I know he's come back. I don't care how; that's your uncle's parish. I just want to know why. All right?"

"Yes, sir. And you both think I can help you. I do care how, though."

"The Doctor reckons if we visit places, people, anything connected with Smallwood and the time I arrested him, and we take you along, then you might be able to pick up, I don't know, atmosphere. Psychic clues. If he's a ghost then he's a supernatural phenomenon and you should be on his wavelength. Might lead us to him."

"Or him to us. Are you saying he's trying to contact you?"

"Why else would he be bothering me? There was no bad feeling between us. He was a villain, I was the law. The law won. End of story."

"No it isn't. You said so yourself the other evening."

I'm relaxed now. I can find clues that are invisible to him. That makes us equal.

"Anyway," I go on, "what makes you think he's after you? He's blown up a couple of safes and left his fingerprints around. No message, is there?"

"That is the message," he says quietly. "And it's for me. I've had this feeling now for two or three months, very strong. And on and off over the last ten years I've known that he hasn't gone away. Can't explain it. You're okay about joining in this thing, are you?"

"Yes. As long as the holiday lasts, anyway."

"Good man. I think your uncle may have plans about extending your time off school if it becomes necessary. That suit you?"

I've surprised myself at how quickly I'm jumping into this. McFee's last comment clinches it. Out here it all sounds simple. It is simple. They'll do the work; I'll be the expert, the consultant, doing what comes naturally.

Supernaturally.

The cold starts on my neck again. There's no warmth in the sun. Be careful, she said; and she was right. If I'm just going to have to sniff old jackets to pick up a scent that's one thing. But it could get weird; nasty.

"That suit you?"

"Er, yes, Mr McFee. It suits me."

He makes to go.

"Mr McFee?"

"Yes?"

"Maybe he wants to tell you who shopped him."

"That's one possibility. So why all this song and dance? A simple ghostly phone call would do the trick. Did the trick for the squeak, didn't it?"

He grunts. "I'm going for a stroll. See you later. Your uncle's got a little meeting fixed for after lunch. Don't go too far away."

I watch him as he walks back over the meadow.

Don't go too far away. Wonderful. I'm pretty far away already, from where I started.

Chapter 13

We're sat round the dining table. Jackson Armitage is handing out sheets of paper with typed carbon-copy lists on them. One list has seven items. It looks like this:

1. Emmanuel Rosenblum. Pawnbroker. Owner of shop where Smallwood arrested.

2. Jack Sidgwick. Policeman with McFee at Smallwood's arrest. Retired.

3. Nightwatchman who guarded Smallwood. Name and whereabouts unknown.

4. Informer who shopped Smallwood. Name and whereabouts unknown.

5. Cellmates and close associates of Smallwood during his last stretch in Pentonville.

6. Family and close friends of Alice Smallwood. All traceable. Some already known.

7. Alice Smallwood. Deceased.

He looks up. "All these people – with the exception of the last – must be found and questioned. In your case, Clement, even Mrs Smallwood may be open to enquiries."

"Does that make me a medium then?" My tone is suspicious and meant to be. There's a moment of delicate unbalance until Shanks says, "It is not a term I approve of. You are a psychic. Shall we go on?"

Berenice smiles at me and I raise my eyebrows to say, how was that? Careful enough? Not quite done yet. "Mr McFee, why don't we know the night-watchman's name? Didn't he appear as a witness at the trial?"

"No. I was exceeding my powers when I left Smallwood in his hands. Less said, the better."

Shanks leads. "Many of these people, if found, may not wish to speak to Mr McFee for a variety of reasons. In that case I shall have to see them. It may involve me in minor deceptions, the kind of tactics I am unused to, but I believe the risks are worth it. Whichever of us makes contact – and it could be both of us – Clement, you will accompany. Your examination may prove the most revealing. All clear?"

"And what about me?"

We look at Berenice. She stares back.

"Where do I come into this?"

"It's not easy to think of a distinct role for you," says Shanks. McFee takes the ball from him. "Some of the merchants we'll be dealing with are a bit uncouth. One or two are complete nutters; nasty pieces of work."

"So they're ratbags. So what? I'm used to rough customers where I come from. It's amazing how reasonable they get when a girl shows she doesn't give a damn. I know how to take care of myself, at least as well as Clement here." She sweeps her hair off her forehead and leans back in her chair. "I pause for a reply."

"I'll drink to that," I say.

More exchanged glances.

Come on, have I got to say it? If I ever got into a tight spot it's Berenice I'd want beside me. She's got it all; tough, agile, rock-throwing, sword-wielding, climbing, riding; and you two have no idea, no clue about how much I like her.

"She's been in on this from the start. You can't leave her out. I appreciate her support."

That's got to be clear enough.

"Company for you?" says McFee.

"Expense," says Jackson Armitage. "I have friends in town, but our researches may take us out of the capital. My thoughts hadn't progressed beyond your staying with Miss Maybury and touring round London while we pursued our enquiries."

Is he smiling? "Extra rooms."

"That's the price you pay for bringing some tone to this business."

"Well said, Miss," says McFee. "We'll need all the tone we can get."

And the rest. I let my breath out slowly.

"One more thing," Shanks adds. "The papers. You can see what the yellow press would do with this story if they got a whisper of it. Not to say how Smallwood's spirit might react to public fuss. Mr McFee assures me his seniors at the Yard – all the way up – have the matter in hand. The Home Office are prepared to exercise certain...restraints. But there are weak links, apparently."

"Such as?"

"Mr McFee knows of at least one junior officer whose professional detachment cannot be relied upon. A question of character. And Alphonse and Ludmilla suspect something. How could they not? Servants are expected to be discreet because they have things to be discreet about. They are not fools but they will be the first targets of press snoopers who inhabit a powerful and sophisticated world. I know the results suggest something cruder, but there it is. For the matter of that, previous employees of mine could be tracked down to provide what I believe is termed background."

"Just like what we're doing, then."

"Quite. What I mean to say is we are working against time. The deeper we go, the more leaks we risk starting. We will be in constant danger of exposure."

He gets up and walks to a window; a tall sash window. The slanting rays of the sun fall around him. Maybe I'm already picking something up; maybe it's just horse-sense, but he seems for a moment to be standing in a strange afterglow of his hopes. It's as if some invisible pattern of him, tall, erect, perpetually disappointed, has been standing by that window, in that light, for the last twenty years; watching the day of his opportunity fade.

He speaks to himself; as though recalling something from long ago.

"It would be very, very bad if this got out too soon. So much of the reputation of this science depends on a successful outcome. A new view of the workings of creation. A new wisdom. The philosopher's stone of the study of the mind. All if we can seek and find and communicate with the spirit of Albert Smallwood. We must do everything we can."

That afternoon a telegram boy on a motorbike brings Christmas greetings from my parents in Nairobi. No card, just a brief message in capitals. The postman leaves letters at the empty lodge house for Alphonse to pick up, so this is the first stranger at our door since I arrived. I put the telegram in my pocket. They've no doubt got my card, sent off so long ago I forget what it looked like. That's about it. To them, no news is good news and I have no particular feelings about it. An hour later come telegrams from Berenice's people and Miss Maybury in London. She shows me them; warm, effusive.

"Well, Mackinnon; going to show me yours?"

"Beg your pardon?"

"You simple creature. The telegram you got?"

She reads it. It doesn't take long.

"Parents of few words, then. Actually you haven't told me a thing about them, have you?"

"I've hardly ever seen them. They didn't want children."

"How do you know that?"

"They told me."

"That's a tough break, Mackinnon. How do you feel about it?"

"I don't. They left me in the care of others. You don't miss what you haven't had."

"Bullshit. Believe me. It isn't true."

"You'd know, would you?"

"Yes. They wouldn't be part of the Happy Valley crowd out there, would they? Bridge, boredom, scandal? We've heard all about it back home."

"Probably. You're not the first to ask."

"Something wrong? Your repartee isn't up to your usual standard. Tell me it's all this Smallwood business. It's getting serious now. Thanks for wanting me along."

It's true. We are simple creatures. It doesn't take much.

"It's okay. Sorry." Now I can look comfortably into her eyes.

"My mother was really cut up because I was born in a railway waiting room in the African bush. It was the last word in embarrassment. If she could have left me there she would have. There was heat, flies and the knowledge that hundreds of curious natives were just the other side of some flimsy blinds. I bet your mother would have loved it – afterwards."

She laughs. "That she would. I was born on the farm myself. Same afternoon I was out rounding up sheep on a half-broken horse. Christmas tomorrow."

"Yup. I do like your name, by the way."

"Well, I don't. Can't imagine what they were thinking of."

"They were thinking of a constellation. Coma Berenices. Berenice's Hair. A constellation of the north. Maybe it reminded them of home."

"They've never been. Could have been the grandparents, I suppose."

"I could call you Fernleaf."

"That's what they called my dad and his mates when he was in the Anzacs in the First War. They call us Kiwis now. Fernleaf. Okay, I'll buy it."

Alphonse has lit fires in many rooms. In the eagle picture room the Christmas tree stands looking reasonably festive, its little twisty candles leaning all ways, ready for lighting. The covers are off the furniture and Fernleaf does her best when she has to be in there.

All evening the phone rings with greetings from Shanks's friends. We play parlour games – harmless ones – and I'm relieved to have no more success in guessing at charades than anyone else. She has a way of moving when she acts out her parts and I see McFee noticing how I watch her. We admire the crib that Alphonse had modelled in his spare time with plaster of Paris and a set of moulds he's picked up at a village hall jumble sale. Under a canopy of real straw the animals stand, kneel and sit and the Holy Family have paper halos stuck on the backs of their heads. Ludmilla sings songs standing in front of the library fire, her hands crossed on her apron. She is entirely without fear or embarrassment while I prepare excuses for when they ask me to perform. Berenice plays carols on the piano by the kitchen and finishes with something by Grieg, or so she says.

We listen to the wireless. Beyond the silence of Inglefield Place the world's in enough trouble for peacetime. A dinner-jacketed voice reports the victories of barbarism across the globe. The continuing religious massacres in India; even I took an interest back in August when this same set crackled with Nehru's independence speech: at the midnight hour, while the world sleeps, India will awake to life and freedom. Not much of that around anywhere this Christmas Eve. Trouble in Palestine, around the place depicted in our plaster crib. Civil war in China, in Greece, in South-east Asia; millions on the march in Europe, homeless, stateless, refugees, prisoners; great cities in ruins; old Allies falling out, new wars, new repressions, atomic bombs, austerity. A tawdry apology for a new world.

I need to get a hold of myself. What's up with me? None of this stuff bothered me before. But images are crystal-clear in my mind; things my memory has barely brushed with. There was this cartoon in a paper at the end of the war. A soldier, bandaged, holding out a wreath with 'Victory and Peace in Europe' written on it. He was handing it to you, but you knew it was meant for the politicians. "Here you are," he says. "Don't lose it again."

I stare at the others. They're sitting there, the way you do when the BBC broadcasts the news. Then I realise the bulletin's over.

"Well, well," McFee's saying. "That wedding was the best thing that happened this year. Had the Force on its toes though. We're going to have a Queen again one of these days, you lucky people."

What's he talking about? Princess Elizabeth and that Greek bloke were married over a month ago. They haven't mentioned that on the news just now.

But they have. Just a few discreet words about the honeymoon. Nice to be able to get away like that. It's just about impossible for the rest of us, her future subjects. Naturally I know about it; you'd have to be living down a well not to, so there's no need to look stupid by asking what they really said. But it doesn't hide the fact that I've just heard a totally different broadcast. A broadcast that hasn't happened, about the sorrows of the world and nothing else.

Is this how it's always going to be? A human receiver picking up nothing but bad news? My heart's thumping. There's never going to be any escape from this, from the intrusions of – what? Of a twisting of reality; a caricature of truth.

"I'm just stepping outside. To see if the sky's clear."

I stand by the box tree in the silence and will myself into calm. The stars are beautiful.

There are lights bobbing in the distance and low sounds of talking. Farmer Symonds's horse and cart comes up the drive, its lamps shining on the wall of fir trees that flank them on either side. That's better. Something normal in this world.

The six of us congregate in the porch while the village kids sing *Hark the Herald Angels Sing* and *Silent Night* – because it is. The lanterns on their poles cast pools of light. Alphonse looks pensive; Ludmilla nods and smiles. So I put my arm round Berenice because her home is far away too and these people have come a long way on the quiet country road under the stars to do this for us; to show that the good things of the present life can go on just a while longer.

Once in Royal David's City. Never mind what's going on there now. *The First Noel*, and *Silent Night* again. Then mince pies, hot drinks and a little hay for the horse as Berenice speaks softly to it and pats its old ridged back.

In the deep, dark country peace our voices make us sound like the only people on earth.

Chapter 14

Christmas Day 1947.

We come together for breakfast like castaways meeting on a desert island after a shipwreck. And the Admirable Crichtons are Alphonse and Ludmilla. Between them they produce a feast such as only the countryside can provide in these rationed times. Ludmilla's spent her life making something out of very little; so the first thing she did when they came in September was to trade for the gleanings that the gardener's wife had collected from that blazing summer's harvest, and keep some to grind by hand to make extra bread. The chickens got the rest. Eggs and that bread are our Christmas breakfast. It's a good beginning.

Afterwards, by the tree, all the presents are revealed in a serious little five-minute ceremony and well received. Out of all of us only the Lithuanian couple know each other closely. The rest of us are still strangers, even Shanks. Now I realise the old truth that the more you learn about some people the more distance it puts between you. So our exchange of gifts is done with the air of explorers or ambassadors. We gauge reactions. "Thank you both," says McFee to Fernleaf and me when he unwraps his. I smile as if I know what he's talking about. When did she knit that scarf? It turns out she produced it in the evenings when she sat up in bed. Seems I unpicked the wool of an old jumper for her.

News to me. "Thanks," I say when we're alone.

"It's okay. You've had other things on your mind. Sorry, but I never asked you if you could knit."

At eleven the faint sounds of the bells of Fingfield Church drift over the woods and meadows. I try not to think of Inglefield's sparse congregation, gathered under their silent, crumbling tower to hear about peace and goodwill while a murderer lies sleeping at their elbow.

Christmas lunch is another Ludmilla masterpiece. This time they sit with us and reminisce with Shanks about the war, their stay in Stockholm, Greta Garbo; while we listen politely. The cider gets to work on me and I ask her if they like Bela Lugosi.

"Bela Lugosi? For the young people, maybe! Only to frighten children. For me is your Herbert Marshall I like." She leans towards Alphonse and pats his arm. "Looks like Mr Stankeivitch!" He shrugs modestly and the conversation settles in Hollywood for the rest of the meal. Then it's time for the King on the wireless.

The phone rings.

After a few seconds Alphonse appears in the library. "Sorry to disturb. Mr McFee, you are wanted, sir. Excuse me."

McFee gets up. His face is impassive but we all stiffen just a little, and meet each other's eye as he leaves the room. The same thought hangs in the air between us: he's got no family, only colleagues. Before I dare let my thoughts improve on that, he's back, looking pale.

"He's done it again."

"Smallwood?"

"Yes."

"To be expected," says Shanks. "Another attempt on a safe?"

"Late last night. But this time it's more, more..."

"More what?" I say.

He turns to me and looks almost accusing. "Close to home," he mutters. "He's done a jeweller's in Marylebone. Only a few doors from where I live."

"Oh Lord," whispers Berenice.

"It means we must get to London as soon as possible," says Shanks. "We shouldn't lose time. Damned inconsiderate, though. Christmas of all days. Barging in on people. I'm sure we can manage on the petrol, though. Well, well."

But McFee shakes his head. His voice is quiet and carries all his authority.

"We'll go tomorrow; by train, first thing. As you say, it's bloody Christmas."

We forget about the King. There's something I have to do.

"Want me to come with you?" asks Berenice; then, "You don't seem sure."

"No, it's all right. I'm only going for a walk."

"Then I am coming. I'm getting to know you, Mackinnon; you shouldn't be left alone."

We step out into that solitude made even deeper by the voices of solitary birds; an Arctic silence of still air beneath a clear sky.

"Where are we going?" as she slips her arm into mine.

"Somewhere I haven't shown you yet. I haven't been there myself this time, with all the other stuff to think about. It's on the border of Shanks's land."

"Mysterious, is it?"

"Yes."

"That why you're being mysterious about it?"

I nod. We enter the hushed woods.

"No. It's called Hob's Pond. I've mentioned it once or twice. About a quarter of a mile away."

"Ah. The only place you couldn't go without Jackson's permission?"

"Not his permission, his knowledge. It was swimming in it that needed his say-so."

"Why?"

"Don't know. I never asked. Right from the beginning he laid down the law and that was it."

"Who's Hob?"

We're just walking, scuffing a few dead leaves. Nothing else is moving.

"Hob's the Devil."

She gives a gasp and clutches the front of her collar. It's like when I did my Dracula impression, but this time I feel less surprised. Almost as though I'd expected it.

"It's all right. Just an old name. An old superstition."

"Why, though?"

"We're doing that whispering again. I don't know. Maybe hundreds of years ago someone saw something here; or thought they did. Drunk, probably. Could even have been some peasants pissing about. No one knows."

She does a tight little smile and we move on. At last Hob's Pond appears through the trees. A stretch of water about a hundred yards in each direction, with bare birches and willows and elders coming right to the edge. There's no path round the shore to give it a visited look, just reeds and rushes here and there.

"Why come here now?"

"Because...because each time – except this time – that I came to the house the first thing I did was to go right round the edge of Shanks's domain. It made me feel it was mine. I was checking on my property; a child's property, that is. And I always finished up here."

"Making sure your world hadn't changed."

I have to think about that. "Yes. That's very good. It's important that it stays the same."

I turn towards her. "I never want it to change. This place hasn't changed in a thousand years. I'm sure of that. It's just that much more of the country looked like this then. It was marshy, watery, mysterious.

Imagine as far as you can see covered with mist in the early morning, dragonflies in the sun; ice in winter. You should have seen this in the winter of '39 to '40. It was my first Christmas here. All this was frozen and silent, locked in a freezing mist. It scared me to death when Shanks brought me to see it. Then last winter it was even colder. I didn't get back to school for days, we were so isolated by ice and snow. By then I regarded the pond as my own. It was even more dark and menacing. The frost on the trees glittered in the gloom. It seemed embalmed, as if a spell – no, a curse – had been put on it. And when it thawed the whole landscape flooded into a great marsh."

She's really listening to me, with eyes as well as ears.

"Then we had that record-breaking summer. Birdsong echoes here like nowhere else. It sounds eerie, but friendly. And no one around; like in the Dark Ages. You hear fish plop in the silence. You see herons standing in the shallows like statues. Sometimes there are kingfishers though the water is still. The halcyon. Halcyon days."

"You like silence, don't you?"

"I love it. I drink it up. I could get drunk on space and silence."

"You're not talking like a Caveman now."

"I don't think I ever thought about it in words that you could speak. All I know is I knew I was happy."

We stand there awhile. A lone bird puts out an occasional snatch of song and it tinkles across the dark face of the pond.

"My grandfather went to sea as a boy," says Berenice. "One day, when I was about ten, he said something to me. It was about growing up, except he didn't say as much. We were just sitting on our nags watching the sheep."

"What did he say?"

"He said: All day you play in the sun without a care. Then you hear a voice calling a long way off and it's saying, the long summer afternoon is over; time to come in."

To this I give no answer.

"I guess you did your journey round the borders at the end of each holiday as well."

"That's right. The day before I had to leave; in the late afternoon; always on my own. Just saying goodbye; you know."

"Like we are now."

"That's right."

"Shall we walk round?"

"No. Stay here. This is the first and last view you get of it."

The day is closing. No breath of wind disturbs the surface of the water. Red rays of sunlight dapple the dark mirror. The rushes stand as if listening to catch a sound.

And my thoughts are clear as crystal; as if all the emotions this place has bred in me are an ancient language, newly deciphered. I know I'll come here again. But I also know that when I turn my back on it this time the enchanted lake will vanish.

Late next morning we board the car for the ride to Oxford. Among the luggage is a wood and leather case containing the Doctor's equipment, which he's placed in the boot himself. Ludmilla stands at the Tudor-arched front door and calls out something we don't understand to Alphonse as we pull away. It might be 'drive slowly'.

We drift at twenty miles an hour to Inglefield, with Shanks and Alphonse exchanging the odd muttered word in the front; lurch over the level crossing and take the concrete way that snakes for a few miles till it reaches the main route to Oxford. Alphonse sits stock-still, head back under his brown felt hat, inscrutable as he steers us ba-bump, ba-bump over the tarred joints in the road. We all know he knows something. With any luck it isn't enough to go on. Not far behind the rest of us, then.

Oxford Station. Alphonse gives us a non-commital farewell and a long handshake for McFee. He clearly doesn't expect to meet him again. Shanks carries his equipment case himself as we walk behind the porter to the platform for London and a long wait.

So here we are.

I leave the others and walk to the end of the platform. This was always the best spot in the station, like the bow of a ship cutting and dividing the gleaming web of rails. Looking back I can see McFee slowly pacing up and down in his mackintosh and bowler hat, emitting clouds of blue pipesmoke that swirl upward and disperse to join the smoke and steam from the one or two locomotives resting nearby. Shanks stands motionless in overcoat and felt hat and Berenice sits on a bench, hands in pockets, legs stretched out. And nobody else with any idea of why we're here. Like spies; acting normal.

The express glides in, a procession of wheels and shining steel rods; sweating oil, precision, power. The Great Western Railway in its last days. Within a week the name will be history. Few people my age are unaware of this. The locomotives will run on, the carriages now in the famous brown and cream livery will run on, but still it will all have changed. I'm becoming history too. As I hurry to board the train I turn to look once more down the tracks that lead to the big city, towards a future wrapped in darkness; like a conscript being carried to a war.

Chapter 15

Journeys in express trains put you in a trance if you're receptive to it. The wheels' metallic rhythms, telegraph wires swooping and rising like a flock of swallows, diving deep in the hot summer days, keeping pace with you at your window. The sudden jangle and screech and jolt as the train slows over a skein of points and crossovers reminds you of far-flung destinations, and all the while the visual tricks of nearness and distance play on you. After ten minutes of this I'm already being carried in a dream.

The country is white with cold and studded with naked trees. The colour and tinsel of our season makes no difference to them. Once, in the mid-ground of frost smeared with brown, a squadron of redcoat cavalry roil after some invisible brown streak practising a little field-craft of its own.

I've travelled in very few expresses in my life. Most of them, I suppose, were on the line between Nairobi and Mombasa, where much turning of wheels produces little speed. But that was in the forgotten time before my life alternated between Monk's Hill and Inglefield, carried to and fro on the one-carriage train that had the same easy approach through its countryside as its cousins on the old colonial railway.

Now the speed of our train begins to worry me. It's relentless. It passes through stations so fast you can't read their names. Tangles of track pass under us with a ripping, machine-gunning sound and the rhythm of the wheels becomes a drumbeat: dada-dum-dum, dada-dum-dum, dada-dum-dum. Faster and faster, London is reeling us in.

As the carriage takes on a swaying motion I haven't felt before, I glance at the others. Doctor Jackson Armitage is frowning over a crossword, Detective-Sergeant McFee dozes and Berenice stares out of the opposite window, looking with what I think is undue interest into the faces of travellers passing along the corridor. I get up and slide the compartment door open. Her eyes meet mine and she raises her eyebrows. Everything all right? I turn down my mouth and make my eyes into question marks. A minute later she joins me in the swaying corridor and we lean on the window rail.

"Something's bothering you."

"I've been bothered since the whole thing started. No, even before that. Somehow, if we were chasing spooks around the woods at midnight I'd feel better about it. It's just the thought of London. Too many people. Dark alleys. Smog."

"You've been watching old films. It's not like you think."

"You'd know?"

"I've been there, drongo. Spent a few days on the way up to Scotland."

"See the bomb damage?"

"Yes. Not the worst of it. That's in the East End."

"I know. I dreamt about it."

"I dreamt it too, don't forget. I'm not used to big towns either. Have you read *The City of Dreadful Night*?"

"Never heard of it."

"Just as well."

I turn and bow my head and our brows touch.

"I don't want to do this," I whisper, "but it's too late to back out. I'm worried. This second-sight business hasn't brought many laughs so far. More kicks than bloody ha'pence. Doesn't it have a good side?"

"I wish I knew," she says softly. "Don't worry, Mackinnon. I'll be watching out for you."

After a long while the scenery changes. Clumps of houses merge like herds going to water. Tall buildings rear up here and there: water towers, warehouses, factories. Stations blur past one after the other. And then the streets begin; endless rows of roofs, battalions of chimneys in fours, bow-fronted shops on corners, backyards touching right up to the railway. Alongside, below, from bridges, we watch acres and miles of dwellings cartwheeling away from us. When you think it must end, the whole pattern repeats itself; one part of one corner of a huge city, the same scenes again and again, further and further in from the peaceful fields; until the train begins to slow, the engine's smoke compressed between embankment walls of dark dirty brick; tall encroaching canyons with glimpses of the sky, longer and longer arches of shadow overhead. The tracks multiply. We pass through tunnels filled with the screeching of wheels, brakes, points, crossovers and trains going the other way.

Suddenly we're out into a clearing, snaking across a floor of gleaming metals. Then people on a platform, then massive arches of iron, blackened glass, pillars, more trains bathed in light filtered through steam.

Paddington.

Brunel's cathedral. As soon as I feel that platform under my feet it's as though I'm standing in a foreign country. It would take all the day's light hours to walk back into a land without houses, streets, endless neighbours, through one quarter of this city; a quarter that lodges more people than the whole of New Zealand. And this is one terminus among many. How many? I ask McFee as I stand amazed amid the stream of travellers. How many? he says, smiling. Oh, there's Marylebone, Euston, St. Pancras, King's Cross, Liverpool Street, Broad Street, Fenchurch Street, Cannon Street, Waterloo, Charing Cross, Victoria; how many would you like? You're standing, my son, in one forum of an imperial city. Still smiling, he lifts his eyes to the great vault of glass and turns his head this way and that, like the lone grizzly raising his muzzle to the piney air of the Wind River Mountains. This is where he belongs; his range; and he's back.

All around, the roar of venting steam and the yammering of the tannoy fills my ears and we walk out into a world whose clamour seems tranquil in comparison. To someone for whom the High in Oxford has been the pinnacle of metropolitan din, Praed Street is a revelation. Jackson Armitage comes up alongside us. In my wonder at everything I haven't noticed him not being there.

"Our bags are in Left Luggage," he says. He sounds different against this background.

We walk. McFee leads us into streets that grow smaller, quieter. With each step it steals in on me that my seasons in the woods and fields, escaping shelter, daring discomfort and the mysteries of lonely twilight places, has amounted all in all to a pretty sheltered life. There are people hurrying by me now who cling to warmth and light and the closeness of their kind, yet their lives are more truly spent under the scrutiny of chance. The high buildings around us are rocks between which they scuttle through fields of danger. Traffic tries to kill them at every turn. The throng of people seems no guarantee of safety. But I only have to look at my companions to see that they feel none of it. They just stroll along. McFee, the metropolitan man; Jackson Armitage, cosmopolitan man.

Berenice, who lives more remotely than most people on earth, scarcely gazes around her. London's a city; very big, full of buildings and monuments; that's all.

I tug at her sleeve. "How goes it?"

"How goes what?"

"It. All this."

"I know. Try to like it." We drop back a little.

"Look," I say, "see it this way. McFee is one man and he's haunted by a ghost. Right?"

"Right. That's why we're walking down this street now."

"You're happy that ghosts exist?"

"I accept they exist."

"And our Mr Smallwood is only one."

"Seems to be."

"So how many other people in London are haunted? How many ghosts could there be here? And how many of them are evil, out for revenge? If ghosts exist, what about the undead? The whole bunch? And I'm open to it; all of it."

She squeezes my hand. "Just keep your feet on the ground. People give ghosts all sorts of strange powers, but we've got far more."

"Really?"

"Yeah, drongo. Because we're alive."

It makes sense and in the way of most sense it fails to reassure. The streets we enter become meaner. The tops of the terraced houses catch the peculiar light of another day departing, but it lacks the comfort, the promise of country evenings. This is a curfew light. The buildings frown. The top of my back begins to tingle; waves of unease flow up my spine, bunching to break in a shudder across my shoulders. I'm about to say something when McFee halts at a dark brown shopfront and fishes keys out of his mackintosh.

I peer into the unlit window display. On a miniature easel stands a board with 'Gascoigne Photographic Studio' in Art Deco letters. It's surrounded by half a dozen framed portraits. Another label says 'Wedding Groups Specially Catered For'. It looks faded. Everything does. Gascoigne doesn't believe in hitting you between the eyes. But the eerie feeling's getting stronger. I'm compelled to study the stale pictures with Gascoigne's signature in squiggly letters across the corners. There's one that holds me; a head-and-shoulders of a man in RAF uniform. He's smiling.

Berenice watches me. "Good to see a cheerful face," she says.

"He isn't."

And as I speak wisps of smoke begin curling up from the eyes and two holes appear, widening and crinkling and splitting as yellow flames reach through.

Then it's over. The photograph is a brown smoking tissue shedding flakes of carbon onto the lino. There's a thick, petrol-fire smell in the air.

It happens too quickly for me to react. I turn to Berenice and her face is pressed to the glass and she's acting normally. When I look at the two men McFee is only just putting the key in the lock of the shop's door. No time has passed while the portrait burned. I close my eyes and turn away. My legs are going and I feel sick.

We haven't been half an hour in this town. What am I going to do?

"Come on, you two."

I turn my back on the window and step to the kerb to take a deep breath. As I move to follow the other three into the dark doorway I force myself to look.

The airman's portrait is intact, complete, smiling. The smell has gone.

McFee is still just inside the door. I keep my eyes down as I squeeze past him and climb a gloomy staircase that reeks of the twilight between damp and rot. "First left," he calls out.

The sitting room is sad and dingy. You can sense how the cold has grown into it like a spreading fungus of ice while its lodger has been with us at Inglefield. Sometimes by turning a light switch you can create an illusion of warmth in a place, but McFee's bright bulb in its shade only makes the cold harder, more crystalline. Our breath clouds around us.

Trying to hide the tremble in my voice I say, "This been your home for long, Mr McFee?"

Surely a detective can afford something better than this? Even single people have visitors. Who would you bring here? Apart from us.

His answer comes from the cubbyhole of a kitchen.

"About ten years. Why?"

"How long has that picture of the airman been downstairs?"

He emerges and tosses his hat onto a corner table. Shanks and Berenice are looking out of the window. Everyone keeps their coats and scarves on.

"Ah, that. Gascoigne put it there on VE Day. Want to know why?" He vanishes into the kitchen again. A kettle fills; cups clink.

"That's his brother Wilfred," he calls out. "Posted missing after a night raid on Bremen in '43. Officially he's presumed killed, but Gascoigne won't have it. Thinks he's still alive, wandering about; lost his memory. You'd be surprised how many people believe that kind of thing. He keeps the photo in the window in case someone spots him. There used to be a sign next to it saying 'Have You Seen This Man?' but he got so many false alarms he took it out. Distressed him, see? Bad for trade anyway. Still, he keeps hoping. Sad, really. Tea all right for everyone? Only got powdered milk."

"You'll have to tell Mr Gascoigne it's no use," I say. I can hear myself sounding flat, tired.

"Eh? No use? I know that, laddie." The other two turn from the window.

"No, I mean it really is no use. Wilfred's dead; burned to death."

I sink into an unyielding armchair. They gather round and I tell them what's just happened. McFee whistles softly and goes back to warm the pot. We're all quiet for a while. Berenice comes and sits by me on the arm of the chair and strokes the back of my head. Only when we're all seated and nursing cups of tea does he break the silence.

"Poor old Mitch. Can't be done, though, can it? I can't just go down there and say, 'You can take the picture out now. Wilf's dead. Burned. A psychic schoolboy told me.' He'd think I'd joined all those other twisted buggers he used to get all the time. No. Better he keeps hoping. Some day he'll know for sure or let it go. Ill wind, though. You're already doing your stuff, aren't you?"

Then I almost smile. Instead of feeling sick I feel warm. It isn't the tea. It isn't even the fingers roaming through my hair. It's like laying down something heavy that I've had to pick up. The glow is relief, but the relief isn't for me.

"Mr Gascoigne – Mitch; I think he knows now. He'll be taking the photo out soon."

It's a moment when no one else need say anything. We drink dreadful tea as the evening darkens, the sounds of the street change and the lamps come on.

"It's pretty chilly in here," says Berenice. Her tone suggests action.

"Hardly surprising," replies Jackson Armitage, "There's been no one here for days."

"You sure?" Berenice speaking, and there's a hint of mischief that I'm starting to recognise. McFee's eyes narrow. "What do you mean?"

"Nothing."

"What d'you mean, nothing? Don't you bloody nothing me. Are you saying someone else lives here? You can be bloody sure they don't. Ask around."

"It's all right, Mr McFee," says Shanks. "No one's suggesting that."

This room is too small to hold an argument in, but it's squeezing my thoughts together.

The doctor doesn't know as much about the sergeant of detectives as he'd like to. Berenice needs to stay on stage because they see her as just tagging along. She knows how to needle, but it's calculating. McFee jumped too quickly. We're not a team. In stories, quests are supposed to unite strangers.

Does Smallwood see us sitting in our coats in this cold, unwelcoming little room? Can he push us apart? Can he make us do things? Berenice hasn't finished yet.

"What I mean," she goes on in a dangerously insistent tone, "is that visitors might have called while you were away. Might have been here."

"No one else's got a key, not even Mitch," says McFee, then his voice trails off. His eyes widen. "My God, you don't mean he's been here?"

His features go slack. "Oh my God," he whispers.

Shanks speaks, sharply. "Hardly helpful, young lady. No one has as much as hinted at such a possibility. This is Mr McFee's home; he has to live here. Such comments from a transient visitor do no good."

So that's two people snappish.

"He hasn't been here. I'm sure of it."

"Are you, laddie?" says McFee. "Thank the Lord for that."

I don't have a clue whether he's been here or not, but a word from the psychic child seems to go a long way. Strange, though. Does McFee want to meet his ghost or not?

"You will look after yourself and light a fire, won't you?" says Berenice. It's a start, but not enough. "When I get back," he mutters.

"Where are you going?"

"We. We're going out to eat. There's a man runs a café near here who owes me a favour. Then we're going to call on Smallwood's latest victim."

"On Boxing Day evening?"

"He won't be going anywhere, or be having visitors. You have to have friends for that."

"After which," puts in Shanks, "we three will retrieve our bags from Left Luggage and take a taxi to Kensington, where we lodge for our stay in London at the house of old associates of mine." This is one of his trademarks; something I'm so used to it doesn't bother me. Correction: except for the business of Raymond and Victoria, which I have so strangely forgotten. He tells you nothing till it's almost on you. On the whole it's saved me years of useless questioning. Did Berenice know? But then I wouldn't have asked her either.

"At nine in the morning we reassemble here to discuss how to proceed. Mr McFee will meanwhile begin using his contacts to track down all those on the list. Any questions?"

"One," says Berenice. "Are we anywhere near Baker Street?"

At last McFee smiles. "Near enough. It's 221b you want, is it? Yes, we'll take a look before you leave town."

"I think it's a good sign," she says. "Do light that fire when you come back in, won't you?"

I think: the maid that is matchless tames the dragons of dissent. It's totally unlike me to see it that way, or say it, and I still can't work out what the hell is happening. The changes and new things tumble over each other. I've become almost another person.

The Sherlock Holmes Café is a dump. Its proprietor finds himself opening his doors to a regular customer at an irregular time. But there are other matters, unspoken, that make us the sole and privileged diners this evening. Just give us what you have, says the detective, and regard this as a social occasion. The owner does not show his feelings. McFee is in the driving seat but this will make it — whatever it is — all square. There's enough tension to make me feel uncomfortable, embarrassed; but not psychic. A rhino could pick up the atmosphere in here.

The bare tables are tucked away in crannies with signs in playbill script over them: The Baskerville, the Sign of Four, the Study in Scarlet. Holmesian paraphernalia and framed prints hang on the walls. It's a good idea, but it doesn't work. Even the presence of Doctor Jackson Armitage, tall, brainy, fine-featured, cultivated, fails to raise the tone or conjure up the proper spirit.

"It ought to be called the Moriarty," says McFee breezily. "The cuisine's criminal." But when the food turns up, served by mine host, it tastes okay. I say so.

They remind me that I eat the bread of a minor public school.

Mine host does a little sweeping-up well away from us. Berenice and I get a slice of fried bread each. McFee looks at him and we get a second slice.

"Was it a big favour you did him?" I ask.

"Sometimes," he says, "what you don't do is the thing you do. Fancy another slice?" Shanks raises his eyebrows. "Rationing?" he says in the same way that aunts at table say 'elbows?'

We get a third.

There is a drifting down of tiny snowflakes when we emerge and begin to walk once more.

Two streets on we stop. H. Dunkley. Watchmaker and Jeweller. An attractive, well-stocked display – for the times – behind a folding steel mesh; well uptown of Mitch Gascoigne. I steady myself, smile at Berenice, check my flies. This is the real start. From now on I'm on the case.

A head pops out of an upstairs window while McFee is still knocking.

Mr H. Dunkley is a little put out, but effusive. We're ushered into the parlour at the back of the shop. "Mr McFee! A pleasant surprise! And a merry Christmas to you, I'm sure. Yes. And your friends? How do you do? Compliments of the season, though I can't see what there is to celebrate. Trade's terrible, and now this. Ah, well; say la gear, as the French say, eh? These your children, Mr er...?"

"This is Doctor Armitage, his...nephew Clement and niece, Berenice." McFee is correct, nothing more. He doesn't approve of Mr Dunkley and nor do I. He sounds like the kind of man who tells you he has a sense of humour, who makes smutty speeches at functions and tickles children even harder when they say they don't like it.

"Berenice the niece! That's good. I like that. Ha! ha! And Doctor Armitage, eh? I bet you're none too pleased with this Health Service business, then, eh? You should hear our quack on the subject. Louise! Kettle on!"

Despite my instant dislike I sympathise with the nervously jovial watchmaker and jeweller. An unexpected visit from an off-duty CID man and three total strangers the evening after Christmas ought to put you off balance. But there's an odour about this room. Can't place it. I try not to look as if I'm exercising my nostrils but I'm on the alert. The smell of Wilfred Gascoigne's fiery death is fresh in my memory. Maybe smell is the way in to whatever I'm supposed to be looking for.

Clement Mackinnon Garner: psychic bloodhound.

Mrs Dunkley appears. Her finery has been hastily applied. The scent's been splashed on a bit but that's not what I'm picking up. What I sense is cheap, guilty, low excitement mixed with decay. Corruption. Gold leaf painted over dirt. Dishonesty. How I'm making all this out is beyond me. We sit down and I'm on guard. McFee refuses a biscuit.

"The Doctor is an old colleague of mine," he begins. "An eminent criminologist; passing through town. I took the liberty of inviting him to the scene of a local crime, seeing as it seems a little out of the ordinary in certain respects. Not too much of an intrusion I hope. He leaves tomorrow, that's all."

Mr and Mrs Dunkley's expressions are fixed. It's an intrusion all right. But it's like mine host at the cafe; McFee's got something on them, enough to make them...biddable. I'm looking at them both with concentration, too late to catch my nostrils flaring.

"Is everything all right, dear?" says the woman. Her smile is sickly sweet, like the smell that's now overpowering.

"Perfectly, thank you." It comes out as a stern croak. She purses her lips.

"Nothing taken, I understand?" says Shanks.

"Yes, that's right. He – they? – must have taken fright and bolted. Don't know what from, I must say. Slept through the lot, didn't we, dear?" Louise nods. You can tell she's the boss.

"What was the intruder's method of entry?" The Doctor's tone suppresses the irritating echo of Dunkley's voice.

"Well, that's just it!" Almost a shriek from Louise and her raised eyebrows. "The police couldn't see how he got in! Fingerprints everywhere round the safe but the doors and windows untouched. Absolutely untouched!"

"So he seems to have exercised as much care in his exit as in his entry. Despite his haste?"

"Well, yes. I suppose so. Didn't do much for our Christmas, I can tell you. But it's not as if it's the first time, is it, Dennis? I mean, we've had break-ins before but they never got away with it. It's a risk you take

113

in the business. But this one gives me the creeps. Honestly, it does." She leans forward and lowers her voice. "It's like he came in through the wall. Know what I mean?"

"Yes, I think so, Mrs Dunkley. You've both been most helpful. I wonder if I could just glance around the safe itself? The work of a moment, I assure you." We all get up. Dennis looks surprised.

"Are you a criminalist too, sonny?"

"I hope to be, some day." I shoot a frown at Louise. She turns away to stand by the fireplace.

The safe is in a little cubicle between the shop and the parlour. Shanks mutters and makes notes on a tiny pad; a convincing act. He's actually rather good. After a bit he asks me in, and it's a relief to be away from the smell. I stand there and try to concentrate. Just in ear-shot, Berenice is asking Dunkley daft questions about jewellery to keep him busy.

But it's a blank. Not a thing. No vibrations, no scent, no feelings of any kind. Just a little office and a safe. Peaceful, if anything.

This charade is going nowhere. I find myself asking: why here? This isn't Albert Smallwood's stamping ground. Sorry, wasn't; or his kind of job. Except that his last job in life was small-time too. Something tells me this is well out of the peterman's orbit. He belongs to that other city lying on the river east of Temple Bar.

How do I know that?

Berenice nudges me and peeps in; shudders and retreats. Dunkley's voice cuts across the peace in this little room.

Then we're outside again. The snow is falling faster, settling here and there, showing the tyre marks of cars and bicycles. We turn up our collars and walk to the corner of the street.

McFee stops and looks around. "So what did you make of that?"

"Nothing much."

"Nothing much?"

"Well, nothing at all, actually."

He blows down his nose. "I see. Listen, all of you. I've just been, for the first time since the early thirties, in the same place that Smallwood has been. I didn't visit his other two jobs because I'm not finding this easy. If this is a blank, we may be barking up the wrong tree altogether. What d'you say to that?"

Shanks waits while a noisy taxi grinds past. "There's nothing to say to that. This is hardly an exact science. We could, as you suggest, be on the wrong track, but surely these are early days. Naturally I am ready to follow any line of action that seems more practical to you as an investigator of crimes. Smallwood is your man, not mine."

McFee's nodding his head quickly. He looks like a gangster boss who's just heard his rival has escaped assassination. "This, for me, Doctor, is more than an intellectual exercise. Consider the realities. Suppose his next appearance is somewhere we can't just stroll into, two men and a boy, and ask to have a nose around. Do we break in? And suppose laddie here gets nothing. How long do we go on like that? There's only so much slack the big bugs are prepared to give me. Does failure bother you as much as it bothers me?"

We step back to let some people pass. So here we are again; not shaking down. I know it means everything to both men in their own ways. Berenice knows it. The snow settles on our shoulders as we stand in uncomfortable silence.

"One or two things did cross my mind back there," I say.

"Really?"

"Yes. Want to hear it?"

"Go on."

"Well, did you notice the smell?"

"Mrs Dunkley was wearing a lot of scent," says Berenice, "but that isn't it, is it?"

"It was the smell of dishonesty."

115

Shanks turns on me. "Why on earth didn't you say so? We've just had words because you said you sensed nothing!"

"It wasn't Smallwood. It came from them."

A bitter laugh escapes McFee's mouth in a cloud. "He's a fence, that's why."

"Fence?"

"Dealer in stolen property, knowing it to be stolen," says Berenice. "What a ratbag! Why don't you arrest him?"

"Proof, my dear girl, proof. Our Dennis Dunkley is a slimy devil. I suppose you noticed that."

"Doesn't take a psychic," I say. "But it's her more than him."

"Is it now? Maybe she's the one after all. We'll watch her from now on. Old Harold Dunkley must be spinning in his grave. No, forget I said that. Anything else?"

"Yes. I was asking myself why Smallwood should bother with this end of London. I'm wondering if location is important. Why this street, for example?" We look behind us. "Plympton Street," says Berenice. "But you can all read, can't you?"

Shanks claps his hands together softly. "Perhaps the street names – or the names of the owners of the properties – have a collective significance. This may turn out to be a matter of decoding. Anything else?"

"One thing. As I turned to leave Dunkley's office a word came to me out of the blue."

They all stare at me, waiting.

"Spiders."

"Spiders?"

"Yes. More legs than are strictly necessary. Eat their husbands."

"There was one in the corner," says Berenice. "I don't go overboard on them. Didn't you see it?"

"No. Just the word. I don't know: eight legs, seventh son of seventh son, sixth sense..."

"I see," says McFee. "We'll call it Louise, then."

Big sigh from Doctor Armitage. "All to be borne in mind. I'm glad to see we end on a lighter note. Report everything, Clement; everything. And try to be serious when it matters."

We leave McFee at the doorway beside Gascoigne's studio. The snow has stopped. Wilfred fixes his smile on me in the lamplit dark.

Back to the station, then a taxi ride, a warm welcome from a Mr and Mrs Shawe-Tritton, and we pass into another world; a convivial supper in their splendid house and an early night.

I'm in a comfy bed in a room below the attic. You can just hear the rumble of traffic and the tube trains plunging into South Kensington station. I've taken in very little of the time since we said goodbye to the haunted detective because my mind is a kaleidoscope of thoughts and pictures. Shanks has reminded me again and again that I must act normally and betray nothing of my powers to our hosts or their visitors; or of our purpose in being here. Fair enough, but why come here, then? This has to be the lion's den, doesn't it? It's asking a lot after what's happened to me. How can I act normal if I know I'm not? *Nothing is normal*. My old self is now no more than an act and I'll be no good at it anymore.

Just as I fall asleep, two images merge in a kind of half-dream. One is Alphonse and Ludmilla doing the last rounds of the house in the cradling quiet of Inglefield Place; the other is Hayden McFee, settling down in his dingy lodging, alone among eight million people, with ghosts for neighbours. I hope he's lit his fire.

Chapter 16

There are times when I forget Sergeant McFee is a detective in his very bones. Not orthodox or obedient, but a persistent and implacable hunter. While we sleep in comfort – no, opulence – in Kensington, he sets things in motion. More than once on that cold, slushy night he picks up his hat and coat, wraps a muffler round his neck and ventures out, riding buses and Tubes till the small hours, hailing cabs, or just walking. Most of the people he wants aren't on the phone. His efforts start movements and messages that ripple out like stones dropped in a pond. They spread, cross each other, and some of them rebound to where he sits waiting in his grim little room. Meanwhile other stones plop into the dark, whose ripples will not return for days.

The result for me is to be hauled out of bed at seven o'clock in the morning. It's Shanks and he's dressed to go out.

"What is it?"

"Our hosts are still asleep. That suits us perfectly. I want you ready to leave in five minutes."

"Why? What's up?"

"Five minutes."

It's still night-time. We're walking the pavements and Shanks is casting about for a taxi. "We are to breakfast in a working men's café on the Battersea Park Road, between the power station and the Nine Elms gasworks. Mr McFee will be there. Clear so far?"

"Yes. Certainly." I look up at curtained windows where there's warmth and people are getting a decent ration of sleep. "Won't they miss us?"

It's started, then. This is supposed to be acting normally so nobody gets suspicious. Shanks on his own, fine. Early morning stroll, bit eccentric; still. But me too?

"I've left a note. They expect this sort of thing with me. Taxi!" He gives me the plan as we head for the river. "McFee's traced the policeman who accompanied him when he arrested Smallwood. Jack Sidgwick; retired now. He works as nightwatchman at the gasworks and he always stops at this café for breakfast on his way home. Apparently his wife works too and will already have left the house. Even on a Saturday. The lives people have to lead! Got that so far? Good. Now, our job is to masquerade as ordinary customers while McFee — who will be there ahead of us — will accidentally, so to speak, run into his old colleague. He will then steer their conversation towards reminiscences of that case, while we eavesdrop. Understand?"

"Yes. So far. How did he contact you?"

"Mr Sidgwick is tall, fat and has a white moustache. I will keep my back to them and you will observe. Don't be obvious. Staring schoolboys are a common occurrence, but not in low cafés at this hour. We need a cover story in case Vic — the proprietor — or anyone else talks to us. Now listen carefully. We have travelled up from Worthing on an early train, changed at Clapham and got off at Battersea Park station. An old aunt of mine is dying in King's College Hospital. She would be your great-aunt. Hence our sudden dash to London. There is a stopping train to Denmark Hill which leaves Battersea Park at eight-forty. We are taking breakfast while waiting for that train. Got that? He rang me last night. Naturally I cannot ring him, not from the house itself."

I repeat the story; then repeat it again, more accurately.

"Is Denmark Hill near the hospital?"

"Of course. Say nothing unless you have to. If I speak to you, just appear to listen. But concentrate on McFee and Sidgwick; without, of course, appearing to listen."

"Why aren't we just taking a bus or a taxi straight to the hospital if it's that serious?"

An impatient snort. "Oh, visiting hours, I expect. It's just to head off anyone who gets nosey. They'll soon wish they'd never asked." I'm not so sure; it sounds daft enough to be dodgy. Vic and his mates won't be maiden aunts. Wouldn't fool me for a minute.

There's a clear pre-dawn light hanging over everything as we cross Battersea Bridge. The crisp air, the empty roads, the strangeness of the hour; a scene for opening credits and staccato music. An invisible hand writes slanting across the screen: Clement Garner, Jackson Armitage. In...*Rendezvous at Vic's*. Also starring: Hayden McFee and Jack Sidgwick. Dumdidi dumdidi dum da daah. At last this thing's coming to life. All it needs is a leading lady.

But for the moment this is more than enough. I want to tell the driver to stop so I can get out and look over the parapet at the Thames; smell it; smell and feel this town while it's still unpeopled and uncluttered.

"I'm giving Wordswords another chance when I get back."

"I beg your pardon?"

"Wordsworth. We call him Wordswords because he goes on a bit. Well, he does, doesn't he? I have to study him."

"I see. No doubt you are referring to his lines written on Westminster Bridge in — 1802, was it? Well, whenever it was. You see the truth of it now. Let me see... Driver! Pull to the side. Thank you. Driver, are you familiar with Wordsworth?"

Good old Jackson, the eccentric professor.

"Wordsworf? Yes, guv'nor, funnily enough. You're not the first to ask, as a matter of fact. Let me guess:

> 'This city now duff, like a garment, wear
> The beauty o' the mornin'; silent, bare,
> Ships, towers, domes, fee- etters, and temples lie...'

"Yeah. Fair enough, guv? No extra charge."

Shanks breaks into a laugh. "Well, I'm damned! Good for you!" He turns to me.

"Who is your English master?"

"Mr Goodship. We call him Lollipop Goodship."

"Of course you do. Next time you groan under his instruction, remember our driver, and reflect that culture is not the preserve of privilege, thank God."

Oh yes. This is getting better and better. I'm almost not missing Berenice. That's because I'm on top of this one. That's because I can look through people with something to hide; like those two last night with respectability painted over their decay.

The river passes out of sight.

"Why," I ask after a moment or two, "do we need this cloak-and-dagger performance with Mr McFee and Mr Sidgwick? They're old friends. What's wrong with a straight-out talk?"

"It has crossed my mind. Perhaps he's concerned about...I don't know. Suppose Sidgwick is a drinking man; starts blabbing all over town? Let's see what happens."

The taxi squeals to a halt. The street and pavements are almost deserted. A pink-and-dark blue sky has overspread the city. Shanks shares a few cheery words with the driver, pays a generous tip and we're left standing in the slush in front of Vic's Café: Hot Meals. Snacks. Teas. It's not a café like the Sherlock Holmes; it's a caff. I've never been in a caff before. The windows are steamed up with greasy moisture. There's moss growing along the wooden sill. "And that, I suppose," says Shanks, peering past the Open sign on the door, "is the eponymous Vic."

The Eponymous Vic? I shake my head. I do wonder sometimes. He thinks we'll merge into the background, does he? I go through a slight failure of nerve, but the little bell on the door is tinkling and we're into the fug of cigarette smoke, warm frying smells and indistinct sounds from a wireless on a shelf. Unlike in the Westerns it doesn't suddenly go quiet and there are no hostile stares. Everyone's eating or reading a paper. Lot of people for a Saturday morning just after Christmas; not that I'd know.

A thickset man in a dark overcoat is stirring a cup of tea slowly and waving a stub of pencil over a folded copy of *The Mirror*. He's alone at a table in the corner by the window. For an instant he looks up, then lowers his eyes.

Shanks motions me to a table next but one to his. Between us a weasel-faced character in brown overalls is wiping a bit of bread round his plate. Good. Maybe he'll leave soon and we can move nearer the window. It'll seem natural, what with the fascinating scenery. I sit down facing McFee while Shanks goes to the counter.

I'm in a film or a play. I find myself watching the detective, studying his indifference. He must do this kind of thing all the time.

"Egg, chips, twice!" Vic calls over his shoulder. "Two teas?"

"How much?"

"S'on the board, mate."

"Ah, yes. Thank you."

Shanks bears the teas to our table and sits opposite me. I flick burnt crumbs into a ring-mark on the green gingham oilcloth as he removes his hat, loosens his scarf and takes it off.

McFee takes a long slurp from his cup. I think he's marking football fixtures to cross on his pools coupon. Be nice if he won. How much is he paying for the Doctor's services? Is paying? Never thought about it before.

A chair scrapes and weasel-face gets up. We wait till he steps outside before I say, "Can we sit by the window?" Nobody takes any notice, but it's amazing how exposed you feel just changing tables. No sign of a tall fat man with a white tash.

We can't just sit here like lemons.

"Do you think Great-aunt Matilda will last the day out?" I say in a conversational kind of way. Shanks looks at me as though I'm the village idiot. I dart a glance at McFee. He's trying not to smile.

"I really can't say," mutters Jackson Armitage solemnly. "We'll just have to hope, that's all."

His eyes are making leave-it-out movements.

"Egg, chips, twice!"

He gets up and collects them from the counter. We eat. It's a lot better than at school.

McFee's tea must be stone cold. Shanks keeps looking out of the window, then at his watch.

He's not coming. He's ill. Got a couple of days off. Been sacked. Surely McFee hasn't left it to chance?

The bell tinkles. Shanks's head jerks up, but the sergeant of detectives sits perfectly still. A deep voice booms over the tinny wireless.

"Mornin', Victor my son! The usual and the usual!"

"Saturday, innit? Sausage, mash, peas once, an' 'ere's yer tea."

"Ta. Just ready for a nice cup o' char. Be nice to get back to bangers every mornin', eh?"

"S'gettin' worse all the time, Jack. Did we lose the bleedin' war or summink? Bloody Food Ministry's still writing the menu in 'ere. Gordon Bennet! Good fing we didn't come second."

Jack Sidgwick puts on an air of authority. "We come in first, Victor my old cocker. Good eight lengths be'ind Stalin an' the Yanks. Uncle Joe's sittin' on 'alf o' Europe. Bloody Uncle Sam's lordin' it over the Nips, little bastards, an' we've just kissed India goodbye. Still, the river keeps runnin' down to the sea, eh? Good Christmas?"

"Jack! Jack Sidgwick!"

The big man's conversation stops. I can sense him turning.

"Mr McFee? Well, bugger me! Mr McFee, 'ow are yer?"

"It's been a while, Jack. Here, come sit down. What brings you in here on a Saturday morning?"

Beautifully done.

"Workin' man, Mr McFee. Night watch at the gasworks. Couldn't keep out of 'arness. What about you?" He lowers his voice. "On the job, are yer?"

McFee nods. "When did you hang up your helmet? Thirty-nine, wasn't it?"

"S'right. April. Often regret it. Still sergeant?" He holds up a huge hand. "S'all right, Mr McFee. I know how it was. Well, well."

"Family all okay?"

They go on like this for a bit and I'm catching most of it. Jack Sidgwick's face is sideways on to me and he's a perfect example of the big, unathletic bobby whose mere existence kept kids like me in order. The war seems to have made policemen thinner somehow. He's taken off his cloth cap and hung it on the back of his chair. I push the black end of a congealed chip around on my plate. Shanks looks at his watch, pulls a pencil and envelope from his inside pocket and scribbles something. I look at it upside down.

'Now 8:32. Forget cover story.'

I already have. The envelope vanishes as Vic's apron brushes past me. Jack's a regular, so he gets waiter service.

"Anyfing else?"

He's clearing our plates and his tone isn't begging us to stay. Our eyes meet. Maybe Vic was born with a suspicious, piercing look. We've got no good reason to be here.

"Er, yes. Another two teas, please." I can hear Vic thinking: what 'ave we got 'ere? Like a duchess orderin' a pint o' wallop. He pushes a cloth in a circular motion round the one bit of the table we haven't used, and I suddenly realise I've dropped off on McFee and his friend.

"...second person I've run into. Couple of weeks ago I was stood next to a bloke in a pub and I knew I'd seen him before somewhere. Took a while to work it out. You remember old Albert Smallwood, the peterman? Remember the night we picked him up over at Manny Rosenblum's? Well, this bloke was the watchman down the road who sat with him. It was him. After fifteen years odd. Small world. You remember Albert."

I'm concentrating again, but the reply's a long time coming. When it does, I find myself frowning, and Shanks is making more frantic eye signals at me. I recompose my features. Something's wrong though. Jack Sidgwick's voice has changed. It's no longer…big.

"Yeah. Yeah, I do. 'Course. Why you askin'?"

"No particular reason. Job I'm on now reminds me of him, that's all. This one can't hold a candle to Albert. They broke the mould when they made Albert."

"Yeah. Yeah, they did."

"Eat up, Jack. It's going cold."

Jack Sidgwick eats like a steam shovel and swallows his tea. Before he's put the mug down he's reaching behind him for his cap. McFee leans back in his chair nonchalantly. His eyes rest on the retired policeman's face. There must be alarm bells ringing in his head but he betrays nothing. When he speaks, there's an edge. What is it? Right; it's a reminder of rank. It stops Jack's hand in mid-movement.

"There's not many uniformed men even remember Smallwood. You're probably the last one who saw him as a free man. I didn't arrest him till we got back to the station."

But Jack Sidgwick isn't playing. "Could be, Mr McFee. What you doin'? 'Avin' a whip-round for a stachoo of 'im?"

"No, Jack. Just going over old times. I remember every little detail of that job as if it happened yesterday. Is it like that with you?"

Jack Sidgwick is on his feet. "No, not really, Mr McFee. Must get on. You know 'ow it is."

"You wouldn't be a bit under the weather, would you, old son?"

"Could be at that. Ain't been sleepin' too well lately. Affects the job. You know; mind wanders a bit sometimes. Long nights at the gasworks, patrollin' round on yer own. You know; smog, 'ooters soundin' on the river, an' that. Couple o' months now." He puts on his cap. "Like yer say; funny meetin' that watchman geezer. What pub was that?"

"Somewhere Stepney way."

"Yeah. Funny, that. Must've bin visitin' 'is old stampin' grounds. Or come back."

"How d'you mean?"

"Well. I used ter run into 'im on the beat now an' then. Last I 'eard 'e was off dahn the Sarf Coast to be a barber. 'Fore the war, that was. Nice seein' you again, Mr McFee, I'm sure. And an 'appy noo year to yer." He almost runs out of the caff. "See yer Monday, Victor! I daresay."

Hayden McFee's face shows no change. He pulls out his pipe and pouch, fills it, lights it and leans back in a cloud of blue smoke. His eyes half-close. How often it must be like this. Dead-ends, cold trails, cold feet. In the movies every informer talks, every line has a fish on the hook. In this world detectives waste time, keep crazy hours and end up sitting over the ashes of failure.

Across the river, gentlemen and ladies now abed think themselves blessed they are not here. No, it's worse than that. Working men's eating places are in another dimension, not thought about. Do they care that work goes on at all while they sleep and throw parties? Hayden McFee and Jack Sidgwick are their night-soil men, removing the unpleasantnesses of their lives. All through the war pamphlets and booklets and films showed everyone doing their bit, pulling together; danger uniting the classes. Maybe it did. I'm not so sure. But now the dust has settled. I think of the visitors at Inglefield Place; posh people in civvies. Afternoon tea on the lawns. War or no war, they're back. And Vic will go on serving amid the greasy steam, and Jack Sidgwick will patrol, uneasy, among the looming silent gasholders in the smog, never quite seeing his wife at home.

"Are you all right, Clement?"

My jaw aches from too much clenching. I demobilise a frown. "Er, yes, fine. Just concentrating."

"I'll say you were. Well, we must be on our way. Come on!"

We walk back towards Battersea Park Station in silence. I mustn't look back. At last we shelter in the doorway of Comet Radio Repairs: 10,000 Valves in Stock. The window is a sepia screen; dust covers the electrical trinkets and gadgets; it's the burnt dust you can smell inside a wireless when it's turned on. All week a man – I can picture him – in sleeveless pullover, baggy trousers and thousand-volt haircut, stands by a paraffin heater at the back of this cave and talks quietly to customers as though they were in a monastery library. There's something inviting about it, as though it's turned its back on the city to nurture in secret the bits and pieces of a better, more modern world whose time is coming.

"Well, Clement? Anything strike you back there?"

"Nothing that wasn't obvious. Like, Mr Sidgwick's a worried man."

"Not much help, I fear. Still, curious coincidence. I wonder if... Ah, here he comes now. I forgot to mention we were to meet here afterwards. Ah, Mr McFee! What now?"

"We keep walking." He doesn't look at us, doesn't slacken his pace and his voice is a growl.

"Keep twenty yards behind me. Sit down when I do."

He leads us past the brick monolith of the power station, over and then under the tracks that feed coal and commuters to the appetites of the city. The rumbling of trains is almost continuous on normal days; I know that from public information films. McFee walks quickly. Blue pipe smoke swirls over his shoulder. Soon we enter an area of bare trees and muddy grass where a few people are walking their dogs. My spirits are low; the morning's promise gone bare and muddy too. The grass here looks sick; a travesty of the countryside. The detective plonks himself down on a bench. It's become very cold, with a raw wind whipping off the river. No sooner are we sat than he jumps up again.

"None too fruitful, I'm afraid," says Shanks, half in surprise.

"There's something wrong there," shouts McFee, straight out ahead of him. He paces up and down in front of us. "Something very wrong. D'you know what I think? I think our friend Smallwood has got at poor

127

old Jack. He's rattled; like me. Both of us, since this whole bloody business started."

"That was the coincidence," murmured Shanks. "What does it signify?"

McFee stops walking, turns and stabs his still smoking pipe at our faces.

"What does it signify? I'll tell you what it bloody signifies! It means, gentlemen, that we are not pursuing Albert Smallwood. He is pursuing us. We are not in any sense going to close in on him. He's already so close to us that he sees our every move. We're going to meet – if that's the idea, and I no longer know what to think about that – when he and he alone is ready. Till then we're supposed to run around like blue-arsed flies, doing no good, going nowhere, and not able to jack the whole sodding thing in, because he is pulling our strings!"

He pauses, barely; looks around him as he goes on:

"John Sidgwick is one of the finest bobbies of the old school I ever met. Most of what I think I know about sheer down-on-the-ground policing I learnt from men like him. He was tough as old boots and brave as they come. None braver. Did you see him back there? Well, we've both just seen him scared for the first time in his life. He can't fight it because he doesn't know what it is that's making him uneasy and ruining his sleep. Is this a game? Eh? Come on, professor doctor, whatever you are when you're sat in your bloody stately home; tell me! What's Jack done to deserve this? You tell me. You're the expert."

Jackson Armitage remains unruffled, outwardly. The length of McFee's outburst has let him acclimatise to his anger. "I agree that this is a riddle; a deepening riddle. But we have to believe that whatever happens does so for a reason. There has to be order in all this. Perhaps we have got the order wrong. What do you suggest? Did nothing come out of your encounter in the café?"

McFee lets out a long breath. "Oh, it did all right. Jack Sidgwick's a dead letter, that's what. We can't go back to him, can't follow up. He already smells a rat. All right, I accept that as an operational fact of life. But actually it's his state of mind that worries me right now."

I'm thinking clearly. It's that wonderful feeling of things happening without obstruction, like exactly the right Meccano pieces jumping into your hand so the model almost builds itself under your eyes.

"There is a plan."

I have their complete attention.

"There is a plan. He was meant to behave like that. Now he's played his part, all his strange worries and dreams will disappear." My thoughts arrange themselves in perfect order.

"Suppose the plan is going as it should. Then we have to ask ourselves what he's done for us. Well; I think he's led us nearer to finding the nightwatchman."

"You are suggesting that that was the correct outcome of the incident?"

"Yes. Were you having any luck finding him?"

"No," says McFee.

"Right. Well, we know he must be still alive; what I mean is, it's part of the plan that he should be. I'm sure of that. How hard will it be to track him down?"

"Easy if you're using all the resources of the Force," says McFee. "But they're not available to me on this case. I'll get onto it."

"Just one thing, both of you." This feels good. They're taking me seriously.

"Yes?"

"It didn't need a psychic to work all that out."

They both grunt in an I-suppose-not kind of way. At least they're in agreement. Shanks gets to his feet. "Well, we press on. I have some calls to make. I understand the Sergeant has arranged another contact for today. You, Clement, are to accompany him. Until later, then." And he steps off briskly towards the river in the sharp cold sunshine. I look at the detective and raise my eyebrows.

"Well. What now, Mr McFee?"

His gaze follows the tall figure for a while. He grunts again, then smiles. "Let's go on the boats. Float around a bit."

We're the first customers on the boating lake. Resting on the oars we drift past islands, pushed by a raw breeze. After a while we see a soldier trying to impress his girlfriend with a bit of fancy rowing. Their voices carry across the copper-beaten surface of the water.

"I hope it turns out well for them," says McFee.

"What does?"

"The peace. After the storm, the rainbow. It'll be the first time if it does."

"Will it?"

"Yes. The veterans' services are forgotten. Always the way." He turns to me. "How well do you know your uncle?"

"He's not my uncle."

"Yes, granted. How well?"

"Not as well as I thought I did. And that wasn't much."

"I see. Yes, I heard about your existence at Inglefield. Swallows and Amazons. Cold fish, isn't he?"

"He told you about it?"

"Berenice told me."

"Right. Well, I really didn't know about his work. But it wasn't my business."

"Did you know most of his ghost society chums think he's crackers?"

"Fine chums, then. No, I didn't. He does get a bit intense sometimes."

"Fact is he holds ideas that the rest of them wouldn't give house room to. He's out to prove 'em all wrong and this is his last throw. That's why this is important to him. It's what makes you important."

"I know."

"You know. Funny what you know and don't know, considering."

"Look, Mr McFee. A week ago I was looking forward to a normal few days doing the things that make me happy. Now I'm a psychic and I'm sitting in a boat in the middle of winter in the middle of London with a detective who's haunted by a dead safecracker. I'm not sure what I am supposed to know any more."

"I sympathise."

Sounds of splashing and laughter drift across the water. That and the cry of a gull wheeling off the river. "What does Shanks think?"

"That's the Doctor, is it?"

"Yes. Does he have any ideas? Like, why doesn't Smallwood just contact you directly? Why the rigmarole?"

"First, I'm not a good psychic subject, apparently."

"Really? But you've felt his presence for years! You said so."

"He tested me. That's what he was doing when you turned up at the house. It's why Berenice — she your cousin or not? — had to fend for herself instead of getting the welcome she deserved. In every test I was a total loss. Ye gods! If I had bloody second sight would I still be where I am?"

"I suppose not. We're honorary cousins, actually."

"The other thing's harder to grasp. You know the tales of Arthur and the Round Table?"

"Yes. They're not true or anything."

"You astound me. Doesn't matter. They went on quests, right? Why?"

"To find things."

"That's right. Keep it simple. Listen...that bloke Gawain...they put him on the Green Knight case. What did he bring back? What did he find? Hmm?"

I decide it's best he answers his own question. It's freezing out here.

"Well, I'll tell you. He brought back his own head on his own shoulders. It was more than he bloody expected, or deserved. And he found wisdom."

"So that's it. Smallwood is sending you on a quest, from which you'll return a wiser man."

"Maybe. And sadder, I daresay. Look at me; look at poor old Jack. Christmas ruined for you and the girl. All those dreams and funny turns you've been having. Don't think it isn't on my conscience. It's bloody freezing out here; let's be on our way."

"Where to?"

"To meet a totter."

I give him a blank look. I know I'll be doing that a lot.

"Rag and bone man."

"What's his name?"

"Never mind. The less I tell you the less you'll make up your mind beforehand. Sound reasonable? Feeling any wiser?"

Feeling wiser all the time.

We walk from Battersea to New Cross, through a narrow band of the reality of life in sub-Thames London.

There are scraggy kids everywhere, not helping their mums.

"They'd tell him to stand up straight, wouldn't they, your place of learning?" says McFee. I'm looking at legs that make an X when their owner stands and stares back. There are women carrying bags and baskets of what the price of victory has left to sustain their families after two years and more of peace. Here and there, on corners and in doorways, stand women who aren't carrying anything but handbags and don't seem to be going anywhere at all.

There are stretches of cleared rubble and cellars open to the sky; walls shored up with timbers; weeds; more kids. And people who look old but aren't.

132

"You are no doubt noting the increased incidence of ill-favoured persons," says McFee in a rather good Jackson Armitage accent.

"Yes. Lot of... It's not Hollywood, is it?"

"That's because poverty is ugly, my son, and its children are not blessed. You're an alien here, aren't you? Born on a different bloody planet."

"Not fair, Mr McFee. There's loads of poor people where I was born. Still are."

"Yeah. And the same bloody reason. Your people. Same crowd that lost us Singapore; clueless gin-swilling clowns. Oh, don't worry. This lot are in the pink. Take a stroll round Belfast, or Glasgow or Newcastle some time. No, I must be honest. Some of them do end up in big houses or posh schools like yours and your chums. As cleaners."

"This would be irony, wouldn't it?"

"Essential ingredient for good eyesight, strong constitution and generally growing up."

I've seen bad housing and weary men and women in Oxford, except I didn't go there much. And bomb damage, and McFee knows it. It just goes on for so much longer here. After two hours I ask him how far we've come.

"About two squares on the map."

"How many squares are there?"

"Many, many. And every one rotten with pimps, whores, black marketeers, used-car barons, petty thieves, spivs, wide-boys and small-timers."

"You don't sound pleased about it."

He stops walking. Ahead of us is a wide double gate made of angle-iron and barbed wire. Behind it an area of broken flagstones and half-buried bricks gives onto a railway embankment. He relights his pipe. "Have we enjoyed our little stroll? No, I could be happier. I used to hunt big game. Now I turn over stones."

As we approach the gate I can see piles of junk scattered round the yard and I hear the clash and jangle of trucks on railway sidings. McFee begins untwisting a strand of wire that holds the gates shut. Suddenly I spot a huge figure rise out of the ground at the foot of the embankment. He has a pick-handle in one hand and shambles over to us growling like a dog. I step back.

"Careful, Mr McFee!"

He looks up and lets go of what he's doing, but otherwise doesn't move.

Our guardian of the yard must be at least six and a half feet tall. His hands and face are all knuckle and bone and red with broken veins. His hair's shaved so it looks like a mist lying on his skull. The pick handle seems like a rounders bat in his fist and when he speaks it's as if his mouth is full of boiled potatoes.

"Wharryawan', hnn? Grrn, groff! Graway orall fumpya!"

"I'm looking for Danny Ogden. Know where he is?"

"Hnn? Wivverorsancar' nnit?"

"When will he be back?"

"Dunno! 'Ooarrya, nnh? Clearorff!"

"Thank you. You've been most helpful. Come on, laddie."

As we walk away I look back. Boiled-potato man's standing stock-still, pick handle resting on the shoulder of his ex-army leather jerkin. Now I get a better view of the hole he's sprung from. It's an Anderson shelter built into the embankment. Suddenly another head pops out. It could be a woman – blonde – but it's hard to tell. A long goods train rolls past, followed by the heavy, easy motion of a shunting engine.

"Who was that back there?" My heart's still thumping.

"That? That was Professor Joad of the Brains Trust. He's part-time."

"It all depends on what you mean by part-time."

He smiles. "No. Never seen him before; must be new round here. One of Danny's ever-shifting crowd of junkyard hands."

"I thought maybe I saw a woman look out of the shelter as we came away."

"Did you? Now that's what I call slumming."

"No, I mean, do you think she's safe with Joad in there?"

"No. By God, no! She's in terrible danger. Look, I'll just keep watch while you go back and rescue her, okay?"

"Mmm. I suppose she's all right. Don't you?"

"Yes. I mean, it would have to be business, wouldn't it?"

A thought strikes me. "Damaged goods. Second-hand goods."

"That'd be about it. Danny Ogden did time in Pentonville with Smallwood. They were cellmates. Ogden got out in '43, unfit for heavy work; no bloody use to man or beast actually. So he turned his hand to totting."

"Sounds as if he was in for a long stretch. What did he do?"

"Stuck a knife into a bookie at Epsom. Didn't kill him, worse luck. Then we'd have been shot of both of 'em. After that he was safer in than out, that being the way it is in the Sport of Kings. He picks up more than just old iron, so he occasionally lets us have the odd tit-bit and we overlook his milder errors. Give and take. There'd be few cases cracked without it."

"But you'd still prefer the world without him?"

"You can take my word for it."

McFee strolls along and chats as we head for a rendezvous with a time-expired attempted murderer. Every now and then he murmurs "wait here" and crosses the street to talk to groups of kids or the odd lone woman just standing around, of whom there seem to be quite a few. Once he spends so long speaking to a beat bobby that I get impatient and join them. We can no longer hear the clangour of the sidings or the whistles of locomotives. As McFee engages a newsboy in conversation I think back to the shuffling music of the night train across the water meadows of Inglefield, reaching into my turret room. Beneath

135

this tar and brick and concrete lies a distant echo of woods and fields. You can hear it more loudly, smell it, where the bombs have fallen.

At noon he invites me to sit on a bombed-site wall and enjoy the sunshine. The wind has dropped and released some of its warmth. A terrace of sad brick houses faces us. I have no idea where we are. From somewhere comes the sound of a handbell. Then:

EEEEEERAIGEEEEEEEBO!

As McFee raises his eyebrows a door opens across the street and a very large woman in a flowery apron steps out. She holds an enamel bucket with no bottom and she gives us a dirty look. I smile back. A dilapidated horse comes round the corner; behind it a cart with four solid rubber wheels. Danny Ogden doesn't need to stop his motive power plant; it just shambles to a halt and slowly waves its head from side to side. Here's a cousin of Farmer Symond's old nag, but it seems more downtrodden and its blinkers make it look blind. I watch the driver as he leaps down. A short, slight man; shorter than me. Tanned face with pinched features and little grey moustache. Snappy trilby. Grey jacket with elbow patches, green spotted cravat, scuffed suedes. Not like I imagine a hardened ex-con. Then again, he has a hint of George Raft; in a distorting mirror.

He throws us a glance and keeps it there a touch too long, then turns to bucket-woman.

"Hallo, my love. Fine morning." You can hear him clearly. A soft, cultivated voice. No forced mateyness. He's recognised McFee, but it doesn't matter.

Danny Ogden regards the bucket. "Haven't you got anything else, my love? Any old thing, to make up a lot?" The fat woman's face puckers into a smile. Her teeth are brown and ropes of phlegm are strung across the gaps. After a second she scrunges her lips up in a doubtful look. "Could be sunnink out the back. Ain't nuffink really."

"I'll have a gander anyway. You never know. Might be an antique, eh?" Danny steers her into the dark passage between the houses and they disappear. We wait. The sounds of the street intrude again. It isn't a motor-traffic kind of area and a small crowd of kids gathers quickly to pat the horse. A boy and girl climb up onto the cart. They obviously know Danny and his old nag so it just stands like a statue with its thoughts, thin steam rising from its back.

Time passes.

Then, slowly, the horse's head turns towards the passageway. Its motion contains a question. At the same instant the curtains twitch and the woman's face appears.

"Jesus Christ!" hisses McFee. "You two! Off!" The kids on the cart bail out.

"Get aboard," he says. Without stopping to think I heave myself up and find him there already, reins in hand.

"Git along there!" The nag begins to amble at a wretchedly slow pace and the juvenile mob surrounds us with shouting and bellowing. "'Ere, where you goin' wiv that? That's Danny's! 'E'll 'ave yer!"

"Stealers! Feeves! Get after 'em!" One little oick with plaster over the left lens of his specs runs along beside me squeaking, "'Orace'll 'ave yer! 'E will! 'E will!"

Last year there was a stink at school when three sixth-formers went on the sauce and stole a car for a ride. Taking and Driving Away. That was it. They got done by the law and then expelled. That was a Morris Eight. Horse and cart can't be so different. But why? What the hell is he playing at? Why risk a song and dance like this?

One kid's hammering at a door. Faces appear at windows. If this gets ugly we might end up in the papers; blown wide open. Smallwood, Shanks, McFee; the whole boiling. I look blankly at the horse-thief beside me. He's lashing the reins, chewing an extinct pipe and muttering. "Crafty little bastard! This'll cost him."

And suddenly we're into traffic. Amid honking of horns and ringing of bicycle bells the pursuit falls away. But the little chap with one-eyed glasses keeps pace on the pavement, intent on his mission to remind us of the horrors of Horace.

"D'you think he's on about Professor Joad?"

"Must be. Horace, is it? Well, then. Tell Cyclops to sod off, will you?"

I turn to the little lad. You have to admire his persistence. Putting on the Bela Lugosi smile I draw a finger across my throat. "You vill leave us now. If you vish to live!"

He stops. "You're cracked, you are!" As he falls behind, swallowed up in unsuspecting pedestrians, I see him tapping his head with one hand and giving us the Vs with the other.

"Ever travelled in style like this?" says McFee. He's smiling broadly for a change.

"Harvest time. During the war. We all had to help out."

"Oh, did you now? Hey nonny no. Well, not many public-school boys get to be rag and bone men. So give it a go. Chance may never come again."

"To do what?"

"Dear, oh dear. A hell of a mind-reader you are. Give it a shout, man! Never mind the bell. Don't want to be held up, do we?"

This is the way the day's going. The presence of strangers gives me courage.

"Any old rags and bones!"

"My godfathers! Doctor Bloody Armitage could do better than that! As for your cousin…"

"EEEEEEEERAIG! YEEEEEEEEEBOE!"

It feels good, being able to shout your face off in public; and nobody taking any notice. "Okay, that'll do," says McFee, twitching the reins. There's no need, though. Danny's old horse is on autopilot. "Look under the seat here. There's a box. Open it."

It's full of newspapers used as wrapping. Some of them are stained with blood. Wet blood.

I peel the papers away. Pork chops. Sausages. Sugar. Nylons. "Are you going to arrest him?" I say.

138

"Why should I? Everybody does it. Look at these people. If they want to put together a few pennies for a little forbidden luxury who am I to stop them? Luxury! We put the top Nazis in the dock and hanged 'em for murdering bloody millions and you want me to do Danny for flogging a few bangers? We're only on rations now because of the war those so-and-so's started. Do me a favour."

The horse ambles on, turning corners slowly enough for us to do timely hand signals.

The street we're now in looks familiar. It's also almost deserted. That's the strange thing about this city. You expect everywhere to be crowded, but there are bits that are as peaceful as a village. Or maybe it's me. Maybe Smallwood has a way of clearing the decks for us, of freezing the action around us so we can act out without interruption whatever affront to reality he's arranged.

The eyeless houses are soldered to the pavement, glinting in the wintry light like brass.

Suddenly the cart lurches. Amid a jangle of ironmongery I turn to see the alarming figure of Horace vaulting onto the back. His face is contorted. For a split-second I think: Magwitch. Magwitch in the movie of *Great Expectations*. Then I think: help. Horace is twice as big and he's leapt out of the screen. This is about to turn very nasty.

McFee shouts "Whoa, there!" but the horse has stopped anyway. He stands up and turns. Both of us are trying to keep our balance as Horace kicks away the junk that fills the six feet between him and us. Lucky he's chosen to come up from the rear, but it isn't much comfort given the meat-eating noises he's making. I decide not to share McFee's fate, and jump off.

Just as Horace reaches out an arm like an oak-branch the detective shoots out a finger right at his nose. The giant stops, sways and stares. He crosses his eyes and stands there like a hypnotised chicken. "Horace!" roars McFee. "Horace! Make another move and I'll run you in." His voice lowers, but the effect on the big man is the same. Horace blinks. His arm falls to his side.

"D'you want to see the inside of a cell again, Horace?"

"'Ow yer know my name?"

"It's only one of many things I know about you, my son. Enough to put you away. Like the sound of that? Not your favourite place, is it, chokey?"

Close up, you can see Horace might be an ex-con. He can't help looking the part. But how does McFee know to play on his fear of going back inside? You can tell it now in his eyes easily enough, but to bring it out on a hunch as the only way of stopping him is, well, impressive. I hold my breath while my heart thumps.

Horace sags; and I see it. The simple-minded giant, all brawn, no brain. Controlled like a circus animal by every sharp operator in sight, too easily held just at the edge of violence with its reward of even more years behind bars. Enough wit to understand the taunts and yet hold back. Charles Laughton caressing the gargoyles of Notre Dame. I climb on board again. McFee's speaking gently now.

"It's Danny I want to see, Horace. He's not in trouble. Nor are you."

With Horace leading the horse the last furlong we approach the wired gate. My heart returns to normal, but the pavements remain empty.

Ogden's Scrap Merchant's yard is about a half-acre of bombed waste ground. This time I take in the lean-to stable and the piles of rubbish that lie around like stooks in a field. One of them's on fire and oily black smoke billows into the breeze. It doesn't look like much of a living and I say so.

"His home's here," answers McFee. "In that shelter. He doesn't need much."

You see what he means. On this sunny winter's day the byways of this kingdom are home to a small army of men – mostly men – discharged from the wars, who just want something other than the respectable paths of inaction that normality offers. They need to go on marching, tramping the roads and living in makeshift shelters because that's where, under strange skies, they found a life that had some value.

Some do it from choice, some from derangement. They have their dignity and mostly they mean no harm.

Danny Ogden has gone through a different fire, but it comes to the same thing. His home is two Anderson shelters placed end to end, in a tunnel he's had dug beneath the railway. Long slow trains of wagons rumble over it, past the stovepipe that peeks out of the sloping weedy earth, and this is his badge of freedom.

Without a pause McFee and I go down a couple of steps and enter. There's a cosy smell of coalsmoke. A board rests on a shelf of earth and both Danny Ogden and the blonde girl are sitting on it. Neither of them looks overjoyed to see us.

I glance behind me to check that Horace isn't joining in. McFee takes off his hat, eases himself down onto a plank opposite Danny and lets out a theatrical sigh of satisfaction.

There is silence for a long time. Fine by me. At the end of this little room an old Victorian kitchen range is blasting out heat and I sit absorbing it, the first real warmth since Vic's Caff.

Just outside the entrance is a heap of broken furniture and great lumps of grey coal. A piece of sacking serves as a door, tied back with an old leather belt. This hole in the ground is full of little creature comforts and the banishment of responsibility. You could get used to it.

Out in the yard, Horace has put a nosebag on the horse and is unloading the cart, picking up impossible weights in each hand and wandering from pile to pile as if unsure where to drop them.

"Brought back your horse and cart for you," says McFee at last. "Visit your lady friends, that's okay. Leaving a draught animal unattended is an offence."

The blonde girl has been staring at me. "What lady friend? Who's he on about, Danny?"

"Come on, Sal." No longer the cultivated voice. "Mr McFee's little joke."

"What lady friend, Danny?" The way Sal mixes a bit of threat into her tone shows this is the normal style round here. Danny starts to get

141

wheedly. "It ain't nothing, Sal. I was just talking to an old biddy with a rusty bucket and she took me round the back to show me some more stuff she had. That's all. Mr McFee's just winding us up. All right?"

Sal looks at him and I look at her profile. She's very attractive. Blonde hair like Veronica Lake. Bright red lips. Perfume that mingles with the coal smoke. All courtesy of Danny's business efforts. Film star effects, and pretty well done. The wellingtons, the oversize tweed jacket that overhangs her shoulders and has to be pulled in at the waist with string, none of that takes away from whatever it is that's doing it for me. Underneath the jacket she's wearing a thin printed dress; a summer dress that makes you long for summer. And she's sitting three feet from me, slim, mysterious; a princess in a pirate's den. Rescuing her would have been a neat move after all.

"Take a walk, Sal."

McFee isn't so impressed. The feeling's mutual, because she doesn't move.

"I said take a walk."

Still no response. So McFee jumps up. I flinch, but she doesn't. Next thing he's grabbed her arm and shoved her out. She storms back in, shouting abuse.

"Sue me," says McFee. "And call your two friends here as witnesses. I'll invite a few of their old mates to watch 'em perform. Should bring back some old memories. Go on, ask Danny and Horace what they think about that."

"Please," says Danny. After a bit she turns, kicks my feet aside, and stamps up the steps.

"You can't tell a girl like that to take a walk, Mr McFee."

"I just did. Actually, Ogden, I talk to tarts like that how I please. Who is she?"

"Daughter of a partner, you might say."

"The one who supplies the goods?"

"I can explain that, Mr McFee."

"I bet you can; just don't overdo it. But that wasn't what was bothering you. The guilty flee when no man pursueth, Danny. What's the story? And what's the tart doing here? Strikes me you're not her type."

"It ain't like that, I swear. She's got plenty of friends her own age."

"You surprise me. Like Horace? Next time you send a welcoming committee..."

"No! Nor him! For crying out loud, he's got ten years on her! He dotes on her, but he's like a child. He just don't think of her that way."

"Now you do surprise me. Unpredictable type, wouldn't you say?"

"He just gets worked up about the law, that's all. He don't like the Bill."

"Nor the firm neither, eh? What was he in for?"

"You won't believe it, Mr McFee. Cattle rustling."

"Well, yeehaw. Where would that have been?"

"Scotland somewhere. They needed some muscle to get 'em into the trucks. He done time in Peterhead."

"And it didn't suit him. Scots, is he?"

"No. Londoner. He's brighter than he sounds, Mr McFee. Some disease makes him talk funny. Look, he's a lot of help to me. Sometimes I send him with the cart and the money to pick up big items I can't handle. Sal shows him the way."

"I'll bet. Money, eh? For rags and bones and old tat."

"Yeah, okay. Nuff said."

Danny gets up, opens the door of the range, goes to the entrance and picks up a piece of coal. Turning, he tosses it right into the flames.

"Well done!" I say. "Good shot."

"Always been good at that." He smiles; seems more at ease now. "The engine drivers throw me the odd lump. No harm in that, is there?" He sits down, wiping his hands. "What's this all about, Mr McFee?"

The sergeant of detectives lights his pipe. I try to shove aside a jumble of impressions and get ready to concentrate.

"I've decided to write my memoirs, so I'm doing a little research. I've got to the chapter about Petermen I Have Known. Remember Albert Smallwood?"

I'm well thrown. Writing his memoirs? A huge neon sign starts fizzing and changing colours above McFee's head. It says 'Bollocks'.

Danny has white eyes. They show even whiter when he's staring hard. Then he smiles and says slowly, "Right you are, Mr McFee; 'course I remember 'im. Shared a cell almost to the day he died. But you know that already."

"So I do, Danny. So I do. Did he ever talk about his last job?"

The sight of two men about to engage in a bit of mutual bullshitting makes me uncomfortable. There's trouble brewing. I can feel it. Danny Ogden's eyes narrow.

"Not a lot, Mr McFee. He was down about Alice. But you know that too."

"Go on." McFee's eyes also narrow. I keep looking from one to the other.

"Who's he?"

"My research assistant."

"Yeah? Where's his notebook then?"

"In my head," I say.

"Looks bloody young to be hanging round the Bill."

"Straight out of school," smiles McFee. "What did Smallwood tell you, Danny?"

"He didn't. He just wrote letters all the time; to lawyers. About property and wills and that. I didn't understand it so I minded my own."

"Not good enough, my son. You did what they all do. You kept your eyes and ears open and your mouth shut. So you looked at them. What did they say?"

"How should I know? In the nick you mind your own; like I said. Reading other people's letters? Give over!"

I'm looking deep into Danny Ogden's hard pale eyes. It's there, the ruthless little gangster of the prewar racetracks. Unmistakeable, because I've seen the films. But this isn't second sight. Any fool could do it. I'm only reading the lines – better than ever – but not between the lines. Maybe there's nothing to read after all. Danny's going down the same road as Sidgwick; puzzled, suspicious, only useful in an oblique, passing way.

I'm no good at this.

A long line of wagons rumbles and squeals overhead. Down here it sounds like a roof-skimming, four-engined bomber. Brief soggy toots from the engine fight through the din.

Suddenly everything's upside-down.

I'm on the earth floor, the smell of damp sacking in my face. Scuffling and grunting is breaking out above me. Crawling out of the way I scramble to my feet.

McFee has Ogden by the throat and his face is smiling with a terrible, calm rage. His voice has changed utterly. "Listen to me, you little shite. One word from me and you won't see this yard for squad cars. And you and that gorilla and that tart of his'll go where you can't hear the dogs bark. Start talking. What was in the letters? What did Smallwood tell you about Rosenblum? In ten seconds I'm going to push your ugly face into that fire."

Danny's gasping like a fish. "Nothing, honest!" His falsetto is unreal, like everything else. "You couldn't read what he wrote! He always tore 'em up!"

McFee isn't counting, but I am.

Four, five, six.

"An' he couldn't spell! Always asking me to spell things!"

Seven, eight.

"Like what? What words? I'm going to roast you, you little shyster."

"Can't remember! Too long ago!"

Oh, lord. Don't want to watch. Stop counting.

"Dunno! Hospital! That was one. Couldn't get it right!"

"Go on, Danny."

Something catches my eye. Danny's hand. There's something differ-ent about it. It takes a long second to work it out. His hand isn't there. Then it flashes out of his jacket pocket. I try to shout, but nothing comes. Then:

"Knife! Look out!"

Both their faces change. Danny's teeth are bared. McFee buries his chin in his cravat as he lets go of his opponent's throat and swings his arm outwards, fist clenched. Danny's left arm is knocked aside but he doesn't drop the weapon. Then McFee headbutts him. With a look of surprise Danny sits down hard before being lifted in one whirling movement. Still his fingers stay wrapped round the blade's handle. Then he lets out a squeak of pain.

McFee's features are in the firelight and they've changed once more, to the look of satisfaction you have when you've tasted something you like. It frightens me. He's holding Danny's knife-hand against the metal of the range. The blade falls soundlessly to the floor. The shelter resounds to heavy breathing. Above, the rumble of wagons dies away.

"Take a stroll, laddie. I need a few moments with Mister Attempted Murder here. I'll see you in five minutes. Close the door on your way out."

I fumble with the belt and the sacking drops over the entrance. My heart's banging like a tom-tom and my legs are trembling so much they can hardly carry me up the steps into the cold afternoon air. Sal is sitting on the embankment above the shelter. She's heard nothing. I look at her with a critical eye. It isn't meant like that; just my expression recovering from the last minute's work. She stares back. A look like that from a pretty woman would have felled me a day ago. Not now. I'm powerful because McFee is powerful. There really are G-men outside the films; men who suspend the constitution for scum who aren't worth it. A freebooter. Maybe that's his secret; maybe the source of many secrets, like the respect he gets from his superiors that doesn't amount to respectability. I know for sure he carried a revolver during the war. Maybe he still does. The thought of what he's putting Danny Ogden through a few feet below us makes me immune.

"Sal. What's your other name, Sal?"

I pick my way upwards till I'm standing over her. The perfume's still there and I'm doing okay.

"What's that to you, sonny? Got a fag?"

I arrange my features in a half-smile and look around me like McFee does; the gesture that says: I'm still deciding whether talking to you is worth the bother. The knees are now more or less under control.

"I thought I was asking the questions."

She looks past me and that makes me wary. I take a guess but decide not to turn round.

"Don't be afraid. But if you want to call people sonny you shouldn't need to look to your boyfriend for protection."

"Well, you've got some neck. And who's protecting you, sonny?"

I sigh. You need to train for bouts like this. Experience counts.

"What's your name then, Sal?"

"You just said it, Popeye. Who's the goon?"

I close one eye and survey the scenery. Popeye. Too much gawping at her earlier on; make a note. "Sally Ogden. You couldn't have seen much of your old man when you were growing up, could you?"

She laughs. "Good try! Four out of ten! Okay, Ogden it is. But he ain't my old man."

I'm feeling pretty creative now.

147

"Your uncle, then. So his partner's his brother."

"Getting colder, Popeye. It's Ogden and Langford. He hasn't put the sign up yet."

"You can't be Ogden and Langford at the same time, Sal." I'm enjoying this. "What's that perfume?"

"My old man ran off. Stan Langford's my stepdad, okay? Haven't a clue about the scent. A present from Danny."

"Hmm. Marche Noir, I'd say. Suits you. You're an attractive girl, Sal."

She explodes into laughter. "Oh, great! Got any money, Popeye?"

"Some. Why?"

"Makes up for looks, you cheeky sod. And I know a bit of French. Surprise you? Marche Noir. Is that what your pal's here about?"

"No; not surprised. I've met cabbies who recite Wordsworth. Where d'you live, Sally Ogden?"

"Prefabs."

"And Horace?"

"With the horse."

"He likes you."

"He looks out for me. He's all right." She's gone quiet and serious. "What do they call you, Popeye?"

"Mackinnon."

"Got a girl somewhere, Mackinnon?"

"Yeah."

"She got a name?"

Pause. A hint of a tremor re-enters my knees. "Berenice."

"Sounds foreign. Nice, is she?"

"Remarkably nice."

"Love her?"

Longer pause. "Don't know." Bluffing's over. I really don't know if that's what it is.

"Then you don't. And she don't love you."

I shoot her a frown. "Very good, Sal. What do you come out with next? 'Cross my palm with silver?'"

A shadow falls by me in the thin winter sun and I turn to face Horace's leather jerkin. He looks down at me as if his face is carved on Mount Rushmore.

"How's the future looking now?" says Sal. "Eh, Popeye?"

"My whole life is flashing before me." Any second now my feet are leaving the ground. I hope McFee's five minutes are up. "Bluto's very light on his pins, isn't he?"

Sal comes over and leans her head on Horace's elbow. She looks straight at me, eyes half-closed, lips parted, a ghost of a smile. Something in me is still enjoying her nearness. I smile back; carefully.

Putting out my hand I look up at the granite face with its raw, veined skin. "We weren't introduced before. I must say I like your place here."

"It's okay, Horace," says Sal, her eyes on me. Both knees are quivering now, mostly because of her. "He isn't one of 'em."

My hand vanishes into his, leaving my knitted thumb sticking out.

Behind us McFee emerges, dusting off his bowler hat. Without a word he strides towards the gate. "Goodbye", I say, with a pang of regret. "Nice meeting you, Sal. And Horace. I hope..."

"Yeah," she murmurs. I pull off a glove and extend my hand. She takes it, softly, while Horace looks at me impassively and I see the dignity in him for the first time.

There are warnings of evening in the sky as we put distance between ourselves and the scrapyard. Bands of red, green and lilac throw the signal gantries of New Cross into dramatic silhouette. Smoke plumes mushroom upwards like trees in a savannah sunset. We take the Tube. I've never been on the Underground before and McFee's silence gives me room to think. I think of Sal in her summer dress; imagine showing her round the gardens of Inglefield on a hot June afternoon; cool, suave, in full possession. Then a jolt, a slowing into another station, another exchange of bodies. The crowd of strangers in the yellow light, rattling through the dark fissure in the earth. I watch their faces, smell the damp of evening in their clothes, try to read their thoughts.

Nothing has come of our visit to Danny Ogden's little commune; nothing that advances our search anyway. How much longer will McFee put up with my failure to sense anything that the rest of us couldn't work out for themselves? Is that why he sits in silence in the swaying carriage which holds more people than the whole of Inglefield?

My failure worries me. We change at Whitechapel for the District Line. More rumbling. More smells of clothing, of pipesmoke, leather; of brakedust as we screech into light from the tunnels. My sense of smell seems to have sharpened. Maybe that's the gateway. Perhaps I really am a psychic bloodhound. Too much has happened today, yet nothing's happened.

Except that I feel stranger to myself than ever.

Opposite me the faces merge, lose their definition. The train seems to slow, to struggle through a viscous darkness. Everything moves more and more slowly. The heartbeat of the multitude dulls into greys and browns and my nostrils become filled with a smell of earth, but not of rich loam; of clay. Imprisoning clay.

I turn to McFee. He's dozing. How much longer here under the ground? I'm desperate to know, so I shake him awake. He points to the map above the windows and nods off again.

What about Berenice? I've scarcely thought about her. Why couldn't she have come? She's been out of it during my excursion into fantasy with Sal. A girl and a woman. I glance at my watch. Scarcely twenty-four hours in this town; getting off another train.

As we walk down the last street McFee says, "Calling on Rosenblum tomorrow."

"It's Sunday tomorrow. Should we do that?"

"Today is his Sunday. He wouldn't see us today if his trousers were on fire. Tomorrow will be fine."

We stop at the foot of the Shawe-Trittons' porticoed steps. Left this place in the dark, came back in the dark. And most of the time between in the dark. McFee looks at the ornate railings and smooth cream pillars. "Still living in style, then. No let up for you, is there?"

"It's been quite a day," I answer, yawning suddenly.

"Average. Average day, average results."

"Look, I'm sorry; that I wasn't more use, I mean. Are you coming in to talk it over with Shanks?"

"Not tonight, laddie. Get some rest. I've got things to attend to. We'll discuss it in the morning. And say hello to Fernleaf for me."

"How do you know that?"

"Mumbling in your sleep. We were going under the river."

"Don't remember being asleep. More to worry about, I suppose. How can you tell, though?"

"Who else would it be? Go on, get up those steps."

Cars glide by. Flashy cars and well-dressed people. I think of Sal in her prefab, of Danny and Horace in the dugout and the stable, about a million miles away. McFee reads my face. "A grand life. For some."

"Goodnight, Mr McFee."

"'Night, laddie. One other thing."

"Yes?"

"One woman at a time, Mackinnon. Easy does it."

I do a you-know-how-it-is smile and he goes on his way, heelcaps resounding on the pavement in the frosty air; then turn and press the bell-push of polished brass.

Chapter 17

The door is opened by a tall, dark-eyed woman with a disapproving look and I step into a different kingdom. There's gramophone music and murmuring from unseen voices.

Some kind of get-together's going on. I walk to a door to look in, but the woman heads me off.

"First you go upstairs. Make yourself presentable."

Her accent's foreign; sounds like Spanish. She eyes me haughtily.

"Are you the housekeeper? Maid? I didn't see you last evening."

"You have been in a field. Go to your toilet."

"Yes, ma'am."

In the drawing room people are standing around, sprawling in sofas, leaning on the mantelpiece. Sherry glasses sparkle in the firelight. One or two characters look familiar; the old Inglefield set perhaps. Everyone's dressed casually for what would still be a black-tie affair in some corners of this world. I can't see Shanks anywhere.

Mrs Shawe-Tritton is a comfortable-looking woman between fifty and sixty with floppy grey hair. She knows all the conventions and enjoys kicking them around. Grabbing my hand she calls for attention. "Here he is at last, back from his mystery tour. This is Clement, everyone. His people are in East Africa." I nod in several directions. They acknowledge me, more or less, and go back to their conversations.

"Where's Uncle?"

"He's in the library, dear. There's no rush. Why not stay and meet some people?"

But I am in a hurry. And I've already met people.

Shanks is sitting on a window seat with a woman in a tight green dress. I wander over. "Evening, Uncle."

"Ah, Clement! At last. You've been out for some time. On your own, are you? Interesting day?" My eyes are on the woman.

"Ah! Forgive me. This is Clement, the young fellow in my charge. Clement, this is Miss Constance Maybury, Berenice's governess." I take her hand. She isn't the first governess I've ever seen but she's the first one who looks human; very human. Her auburn hair is gathered back in a chignon and sets off her classical features perfectly. A Greek goddess. And Shanks is enjoying her company. Plummy tones and braying laughter erupt from the corridor outside. Just don't come in here. Not yet.

"I'm very pleased to meet you, Clement." A rich honey voice. I gulp. "Jackson's been telling me about you. Are you missing your parents this Christmas?"

"No more than usual." I search her features for a look that might say: tut-tut. But she just wears a knowing smile that's all for me; I can tell. Goodbye, Sal. It's time for a witty, sophisticated remark or two but I'm all out of stock.

"Where's Berenice?"

"Up in her room. She has a headache." She gives me a huge wink and parts her lips and I can't stop myself.

"I bet you're a lot of fun. You don't sound like a New Zealander though."

"No, I'm not. But I've lived there most of my life."

"Do you live on the farm too?"

"Nearby."

"Do you ride and all that?"

"Of course."

"Berenice's headache, is it bad?"

"Oh, terrible." She smiles again.

An amusing headache. Wish mine were. "Excuse us, won't you, Clement?' says Shanks.

Her room's on the fourth floor, opposite mine. Portaits, prints and framed photos cascade down the walls of the staircase. On each landing stand little Chinese tables, decorated urns with big-leaved plants flopping over them. The first-floor landing opens into a conservatory with cane blinds and bamboo chairs. But it's the wallpaper that keeps making me stop and look. It never seems to repeat its pattern; greens, reds, yellows; trees and creepers and birds of paradise follow me silently until I feel I'm climbing a path in a Celanese forest. It gives out warmth in this dark season and you knew it'll refresh you with hilly breezes in the days of heat.

Nothing like the quiet, sad dignity of Inglefield Place; nothing like the wasteland of institutional dinginess at Monk's Hill; and a long, long way from the sour cream and washed-out flowers that make almost every other house in England feel like a boarding-house parlour. The Shawe-Trittons are rich enough to play at being interesting. They've got my attention anyway.

George and Damietta Shawe-Tritton. Photographs of their progress through other people's lives hang everywhere. One of her taken in 1935 is signed 'Sybil Cumana' with 'Gentlewomen's Directory' written underneath. She still writes under that name; an advice column, apparently. I can imagine her advice: scandalise the neighbours; if they think you're letting the side down you're probably doing all right.

For the moment it's exciting being here. But it can't make me forget New Cross.

Berenice is sitting up reading; intently. I sit on the end of the bed.

"How's the head?"

No reply.

"Listen. I was dragged out of here at seven o'clock this morning. It was meant to be just Shanks, McFee and me. Between us we ran into some strange people. I wanted you to come, but there it is." She wriggles further into the blankets and turns a page.

Okay.

"I'll leave you to really read your book, then. See you later." She doesn't look up.

"You haven't got a headache at all, have you?"

Her eyes meet mine. "Oh, really? Ah, yes. Clement the psychic; I'd almost forgotten. How could I hope to conceal such things from you?"

"What happened to Mackinnon?"

"He slunk out this morning."

"Look, what d'you want me to do? Re-run the film? If they'd wanted you along they'd have said. They didn't. So that's it." I close the door softly behind me. No matter. Today I've met Sal Ogden and Constance Maybury. I'm walking upright. Sort this out later.

Halfway down the stairs, just within earshot of the music and talking I pause to look at yet another framed photo. A couple who look like our hosts in their prime are standing either side of what looks like Rudolf Valentino on some kind of film set. George is wearing a white suit and Panama hat, Damietta has a turban like women wore in the early twenties and he's in jodhpurs and an Arab headdress. I peer at the autograph. It *is* Rudolf Valentino.

"They got around, didn't they?"

I turn. It's Miss Maybury. She's as tall as me and when she leans forward to study the picture more closely I'm enveloped in her scent. Her face is level with mine. A faint buzzing fills my head, which begins to exist separately from my body. That isn't just perfume from a bottle. It's blended with her; essence of Constance Maybury. Politeness dictates that I step aside. I stay where I am. But embarrassing things are happening to me. Without taking her eyes from the picture she murmurs "How's Berenice?"

Who?

"You've just been to see her?"

"How do you know?"

She laughs; softly. It caresses the back of my neck and tremors affect me in several places.

"Your whole look says you have. Frustrating little madam, isn't she?"

"Do you know, she hasn't got a headache at all?"

This time she looks at me. "You poor boy. Of course she hasn't."

"What has Shanks told you about me?"

"Shanks? Suits him, doesn't it? He's told me enough, Clement."

"That why you said 'Poor boy'?"

She puts her hand to my cheek. Cruel kindness. "I'm going to fetch her down for dinner. We'll see you presently. What do you think of this wallpaper? Hand-printed to order. See you later."

I watch her continue up the next flight of stairs. Teach me; be my teacher. I'd drink in every word, so help me I would. How much I've lived in a day.

The next few minutes cure me of all desire.

Back in the drawing room an extremely short old woman with sparse white curls and many chins detaches herself from a group and advances on me with a dot-and-carry-one movement. I think: wooden leg. She wears what I've come to regard as standard medium's uniform. It trails around her with no shape. A smile fights its way onto my lips and I desperately fight it off. She looks like a pale-tentacled sea anemone shifting position on a rock. Thrusting her face up at me she speaks, very loudly.

"You're Clement, aren't you? Jackson has charge of you." She nods furiously and chews her gums.

"Yes, that's right."

Her eyes widen and she glances furtively right and left, then whispers: "Do you believe in fairies?"

"Er, no. That is, I've never seen any."

"That's because you've never looked! They're everywhere, the little folk. I often see them. But Chu here sees them all the time, don't you, darling?"

She focuses on my right elbow and chews vigorously. Crazy, to hell and gone. I've been cornered by a lunatic. Then a tangle of fine greyish hair begins to emerge from the folds of her costume. A pink ribbon grows round it, and an eye like a luminous brown marble. There's only hair where another should be. A Pekingese. I can take most dogs or leave them alone but I draw the line at the kind you carry around. I stare back at the eye as she babbles on. "Heaven-born Prince Chu of Pimlico. Isn't he regal? So much more intelligent than the majority of humans; and he talks to the little people."

"Is that so? How interesting."

"It should be, young man. I've heard you're one of us too."

"I am?"

"A sensitive! I'm surprised they haven't revealed themselves to you. Jackson's place is teeming with them. They prefer children and clever animals as a rule. Have you heard of Conan Doyle?"

"Naturally. I enjoy all the Sherlock Holmes stories." Firm ground at last.

"Silly boy! He was a believer. Our greatest convert. I knew him, you know." Heaven-born one-eye begins to wheeze and snuffle and growl from her armpit. "Chu's not sure about you. Are you, poppet? Are you really a psychic, young man?"

Cunning old hag. What do I say? Is she guessing, making conversation? Then I can deny it. But if Shanks really has told her then denial makes me a liar. This is what McFee does to suspects in dimly lit concrete rooms.

"You can come to dinner now!"

Saved, by La Pasionara standing in the doorway with her look that servants reserve for the idle and unworthy. To my horror Anemone Woman shoves the whining dog under her other elbow and offers me her arm. Everywhere men and women are pairing up and drifting towards the door; a charming scene if my mind weren't full of the prospect of an hour's interrogation. Suddenly Shanks rides in, coming discreetly between us. She smiles at him, hisses "Do be quiet, Chu!" and leaves me to follow on my own.

There is candlelight. Berenice and Constance are already there, admiring the decorations and centrepieces while I admire their faces in the glow and sparkle. All new things; the atmosphere, the surroundings. Luxury and privilege; they too caress the back of my neck and make me tremble.

Fourteen of us sit down. At the ends of the table George and Damietta preside. There's plenty of time to talk because the dark-eyed woman seems in no hurry to serve us. Twice I hear, "Thank you, Amelia."

Despite the novelty of dinner by candlelight among these fine people, my thoughts stray to the events of the day. Then a burst of laughter brings me back and there'll be Shanks with a look that says: snap out of it. So after a while I concentrate on one or two of the party to see if my powers can reveal them to me. They can't. Staring at the two women in my life will look bad so I settle to what I should have done all along: listen.

George Shawe-Tritton is an old buffer. Chubby, florid-faced, little white military moustache, expression of perpetual surprise. He says little, looks at everyone and eats carefully. Every now and then he nods to Amelia and she approaches, leaning to hear him whisper, her eyes flashing at the diners; the harmless-seeming patriarch murmuring instructions to his hired assassin. I begin to like him. Damietta on the other hand is witty, knowing and hard to ignore. You can imagine people thinking she's the strong one, but I guess she floats on a sea of her husband's patience. They make a good couple, and I surprise myself by my own thoughts. Insight rather than second sight. Whatever it is, something's going on in my brain that hasn't been part of me before.

Of the guests I don't know, two in particular – a man and a woman – seem just plain unadorned obnoxious. They complain about everything the war's imposed on them. Everything except what matters. The whole conflict's been a conspiracy got up against their own convenience, and peace has only rubbed it in. They call the world war the 'recent unpleasantness'. Limp-wristed bollocks. No one argues with them much, here among the crystal and candlelight. Maybe they've heard it all before.

But the day has changed me. Once I'd have been happy being seen and not heard among my elders and betters. Now I've been places. I've walked down the mean streets where a man must go. And most of this lot never will. The spirit of McFee enters me.

It's a male decade, the forties; a man-made world where if women are heroes or villains it's only after you stop to think about it. So I concentrate on the bloke.

At which Constance changes the angle of the talk. "Looking forward to the Games this summer? It's been over ten years now since Berlin. And it'll be right here on your doorstep." I stand my thoughts down and smile at her. Just as well; better than arguing. "Well, I wouldn't cross the street to see any of it. Bloody hearties performing like seals. What does anyone see in it? What's it supposed to prove?" Our poor war victim's going to push his luck. The wine inside him's already perspiring on his face.

"Surely sport's good for us?" I say. Oh, yes. A real Humphrey Bogart line.

"In what way, pray?"

There's a whole speech about why it does us good which has been tattooed on my behind since my first schooldays, but this isn't the moment to recite it. "Didn't you do sport at school? For your house?"

He explodes in derision. His companion laughs and looks away and up. "It's my proudest boast that I never lifted a finger for my bloody house. What a load of balls! Go on, tell us, what do they make you do?"

The atmosphere's gone half tense, half amused. "I box. House and school."

"God, what a little thug. You proud of that? I find it disgusting."

"Come now," says Damietta. "Time to change the subject."

159

"Ha, ha! Time! Ding, ding! Seconds out! There ought to be a bloody law."

Constance speaks. "I believe Clement also plays tennis." She gives me a surreptitious wink. "And athletics. And cross-country running. And chess. Not a complete oaf, then. School vice-captain; isn't that right?" I nod, modestly. Right.

"Well, well! The gorilla with a bloody violin. Doesn't change a thing, old bean. Same old hairy-arsed waste of time and effort."

"Now that really is enough, Quentin," says Damietta. "Come on, Violet; keep your fiancé in order, there's a good girl." From things revealed on this day I draw on a new-found dignity. Quentin is drunk. I gaze steadily at him and speak to Fernleaf.

"Berenice, you're pretty athletic. Let's write to – oh, Jesse Owens, Paavo Nurmi and Fred Perry. Tell them they're gorillas, and get Quentin here to sign it. Oh, and Quentin, why not invite them to dinner, here, so they can be seduced from their ways by your example. I'm sure they'll love to meet you. Quite a party. Chimps' tea party, eh? Ben Hogan, Joe Louis, Henry Armstrong, Gene Tunney..."

"Point made, Clement."

No. Not done yet, you jellyfish. "On second thoughts, write to Thor Heyerdahl and ask to join his next voyage..." And I'm about to say 'as sharkbait' when I realise I'm over-exposed. My feet are dangling in fathomless green deeps.

That'll better do, then. But he doesn't rise to it. Hasn't he heard of the *Kon-Tiki*? Only a few months ago, for God's sake. No, they're just ignoring you; sophisticated brush-off; no longer amusing.

"I agree with Dame," says Jackson Armitage. "Let's find another subject."

George harrumphs quietly and silence follows. I keep my gaze on Quentin until I'm sure he isn't playing any more, then do the same to Violet. She's pretty, but not attractive. They're made for each other; their lives will be full of pleasure and they'll set no foot in any wild place or any arena spotted with real blood, or any contested field.

The damage they do will be serious just the same and no handshakes afterwards.

She stares back angrily and I give her a little smile, enough to start a fight at Monk's Hill.

Lordy, but this feels good. Until I see Constance frown and slowly shake her head. I smile at her too. Okay, show's over, folks; nothing more to see here. Move along.

Conversation starts up again. Amelia clears away and serves and all is proceeding once more in harmony, when Anemone Woman leans forward. The whining and snuffling and wriggling from inside her sleeve has been getting worse, but it turns into a sudden yelp as she presses against the table. Her features are thrown into relief by the candlelight and for a nasty split-second I see what a bunch of gargoyles some of the rich really are. She bellows into the midst of the talk.

"Queer goings-on at Scotland Yard! Have you heard?"

Everyone turns towards her except Berenice, whose eyes widen in alarm.

"Well, you do all know my nephew Cecil is on the *Chronicle*? Well, my dears, he has word that the Yard and the Home Office are sitting on something. It's to do with a series of crimes; unexplained crimes…"

"What, murders; that sort of thing?"

"Not another Jack the Ripper episode? We'd have heard, surely?"

"No, no!" She's enjoying herself now. "No, nothing awful like that – at least he doesn't think so. Still, it's a bit odd, don't you think?"

"Unsolved crimes are hardly new," says Shanks.

"I didn't say unsolved, Jackson; I said unexplained."

He's doing well not to sound guarded. "Not much to go on, is it? Fleet Street rumour? The public will want facts. Rumour and gossip are the messengers of…"

"Yes, I know, Jackson; confusion. You often say so. But really! I don't suppose Cecil would be on a wild goose chase. Something is going on."

She presses even further forward. Yelps of discomfort punctuate her words. "He's got a source! Watch this space, eh?"

Murmurs of speculation follow. Shanks wipes his mouth on his napkin, leans back and admires the ceiling for a long time.

"Will you tell us about meeting Conan Doyle?" I ask. My heart's banging.

"Why should I do that?" she retorts.

"Well, er, he would have enjoyed a mystery like this, don't you think? What would he have made of it?" As I start to sound stupid Berenice rides in. "Hey, I'm a real fan of his! Did you really meet him?"

"Go on, Petronella. They haven't heard your tall stories," says Shanks. It takes a while, but she starts on the reminiscence trail and I risk a few questions about fairies.

This isn't a household that goes in for passing the port or leaving the men to talk smut in private, so half an hour later we're all arranged round the drawing room fire again. Shanks touches Berenice's elbow and says, just loud enough for everyone, "So you both like Sherlock Holmes? Come on, I'll show you something. In the library."

The green baize doors close behind us and Jackson Armitage's face changes. With an expression of fury he marches up and down, grinding his fist into his palm. "Damn! Damn, damn that old vampire! And that useless alcoholic scoundrel of her nephew. That whole family should have been strangled at birth! God alone knows what McFee will say to this. This is our worst nightmare!"

"Do we have to tell him?"

"Of course we have to tell him! Who the devil is leaking this? We can't even investigate that without inviting suspicion."

No, wait. "Uncle, let me get this straight. What we're talking about is a series of robberies with fingerprints that can't be matched to any living person. That simply adds up to a load of unsolved crimes. Where's the problem in reporting that?"

Shanks reacts quite patiently, considering. "Clement, we have to consider the possibility that one or more of the few men who do know whose prints they are, have not kept the matter to themselves."

"Clement hasn't told us about his day yet," says Berenice. "I know he hasn't had a chance, but maybe this is the moment. Where are the Holmes books? We ought to look convincing if anyone comes in."

"Too risky. You don't know these people like I do. What's the time? Twenty to ten. Come on; we'll go and see the lights in Knightsbridge before we retire. Does that sound plausible enough?"

"Yes," she replies. "I'll insist."

Nobody in the house cares much, except Constance Maybury who bids farewell to us in the hall and says not to be too long. Each one of us would like to have her with us. Five minutes later we squeeze into a phone box. "Hallo, McFee? Thank God. Armitage here. Armitage. I have the young people with me. Eh? Yes, yes. Listen, there's been an unwelcome development. Someone at dinner tonight has a relative on the *Chronicle*. What? Yes, the *Chronicle*. This person has got wind of something. A series of unexplained crimes is how she put it. The Home Office are keeping the lid on it, according to her. Eh? She's called Petronella Lendery; a medium of the worst kind but very fashionable. Look, what do you make of it?"

McFee's reply is long enough for the telephone box to mist up competely.

"His name? Cecil Lendery. A complete scoundrel. They all are. Yes, yes. I take your point; we must assume the worst. Look, it's no use like this. We're meeting tomorrow when? That's earlier than we arranged. Albert Memorial; eight. Very well. Yes. Good luck. Till tomorrow, then."

We talk it out as we wander down Knightsbridge. The scenery doesn't matter. I describe what went on after Shanks left me with McFee that morning and try to answer every question. There's little to cheer us. We're floundering and we know it.

"Clement?" says Shanks as we turn back.

"Yes?"

"Do not repeat your performance at dinner. You drew attention to yourself."

"Come on," mutters Berenice, "they were ratbags, both of them."

"Oh, I grant you that. Listen, the pair of you. Everyone at that table has the power to make things very difficult for us. Petronella Lendery is the least of them. Your two friends, Clement – and I'm not saying you didn't acquit yourself well – are among the worst."

"Even George and Damietta? Then why are we staying there? No, never mind."

"It's a snakepit. Just use discretion; all right?"

I'm a *voyageur*. My canoe is bucking and tossing in the rapids. The cries of my beautiful companion ring loud in my ears. Thrown into the foaming freezing water we cling to each other. Her hair sweeps into my eyes; my mouth fills with choking foam.

"Wake up, you useless lump!" comes hissing through the confusion.

Berenice, in yellow silk pyjamas this time. I lie back, her hands still gripping my shoulders, and take in some reality. "You seem," I murmur, "to be making a habit of creeping into my room at midnight. What is it?"

That serious look again. "Constance has gone missing."

"What! When?"

"We don't know. She was last seen in the company of a youth, about fifteen or sixteen."

I shake my head.

"You were calling out her name, drongo."

"Sorry. I like her, that's all."

She ruffles my hair. "Well, it's your sheets, not mine. Oh, stop blushing! I came for a chat. Is that okay?"

"What about?"

"Lots of things. Are you ready?" Without waiting for a reply she shoves my legs aside under the blankets and sits on the bed cross-legged, facing me, her hands in her lap; all in one graceful movement. The room's cold and she's ignoring it.

"Are you in that Women's League of Health and Beauty by any chance?"

"No. Connie was, though."

"Was?"

"It got a bit, I don't know, political. Never mind, she doesn't need it."

I leap out of bed, get my dressing gown off the hook and put it round her shoulders. She doesn't move or say anything till I'm back under the covers.

"I guess you are awake, then."

I am. And suddenly very receptive; very glad she's come.

"What time is it?"

"Twenty past two. The last of them turned in about an hour ago. Connie came and chatted a bit but she's asleep now."

"Connie. Doesn't fit her somehow."

"Clement doesn't fit you. But then, you don't see her in quite the way I do." She gives me a big, open-mouth wink.

"Fernleaf, will you do something for me?"

"Go on," she says, a wary smile spreading over her face.

"Remember I said I needed your horse-sense to keep me on course?"

"Yes."

"I need you now. To help me make sense of what's happening; and to tell me when I'm thinking clearly and when I'm not. Is that okay?"

She spreads her arms and bows till her forehead touches the blankets. "Your genie is here at your command, O Wise One."

"Well; if only. Look, I'm having trouble with all of it. Can you start us off?"

I noticed her loose pyjama jacket when she arched her body and when she rose again. It gives me fresh reasons for admiring her. Berenice is attractive because her gestures fit her so well. Generosity from a stream in flood. Sal Ogden was too hard-edged, too showy to be like this, with her defensive gestures copied from a world itself unreal. Whatever Lauren Bacall looks like with a cigarette, on Sal it just looks feeble-minded. Trouble is, I'm still too much like that myself, a copier of gestures, trying on borrowed styles. It's time to baptize myself into a new religion. That of having your own style. I wait to hear what Berenice has to say.

"Okay. Question one. As far as you know, how many people are in on McFee's secret?"

"Right; hang on. His associates; fellow detectives. Don't know how many exactly. Then, er, his superiors at the Yard. One or two people in the government maybe. They're protecting him by keeping the press off his back and giving him sick leave to sort it out. I don't really see why, though. He's not very important and he thinks he's being haunted. Do you reckon he's crackers? All there, I mean?"

"Later. Stay with this. Who else is there?"

"You, me, Shanks. McFee himself. That's it."

"Okay. And how many of those do you know personally?"

"Just the last ones."

"And how many of those are still thinking straight about the whole thing?"

"Sorry, lost you now. What d'you mean?"

"Come on; try. It's important. Start with McFee. Since we came to London you've spent more time with him than anyone else."

"Except for Smallwood, maybe."

"Yes, maybe. What do you think about him now?"

I bring my knees up to my chin. "He's edgy. He doesn't show it, but he's more on edge than ever. I sometimes wonder whether he really wants to know what Smallwood's after. That sound strange?"

"No. Tell me why you think so."

"Well, I'm sure I've heard Shanks say that hauntings die away after a while. Years, usually. McFee's had this trouble for ten years at least. Could be that half of him is thinking that all these psychic reinforcements — us, I mean — have weakened Smallwood. If he hangs on a bit longer he'll go away. But it's like you get more nervous nearer the end of the game. More worried that some small thing could happen at the last minute. You know, the bullet just before the Armistice. In his case the bullet is the press and the danger is that Smallwood is frightened off but never stops haunting him. That make sense?"

"Go on."

The thoughts are coming now in the same well-ordered way that felt so good in the park by the river. "Like, yesterday we visited Danny Ogden, right? I can't believe Danny, Horace and Sal are going to keep it to themselves, can you? It'll be all over the place; every pub, every garden fence at the prefabs. McFee asks about Smallwood. He roughs up Danny. Smallwood was a safecracker. Safes are cracked for no obvious reason round London. People aren't stupid, for God's sake. Why did McFee do it unless he's rattled? Why hasn't he even hinted at what happened in the shelter after he told me to get out?"

Her expression doesn't change. It's as if she can read my thoughts, not the other way round. "Then there's this feeling he's got that he's sunk low. He said something to me, like he used to be a big white hunter and now he just turns over stones."

Still she looks.

"And then there's the bit about how he thinks he's being sent on a quest. Not just him either; me too maybe. We're being put through this to make us humble; to improve our characters. But there was nothing humble about him beating up Danny Ogden. He didn't care if it got him into trouble; as if he was above the law. That's the opposite of humble, surely. Anyway, my bloody school is supposed to be improving me. Doesn't need a dead jailbird, does it?"

I look back into her eyes.

"After all that he called it an average day. I guess I've been living a sheltered life."

At last she speaks. Almost a whisper.

"Don't you think he's a bit strange anyway?"

"Well, he's a bit seedy. Living all alone in those rooms. He could do with looking after. But being a detective isn't a normal kind of life anyway, is it? Look at the kind of people you have to mix with."

A silvery ting, ting, ting floats up from the hall, up four flights of stairs; past the sleepers, past the birds of paradise and the photographs of an age of pleasure. I smile to think of it. "It's not a normal life being us."

"Look at the people we have to mix with."

"Is it three o'clock already? You only came in a minute ago."

"Conversation quickens time. Now tell me what you think of Uncle Jackson."

My mouth has gone dry. I pour from a decanter of water by my bedside. When I offer her some she shakes her head.

"Not many new thoughts about him. One thing puzzles me. He's promised to help keep things quiet for McFee, but his whole life's purpose is to publish his success – if he gets it. How can he do both? Suppose McFee suspects that Shanks'll be tempted to reveal all the facts? Well, he will if it's research, won't he? Mightn't that stop him giving us the whole story? What's he kept from us? Seems we're all keeping something from each other."

"Are we?"

"No, not between us. Can I talk about me?"

"Yes."

"Why hasn't Shanks carried on doing his tests on me as we go along?"

"Because this is hardly the place, after what he's told us. Anyway your performance at Inglefield was pretty conclusive, I'd say; wouldn't you?"

"Oh, yes. So why doesn't it work most of the time? Why can't I read your mind? Ought to be simple enough. No offence."

"You're not thinking, Mackinnon."

"Only leaves you."

"Mmm. And I'm not a detective or a ghost-hunter or a psychic. Come on, drongo; when don't your powers operate?"

"When I'm under emotional strain?"

"Right."

"Wrong! I've been under bloody emotional strain since I got off the train at Inglefield. My little world all changed. And I was angry with you after all that showing off you did, remember? And scared witless when I did the card trick."

"Were you?" She looks startled; it's the first crack in her composure.

"Yes, I was. Even more than that turn I had at the Holland tomb. That's when it started. Some incident, Shanks said. Mixed with, er... growing up."

"Puberty."

"That's the word."

She nods. "I'd like to think you were a bit past puberty. But he does think adolescents are transmitters as well as receivers of psychic signals."

"Does that mean I can influence what people do?"

"Don't get carried away. He also said it's involuntary. You've got no control."

Tiredness is stealing back over me. But there's something I have to do. I have to remove a barrier that's making everything difficult for me. This is the ideal moment; it may not come again. My heart's thumping and my chest feels tight. Are all my words in the right order? Are they the right ones? I open my mouth and look directly at her.

"Where are we off to tomorrow?" She looks around her at the wallpaper.

"Eh?" I croak.

"Who are we seeing, tomorrow?"

"Er, Rosenblum. The pawnbroker."

"Just asking. You all right?"

"Fine. Tired, that's all. It's the three o'clock in the morning thing with me; you know."

"Me too. See you later." She slips my dressing gown off her shoulders, stretches both arms out beside her and slowly wriggles her body down to the waist. Her fringe falls over her brow and she sweeps it back.

"Don't go just yet," I say quickly. "There's something else."

"It's getting late, Mackinnon."

"I know. Just hang on a bit. You know I said Danny Ogden had a girl with him?"

"You used the words 'young woman' at the time, I believe. It was just before Harrods."

"Did I? Was it? Well, anyway, I got talking to her at the scrapyard."

"So you said."

"Well, she asked me if I had a girlfriend." My heart's banging so hard I can hear it. My whole body buzzes with tension and my skin is cold and dry.

"And have you?"

"I told her I did. I said it was you."

"What's wrong with that? I'm a girl. I'm a friend. Do you know any girls better than you know me?"

"No. No. But I wasn't kidding her. I wanted it to be true. I want it to be true. She asked me if I loved you. I said I didn't know. So she said, 'Then you probably don't'; something like that, 'And she probably don't love you.' That's all."

I look down at the blanket between us, frowning deep. She doesn't move or say anything. When I look up again she's just gazing at me. Confession has given me courage. I push the covers away and sit cross-legged like her so that our knees touch. The bed goes twoing, joing, and falls silent. The jacket of my pyjamas is fluttering in time with my heart. I take her hands in mine, leaving her fingers free. Her skin is warm, but there's no encouragement, no moulding of her hands to mine. I lean forward to kiss her face.

"May I?"

She draws her hands and face away. "I don't think you should," she whispers. Yet I feel no disappointment. Out of nowhere I hear myself murmur: Would you close your eyes for a moment?

And she does. Her eyelids slowly fall; without fluttering, without apprehension. I rise from my knees.

Twang, joing.

Putting my hands gently on her shoulders I kiss each eyelid. Softly, because my lips are dry and hard as a bone. Leaning back I sit on my heels and wait.

She opens her eyes. Is she thoughtful, or frowning? "I didn't mean to offend you," I whisper.

"You haven't," she whispers.

"Why are we whispering?"

"I don't know," she whispers. We both smile. This is too serious for laughter.

"Lie back," she says. As I do so she pulls the covers up to my chest. With a soft click the room becomes dark. My heart misses a beat. "Are you going?"

"Lie still," she murmurs. I feel her fingers touch the top of my nose, then travel up into my forehead in small spiralling movements. My heart should quicken to this intimacy but instead it falls quiet until the fingers begin exploring my hairline and other things begin to happen.

"What are you doing?" I say. It feels terrific.

"Something I learnt far away from here." Her words float out of the dark. From below comes a single ting, for the half hour. "It'll help you sleep."

Her lips touch my brow and she's gone.

I float in a warm sea of happiness. But sleep is out of the question. Every feeling, word and gesture must be imprinted on my memory; every response weighed and measured.

Berenice is still a mystery, but now she's given me the key; strangely and intricately wrought, that changes before your eyes, as these things do, and feels different each time you hold it. But a key. And all the thoughts that follow become very clear.

Trickles of this crystal stream find their way between the obstacles that have beset us. Some vanish into the sand but others come together to form pools; pools into which I look. So the crystal ball is not a myth after all. Freed from part of my mortal concerns, I'm allowed a glimpse of a reflection of truth.

Now it's my turn. I creep across the landing and tap on her door.

"That you?"

"Yes. I'm coming in. Turn on your light."

An amber glow floods the room. She's raised on one elbow, blinking.

"I've been thinking. You ready to hear it?"

"I'm all ears. Better be good."

"We'll see. This time I ask, you answer. Okay?"

"Fire away."

"One. Is McFee happy about this Smallwood thing?"

"No, of course not. He wishes it had never happened."

"Correct. Two: does he care about what Smallwood might be trying to tell him?"

"Depends. He'd like to know who shopped him. But it's hardly worth all this trouble to find out."

"Okay, I'll go with that. But suppose this has nothing to do with the law?"

"You'll have to explain, Mackinnon. You're ahead of me."

"Look. All along we've assumed that the only relationship between McFee and Smallwood is the one about the villain and the cop; that they're on opposite sides of the law."

"Yes, we have. Shouldn't we?"

"Until now maybe."

I take a deep breath. "I think there's another connection. And I think we need to find out what it is, or we're all wasting our time. That's it."

"That's it." She isn't agreeing with me; just repeating the words. "Another connection. Another connection." She says it five more times, each time softer than the last. Tasting the truth of it.

"What do you think?"

"I think there's no reason why not. But it must be something pretty secret, or someone's got to know already, and we'd have been told. Because it would help. So it has to be very personal." She's concentrating hard, lips tight. "And if you're right, Smallwood must be in on it too."

"Don't know about that," I say. God, this clear thinking. Is this the bonus end of all the psychic...crap? "What if...what if Smallwood knows it *now*, now that he's dead?

She whistles softly. "We can't let McFee know you think that. Can we?"

"No. And we can't let Shanks know either. It would muddy everything up."

"Why not just bring them together and say: come on, how about all the cards on the table?"

"Because McFee doesn't want us to know. I reckon he thinks it'll, yeah, muddy the waters. Our ignorance is supposed to help make it happen. Only we do know."

"Are you sure? Dead sure?"

"Yes."

She lies back and stares at the ceiling. "Getting complicated, isn't it?"

"Isn't it, though? Plus there's the business with the papers, and how this whole thing will affect Shanks with the rest of the ghost society."

"And with Connie," she murmurs.

"Really? They getting close?"

"Nothing serious."

"Not like us, then."

She puts a hand on my arm. "Mackinnon, let's just keep it the way it is."

"I feel stronger, now you know."

I can't remember taking off, but I'm gliding down a great wide tunnel, full of unnatural light. My arms are outstretched like wings, my body just skimming above the ground. Down and down slopes this endless cavern, curving and flattening so imperceptibly that I know it will never end. I feel the distance I've travelled, the weight of the earth above me. The tunnel begins to narrow and darken. And with every second I realise the agonising lifetime of crawling upwards that faces me before I can see the daylight again. If I ever stop. But I can't stop.

Down, down I swoop; and I begin to scream. The scream flows out behind me like a banner, and the dark ahead remains silent, frictionless, without end.

I sit up, sweating and shaking. Embracing the cold quiet shadows of my room I wonder if the scream was real and whether it woke me; or others. But nothing stirs throughout the house, no consciousness seeps under the doors and up the stairway past the stone-still ferns. I lay back and enter a world of better dreams.

Across the river in Camberwell, in Coldharbour Lane, the buckled safe door in the manager's office of Binney's furniture store swings on its one remaining hinge. Around it the fumes of nitroglycerine gather in a long veil and pass through a ventilation brick, emerging like the birth of a pestilence into the sharp pre-dawn air of the last Sunday of the year.

Chapter 18

Shanks, Berenice and I sit round the breakfast table. It's a large table and there are gaps between us. The gaps are inhabited by empty chairs. We eat in silence.

A Shawe-Tritton breakfast lasts all morning. House guests turn up at random. The early risers eat alone. Slugabeds or those with discreet reasons for staying out of sight might get theirs in their rooms and not appear fully dressed till lunch.

Something's irritating Doctor Armitage; there's tension in the air. When Amelia offers him the morning paper he waves it away. He treats her so disagreeably I feel I need to make up for it. As soon as I can I excuse myself and find her in the kitchen.

"Amelia, where are you from? What country?"

"From Portugal. Why?"

"Just interested. Which part?"

"Santarem. Near to Lisboa."

"You must miss the sunshine. The weather in England is not very good."

"Yes, I miss the sun."

"When you go back you must take me with you." Harmless, inconsequential remark, but Amelia's face suddenly twists into an expression of contempt.

"I never go back!"

"Whyever not?" Seeing my surprise her look changes into a proud, cold sneer.

"The assassin, Salazar. When he is killed, I go back. Till then, can snow every day. I stay here."

Salazar; Salazar. The name comes back to me. Dictator of Portugal. His name's often on the lips of my housemaster, Toady Hopwood. As I look at Amelia I remember why.

"Would that be 'gracious Salazar'?"

This is a mistake. She snatches up a large knife. "Who says that? Show me him. I will kill him!" At least the knife isn't for me, so I stand my ground.

"A master at my school calls him that. This man fought in the civil war in Spain; for Franco. Salazar supported the Nationalists, so he admires him. That's all."

"That is all, huh?"

"If we could get him here, would you really kill him?"

"I would cut off his testicles and send them to Doctor Antonio Oliveira de Salazar with my blessing."

"That would please some of the Lower School boys. It's a deal. When I get back we'll have a whip-round for his ticket. This could solve a number of problems. We hate him as much as you do."

"Do not joke. You know nothing."

I don't hear her. I'm becoming aware of an odour in this kitchen. A slaughterhouse smell. Blood. Bones. Flesh. The smell you get in a butcher's shop. I look quickly round the kitchen but there's no meat anywhere. Amelia stands there with her unspoken history.

So the power's still there.

"I won't mention him again. I don't suppose you have any other enemies?"

"Leave now."

Well wrapped up, we gather once more on the pavement in front of the house. This time there's no problem about Berenice being with us. We're going to see a harmless, law-abiding old Jewish gentleman.

The big surprise now is the thick, clinging mist. Breakfasting behind drawn curtains we haven't been aware of it. We pull up our collars and set off along the eerily quiet Sunday streets towards Hyde Park. Now and then a pair of headlights emerge squinting out of the fog and grope past us with the damp chugging sound of an engine in low gear. We meet a few early birds as we pass up Exhibition Road beside the great museums, and walk between the red sandstone buildings that flank the Albert Hall as though entering a canyon in Colorado. Crossing Kensington Gore we ascend the wide steps of the Albert Memorial.

There he sits, deep in thought; not quite dressed for this weather; poorly sheltered by his pointy canopy. Berenice and I walk round it a couple of times. You can sense the spaciousness of everything here. This is the monumental London, where the comfortable might feel comfortable, taking their ease among the patrons of empire.

"I think the psychic stuff is working again," I tell her. "Thanks for last night." We hang about next to Shanks, shivering and sending our breath ballooning into the murk.

"We're early," he mutters. "I hope to goodness he isn't held up."

Time to make conversation. "Amelia's a strange woman."

"No stranger than most of the foreign crackpots they like to take in."

"How do you mean?"

"I mean our friends the Shawe-Trittons like to pose as protectors of the oppressed by sheltering those deemed undesirables in their own country." He allows himself a sardonic laugh. "Sometimes they employ them. As servants of course."

"Er, like Alphonse and Ludmilla?"

"Don't be impertinent. Their case is entirely different; as you would recognise if you cared to think about it."

"Sorry."

"Hmm. Well, don't get dewy-eyed about Amelia. She comes from a long line of revolutionaries and bandits. Most of her relations have blood on their hands."

"What about the enemies of her relations?"

"Mm? Oh, so do they, I've no doubt. We live in a bloodthirsty age, my boy. Everywhere the blood of nations cries out of the earth for vengeance. George and Dame enjoy the company of dramatic personalities. Twenty years ago it was Hollywood. Now they roll up bandages for the bleeding hearts of exiles in the safety of Kensington." He clears his throat. "And they also happen to be leading lights in our society. Dilletante but influential. You've met some of our choicer specimens. So you see, it's an amusing social mix for them. A menagerie of dangerous political animals and a bunch of mediums. The deluders and the deluded. Difficult to tell which is which." He mutters something inaudible and walks off.

"What's eating him?"

"Can't you tell?"

"No. I should be able to, shouldn't I? He's not giving off any signals, apart from the obvious."

"None that a man would recognise. You're all the same. What's the opposite of psychic? Or intuition for that matter. Is that why men spend their lives bumping into the emotional furniture? Last night, before we had our talk, I had a chat with Connie."

"Yes. You told me."

"Well, she said he'd spent some of the evening putting the moves on her. Nothing she couldn't handle, but she as good as told him not to bother. He must have taken it bad."

"Now there's a thought. Old Shanks getting fresh with Connie; can't say I blame him." I grab her hand. "Hey, think of it! Shanks marries Connie and we all live together at Inglefield. Or New Zealand; I don't mind. What about that!"

"You can dream, Mackinnon. She did listen to something he said, though. His sob story about him and the rest of the League. The whole shooting match is what's getting to him."

There's a sharp sound of heelcaps and the blurred form of McFee heaves out of the mist. He's not alone. At first I think it's Shanks with him, but it isn't.

"Good morning, laddie; 'morning, Miss. Where's the Doctor? Must have missed him in this damn fog."

"Over here," comes Shanks's voice, and he materialises as though behind frosted glass.

"Morning, Doctor. This is my colleague, Detective-Constable Davies. John, these are Berenice, Clement and Doctor Jackson Armitage."

"How do you do?" we say. He shakes hands with Shanks and touches his hat to Berenice and me. He looks smart; well-pressed pinstripe trousers, crisp trenchcoat. McFee's in his usual coat and bowler and a curly end of shirt collar peeps out from his scarf. He looks about three times as old as John Davies.

But, grumpiness apart, you can tell Shanks isn't happy about this development. We all know McFee places great confidence in Davies and trusts him with a lot, but no one's been warned about him coming along today. The three men walk a little way off and there's some talk among them. Then McFee says we'll cross Kensington Gardens and take the Tube at Lancaster Gate.

"Isn't there a Tube station near where we're staying?" asks Berenice.

"Yes."

"Just asking."

She and I keep a few yards behind the others as we set off into the thickening mist. For some reason my hearing seems very acute this morning, so I listen in to their invisible conversation and repeat it quietly as we go along. It seems to be like this:

"Smallwood's struck again; that's four so far. It's the first one south of the river. McFee's ranting on about how many more jobs there's going to be. Says he's pushing us to the brink. Could go on for ever; nothing to say he won't. Shanks is trying to reassure him."

We're on the footpath near the centre of the gardens. I suggest we drop back a little. "It's okay, I can still hear them. I'll just give you the gist. Seems like, oh, right; all calls about safecracking jobs in the capital are being routed to John Davies. We didn't know that. And fingerprints are handled exclusively by Phil Waterman. They're the two he trusts. It's how they keep it under close wraps, with the top people being told only what they need to know. It's…it's not watertight."

The path comes to a junction. The group in front quicken their pace, past the Peter Pan statue, heading for Lancaster Gate. Bare branches reach up into the mist as though drowning. Among the trunks of trees the occasional dog flits like an apparition in a marshland and the effect of travelling through some Siberian half-world is heightened by the sound of wings whirring and beating cold, still waters on the Serpentine.

"Can you still hear them?"

"Yes. Clearer now."

"But they're further away."

"I know. Don't make me think about it too much. Will you take my arm?"

They're talking too quickly for me to stop and repeat it. I squeeze Berenice's hand to say: be patient.

"John here's been doing some checking up; unofficial of course. Just between us, this, all right?" "Perfectly, but what do you intend to do about it?" "Nothing. There's bugger all I can do. Can't confront him, can I?" "Can't you have him removed? Other duties?" "That'll look good, won't it? Either way we're jiggered. It's best we do nothing. Give him so little they'll go cold on him. News has to be hot, Doctor; well, here in London it does. A week old's good enough for the North Oxfordshire Gazette. Not here, believe me." "But he's compromised his career, surely? No one's going to forget disloyalty on this scale."

This time Berenice squeezes my hand. Her eyes ask: well, what are they saying?

I hold up my hand, asking her to hang on just a little longer.

"Well, that depends, doesn't it? On how big this thing gets. If the Yard comes under enough pressure it'll be us that go first. I'm their beloved infidel for now, but it needn't last. Some of my – notoriety? – is starting to rub off onto you now; eh, John?" "Maybe, Hay. It's not easy working alongside him and watching him at the same time. I reckon he's feeding them less than he knows. Keep 'em gasping – and paying." "Ah, you're learning. Still, not fair on you, is it? Career on the line before it's decently started?" "What do you think, Doctor?" "I think your Mister Hartington will go far; if not in the CID then as a reporter on the *Chronicle*. There's a warm welcome there for vipers like him."

I turn to Berenice. "Shanks wouldn't look at the paper this morning, would he?"

"No. What have those three been talking about?"

"One of theirs. Hartington. Slimy, apparently. It's him. He's the squeak."

"Do you think he's talking to more than just *The Chronicle*?"

"God, I hope not. Say it ain't so, Joe."

"Let's hope Mr Rosenblum can help us then, if time's running out."

I stop walking. The backs of Shanks and the detectives vanish, along with their voices.

"Fernleaf."

"What? What is it?"

"I'm feeling…strange. There's shivers going up my neck; but I don't feel frightened. This has been a strange walk in the park. I've heard what I shouldn't hear; and now."

"Yes?" She has that beautiful, wide-eyed look that I could fall into.

"It's coming together. Something important. Give me time."

She turns her head from me. "We'd best be after them, Mackinnon, or we'll be lost. We don't know the way."

They've waited, but without patience. Below ground the clinging mist loosens its hold on us. The strong draughts of air that keep the tunnels ventilated are more than a match for the sea of cloud that's draped itself silently over the city.

Still, there are other mysteries, and few trains mean a long wait. My mind's still trying to construct an idea from materials I can scarcely recognise. Berenice and I walk to the mouth of the tunnel where the rails shine for a few yards before disappearing into the gloom. There's no dripping decay here, just a dry oily smell from the dust shed by brake linings.

"I'd never been on the Tube till yesterday. Read about it, though." I'm talking to myself. "Hundreds of miles of tunnels. And after the last trains stop running all the tunnels go quiet. They turn off the current and men patrol the tracks with lamps. Rather them than me. They go under graveyards, under slums, under the dark swirling river where men have drowned. They hear footsteps, unexplained noises, sudden breezes. Suppose this is where Smallwood goes at night? Suppose he stalks the long dark passages and comes up only to blow another safe? What if he's there now, merging into the tunnel walls, watching us go by?"

Berenice puts her arm round me.

"Don't, Mackinnon. It doesn't do you any good."

"It's okay. This isn't where Smallwood and McFee will meet. I think I know now."

A distant roaring and a strengthening rush of air makes us step back and run down the platform to the others. "Find an empty carriage!" I call out. "I need to say something to you!"

We get only two stops entirely to ourselves on the way to Bethnal Green. It's enough.

"I've just had the strongest sensation about where you and Mr Smallwood are supposed to meet. It's really strong."

"Well, go on." We're all leaning forward as though praying.

"You're going to meet in the same upstairs room that you arrested him in."

"It's not a new idea, laddie. It's crossed my mind more than once. How do you know we're even supposed to meet face to face?"

"I'm certain, Mr McFee; and I'm certain about the place."

"All right. How does it get to happen?"

"Well, that's the thing. These robberies hold the key. Can't we visit the one that happened last night in Camberwell?"

They all exchange glances. "How did you know that, Clement?" says Shanks.

"I heard you, in the Park."

"I see. Well, let me answer then. It's too risky for Mr McFee to be seen there. The only one he has visited is the one that occured near his home, for obvious reasons. Let's trust that Mr Rosenblum may prove helpful."

After Oxford Circus the carriage starts to fill and we speed under the great landmarks of the City towards Bethnal Green. At each station I watch faces rush past, slow up, then move towards the doors. Six, seven years ago these people came down here to shelter from the bombs. Their clothes were brighter then. They brought bedding, chatted, sang, slept, peed over the platform edge, got noisy, got shouted at, hushed babies, formed committees, cried out in dreams and listened to the thump, thump above their heads. Now with the peace they've reverted, but they're not the same. A less dramatic adversity grips them: a thorn thicket of regulations, the fairness of Fair Shares and the urge to get round it. These people never saw themselves as heroes but now they feel demeaned when they should be exalted. It's not what our elders hoped for, but it's what they have. And we children, on whose behalf they worry, we feel it least. Few of us can remember anything else. The adults go shopping with their ration books like they always have. It's hard sometimes to see what all the fuss is about; till now. I study the faces of the people in the carriage and hope for a future free from the affliction I'm undergoing; and free from the memory of it; something more carefree altogether.

More of these heavy thoughts. I wish I could shake them out of my head.

On the Cambridge Heath Road the mist smells more of coal smoke, and I manage to get a few words with John Davies as we follow McFee into territory only he recognises.

"I couldn't help overhearing you as we crossed the Park."

"Well, you surprise me. I looked round once or twice, you know; couldn't even see you."

"Yes, well. I did overhear about the new safe job."

"Ah, that. Well done. Anyway, your sharp hearing was wasted on the rest; a very dull conversation." He smiles a boyish smile. I smile back because I think he's playing games.

"Oh, I don't know."

"Really? Our taxation system is a particular interest of yours, is it?"

"You weren't talking about your CID colleagues?"

"Well, hardly. Supertax, actually. Tax-dodging. And the dollar crisis. We must have a chat about it all sometime." He smiles again; a poor-deluded-youth kind of smile.

"Must have misheard you, then. Sorry." He goes to catch up with the others. I tug Berenice's sleeve. "He says they weren't discussing Hartington!"

"Does he? What was it then?"

"Paying tax or something."

"He was just putting you off. Why believe him?"

"Oh, I do; no reason not to. We've got as much right to know who's telling the press as they have; well, Shanks anyway."

"You sure, Mackinnon? Thought we agreed that maybe people weren't being completely straight with each other?"

"I know, but I believe him anyway. I just heard a different conversation, like with that news broadcast back at Inglefield."

"Don't remember you mentioning that. Hey, we're there. Better keep quiet."

A neat little house fronted with flowering shrubs in pots and barrels; an oasis of well-tended colour in a street left untended, waiting for spring. McFee turns to face us.

"Listen, all of you. These are good people. I don't care much for most pawnbrokers but Manny helped a lot of his fellow men during the Depression and the war and he still does. I'll do the talking. They're expecting a small crowd but he's an old man. Get my drift?"

We nod. He lifts the knocker. Several seconds pass and he knocks again. The door opens and the three men remove their hats and step forward. But a new sense of unease has got hold of me. A short stout woman closes the door behind us and we file into the front parlour.

As we arrange ourselves to be introduced I find myself closest to her. Her eyes are red; the face she greeted us with is collapsing. In her hands she twists a small soggy handkerchief.

"What's wrong, Mrs Rosenblum?"

She breaks into sobs.

"Not Manny, is it? Is he all right?"

"Yes, he's fine, Mr McFee; I hope to God. Please sit down." She takes a deep breath.

"About half-past six we get a call. Emmanuel goes down to the front door. It's dark and foggy; night and mist. That was a bad thing to start with, Mr McFee. You know how it is with us and knocks on the door in the night."

"Yes, I know, Rachel. Go on."

"It's the police. They say can we come to the shop straight away. You know he's only got the one now? Well, of course he says, has there been a robbery? But no, it's worse even than that. I'm at the top of the stairs by now. "What is it, Emmanuel?" I call down. He turns to me and he says, 'It's the shop; it's fallen down. Collapsed in a heap of rubble.' So he tells me to stay and wait for you while he goes off with the police." She can't say any more, and buries her face in her handkerchief.

McFee sits there, his hat in his lap, just staring forward. What's he thinking? I know what he's thinking: sixteen years ago he catches Albert Smallwood in that same shop and this morning while we go to visit the owner I tell him I'm sure he and Smallwood will meet there again. And it crashes into ruins. What kind of stunt is this? Can a dead man strike down whole buildings? Why? Has he got it in for the Rosenblums too?

I'm thinking: We can't fight this. Why go on? If we stop, he'll stop; won't he?

Berenice breaks the uncomfortable silence. "I'll stay here with Mrs Rosenblum," she says quietly. "You gentlemen continue with the purpose of your visit." The way she says this; the way she commands us gently not to despair, reminds me of how she's done this before, back at Inglefield and in McFee's rooms. She's got something, but it's not all that chivalry stuff about innocence and virtue prevailing over brute things. Innocence and virtue have had a raw deal during my lifetime. I don't know how innocent and virtuous she is, anyway. Just that in dark moments we need this kind of thing. As one, we get to our feet.

Then John Davies says, "I'll stay too, Hay."

"Yes, please do," Berenice answers, and she says to Mrs Rosenblum, "I'll make the three of us a cup of tea."

"You are kind," says the old lady, smiling and blinking. "What's your name, child?"

"I'm sorry we weren't properly introduced. I'm Berenice."

"That's a lovely name."

"Thank you. It's the name of a constellation, I'm told." She gives me a shining smile. I know I'll be forever lost without her.

187

There's a murmuring crowd, a fire engine and a handful of police as we approach the wreckage of Rosenblum's shop. We've had a job getting here. The mess is astonishing; it's as though the whole place has fallen inwards, with hardly a brick on the pavement or the street.

A picket fence has been set up and a bobby's strolling up and down keeping kids and rubberneckers behind it. McFee mutters a few words to him and we all pass through. "Be careful now," says the bobby. "Brigade's checked for gas, but you know how it is."

In the debris of what must have been a back lean-to a rotund little man is sitting on a bentwood chair. His thinning wavy hair is pure silver. He wears a black coat and fiddles with a dusty black Homburg like a man with rosary beads. McFee steps over a jagged pile of bricks, pushes aside a wooden beam from what looks like the remains of a staircase and places his hand on the old man's shoulder.

"Hello, Manny. I'm sorry to see you like this."

The little pawnbroker places his own hand over McFee's. It isn't trembling. Mine are, deep in my pockets. He doesn't look up.

"When I was a child," he says, "I saw the pogroms in Lodz. Half the family murdered by Cossacks. So I left; I escaped the Tsar. When I was set up here I was robbed – twice. Then Moseley's gang broke all the windows in '36. But that was all the trouble we got. It wasn't Cable Street. Then in the bombing one fell on either side of this shop and left it standing. So I escaped Hitler like I escaped the Tsar of All the Russias. But the bombs were just waiting; delayed action, huh?"

"It wasn't a gas leak, then?"

"No, Mr McFee. Subsidence. The bombs did something to the ground underneath. The whole shop fell into a hole. The earth opened and swallowed it." He turns and looks up.

"Tell me there's any justice in the world, Mr McFee. The camps took what family the Cossacks left. I begged them to come over. It's not paradise, I said, but they keep their police under control here. I sold the other place; one was enough for my old age. Now this. They got me in the end."

"You were only robbed once," says McFee mechanically.

"Eh? Oh, yes. Was that what you wanted to see me about? Long time ago now."

McFee looks around wearily. A pigeon settles and looses a small cascade of plaster dust near him. "It doesn't matter, Manny. Not any more."

"Tell me there's any justice, Mr McFee."

"There's no justice anywhere, Manny my son. I've never said there was."

I'm standing close to them, and the bitterness in McFee's voice cuts through me. Just don't kid yourself anything's fair and you'll get through. Not happy; but spared.

With a clinking of dislodged bricks Emmanuel Rosenblum rises slowly to his feet and holds out his hands, waving his hat from side to side. "All these pledges," he says. "Unredeemable! Every one!"

"They're not the only ones," says McFee. The old man doesn't hear him. "You get back to Rachel. This'll sort itself out. Good luck, Manny; I wish you happier days. I'll be in touch."

We pass back through the barrier. "Where's Shanks?" I say suddenly. He's been forgotten.

We go round the corner and there's Jackson Armitage, looking at the road.

"Is this where the nightwatchman was?"

"Yes. Roughly."

"Thank you."

The three of us stand there, away from the unhurried drama of this misty Sunday morning. McFee keeps gazing round him, but he isn't really looking at anything.

"So you reckon Smallwood is angling for some sort of confrontation here, do you?"

"Yes." I sigh because I know what's coming, but the feeling is still too strong, too real.

"It's meant to happen here. In the upstairs back room where the safe was. I'm certain of it."

"Oh, I don't doubt your instincts," says McFee in his looking around him way. "And I'm sure the Doctor doesn't. Trouble is, 'here' isn't here any more, is it?"

"No," I say. "It isn't. What the hell are we supposed to do now?"

Chapter 19

When we take our leave of McFee and John Davies outside Bethnal Green station I can easily believe we'll never see them again. No one speaks or looks at each other much as the train carries us back through halts and changes to South Kensington.

There seems no point in going on with it. Smallwood's waving his matador's cape and we're charging blindly till the second he snatches it away. So drop it; it's him reaching out to us from wherever he is, not the other way round. Just stop playing the game. Tough on McFee, but there are other lives to get on with.

And there's the problem. I'm now saddled with powers I never asked for and don't want and the only satisfaction I'll ever get is in using them to some purpose. The puzzle of the peterman would have been one way, might have been enough.

Lunch is even more miserable than breakfast was. Shanks eats in grim silence and our hosts catch the mood. Amelia broods over us, dark-eyed and tight-lipped, and a couple of house guests who've stayed on find themselves crawling through a no-man's-land of embarrassment. Connie Maybury never has lunch and Berenice elects to take a boiled egg upstairs and join her. It's one of a dozen we've brought with us from Ludmilla's hens; which is no more legal than the hidden stuff on Danny Ogden's cart is legal. We're grubby with evasion and failure.

At two o'clock I knock on Berenice's door to talk it all over but she says, "Not here. Let's go down to the conservatory."

"But anyone can see us there."

"And we can see them. We can't be jumped." We push aside plate-glass sliding doors and go in. Great fronds of things hang everywhere; there's a smell of rampant jungley growth, a silent warning of the strength of cells multiplying in millions till they can bend iron or pull down buildings.

We're surrounded by glass and beyond it the yellow-grey fog, thicker than ever. It lies unmoving except when an eddy from the kitchen waste outlets disturbs it like a deep current of the ocean. The whole conservatory is suffused with strange light and it feels like we're in a craft drifting in a mobile, alien element.

"It's like *Twenty Thousand Leagues under the Sea*."

"Or the atmosphere of a new planet."

We pull two wicker armchairs next to each other and face the outside.

"Landing in twenty seconds. Prepare the air lock. Instruments, Professor Berenisov?"

"Scarcely breathable." She twiddles invisible knobs. I ease back the joystick, rock a little in my seat.

"We have landed. An historic moment, wouldn't you agree?"

"So long as we are indeed first."

"What do you mean, Professor?"

"I mean, my dear Gordon, that the mad Doctor von Armitage may have preceded us."

We both need this. "Indeed, you could be right. My God, what's that?"

"An alien creature, no doubt."

"No, I'm not joking! Look!"

Berenice gasps. A face is coming out of the mist. It has terrible staring eyes and contorted features. It's on the window now. I turn and get a worse shock.

There's Amelia, her face pressed against the plate glass behind us. The pane at that point is flawed, making her eyes into ovals standing on end. As we stare at her she steps back and continues on her way downstairs. I go out on the landing, put my face to the same spot and my reflection appears in the outer window.

"Wonder how many ghosts are only reflections in mist," says Berenice. "She's a weird woman."

"Weirder than you know. There's an aura of blood round her. Hatred and revenge."

"Hatred? You watch if they ever put a bowl of tapioca in front of me."

"You know what? Your New Zealand accent gets stronger every day. Does Connie give you elocution lessons?"

"Sure."

"Not working, are they?"

"Yes they are. The trick, Mackinnon, is not to be a type, known only for one thing. The trick is to be capable of many things and to choose when to be them. Her words, and I agree with her."

"Right. I'll keep that in mind. Let's turn our chairs around and talk. After you."

"Okay. You remember John Davies stayed behind with Mrs Rosenblum and me yesterday?"

"Oh, yes. Enjoy it, did you?"

"Be serious. He is nice, though. I had a quick urgent word with him when she went out for a pee and a nose-blow."

"Charming turn of phrase."

"You don't get around enough, Mackinnon."

"Really? I'd have agreed with you once. Go on."

"I asked him to help us; check on a few details."

"Who's us?"

"Us is you and me. It's about things neither McFee nor Jackson seem to think are worth knowing."

"Or telling. Like what?"

"Like about Danny Ogden; those missing minutes when McFee was roughing him up. Or was he? Why hasn't he said what went on? If you or I tried to leave anything out we'd get curry all right."

"I thought maybe it was about his black market stuff; not my business."

"I think you need to stop thinking like that."

"Yup. Anyway I had things on my mind too."

"I'm coming to that. I asked John Davies to find out about Sal too. And Horace."

"Why? They're just around, that's all."

"Is anything in this business mere coincidence, Mackinnon?"

"Some things must be."

"I say again, you've got to stop thinking like that."

"Okay, then; for the purposes of elimination."

"Good. I asked him to find out what he could about McFee's early life. He's a Londoner, so he might have known the Smallwoods when he was younger; you never know. And finally, who would be the easiest people to get hold of?"

"Um. No, you tell me."

"Smallwood's relatives. Old crocks mostly, I guess. Why hasn't McFee even mentioned them?"

"They might smell a rat if there's no obvious way in. I'm with you, though. What are we going to get out of it?"

"Everything or nothing. Listen; this bit of the hunt is strictly ours. Using the leads John Davies gives us we're going to sniff around on our own. Jackson and McFee no longer have open minds and they're discouraged. We have to be careful, that's all. Okay?"

"If you say so. But it sounds disloyal; underhand."

"No more than the reasons why we're having to do it, Mackinnon."

"No, you're right. Sometimes I see everything clearly; other times I need you. Fernleaf, you are as wise as you are fair. Let us go forth together. You supply the conscious; I'll handle the subconscious."

"Unconscious more like, drongo. You haven't asked how I got John Davies to stick his neck out just for me. It could land him up a tree."

"No, I haven't, but I'm broad-minded." I duck as she takes a swing at me. "Hey! No, seriously; you just used your well-known power over men, that's all. How's he going to let us know?"

"We phone him."

"From here? Hardly!"

"From London, you oaf; that place out there. We're visiting it tomorrow."

I feel like being idiotic; jump up and dance around, clapping my hands. "Whoopee!" George Shawe-Tritton appears on the landing and looks at me in surprise. I wave to him and he gives a wary little wave back before lolloping off down the stairs.

"Nice idea, Fernleaf. Suppose Shanks and McFee have other ideas?"

"I've dealt with that; spoke to Jackson earlier on. There are no plans for tomorrow. We just have to phone in regularly to say where we are, in case of developments."

"White lie country, then. What about Connie? Paid companion; should go with you."

"All sorted out. She's going to the West End with Damietta, and Jackson and George are going to stay here for a man-to-man about their Society." She leans back, steeples her fingers in front of her nose and gazes over them at me. "So it all comes together rather neatly, doesn't it?"

The atmosphere brightens during the afternoon and the fog begins to lift as a breeze springs up. Shanks and Connie sit in the library and seem to be getting on very well. Damietta announces a New Year's Eve bash and George suggests it should be a Hard Times party. Luckily he's voted down on grounds of bad taste after I offer to get in a Forgotten Man or two for the amusement of the stiffs. After dinner I have Constance Maybury to myself for half an hour. What with her scent, her mellow voice, perfect features and Puccini in the background, I'm as happy as anyone in my place has a right to be. We talk about families, and I remark that Berenice only ever mentions her mother.

"Her dad's a dreamer," says Connie. "You either get dragged along willingly in his schemes or live a life of constant exasperation."

"Which do you do?"

"Neither. I get dragged along in the adventure of turning my pupil into a cultured young woman."

"Like you?"

I want this moment in an armchair by the fire to go on forever.

She smiles. Her dress hugs her perfectly. Her crossed legs are perfect. I dare to look deeper and deeper into her eyes, with no illusions about what she sees, but I wouldn't ask for more than this: the favour she bestows on me by just sitting there and letting me lead in this slow dance of words.

"Berenice is an extraordinary girl," she says. "Born on the farm. She has the landscape in her blood."

"And yet she moves through society like this as if she was born to it."

"That's right. I can't claim credit for that. It's how she is."

"To be capable of many things rather than be one thing."

"Well done, Clement. Just what I'd have said."

"You did say it. She told me." I can see her now, talking with a foreign-looking man by the gramophone. "She's a bit younger than me, but she seems older."

"In a manner of speaking, Clement. You like her, don't you?"

"Who wouldn't?"

"I'm talking about you, though."

And I'd like to be talking about you, too. I could say the same thing about you. But you'll always be properly distant; so many ways of being attractive, of answering desire.

"I'm very fond of her."

"A phrase that means more than it says, Clement. You're letting courtesy rule your courage."

"Perhaps my courage chooses to enter by the door of courtesy."

She laughs, but her eyes change for a moment. A perfect reverse turn in our dance.

"Will you excuse me now? I'm going to suggest an early night. I do hope you have a good day out tomorrow."

"We both deserve it," I reply.

I rise to my feet as she leaves me and crosses the room.

Chapter 20

We hit town. London has woken up from Christmas and shaken off the emptiness the festive season lent its streets. The whole place is crowded. Cars, buses, taxis, trolley buses, bikes and vans move in streams. Rich and poor throng the pavements. If you look you can spot an occasional wearer of the New Look braving the mild overcast weather and the public gaze.

We sport the old look. She's in her skirt, jumper, overcoat and beret and I've dug out my brown plus-fours to go with the jacket. She carries the rolled umbrella, I the soft haversack slung across my chest with our supplies for the day. We're well equipped: Spam sandwiches, two apples, four leftover not-exactly-mince pies, a shilling's worth of pennies, Vest Pocket Kodak with full unexposed roll of film, a quarter of barley-sugars, penknife, folding map of central London and – the key to infinite possibilities – a ten-bob note.

For the first time in our lives we see the real Big Ben. We take in the Houses of Parliament and Westminster Abbey. At half past nine I correct my watch.

"Scotland Yard's over the road," says Berenice.

"Take my arm." This is a reminder of serious business, but she's beside me. It all feels right; today the big city's doing fine.

We stand beneath Boadicea in her chariot with the scythes on the wheels and look across Westminster Bridge towards the curving front of County Hall. "That's where the London County Council meets," I tell her. It's one of the things I know about. "Whoever the chairman is, he rules over four times as many people as you've got in New Zealand."

"I thought King George ruled. But you're right. This sure isn't Auckland."

"What's Auckland like?"

"Only seen it a few times. We sailed from Wellington." She gives me a beautiful ironic smile that makes my eyes travel all over her face and come to rest on her mouth. "You can do Auckland in a morning, Mackinnon. I'm just a hayseed. My grandparents talked about the mother country but it didn't mean much to me."

"Are you enjoying this as much as I am?"

"It's the world. I love it."

A few steps along the Embankment and we're looking up at Scotland Yard. "I expected it to be bigger," she says. So did I. "John Davies could be in there now. Seems crazy having to phone him; he could open a window and call down to us."

"Yeah. Well, so much for the tourist bit. Let's get the map out."

The Tube to New Cross Gate. Either I'm getting used to it or the other passengers look as if they're going somewhere too; but this dose of reality is doing me good. Today the surface doesn't seem so far above my head.

This feeling lasts until we get out into daylight again; and suddenly I'm in territory that holds fresh memories: the shabby streets haunted by people with less than their share of luck. We're our way to meet with dodgy characters; unpredictable types working on a different system of morality and even logic. After a bit of asking we enter the road where Horace jumped on the cart and my legs begin to have second thoughts.

"You sure about this, Fernleaf? I've met these people. We haven't got McFee with us now."

Her unconcern worries me. "That's in our favour. He's the last man we want."

My heart's banging – doesn't it ever get used to this? – and my mouth feels dry as I curl my fingers round the barbed wire of Danny

199

Ogden's gate. We've walked past it once on my insistence so I can get myself together.

The yard's empty; I can't see the horse and cart. Then an old man comes round from behind the stable shelter, rolling up a joggling bunch of chicken wire.

"Excuse me! Is Danny about?"

Without looking up he calls back, "No, mate. 'E ain't."

"Er, Horace about?"

"No, mate. 'E's out wiv Danny."

"Sal?"

"No, mate."

"Any idea where we might find her?"

He tosses down the chicken wire. We've irritated him. "'Ow should I know? Tell me that. Not my business, chum; s'pose you try lookin' fer yerself?"

Berenice joins in. "It is rather important that we find her. Do you have any ideas?"

I almost laugh. She's doing her elocution bit, like some debby BBC announcer. The old bloke's attitude changes. He looks at her, then gazes down as if he's giving it some thought.

"Ah, well now. Monday innit? She'd be at her mum's, more'n likely. Yeah, 'course she is."

"Of course, Monday!" she calls back.

"Oh, jolly hockey sticks!" I whisper. She elbows me hard.

"It's the prefabs, isn't it? I wonder, could you tell me which number?"

He wanders over. His eyes shift between us before he answers slowly. "Second on the right, right again. Third on yer left. 'Sgot an 'orseshoe nailed on the gate."

I answer, "Thank you; you wouldn't be Mr Langford, would you?"

"'Oo?"

"Stan Langford. Danny's partner."

"Dunno any Stan Langford. Danny's on 'is own; 'e ain't got no partners."

Round the corner, out of sight, I turn to Berenice. "Sal lied. She said her stepdad was called Langford and he was with Danny in the business. Why?"

"Don't know, Mackinnon. Maybe her stepmum's called Langford. When we get there let me do the talking, okay? Woman to woman."

"Woman? I like it."

"Don't you think I'm a woman?"

"You're fifteen. Why are you looking at me like that?"

"It's not your fault. Like McFee says, they don't teach you anything worth knowing."

After an uncomfortable pause I ask her why she thinks Sal will talk to her at all, a complete stranger, never mind want to say what went on between McFee and Danny, even if she knows.

"Leave it to me. I'll be careful."

A gaunt woman in pinafore and knotted headscarf answers the door. A damp cigarette dangles from her bottom lip. She screws up her eyes.

"Yeah?"

"Is Sal in?" The chirpy young thing bit. I couldn't get away with it in a million years. There's a smell of cats and cats' fish boiling. A fresher, laundry smell mingles with it but on the whole it doesn't help much. The woman turns and bellows, "Sal!"

"What?" from inside.

"Two visitors for yer!" She squints at us again and wheezes, "'Ere, you ain't the Band of 'Ope, are yer?"

"No. Just friends." Sal's face appears over her shoulder. "Well, well! Popeye! What the 'ell are you doin' 'ere?"

"Just visiting. Can we come in?"

"Why? What for?"

I don't know what for. This is Berenice's shout.

"Mackinnon's told me about you. We were in the area so we thought we'd drop in. Rest our feet; you know. Would that be all right?"

Sal pushes past us and looks up and down the road. "'E ain't with you, is 'e?" she mutters.

"Oo's that, Sal?" says the older woman. Cigarette ash cascades down her front.

"No one. Come in. I'll give you an 'and with the mangle in a minute."

She leads us into a tiny room stuffed with utility furniture and bric-a-brac that must be off the cart. Three or four cats lay about and soapy steam wafts in from a zinc tub on the kitchen stove. Mum prods into it with wooden tongs and hums to the music on the wireless. Sal shuts the door so only the squeak of the mangle penetrates. For my money this has been much too easy and my suspicions are quivering like a shrew's heartbeat.

"What can I do for yer?"

A cat lands on my lap. I stroke it. It seems to know that I'm not fussed about cats; but I need to concentrate on the young woman opposite, who no longer appears very seductive. She's ill at ease; not with me, though. With Berenice. The cat starts to nose into my haversack.

"I'm from New Zealand. This is my first time in the mother country. Mackinnon told me you were a rag-and-bone lady. Is that true? I've never met one."

"Popeye told you that, did 'e?"

"If you mean Mackinnon, yes. How else could I have known?" She smiles. "I'm not clairvoyant."

She's — what? — five or six years younger than Sal, but firmly on top of this. I settle back. This is in good hands. The cat relaxes, and I start

202

to get a strange feeling. It's as if my senses are working by themselves, outside my body, unconnected to my nerves. They don't need memory or experience; just work, smoothly, like you think they do when you're a bit drunk. I can no longer hear either Berenice's questions or Sal's answers. Because they don't matter.

It's taken a long time to get here, but at long last I'm functioning as Doctor Jackson Armitage hoped I would. Maybe now I can start making some sense out of the case of Hayden McFee and the peterman.

Sal's neither arrogant nor self-assured, but a frightened child; a child who belongs to no one. She doesn't belong to this temporary house any more than the house belongs to the cleared space it sits on. Her whole life is a quest for protection and she buys it with the only currency she has. Left alone she grows terrified, curls up. I sense her warming to the fifteen-year old girl. Girl? Woman. Woman to woman. Woman to girl. Berenice is offering something in place of brute strength that needs to be manipulated and used. Sisterly stuff.

My power speaks to me and astonishes me with its subtlety. Leave these two to each other, it says. The channel to you can be closed now; you've heard enough. It will come right without you.

I stand up. "Will you excuse me?" The cat suddenly finds itself clinging to the north face of my plus-fours. For a second my eyes water a bit. With a miaow of disgust it drops to the floor. "I see you two have a lot to talk about. I'll just take a stroll, okay?" Their look tells me it's okay; and timely. Knowing when you're not wanted is a rare gift. "Where," I ask, "can one do a bit of train-watching round here?"

"Tried the railway?" says Sal.

Ah, good try, Sal; but I know you now. I fix her with a slow smile.

"'Undred yards this way from Danny's. There's a footbridge. See all yer want from there; if that's all yer want to see."

The breeze up on the bridge has a hint of drizzle in it. I'm thinking: I've left Fernleaf on her own. Suppose Danny or Horace walk in? Actually I can just see into the totter's yard from here. Go back in half an hour if she hasn't turned up. I start on a sandwich and watch long lines of coal wagons as they squeal, jerk and buffer below me. Undramatic but compelling. The tracks could lay empty between trains all day and I could observe without impatience. Why is that? I let my mind take a holiday among the things that are real to us, my generation: the movement of wagons on railways; the promise of wagons moving on railways. Crawling around goodsyards or hammering through the night at eighty miles an hour. Locos with muscles, lungs and voices; the aristocrats of labour on the footplate. A romance for the unromantic. Forty minutes pass.

A watch ticks in my head. Fernleaf! Clatter down the steps and walk very fast to the horseshoe on the gate. Holding my breath.

"Yer too late, sonny. Left ten minutes ago. Yer've missed her on yer way." The door slams shut.

She's standing on the bridge where I was. I laugh with relief, running fingers through my damp hair, wiping anxiety away. She just gives me a puzzled smile. I almost shout, "You have no idea how much I care about you, do you?"

"Of course I don't. Don't want to either."

"Eh?"

"It's like climbing a peak, Mackinnon. Where do you go when you reach the top?"

"Well, it's okay while you are climbing. You climb real ones, don't you?"

"Mmm. One day I'll get to the top of Mount Cook. And Mount Aspiring."

"Where do you go after that?"

"Higher mountains. There's plenty around."

"Yeah, I suppose. Just like people, then."

She looks up and down the tracks. "Don't ask me yet about my chat with Sal. I want to check on my hunches. If I'm barking up the wrong tree you won't have extra things to worry about. Will you trust me? Now we need to get to a phone box."

Four pennies in the slot. Whitehall 1212. Never thought I'd actually ring the most famous number in England. Just as I push button A there's a knock on the glass. Big woman with a brolly mouthing something; really awkward moment. I hand the receiver to Berenice and open the door. Switchboard and all, this could take a while.

"Yes?"

"I wish to make an urgent call!"

"We shan't be long. Honest."

"You better hadn't be. I know you kids; making disturbing calls to lonely old folks just out of devilment! Hurry up or I'll get the police!"

Talking tough doesn't bother me; not any more. I narrow my eyes. "That, madam, is what we are doing in this phone box."

I put my ear near to Berenice's. "Lordy!" she's saying. "Where?"

John Davies's voice crackles faintly. "I don't think you need worry about that."

"What! Not worry? What d'you mean?"

"No, I don't think so."

"Hold on, please." She puts her hand over the mouthpiece. "He's talking weird. Someone must have come into the room, or it's the switchboard. Hang on."

I glare at the woman outside. She looks away.

"Mr Davies, is someone in there with you? I see. Have you found out anything? Right. Do you think we should meet somewhere? Okay. Hang on please." Her hand covers the phone again. "What's a good place to meet John Davies?"

"Don't know. Somewhere near a place we'll be visiting."

"But that's it! Where we go depends on what he's got to tell us! Only now he can't. Oh, never mind. Mr Davies, what about under the departures board at Paddington? Okay, yes. Oh, er, four o'clock? That suit you? Right. See you there. Thanks. 'Bye." She puts down the receiver. "Tell you outside."

The drizzle's heavier, sifting down from a darkening grey sky. It coats pavements and buildings in a greasy sheen. We put up the umbrella and squeeze together under it. How much closer can you get than this? I find myself closing my eyes, carried away by the warm excitement of being near her.

"What's the news from the Yard?"

"Smallwood struck twice the other night."

"Twice! Where?"

"The one we know about, when you heard them talking yesterday, and one in Brixton. Coldharbour Lane. They didn't discover it till this morning, but they reckon it happened before the other one. It was in a furniture store. That's five so far."

We walk the length of a wet downtrodden street with our own thoughts.

"You know," I say, "I've never thought Smallwood had anything against us personally. You and me, I mean. But now we're at the head of the hunt; we're the ones who are pushing it. This is turning into a long, cruel game. People like Jack Sidgwick are getting put through it. Oh, no!"

I stop. "What?" says Berenice. "What is it?"

"It can't be coincidence, can it?"

"What?"

"We find out about McFee being haunted and that same night we have the dream; then it's the Holland tomb the next day, then the card game. All this stuff started for me when McFee brought his bloody problem along. I'm being put through it too. It's got to be! Smallwood chose me to be the one who leads McFee to him; turned me into a psychic for the purpose. Nothing personal. Just any poor sucker who happened to be around. You said there were no coincidences. It was either you or me. So he got me."

"Why hasn't this occured to you before? In one of your clear thinking bouts?"

"Don't know. I'd convinced myself it was just me having the power."

"Well, Mackinnon; if you're right then he'll retire you when it's all over."

"Oh, right. But look at the damage he's done already! What about old Manny Rosenblum? His life's work in ruins."

"Maybe not. Come on, keep walking. It's the one thing that ought to convince us Smallwood isn't evil."

"Go on; impress me."

"No, just reassure you. His shop could have collapsed any day. It was waiting to fall down. It fell down when Manny wasn't there; or anyone else."

"So he saved his life."

"If we believe nothing is a coincidence. I prefer to think it anyway."

"Maybe we're all being saved, then."

"Maybe."

"I don't know what to think anymore."

"Just trust me."

"Do you need the map?"

"We're off the map. This isn't tourist territory."

"Why didn't we bring a map of the whole town?'

"Because we were given one for people doing what we told them we were doing."

"So what do we do? Ask people the way?"

"Unless second sight can help us, yes."

We ask the way.

"So," I say, "no more mystery tour. It's Ladywell Cemetery. Dare I ask why?"

"Alice Smallwood is buried there, I think. We're guessing."

"We being…"

"John Davies and me. He says she died in Lewisham Hospital. It's nearby. Don't worry; he felt pretty definite about it."

"Is Albert there too?"

"We think so."

The drizzle's stopped. Berenice lets down the umbrella and we stroll arm in arm down Brockley Road. Suddenly she asks, "How old would you say Sal was?"

"Don't know. I can't tell women's ages."

"Guess."

"All right. Twenty-two "

"She's twenty-eight."

"So?"

"So she was born in 1919."

"Right. "

"It's part of a hunch, that's all. Let's leave it till we see John Davies."

Deptford and Ladywell Cemeteries stand side by side. Our route to the second lies through the first. The chill and damp begin to affect me. A mass of dark cloud shoulders its way into the overcast and the light everywhere becomes sad and desolate. I'm not surprised. The place seems deserted, but after a while you notice the odd figure wandering among the rows of graves. They're women, mostly, with headscarves and little bunches of crysanthemums.

We need a guide. So down the path comes a man with a pick and shovel over his shoulder. He wears wellingtons and an old greatcoat that nearly reaches the ground, as well as a haversack like mine slung across him and an unspeakable cloth cap rammed down to the ears. His face is weathered and dirty and his eyes almost too close together. Without the tools you'd take him for a tramp.

"Excuse me," says Berenice. He stops and stares at us, eyes showing up white in his walnut face. "We're looking for the grave of Alice Smallwood."

"You've got ter tell me when she was buried, then." A slow careful country voice.

"April 1932."

"Ah. Well now. Yer've to go up past the Old Germans an' turn right fer 'undred yards."

"Do you know that particular grave?"

"Ah. Dug 'er meself, more'n like."

"We're from out of town. Could you possibly spare the time to lead us to her?"

His face reminds me of the travellers who used to put up in one of the water meadows each summer. I remember their horses standing in the shallows and me seeking out *Lavengro* and *The Romany Rye* on Shanks's library shelves to see if it was all true. He turns back up the path and I wonder if he understands about the things and natural places. This is no levelled park we're walking in. It's a piece of that ancient forest that was here since before London was a ferryman's hovel. A few holes have been dug in it; the trees have fallen and the city has washed round it; but that's only skin deep. The gravedigger looks as if he knows this and knows what it means. Is he part of Smallwood's design? Is he here to hand us on to the next guide – Alice herself maybe – and then leave the stage?

I wait to hear whispers from the tombs.

We pass the Old Germans; a dozen stones in the shape of the Maltese cross. The dates are from 1915 to 1919. These were the war prisoners and internees; eight of them died in 1918. The Spanish influenza. Somewhere in this graveyard are the New Germans. Thousands of their living compatriots still toil on British farms, still wait to go home. Take those in the dock at Nuremburg, someone said, and put them to work in the war cemeteries. Might have done some good. Who knows?

Our guide stops and nods towards a plain headstone two rows back from the path.

"I wonder," asks Berenice, "would you be able to tell us anything about this grave? How the funeral was; that sort of thing?"

The man doesn't answer. He takes off his cap and seems lost in thought. I go forward and read the inscription:

Sacred to the Memory
of
ALICE EDNA SMALLWOOD
20 · II · 1897 - 8 · VI · 1932

. . . .

and of
ALBERT GORDON SMALLWOOD
7 · II · 1885 - 27 · XI · 1933

Fear Not For I Am Coming

"Ah. I did this one; normal sort of two-deep. Very early in the mornin' they did come. The more I think on it the clearer it gets. There wasn't supposed ter be too many people about, see? On account of they'd brought the 'usband from out of prison. Forget what he'd done. So there's 'im an' two policemen. 'E's 'andcuffed ter one, see? Priest, bearers an' me. That was all. Couple of people turned up after, like."

"When you'd gone?"

"Ah. Then it was next year I was told off ter do the openin'."

"Opening?"

"Yer digs out the spoil that's over the coffin. Should be easier on account of it's not so firm. Not fer a few year at any rate. Anyways, that was fer the 'usband. 'E died in prison, like."

"D'you remember that too?"

"Ah. More'n the first; yer got me recallin' it now. First the priest comes up. 'Twas very misty, very thick, an' very early in the mornin'; almost before light. 'E come swingin' up the path with 'is cloak out behind 'im. Then the 'earse. An' we committed 'im to the earth. Just the chaplain an' the bearers an' me."

"No one else?" Berenice is whispering now.

"There was a woman. She stood a ways off, up by the tree there. Grim, she looked; didn't cry. I know yer'll ask, so I'll tell yer. She were 'is sister. She went off straightways after; an' we was left alone. That's all."

"Does anyone still visit?"

"One or two. Never seen the sister, though."

"Anyone in particular?"

The gravedigger rubs his chin and shoots us a sideways glance. "One's a woman. Youngish, like." There's wariness in his voice.

"Twenty-five, say?"

I decide to look at something else. My hands are clenching in my pockets.

"'Bout that."

"Blonde?"

I close my eyes and start to breathe slowly. Careful, now; easy. Don't push it.

"Dark. She puts a few blooms there now an' then."

"Anyone else?"

A long pause. "One. Comes regular."

"Can you describe him?"

I start shouting silently: go easy, don't lose it. He's suspicious.

"Why? Didn't say it was a man, did I? What are you after?"

I open my eyes and stare at him, and for once Berenice hesitates. "We…we think we might be related. Old family business; it's hard to explain. We just wanted to find out…"

"Then yer can ask 'im yerself. 'E comes Sundays. Ever since they buried 'er." He puts his cap back on, touches the peak, and swings off down the path.

"You pushed him too hard. Where's all this going?"

She puts her hand on my arm. "Try to concentrate on this place. This is where he was laid to rest. Only he doesn't rest. He goes out from here and leaves clues and warnings all over this city. He breathes on ordinary men and women and makes them part of his puzzle. He makes things happen so people behave in certain ways. Including you and me."

"I prefer it when you talk as if horse-sense is the answer." I'm all unease now. The drizzle's returned, pushed by an insistent wind. The gravestones gleam in the grey light with the whiteness of bleached bones. I try hard but it's no use.

"Maybe he's not at home."

"Mackinnon?"

"Yes?" I know what she's going to say. "No," I mutter. "Don't ask me to touch it. I'm not very good with tombs."

"I'll hold you while you do. I'm with you." She places her hand over mine and I approach the headstone.

Fear not for I am coming. Right.

A last look into her eyes and my outstretched fingers run lightly over the curved top that's wet with rain.

Nothing. But I don't linger.

"She was younger than I expected; thirty-five. I thought of them as round about the same age. Wonder what she died of?"

"It wasn't sudden, anyway. By the way, Mackinnon; well done. I know it wasn't easy."

"Worth a try. He was locked away knowing she was dying, then let out at dawn for a secret funeral. The informer must have known. He must have really had it in for Albert, mustn't he?"

I gaze around me. Everything looks merely desolate. "It matters who the visitors are."

"Yes. I must admit I thought the girl might have been Sal, but she obviously isn't. When I was talking to her I sensed something, though. That's why we came here. So who's the man?"

"God knows. Old gravedigger chap made out he came because of Alice. We can't hang around till next Sunday to find out, even if it was that easy. Won't be, though, will it?"

She bites her lip. "Let's go. Next stop Smallwood's sister; if we can get John Davies on a phone and if he's been able to trace her."

We turn up our collars, open the umbrella and march along past an avenue of those chest-shaped Victorian tombstones that always seem on the point of capsizing.

"My God! Look!" I shove Berenice off the path.

"What?"

"Coming up this way!" I scramble her behind a monument. People never move quickly enough.

His head bowed against the squall – or he would surely have seen us – comes a hurrying figure in a dark mackintosh and bowler hat.

We crouch, holding our breath, and move round so as to stay out of sight. There's no need to guess his destination, though he holds no flowers.

"Let's get out now," hisses Berenice; but it's my turn to take over. "Wait. Let's go back and see what he does."

"You're going to follow him, are you? He knows all about tailing people!"

"Stay here then. I'll be back."

"Why the mystery, for God's sake? McFee can be here if he likes. It isn't Sunday so he can't be the regular that bloke was on about; so let's go! He's got more reason to be here than we have."

I hesitate. She's right; no, not right. "He was with us yesterday!"

"Not all day, he wasn't. He could easily have come here if he wanted."

This time I fix her with my not-very-grey eyes. "Maybe he did."

She sighs and lets go of my arm. "Be careful. He sees you and we're finished. The whole bloody go'll be finished. I'm staying here."

Short rushes from one stone to the next; try to walk quickly; try not to crouch. Too easy to be spotted from the flank. Remember your fieldcraft from the cadets; about time it came in handy, not just running around in Shanks's woods. Keep to the shade. Not difficult in a sunless graveyard. Make use of dead ground. Ha, ha; very good. Avoid isolated cover. There's a big chest-type monument just by the path where we stood to look at the Smallwood grave. It's on its own. One last look all round and I cover the ten yards up to it and sink down on one knee. Then I peep round. He should be there by now.

He isn't. A spasm of panic shoots through me.

He knows. He's doubled back and now he's watching me.

An age passes as I search every corner of my field of vision, expecting any second to see his face. But hold on; hold on there.

Maybe he's not visiting Alice or Albert. Maybe it's someone else. Why shouldn't he just have walked on to another part of the cemetery? He must know dozens of people buried here. What's the deal? Are we getting too clever? Minutes begin to pass very slowly.

Then I jump so quickly I skin my face on the stone.

"Hallo there!"

It's McFee's voice. Keeping my head in contact with the rough, cold side of the tomb I swivel my eyes. The grass smells sour in my nostrils; the last smell I'll experience before the whole shooting match collapses in ruins.

"Not yer usual time, sir."

I close my eyes and press my fist hard over the patch of lichen nearest to me. The gravedigger! He'll tell McFee everything. What couldn't get any worse has just got worse.

But there's no further talk. I edge round till I can see the Smallwood grave once more. He's standing there on his own, his hat in his hand in the driving drizzle.

So this is the connection. For sixteen years Hayden McFee has been making a weekly pilgrimage to the resting place of another man's wife; has done so even while her husband lay in prison. Why?

I feel a hand on my shoulder. This time I'm perfectly calm. "Hallo, Fernleaf. Glad you could make it."

"Cool customer, Mackinnon. I watched you stuck here with those two on the other side. Quite a performance. They had you rattled, eh?"

Before I can answer she hisses, "Down! Here he comes!"

We retreat round the monument as McFee crunches along the path and disappears from view; then we stand up. I'm stiff from the tension. This is the moment when Berenice laughs out loud. There's the grave-digger, sitting on the bench, his back against our tomb. McFee must also have sat there peacefully while I crept up on him like a Red Indian in a movie; and only a yard between us while I was nearly wetting myself.

"'Allo again," he says with a sly smile.

"Thanks. We are grateful, aren't we, Mackinnon?"

"Oh, er, yes. Thanks." I raise my eyebrows.

"I'll be away, then. Shan't see you again, I don't suppose. Behave yourselves, now."

He touches his cap and strolls off with his tools over his shoulder and his haversack, like a mercenary in some old European war.

"Let me tell you a story," says Berenice. "Are you comfortable?"

"Yes. You are about to make game of me; I can feel it. But I'm too relieved to care."

"Well, when you were playing hide-and-seek among the tombs I got to thinking there must be an easier way to get a look at McFee. So I got up and went round on the paths, like a normal person. He couldn't possibly have seen me. But then I suddenly ran into Mister Carey."

"The gypsy rover."

"Yup. He asked me what I was up to. D'you know, he'd crept back because he thought we were up to something? So I had to hold him up by talking to him, or he'd have run into McFee and told him the lot."

"And all the while I was sweating it out here."

"So it seems. He doesn't live in a house, you know. His mates call him Caveman Charlie."

"Really? Well, fancy that. Your life's full of cavemen, then."

"Mmm. He keeps an allotment and lives in his own toolshed. Completely against the rules, but it suits him. Ten bob a year! 'Course he has to spend getting up and going to bed times doing a spot of work on his plot so as not to raise suspicion. They think he's daft anyway. As far as his so-called mates know, he sleeps rough; or they'd shop him. And he can't read or write."

"Phew, it's a man's life, this. See exotic places, meet interesting people."

"Oh, do leave off. He said we were only kids and we couldn't harm the living much and the dead not at all; so he'd leave us to it so long as we didn't offend the dignity of the cemetery."

"Big of him."

"Well, I think so. He gives racing tips. Looks up at the vapour trails of planes and tells you who'll win the two-thirty at Doncaster. Beats being a psychic, eh? He doesn't gamble at all; just gets a little commission if you win. Clever man, I'd say."

"Well, splendid. Now can I remind you why we're here?"

"Okay. I just thought you needed to relax, that's all."

She takes my hand in hers. "He told me about the two people who regularly visit the grave. McFee is one; we know that now. The other is the dark-haired young woman."

"Go on."

"He said sometimes they meet here, at this seat, then spend a few moments together at the graveside. He said one more thing too."

"Please don't spin this out."

"Sorry. I shouldn't have said that; trust me a little longer. I need to check on one last thing. Okay?" A squeeze of the hand. Okay, then.

"I know better than not to trust you. Have a tasty Spam sandwich. You haven't eaten all day, and it makes a change from all that roast lamb you have to put up with back home."

We eat in silence, but in one way I'm satisfied. I was right about the connection, but we still don't know what it means, or whether it makes things easier or more complicated.

"When McFee was sitting here in the rain, d'you think he was waiting for her to come, only she didn't and he went away?"

"I don't think so. He didn't wait that long. Wrong day, anyway."

"Good of Caveman Charlie not to give us away."

"Yeah. Perhaps it was meant to be like that."

"Let's go and phone John Davies."

"Hang on; just had a thought. Wait there." I get up and go over to the grave. I was right. There among the dead and dying chrysanthemums is a posy of immortelles. They look new; fresh isn't the right word for immortelles. Berenice stands beside me.

"It means she'd been here already."

We both shudder. The onset of evening. Crows glide in great circles to land and rock unsteadily on headstones. The peace of the cemetery becomes a hush. We walk out into the city once more.

There's still much to know about the Alice Smallwood connection, and it's in Berenice's hands. I'm content to be patient, but something's amiss for sure. Within – or outside – our supposedly united efforts, McFee's playing a lone hand. And so are we.

"They say graveyards are one place where you never actually meet ghosts."

"Well, I don't know, Mackinnon. I think we both saw one back there. Let's walk a bit faster." The drizzle encases us in a shell of damp and the sky presses down.

"Hello, Mr Davies? Berenice here. Oh, okay, thanks. We're heading for Smallwood's sister's place; just need the address."

The line isn't good. Our heads rub together by the earpiece.

"No, I'm afraid not."

"Have you not got it?"

"Can't help you at the moment, I'm afraid."

"Mr Davies, is there someone with you again? Oh, bad luck. Hold on, please."

"Why doesn't he move to another phone and ring us back?"

"I'm sure he would if he could."

"Ask him to cover it up somehow; say it in code."

A pause. I watch the water run down the glass and collect on the crossbars. Passers- by ripple across my vision. The world's in mourning for something.

John Davies's voice suddenly becomes clearer and the clicks and hisses stop. "Mr Lane? Yes, he's a brick, isn't he?"

I take the receiver. "Do you mean Brick Lane? Is there a place called Brick Lane?"

"That's right. Close to that, I'd say."

"Close to Brick Lane?"

"Yes. I hope he's in town. I said I hope he's in town. Shocking line, isn't it?"

"Thank you. Hang on, please." Berenice's frown changes to a confident smile and she takes the receiver back. "He said 'hope' and 'town' twice. He emphasised them."

218

"Hallo, Mr Davies. Hope and town; is that right?"

"Yes. Together."

"Hopetown?"

"Yes."

"Just that?"

"Flat cap."

"Hopetown Flat? Flats? Right; we'll find it. What number?"

"He's about thirty-two. Twelve stone. Listen, I'm rather busy at the moment."

"That's all right. Hopetown Flats, near Brick Lane. Flat twelve of number thirty-two, or the other way round?"

"The first. Goodbye."

We get the Tube for Whitechapel and Shoreditch; familiar names now.

"That was a rigmarole, Fernleaf. He could have just said it out straight; unless Hartington or Waterman was in there. Who else would care?"

"Well, maybe they were. Look, couldn't you tell? He was enjoying himself. He still doesn't know how seriously to take us. McFee is the man as far as he's concerned. All he's worried about is that we don't upset the apple cart. So we act very calm, very harmless."

It's easier to find than I expected. The Flats are grim; a grey tenement in a grey world. Some time in a harder past they promised warmth, safety, progress. People counted themselves lucky to live here. Two men are leaning against the wall at the bottom of the stairwell. They're reading two halves of a *Daily Sketch* but I feel their eyes on my back as we mount the stairs. Something's telling me we've overplayed our hand.

Each floor has three doors and the paint's peeling from every one. Each door hides a scene of damp, dismal washday squalor; coughing, crying and yelling rebounds across landings where prams huddle against the walls.

The prefabs of this morning had all the same possibilities but they've got little gardens and spaces in between so people can be human. And the perfumed staircase of the Shawe-Trittons? The fashionable conscience thrives on distance. Better a Gorbals in the mind than actually feel these steps beneath your feet.

Number twelve. I look down the stairwell. The two men haven't moved. Maybe I'm getting too melodramatic. Calm down. You've got be calm for this old dear.

The door opens an inch, then another. A woman bent as only a walking invalid can bend looks out with a staring, frightened face. Three fingers, all bone, clutch a shawl round her and she twitches all over. Her eyes jump constantly, from Berenice to me.

"Yes?" she whispers. All her facial muscles are out of control.

It only takes a little thing. Done differently, who knows? But I speak first, and maybe I look and sound a bit rough, a bit up to no good.

"Miss Smallwood? Albert's sister?"

She lets out a little squeak and tries to close the door. She tries to close it on a caller who's damp, cold, a little perplexed and never quite free of the feeling that up to a week ago he was reasonably happy and normal. I'm not in the mood. I put my shoulder against the door.

"We only want a word."

Poor old lady. She doesn't see two personable young people. God knows what she does see. But she starts shouting unbelievably loudly. "Help! Go away! Leave me alone!"

"We don't mean you any harm," says Berenice.

There's a scuffing noise coming up the stairs.

"You're from him! Help! Somebody!"

The two loiterers are on their way, and they didn't strike me as good listeners when we passed them in the hall. I push the door wide and grab Berenice's arm. The old woman backs away, holding her shawl to her mouth and gibbering quietly. I slam the bolts home and turn the key and everything is wrong. I'm filled with a mixture of terror and excitement. "Who's him?" I bark. "Who are we supposed to be from?"

She begins weeping silently. The door handle suddenly leaps and twists. "Preston," she mews. "Preston."

Berenice is just a presence somewhere behind me; I don't look to see if she's following; just run across the little room with its reek of mouldy rugs and throw up the window.

Drizzle swirls in, but it's there: a fire escape, by the next room; the old lady's bedroom. I jump on the bed and wrestle with the window catch. The rule book's been tossed aside; it's nowhere. This is a criminal act, and I've crossed the threshold into the world of the maggots that McFee despises. They can set the law on us for this and the law can, if it wants, pursue us to the ends of the earth.

The catch is painted in. Solid.

At the fifth blow it gives. A crack races across the corner of the window. Why isn't the room filled with pursuers? Are they in? We climb out and skitter down the iron steps.

The yard. Home base; but I think too soon. The two heavies suddenly appear at the other end and we're trapped. We run the other way among dustbins, rolling a couple over to slow them down; like in the films. I snatch a lid just to have something in my hand. We rush round a corner to be met with an eight-foot brick wall topped with broken glass.

I sky the bin lid at the first head to appear but it bounces off the angle of the wall with a load of noise that so far doesn't seem important. Berenice regards them with narrowed eyes. Dropping the umbrella, her hands fly down the front of her coat; rolling it up, she tosses it to me. "For the glass!" Then she makes a stirrup with her hands.

"Don't be so bloody stupid!" I shout as I run at her, shoot upwards past the courses of brick and ram the coat down on the top of the wall. It holds and I scramble up with Berenice shoving from below.

Crouching above her I can see why our pursuers have taken so long. There's no way out for at least one of us, so no need to hurry. Heads poke out of windows as they saunter towards her. One of the goons grins at me. They both have the standard working man's uniform of second-best suit, cap and choker; but they lack authenticity. Loafers; low-life. Bookie's runners, deserters maybe; there's thousands at large in London. Just the job, a bit of casual violence on the assailants of a defenceless, crippled old woman. And an appreciative audience thrown in. The grinning one opens his mouth to speak.

Next second he's staggering back, hand to his face. His henchman doubles over, choking; and Berenice is turning, umbrella at the recover position. She's stabbed one in the eye, the other in the throat; like lightning. Throwing the umbrella over the wall, she backs almost as far as her victims, then nods.

We nearly make it. I've almost dragged her up to me when one of the bruisers, his hand over his eye, lunges at her. She drops down, gives him an almighty kick in a tender spot and dodges past him. But partner's back in business now. Berenice scoops up a dustbin lid with both hands and clangs him round the head with it. When she sees how little effect this has she swings it again and catches him on the bridge of the nose with the rim. With both of them out of it, she runs for the corner and disappears from sight.

I'm breathing hard and trembling, and I'm perched on top of a wall like an escaped circus monkey in full view of the street. Taking my eyes off the coughing, cursing layabouts I turn and look behind me. An old man and two women with shopping bags are all shouting at once. One of the women brandishes the umbrella.

"This nearly 'it me! Could 'ave 'ad me eye out!"

One eye's enough for today. "I'm coming down. Look out!" Jerking the coat off the glass, I crouch on the points and jump. Snatching the umbrella I gasp, "Thank you. Sorry," and run.

My haversack bounces beside me as I head for the entrance to Hopetown Flats. I can't be sure our opponents haven't recovered or someone hasn't called the police. Berenice should have appeared by now. Where is she? I skid into the hallway and stop dead. She's there all right, struggling in the grip of a huge man. He has his back to me. There's been enough mayhem; probably he's just a resident alerted by all the fuss. I'll talk to him; explain, apologise, sort this out. Then he starts slapping. Her head jerks with the blows.

I run up, jab the umbrella into his neck, and he loosens his hold and turns. I could leave it at that but now I'm mad. I throw down the coat and, as he starts to say something, give him a short uppercut to the jaw. Something makes me pull my punch, but it's enough. He must have bitten the tip of his tongue off. Berenice wrenches free and we run. Being a bit overloaded I have a job keeping up, but we don't look back. It's not only the people I'm fleeing from; it's the whole business, the whole useless, unnecessary mess we've made for ourselves.

A bus trundles up to a request stop and nothing matters less than where it's going. We collapse together in a seat, gasping, hair plastered with wet; eyes closed. The conductor takes our penny fares and says he'll let us know when to get off.

We get down from the bus somewhere near the river among the docks as the dark closes in. Street lamps come on. Mournful hooting floats through the wintry dusk from the crowd of shipping invisible on London's river. We're still finding holes in Berenice's coat; it's badly gashed all round the left pocket.

"Can it be fixed?"

"It'll have to be. A lot of somebody's coupons otherwise."

"How are we going to explain it?"

She looks down. "I think we should tell Connie. Our part of it, I mean. Might be best."

I'm feeling sick. Both of us are pale from fear and flight, and all for nothing.

"So why did she think we were from Preston? Do I have a northern accent?"

"You could have been a Mongolian goat farmer; it wouldn't have mattered. She was crazy. Ought to be in a home."

"Well, she could be, couldn't she? She must have come in for some of the money Albert put away. Care for a mince pie?" Sick or not, I want to taste something sweet and ordinary; but as I bite into mine the face of Albert Smallwood's sister shivers into my mind. The old woman lives in a nightmare and now we're part of it. I feel dirty, and a cold pit grows in my stomach the more I think that a hue and cry's already begun and that we're being hunted right now. I mustn't wear these clothes again, or ever come here. We've punched a hole through the fragile secrecy that we all depend on and it can't be fixed. What the hell did we think we were doing? She might be crackers, but that wouldn't stop her getting on the grapevine. What if she's on McFee's list? I'm going to look a right fool when I'm introduced to her then. The mince pie has an acid taste of callousness and the old woman's eyes bore into me.

"Someone was after her, Mackinnon, and she thought it was us. What were those two drongoes doing hanging around? More coincidence? Or keeping watch against Preston?

Maybe John Davies can tell us something. What's the time?"

"Twenty to four. We'd better get over to Paddington; it's getting late."

"Late! I'll say! We'll never make it. He won't wait, you dill! Where are we, for God's sake?"

"No idea. Find someone and ask."

"Do you see anyone?"

"No. Weird, eh? Never anyone around when you…"

"I mean, Do-you-see-anyone-of-course-you-don't. You never do! Just run!"

But there are people. Soon we're running, panting, legs and chest aching, down the darkening back streets and past bombed sites to Wapping station and the Metropolitan Line. Everything eats away at our precious minutes: buying tickets, waiting ages for a train; changing at Whitechapel and looking in dismay at the map with its string of halts before our destination. My body trembles with frustration at the steady speed, at the unknowing, placid passengers. On foot you can urge yourself on, faster and faster. We bump and roar through the tunnels and the stations drop away with heart-rending slowness. As we rattle into Farringdon my watch says four o'clock.

"We're on borrowed time. Hope to goodness he waits."

But she's asleep, her head resting lightly on my shoulder. I look at her reflection in the opposite window. I kissed those eyelids once; this tough, trusting girl.

There's nothing to do now but surrender to the force of events, like I did once before back at Inglefield when everything went belly-up. On this damp evening in a carriage filled with the unanswerable argument of time I sit and just stop worrying. When at last the train pulls into Paddington Underground I wake her ever so gently and murmur, "We've arrived."

John Davies isn't there, under the departures board or anywhere else. "He hasn't been and gone, surely. He knows we could be held up. Let's wait," she says.

"Why not? Nothing to lose."

This is the calm before the evening rush hour, but you can feel the approach of the flood. The to-and-fro pageant of the railway public passes before us. Thin men in chalkstripe demob suits, soldiers and sailors with kitbags and warrants; well-dressed women, some of them in waisted New Look coats, followed by porters wheeling trolleys piled with luggage and hatboxes; and less well-dressed young women looking around for the first time at the big city. They especially attract my attention, these girls with their drab outfits and close-fitting hats and cheap suitcases, because I also stood on these platforms less than a week ago as if entering a strange land. They've come from villages and country towns and hard cities to seek the better life and they're all beautiful with hope, anxiety and courage.

All these people come and go to a background of sounds that will, I know, vanish as utterly as the street cries of Old London: venting steam, locomotive whistles; the whoosh, whoosh of the departing train's smoke mushrooming into the iron tracery of the station roof, the tannoy yammering in Serbo-Croat, the dull slamming of carriage doors. It feels as though there's never been a time when I haven't been at home in this; the kingdom of steam. I wait there beside Berenice, weighed down with worries, and drink it in. The footbridge near Danny's scrapyard is one with Paddington, one with the Canadian Pacific clinging to the canyons of the Fraser, the Trans-Siberian traversing endless steppe and forest, the great enterprises running arrow-straight to the horizon, or stopping for a brief minute at quiet halts with a crossing, a lamp on the platform, a fire in the waiting room and a voice calling in the disturbed silence: Inglefield! This is Inglefield!

It's happening again. I shouldn't be able to think like this, even if I feel it.

"Daydreaming? Sorry I'm late. Been waiting long?"

Berenice answers as I come round. We find a table in the buffet and sit with a cup of hot tea each. After the people we've met today John Davies is reassuringly young and good-natured.

"What's happened to your coat?"

"A little accident. Any news?"

"I hardly know where to start. How about Sal? Want to hear about Sal?"

It surprises me there's much to reveal, other than what I sensed back in the cluttered room with a cat on my lap. "Here goes, then. Sal's real name is Adamson. She's an orphan, at least in the sense that her parents are unknown. A foundling, you would say."

"How do you know it's Adamson, then?"

John Davies sips his tea. "She was left on the doorstep of an orphanage in the East End on a cold autumn morning in 1919. A week old, and very small. It was run by an order of nuns. There was a note in the basket which said something like: this child's father wanted a son; please look after her; I can't. Something like that. So they came up with Adam because it was a man's name. They would, I suppose; and 'son' because that was what it was supposed to be. Sally was, well, a name for what she really was. Baptized into the faith as Sally Adamson."

"Adam's sons were Cain and Abel," says Berenice. "Not the luckiest choice."

"No." John Davies looks tired now. "Anyhow, about ten years later a woman turned up and asked if she could watch the children while they had supper, or played or whatever. Seems they got a lot of that sort of thing; nobody ever wanted to adopt, apparently. They kept an eye on her and it was obvious she'd come to look at Sally. One of the novices asked her straight out if that was it; Miss Tact 1929, eh? – at which she rushed out and they never saw her again. They said she looked ill, wasted."

He swirls the last of the tea in his cup. The buffet's filling now. "I'm sticking my neck out, all right? The nuns' description tallies pretty closely with what Hay's told me about Alice Smallwood."

"That's mad." I shake my head. "We go to see an ex-con called Danny Ogden and run into the daughter of Albert Smallwood?"

"I didn't say Albert. I told you I didn't know where to start."

"Still, it's a bit rich, even for coincidence."

Berenice looks round at the commuters spilling past the doors. "That's because it isn't a coincidence. I keep saying that. Nothing happens by chance in this." A smile of resignation passes between her and John Davies and for the first time I feel the tiny itch of possessiveness.

"Do you have the address of the orphanage?" she asks. "No, of course you have. You spoke to them, didn't you?"

He hands her a card then goes to the counter for another three teas. I drum my fingers on the table. This is getting hard to follow. Still, a thought keeps niggling in the back of my mind and I can't retrieve it. What is it?

"Here you are. No, it's on me. Next; how would you like to hear about your friend Horace?"

"I know as much as I want to know about him. He's got something going with Sal, right?"

"Has he? Ah, well; love is a mystery. Look, I haven't got all day. Danny Ogden told you he'd done time in Peterhead for cattle-rustling, right? All lies. Horace has never been to Scotland in his life. Nor is his speech impediment the result of disease but of an accident. I don't know the details. And his given surname is Pressman."

"Preston!" I shout. Several heads turn towards me. John Davies smiles enquiringly.

"Of course!" shouts Berenice. Heads that were turning back jerk round again. "The old woman we went to see – Albert's sister – she thought we were from Preston. She meant Pressman. She was terrified. Those two heavies…"

"What heavies? Have you been in some kind of trouble?"

I try to play it down. "When we went to visit her there were a couple of rough-looking types hanging round downstairs. She started kicking up a fuss and they came up the stairs. We had to leave in a hurry, that's all."

"They weren't solid citizens," says Berenice.

"I see. Well, if someone's being menaced that's police business. If we're free to pursue it."

"Do you have to?"

"Meaning?"

"We've got to tell you; it's been on my mind. When we left in a hurry it was through her flat and down the fire escape. I wrecked a window to get out. The old woman was terrified; she wasn't in her right mind, Mr Davies. Apart from forcing our way in past her we might have given her a heart attack or something. And we had to fight our two friends."

He makes us go over it. In detail.

And a heavy lead weight settles inside me, about six inches above my seat.

Part of it is impatience, loss of time; wondering why a man who's supposed to be in a hurry needs to know about stuff that doesn't matter.

What were they wearing? What time was it? Did they smell of drink?

The other part is that sick taste of violence. One day all the films will be in colour and they'll be able to put in the smells. Smell-o-Vision. And you'll taste the sweat and the stale urine and the way old people who are poor and demented get in your nostrils and stay there long after you've forgotten all the rest.

Will that cure violence? The honk of blood, of fear? No, it'll just cure cinemas of customers. The whole telling of stories hits every bit of your imagination except the part you can never shake off. A few Smell-o horror films and you'd never go again. And they'd have to clean and disinfect the seats after every showing. No, forget it.

Fernleaf is being very patient. She answers each question fully so he doesn't need to go back over it. And she keeps calm because she needs him calm, open, unoffended.

So do I, but I'm not right just now. My mind races through her answers stirring up nothing but sludge. I wish I could take a walk, sniff some coal smoke to clear my head. Stay with this, for God's sake. No skin off his nose to up and walk away himself, into his own proper concerns, and leave us sitting here like the clowns we probably are.

Clowns and Butterfingers. I close my eyes and suddenly Fernleaf stops. He's done.

John Davies isn't happy. "It's unlikely," he says at last, "that she sounds mentally capable of lodging a complaint or of helping us with our enquiries. And I don't suppose your two heavies would be willing to. You're probably out of danger."

"And the people in the street? And the people hanging out of the windows? And the bloke I punched?"

His eyes widen. "My God, you don't make it easy on yourselves, do you? What bloke?"

"He attacked me first," says Berenice. "Hit me round the head."

"Well, there's one thing in your favour," he mutters. "At least I know who you are."

"So if there's an investigation and it gets too close to us you can head them off?"

"That's perverting the course of justice, young man. I would do no such thing."

"So…"

"So you don't come from that part of the world, you're strangers to London, you aren't here long, you have no previous record, you are – more or less – of good character, and that will save you. From me."

"Thanks, Mr Davies."

"What won't save you is that you've alerted Sal and, by implication, Horace. Your names are being taken in vain on their bush telegraph right now as nosey kids, slumming around on behalf of my boss. If no one makes waves with that little lot you can consider yourselves damn lucky; luckier than you deserve." You can tell we've offended his code. There's nothing we can say and I feel stupid.

"Okay, next. Albert Smallwood the soldier. Ready?"

"Just a second, Mr Davies. How do you know all this? I get it about Sal, but…"

"Files."

"You mean Mr McFee knew about Horace already?"

"It's possible. It's also getting late. Can we get on? Albert wasn't demobilised in 1918. Or 1919 either. He had a short spell of leave in October 1918 and that's when he got engaged. They agreed to get married when he left the Army. Then the following May he did a strange thing. He volunteered for service in Russia. We had some military stores up in Archangel and the Bolsheviks looked like they'd get their hands on the dumps. So the Army called for volunteers to defend them. Albert was due for release but instead he elected to postpone his wedding indefinitely and go to north Russia for who knows how long? He wrote to Alice and said they needed experts to check on the state of the explosives. And Alice gave him her blessing."

"Of course she did," says Berenice. "She needed him out of the way so she could have some ratbag's baby and get rid of it. Convenient, don't you think? And she got it after she was engaged to Albert! Bit of a player herself, eh? Didn't he suspect anything?"

"Seems he didn't. The Allied Intervention ended for him in early 1920 and they got married. Had a daughter the same year."

"So Sal unknowingly had a half-sister. Quick work," I interrupt. I know how long it takes; bit hazy about some of the details.

"Very quick. But that's men home from the wars for you. Didn't Hay mention Albert's daughter when you were at your Uncle's?"

"No. He didn't."

Berenice lets out a long sigh. "Which brings us to Caveman Charlie Carey. No, please don't ask. He's a gravedigger; dug the Smallwood grave. There's a young woman that visits sometimes and meets Mr McFee there; she's dark, mid-twenties, and he said they had a very strong resemblance; a family resemblance. Like father and daughter, in fact. That was what I didn't tell you about, Mackinnon."

I let out a whistle and see John Davies flush. His mouth tightens and his brow darkens. There's the beginning of a ginger moustache above his lip. He sits back and looks at Berenice and so do I. Then he clears his throat. "Do you mean to tell me," he says slowly, "that the woman Smallwood took to be his daughter is actually the child of Alice and Hayden McFee?"

She nods.

"In the opinion of some gravedigger?"

"Don't let his nickname put you off, Mr Davies. He's seen them over many years. I believe him. I'm sorry; must be a bit of a shock."

He bites his lip. "I'll have to reserve my judgement. Do you want me to go on?" But his tone's changed, as though he's speaking one thing while thinking another.

"Very well. I did a bit of chasing up on the informant who shopped Smallwood. Nothing new; the report says he called from a telephone box and he was drunk. Not unusual; they often need a bit of Dutch courage."

I'm not listening that hard. "So that's the story. That's the connection. No wonder."

"Hay and Alice Smallwood. And their mysterious daughter? If it's true."

"Oh, it's true," I say. "Can we go on like this? What will it do to everything?"

It's a chance to pull back some of our reputation. "We suspected that Mr McFee might be, well, keeping something back; something that might be relevant, that might help us to help him. That's why we were being nosey, as you call it. What's the point if people aren't being honest with each other?"

He looks only half convinced, but the words have straddled him even if they haven't hit home.

"Let's get this much straight. I'm doing more for you two than my job's probably worth at this moment. Nor is it my ideal of professional loyalty. I've had to accept your reasons. God help you both if you don't keep this to yourselves; understand?"

We owe him too much, and have loaded too much on him, not to feel grateful or guilty.

"You may ask why Hay doesn't get promoted. I know enough about him now to tell you. Fact is, he's not a terribly good policeman."

"What!" Hayden McFee is almost certainly the father of one of Alice Smallwood's illegitimate children, but that pales against what I've just heard. "You're not serious?"

"Don't misunderstand me. He's a great detective, but petty crime bores him. He hates all the little laws and regulations that war and rationing brought in. It makes millions of people into criminals. You've seen it yourselves; a barrow boy can be had up for selling rhubarb off a fruit stall; you can be done for buying a second-hand car and actually using the petrol in the tank to drive it home. Are you with me? He thinks either the spivs are maggots or they should be left alone. It's a mess. And he thinks it'll stick even when things return to normal."

"So big crime interests him and little crime doesn't," I say. "Fair enough. He'd go after Black Max Intrator but turn a blind eye to Danny Ogden. What's the problem?"

"What's wrong is that we're paid to uphold the King's Peace. You can't pick and choose." He can see I'm finding many things hard to take. "Look, if this had been someone else's ghost he'd have enjoyed the hunt; worked harder than anyone, even without psychic help, because it would have caught his imagination. But he knows a lot of it already, doesn't he? And much that he hasn't told us, apparently."

"So you believe us about him and Alice?"

"I may have to. Does it bring the end any nearer?" He gets up, puts on his hat and turns up his collar.

"Thank you, Mr Davies. You've done wonders in such a short time."

Suddenly he turns back. "One other thing; almost forgot. There's a rumour – only a rumour, mind – that your uncle was mixed up in something hush-hush during the war. If it's true it'll be classified. Just so you don't waste time thinking about it. Good luck."

As he passes through the crowds and the sounds of the station reassert themselves we just sit there. But the nagging, insistent thought worms its way into my silence.

Something important.

We get up. The complications multiply and I can't tell what means what. When I felt the power at Sal's mother's house, what did it lead to? Has Berenice discovered anything that matters? And how did she get a professional detective to spend valuable time feeding a couple of kids with high-octane information about his own boss, unless he wanted to? Why did neither of us ask about McFee and Danny Ogden in the shelter, or doesn't that matter anymore? It seemed to, once. I stare in front of me and consider coincidences. Sometimes there aren't any. There are blind alleys. People are behaving out of character. Smallwood's constructing the maze ahead of us even as we try to find a way through it.

In the corner of my eye a young woman; cheap suitcase, seeking the better life, is in a phone box putting pennies in the slot.

I smack my forehead.

"Oh, God! We never phoned them to say where we were! All day! They'll be livid! We'll never be let out... Oh, Lord!"

I'm submerged in our stupidity. Luckily Amelia answers the phone and we keep it very, very brief, then race, ride the Tube with hearts beating and race again to the Shawe-Tritton house. Unconcerned pedestrians stroll by towards warm welcomes and peaceful evenings. We're dishevelled, ripped, stained with violence, rotten with irresposibility, loaded with uncomfortable secrets and inescapably guilty as hell. Surrender to the force of events isn't going to work this time. All I have is Berenice to share it with me; Fernleaf, Fernleaf; we're on one side of the fence and everyone else on the other. Let justice be done, though the heavens fall. Well, here is the news: the heavens are about to fall and justice will certainly be done. To us. We compose ourselves. A last thought comes to my aid.

"We're not the only ones who should have made contact and didn't."

She puts a hand on my shoulder. "Ay, now the plot thickens very much upon us."

"Sounds about right. Who said it?"

"The Duke of Buckingham."

"Not the one who got murdered?"

"No. The second one."

"Better off than us, then."

I press the bell and wait for Amelia to answer the door.

Chapter 21

The sun rises on our disgrace. Last night's Inquisition behind closed doors is history; Shanks and Connie tearing us off until we stood so drained we didn't hear them anymore, then taking us off separately to do it all again. But I know the worst was kept for me. Connie's heard the truth in private and can only be more forgiving now she knows. At least I hope so; because it's been solitary confinement since then. For twelve hours Fernleaf and I have been kept apart with Amelia holding the keys, and like many would-be liberators she makes an efficient jailor.

But it surprises me how quickly the effect of their anger wears off. Their abuse was nothing compared to the fight at the Hopetown Flats. Mainly, though, it's our own strength and solidarity. We occupy the high ground now. Below us the others are losing their grip; coming apart; keeping things from each other and from us. Our knowledge is military intelligence, gained in the field. If we ever get anywhere with this thing it'll be because of our efforts, and despite theirs.

I lie in my room going over all the events of the day, adding them to every other thing that's happened, trying to build a jigsaw. Sorting out the puzzle set by Smallwood seems the least complicated part; a straightforward set of clues that somehow point to a meeting. Only thing is, none of us has the faintest idea where to start.

A key rattles in the lock and Amelia enters with a glass of milk on a tray.

"Hallo, Amelia. How are things?"

"You are wicked boy to make your uncle worry. May God forgive you. And to you I am Miss da Costa. Drink your milk." She watches me, this tall woman of Portugal in her black dress. Everyone who's brought me something on a tray seems to have had a tough life; dangerous escapes, losses, memories.

"Are you looking forward to the New Year party? Should be fun."

"I know what you are up to. You think I am stupid, a stupid servant. Before, I did not like your uncle; then I see him worry for you and the girl. He is a good man. You are both bad children. May God forgive you."

"Yes, I hope so. Miss da Costa, could you take this note and slip it under the girl's door? I shall ask you no other favours. I promise."

She looks at me with quivering disdain. I can almost see up her nostrils. Her glare intensifies.

"I'm sure you're the soul of honour, Miss da Costa. A true Portuguese."

"And you have no honour. To you, promises are nothing."

"You always keep your word?"

"Yes."

"You are very upright."

"What is that?"

"Very honest. But this is important to me."

"All this makes nothing. Your cousin is in the bath. Drink your milk. After her, you must have bath. Now drink; no more of this asking." Half an hour later she escorts me to the bathroom, hands me a towel, waits outside and escorts me back. She takes her duties seriously, probably more than Shanks and Connie intended. I see nothing of them all day, or anyone. It becomes even easier to imagine they all have designs of their own and are telling us nothing.

But as the day wears on I begin to appreciate this rest and realise how much I need it. Amelia looks in on the hour and brings me books from the library, and as dark descends outside she tells me our punishment will end at eight in the morning and not a minute before. On her final visit she takes away my supper tray, escorts me to and from the bathroom again, and shoves a chamber pot under the bed.

"Any chance of a hot water bottle?"

"Go to sleep. Think of hell and pray for your soul."

"That should keep me warm. Thanks, Miss da Costa. Goodnight."

The minutes pass and become hours.

Staring at the ceiling my mind starts to undergo that strange, cool sensation of clutter falling away. The decks clear; the thoughts marshal themselves into some sort of order. I can almost watch their evolutions as they flow round each other like a well-rehearsed parade. All I need now is to see Fernleaf in her room, or for her to visit mine. The risk has to be taken. I lie awake and wait and the crystal thoughts don't go away.

Footsteps on the stairs, doors closing and the noise of the tank refilling above my head tells me the Shawe-Trittons and their guests are retiring. When the rumbling of the Underground trains finally ceases I'm left with the ticking of the alarm and the silver chimes every fifteen minutes from the hall clock far below. The house lies in silence, but not the deep, ear-penetrating stillness of Inglefield.

We've been away almost a week. When I allow myself to consider what that week, and the days before it, have done to us my thoughts become muddied and confused. For a moment I'm filled with panic, but I need only to concentrate on Smallwood for order to return.

By two in the morning I'm ready. Fernleaf must be asleep. I put on my dressing gown and slippers and open the door.

All quiet. A half-dozen steps will bring me to our meeting. Thirty-odd hours have passed without seeing her face; a heavier indemnity than they realise.

But I don't cross the landing.

It must be Smallwood whispering to me, and his message is strange and seductive.

237

Think about this house and its imperfect sleepers. They have handed it to you. Tonight it's empty. Move through it; intrude in its spaces. Remember your freedom in the forest. This is a new forest.

So I descend the stairs and stop for a half-minute outside each bedroom door. Behind those thin barriers they lie dreaming, all unaware. A sense of liberty and power grips me as I think of them.

Four floors down I turn, rotating slowly with arms outstretched to the clock's music. The chequerboard of tiles and the wooden panelling mingle the fragrance of their years of polish into a tingling sensation of wealth and ease, unearned and undeserved. I range through every room, turning on lights that fill niches and cantons with their glow. Elegant talk echoes silently from corners and from portraits in gilt frames, while other pictures look outwards onto still, dusk-bronzed rivers where lone anglers sit in boats amid crack willows and their reflections. I sit in every chair, wander among side-tables with their ashtrays and magazines waiting to be cleared away in the morning. There's only one place I avoid: the conservatory off the first floor landing. It's too close to the night.

In the library I settle into the wing chair from which Doctor Jackson Armitage so lately delivered judgement. But the place is mine now and I understand the excitement that drives the peterman and his lesser brothers. It's the intruding, not the thieving, that's the thing.

Now the house is mine; and all its inhabitants lie as if drugged and cannot touch me. I breathe in deep, take down a book without bothering about the title and flick through it, looking for pictures. But there aren't any so I settle back and grow into the room.

And suddenly I feel no longer alone. Something has changed. My neck begins to prickle and I turn my eyes towards the door.

There should be more light from the hallway. In fact the whole house seems to have silently and eerily grown darker. Darkness is following me and it's going to meet me here, bringing back the fear I thought I'd put aside with my childhood, giving it back to me; the Faustian bargain that I never agreed to. My body shrinks and I can't take my eyes from the point in the hall where the library's cone of light dies away.

There is a figure standing at the edge of the dark.

She comes forward in a long white flannel nightdress, barefoot, her eyes wide, her mouth half-open. For a second I think she's sleepwalking.

"Fernleaf?"

She approaches without a word, surprise frozen in her face.

"My God, I'm glad it's you." It's hard to say because I feel as if I haven't spoken for years. "Are you all right?"

"I'm fine, Mackinnon," she answers in a small faraway voice. "What about you? I couldn't find you in your room so I followed the lights down; turning them off as I went, by the way. What are you doing here?"

"I took a stroll, that's all."

She crouches at my feet and puts her hand on my arm. There's something about a girl's face looking up into yours. "Are you sure everything's okay?" she asks softly-sleepily. "Is this all getting too much? Is it getting you down?"

"Too much has happened," I reply, "for everything to be okay. If it was things that had changed and I was the same, I'd just have to wait till it was over. But I've changed. No, I've been changed. Lumbered with more senses than I should have; and worried about what it's doing to the ones I had already. If that makes sense. I haven't been apart from you for so long since we met."

"That's true. There's one thing I've never really asked you. What were you going to do with your time at Inglefield? Before this started? If I hadn't been there?"

I can hardly remember the answer. It's a long time coming.

"What I've always done, but gone further out. Noticed changes in the woods. Spent nights holed up in lonely spots. Shanks would have been all right about that. I used to sneak out at night anyway. Watched

239

foxes, badgers, birds. Watched stars. Got better at moving through the landscape; started taking photographs; I'm getting into that now. Forgotten about school."

"Are you worried you might get crook?"

"Sometimes. But not tonight. No, I feel fine, after that little fright you gave me. I think I've finally worked it out. From now on everything's going to be easier."

She keeps looking into my face, her eyes searching all over it. And my feelings about her become the more important thing.

"You're cold," I murmur. "Come and share this chair with me; curl up in my arms and be warm."

"Thanks, Mackinnon; but I'm all right. I don't feel the cold."

"I feel it for you. You sit here; I've warmed it a bit." So I stand up and she slips into the chair and draws her feet up, while I crouch down, my hand over hers.

"Mmm; that's nice. Thanks. I'm glad you don't mind."

I do, but there it is.

"Fernleaf, do you really play chess?" The library is so completely ours that time no longer matters. We speak in the unhurried way of those who own the moment.

"Mmm. But I know I'm not as good as you. Why?"

"You mean, back at Inglefield you didn't play me because...?"

"That's right. No, I was annoyed at Jackson more than anything. What's your drift?"

"Just I think I sometimes make it too complicated for myself. This business, I mean. I worry about every angle, every possible combination; three or four moves ahead. How does this affect that? It isn't necessary, that's all. This isn't chess."

"Jackson might think so."

"Smallwood doesn't play chess. Nor does McFee. You said once, cavemen's heads weren't full of horseshit or something. They had ordinary clear sight and we call it clairvoyance. Well, tonight I lay there thinking and the whole mess sorted itself out and it's simple. Want to hear it?"

"All ears, Mackinnon."

"Right, I'll take us back a bit. We're pretty sure now that McFee has a guilty secret that connects him to Albert Smallwood. We're also pretty sure that Albert didn't know what he and Alice were up to and died still not knowing. But none of it amounts to a complication. It doesn't make any difference to what's got to happen. McFee has cause to worry about it, but that's his personal problem. It might make him leave out the clues that embarrass him and that makes it harder to work out the whole thing; but it will be solved anyway."

"We've got to stay with the spooky robberies, then. Well, not robberies. You know what I mean."

"And they'll lead us to the upstairs room at Manny Rosenblum's shop."

"Which isn't there anymore."

"Yes. And here's the simple bit. Somewhere in this city, some day, McFee and Smallwood will come together in a reconstruction of that room and of the moment when he found him kneeling by the safe with his lantern."

"How do you know that?"

"Because I do, Fernleaf. It's clear in my mind. Nothing matters now but following the clues."

"So all the drama we had yesterday – no, the day before – was a waste of time?"

"It can't have been a total waste of time. Like you said, no coincidences. We've got to treat it as part of the key to understanding the safebreaks."

"Does that mean sharing it with the others?"

"No. No, you're right. We can't."

The great simplicity isn't quite the shining monument it seemed. When you look closer there are fallen stones round the base. Fernleaf picks one up.

"When McFee came to Inglefield to see if Jackson could help him, what do you think he was expecting?"

"I don't know."

"Well; he might have thought Uncle would get together a medium or two, hold a seance and contact Albert there and then. What about that?"

"Okay; for a start, Shanks would have put him right about mediums. Second, I just don't see McFee believing that kind of stuff himself unless he was desperate."

"Fine. And he might have expected nothing at all, or a long shot that was better than nothing, or just a therapeutic chat. Don't forget Jackson was a psychiatrist. So what did he actually get?"

"He got to tell his story to two eavesdroppers."

"Two eavesdroppers who had nothing to do with him, no influence, no importance. Children. But at least he could tell someone."

"He'd told Shanks."

"Not the same, Mackinnon. And for that moment we weren't children. We aren't children now. You know he really was leaving? Shanks had told him he could do nothing. And then Clement the psychic made his amazing appearance."

"You know what I think about that."

"Yes, I know. But how did that make McFee feel?"

"Relieved that something could be done after all. And, ah, I get it; worried that I would pick up little hints about the business with him and Alice along the way; hints left for us by Albert to turn the screw on him? Or even worse, read his mind directly?"

"But he's still in the hunt, isn't he? Why?"

"Because I'm supposed to sniff out psychic clues only at the places he chooses to take me. Places with no connection to his secret. Only... only he came unstuck because of Sal. He doesn't know about Alice and Sal, does he?"

"No, he seems not to. Doesn't that worry you a bit?"

"How would it?"

"Listen. I know you're male and you've only got a limited education, but...how can I put it? If you've just had a child it's difficult to hide."

"What, the child?"

"No, you drongo. The fact you've already given birth. Even if you'd gone away to escape the neighbours, and there wasn't a whiff of scandal for even a local bobby like McFee to hear about, a man would know if the woman he was with had, well...had it. Whether she'd got pregnant or not. Had it. And more so if you had actually given birth. I'd be surprised if Alice was his first. Do you read me?"

"Right. I think I've got that. I'll take your word, anyhow. So let's say young PC McFee knew Alice had, er, had it already, assuming she hadn't told him anyway; he still needn't have known that she was talking about Sal. Sal is a total stranger to him. I saw them together."

She puts on a furrowed-brow look. Whatever her face does, it looks good. She smells good too; here in this forbidden room.

"Mackinnon, I still need to clear up one or two questions. It means visiting people. I know after what we've said it sounds like raking over old ground, but if it comes to nothing there's no harm done. I just need to be sure; for our sakes. Maybe just my sake. All right?"

"Fine by me. But Shanks and Connie aren't going to let us out together on our own. You heard them the other night. It makes what we're doing here deliciously risky. If they caught us now we'd never be let out at all. For days."

This time she looks at me as if expecting me to be angry. It's even better than her thinking look. "I told Connie all about it. She's a very upright young woman, you know."

"Don't talk to me about upright women. What did she say?"

"She promised to ask Jackson if I could go out with her tomorrow – today – and get the coat mended."

"Good move. It'll get me out of the house."

"No it won't, Mackinnon. Uncle holds you responsible for our crimes. You'll still be under house arrest for a while."

"Right; no point arguing, I suppose. Yes, there bloody is! Suddenly I'm meant to be your bloody guardian!"

"Relax. It'll come right."

"But you'll be without a psychic to help you."

"The answers I want are simple ones, Mackinnon; things to put my mind at rest. Don't get upset; not like I did when you went off without me."

The clock in the hall chimes three. For a minute or so we remain just as we are, our hands touching, our fingers on their own exploring their spaces, like the wavelets of a calm sea. The quiet fragrances of the room and of her fill my head; its shapes and shadows cradle us. My eyes read the library as if it were one big book, pausing now and then to rest on her, on her hair, on her look, which is very far away. Each time they do I want more and more to say what I feel, and each time the surroundings draw me back and the feeling grows stronger that there's a message here for me too, in this room.

Her voice moves through the silence.

"Uncle had a row with George and Damietta about their society while we were out. Very polite, but it left him in a foul mood. We got the rough end of that. Connie said he was on the point of resigning as secretary. And what about this hush-hush war business? Are they connected? Are they going to mess things up? And why aren't we in more danger from the papers? Back home they'd get their teeth in and hang on. What's the answer, Mackinnon?"

I hold her hand a little more tightly and look right into her eyes.

"All taken care of. This is when it feels so good. They are connected, and instead of complicating everything they all cancel out."

"How?"

"Whatever Shanks did during the war is what stands between him and the rest of the society. They didn't approve or agree with it, not the big cheeses anyway. And it was top secret; still is. Remember him saying the Home Office could call the press off if they got too near McFee? Well, I don't know much about the papers but I know they come in two sizes. One sort lives off this kind of story and they won't hold off forever just to please Scotland Yard. But if Shanks gets dragged into it, what have we got? National security is what. The papers can't touch it then. Not the patriotic ones, anyway."

"Lousy but loyal."

"Something like that."

"That's very good. I'm impressed."

These words affect me like the sweetest music.

"Thank you. But it's just the clear thinking trick again. The sort of thinking I've only been able to do since, well, you know." I smile at her.

She smiles back. "Do you know what would really get my undying admiration? Telling me what Jackson's secret work was. What was he up to, d'you think?"

My smile vanishes. "Got it. I've seen this on the films; the hero does something smart, risks his life, and the woman says, go on, show me something else. Jump through another hoop; go fetch one more stick if you want to keep me interested. How much of your admiration do I have already? Can't be the undying sort."

"Admiration can always die, Mackinnon. What about your admiration for me? What have I done to deserve it?"

This is the moment. But I'm only half prepared.

"Everything I know about you."

She just carries on looking straight at me. What makes the difference in a look? The tiny displacements that move your expression from shadow to light, from monologue to dialogue though only one of you speaks? I take a deep, silent breath.

"First it was your face. If a thousand years ago I'd got only a glimpse of you in some lonely place, it would have made that place enchanted. And I'd have gone searching for you, hoping you were real, hoping to see you again. For the rest of my life."

There's a smile somewhere in her eyes; but there are other things too.

"Promise me one thing."

My heart's banging. It never learns.

"Go on."

"That's good. You didn't say, 'yes, anything'."

"No. I might have, once."

"Mackinnon, promise not to tell me you love me."

The words I've tried for whole wakeful hours to weave into a pretty speech, turned round and given back; yet still exciting to hear, still a long way from just 'no'.

"I want to tell you. But I don't have to tell you if you know it already."

"You'll have to, one day."

I'm uneasy, almost frightened again.

"Then how can I promise not to, ever? How can it be never?"

"I didn't say never."

"Have you got someone back home?"

"No."

"Are you asking me to be patient? Is that it?"

"Please promise."

Now this matters more than anything. The spoils of adolescence are meagre, but they're all you have. You lay them before someone and they tell you to take them away. And you say: but you possess them already; in the offering they become yours. They won't be mine again just because you return them to me.

"Fernleaf, I'm going to earn my freedom from this promise, or keep my word because by then it'll cost me nothing." She doesn't answer. But there are many emotions in her look now, and I know I've said all that I should say.

I love her more than ever.

Putting just enough emphasis on the last three words I say, "Fernleaf, Berenice; I promise not to tell you I love you."

She takes both my hands in hers. "Thank you, Mackinnon, Clement."

My mind lies strangely at ease. We've done this before; something like this. I feel the freedom from all worry, all necessity; so strong it's physical. The room itself seems to take me by the hand and I rise – no, my body rises – from the floor and without a word walks to the part of the shelves from which I'd casually taken the pictureless book. Because no thought is involved in these movements I pick up every influence from my surroundings. I feel the house itself sleeping; the dying of the ashes in the grates; the uncoiling of time in the clocks; the eyes of Fernleaf on me.

I pull the same book out again and peer into the space behind it. There, encased in shadow, is a glint of metal. Three thick volumes conceal the rest: a square blue-steel door with a stainless combination lock.

She lays a hand on my shoulder. "What are you doing, Mackinnon? How did you know it was there?" Her voice sounds strange.

I'm concentrating; calmly waiting for the numbers to come. I know they will. Poor old Albert! Fiddling with stolen gelignite in the dark; groping with dishonest keys! Clement Garner, psychic peterman. No fumes, no prints, no clues.

I chuckle softly. Her fingers dig into my arm, then loosen. "Please leave it. Leave it alone. This isn't right."

Oh, yes it is. Too much to enjoy in this intrusion business; the gift of revealing what is forbidden.

I wish for six numbers and they appear. As the last one fades from my mind I reach my hand to turn the tumbler. Suddenly there's a broken series of clicks and the door swings open. By itself.

The trance ends and I find myself staring in horror at what I've done. No, not done! Turning, there's the same look on her face. We were talking about love. Love! Now tears are running down her cheeks. I take her face in my hands and kiss them away.

"Ever since I knew," I whisper, "I've wanted to be able to make things happen, to balance up the things that I couldn't stop happening to me. But it'll always be out of my control. This is robbery, isn't it?"

"Not if we close it and go," she says.

"We're not meant to, are we? This is happening for a reason. You said I'd impress you by saying what Shanks did in the war. The answer's got to be in this safe, hasn't it? Why else? We'll look, then put it back. Nothing taken; not robbery after all."

"Please be careful."

I ease out packets of papers, a notebook and a padded envelope. One of the packets is marked MOST SECRET. Cover your tracks, says an inner voice. So I undo the elastic bands and memorise the way they've been put on, hoping they aren't perished. The first sheet of paper trembles in my hand.

It's covered with grainy typescript and looks like a bottom copy. The signature underneath is illegible but the hyphen clinches it. We stand directly under a wall bracket to read all the sheets more clearly. Fernleaf puts her arm round me and leans her head on my shoulder. She's completely with me now. This is not for the eyes of children or adults or anyone. Most secret.

Much of it makes little immediate sense. George Shawe-Tritton has most of the vices and few of the virtues of a rotund literary style. But the seventh page tells us what we need to know:

"In summary, I suggest that Dr Armitage's argument for the establishment of an - albeit experimental - Psychic Warfare Department is fundamentally flawed. The dangers may be seen to outweigh by far any possible benefits, as follows:

(i) Mass psychic transmission over long distances.

Assuming this to be achievable, the enemy's potential for retaliation rests on their greater population and evident regimentation of thought, not to say fanaticism.

The whole idea is therefore far more useful to them than to us.

(ii) Peacetime uses of a Mass Psychic Warfare Unit.

How would such a unit be demobilised and disarmed? What would happen if an unscrupulous government or other agency were able to command the services of even a proportion of such a unit?

(iii) Psychic derangement of enemy electronics and communications.

The arguments against (i) apply. Conventional means are understood to be well in hand, and be more easily controllable. (see (ii)).

(iv) Psychic interrogation methods: prisoners and enemy agents.

Whatever merit this idea might possess, it would favour the enemy who at present hold far more prisoners than we do and are known to operate far fewer agents in the UK than was previously feared. The idea is more use to them than to us.

(v) The double-edged sword.

The experience of 'war-winning' contrivances such as the magnetic mine ought to teach us that new weapons can be counteracted or turned against their originators. How could we measure the results of psychic warfare methods, or judge whether our efforts had been detected, analysed and turned against us?

12. 4. 41

We turn over page after page; more notes, reports of meetings. George must have been high up in the intelligence services, but he never managed entirely to kill off Shanks's ideas. Committees were set up to look into them and each time they were pronounced unworkable.

All but one. Again and again the notion of using psychics to sit in on interrogations of prisoners and suspected agents, or to keep tabs on them, kept coming up. The last sheets in the bundle are dated 1945, but George Shawe-Tritton's criticisms never stopped and Jackson Armitage pressed on regardless. No wonder the rifts in their ghost-hunting society run deep. I put the papers back in order and replace the elastic bands.

"Churchill let him get on with his experiments right till the end of the war. Maybe he believed in them, maybe it was to keep him out of mischief. Do you know where the headquarters of the Experimental Psychic Warfare Unit was?"

"Yes, Crewe. It said so in the notes."

I smile wearily at the wallpaper. "Crewe was a codename; for Inglefield Place. All through those years he was working to prove we could combat the Axis by psychic means. All during the holidays when I was hiding and seeking in the woods with the gardener's kids, and eating with him in the evenings when he had no visitors, and playing chess with him. That's why he didn't take in evacuees. One child round the place would be enough good cover for a secret establishment; especially a child who lived a life of his own. Raymond and Victoria must have been in on it; must have been Secret Service people or something. Were they guarding him, or watching him? Or both? All those visitors, eh? Must have been big bugs, some of them."

She lets me ramble on. Years of hidden truth need something said about them. And it's still happening. The coming of peace hasn't stopped Shanks trying to prove his theories right; hasn't removed him from the secret lists of the government. There are new enemies, after all. And how do Alphonse and Ludmilla fit in? They have no love for our recent Soviet allies. Are they undercover operatives too?

"No, I don't think so," says Fernleaf, answering my unspoken question. "I really don't."

"You're right. I want them to be just what they seem. All Shanks needed was an ace up his sleeve: one first-rate psychic and a few really convincing demonstrations. But he never found one until it was all over. And there I was."

"Poor Jackson. No wonder this case is so important to him. Now he can be right at last."

"If we succeed; and if it's allowed to come out. Or he may never get the credit after all."

"Put them back now."

But something fails in me, and I'm gripped by blinding reality. All I see is I'm in the library of a strange house in a strange city, with an opened safe and secret papers in my hand. I move swiftly to the shelves, thrust the bundles in, then pull them out again, trying to remember exactly how they lay when I found them. Shaking, breathing hard, I finally push the blue-steel door shut. Then freeze.

"What is it? Why have you stopped?"

"I've forgotten the numbers! It's like I never knew them!"

"Oh, God," she whispers, and we fall into desperate inactivity. Compared to this, our past sins are nothing. No explanation can ever save us.

She hears it first.

Her fingers squeeze round my wrist, the nails digging into me. Her voice is horribly calm.

"There's someone coming. I can hear them on the stairs."

There's only one way out if you don't count the window and who-ever's approaching is already too close. Our number's up. Huge voids of time pass, full of space for our discoverers, a desert of irresolution for us. My mind begins to converse with itself. There are two ways to go, it says.

The presence must be on the last landing now; and they can see the light from this room.

One way is in panic.

They're halfway down the last flight of stairs.

The other is to take calmly the evasive action for which there is not enough time; steady and deliberate until disaster overwhelms you.

Now they're on the chequerboard tiles of the hall.

The result either way is the same, so you may as well consider the manner of your going: like a headless chicken or with dignity and clean trousers. Throwing off a hill of inertia I speak and move slowly so as not to stumble in either.

"Crouch down behind that sofa," I mutter, and turn to put the books in their place to cover the telltale safe. Time has run out. When I turn again they'll be there. I have no words for this moment. The adventure has ended.

The doorway is empty.

I take three steps away from the shelves, throw a glance sideways to be sure Fernleaf is out of sight, and begin to walk towards the door. Our discoverer's delay is beyond reason, but it can't change anything. I take another step, and an idea begins to work on my body almost before it introduces itself to my brain.

Two steps. All traces of a jerky start from standing are gone. I stare forwards.

The figure of George Shawe-Tritton himself stands before me, in green silk dressing gown, clutching a rolled umbrella. His decision to arm himself from the hallstand has given us priceless seconds.

I keep walking, staring fixedly, not blinking.

George looks saggy and florid, his tonsure of white hair disordered. He looks like a character in a country house whodunnit: Colonel Plum in the library with a brolly. It would be funny anywhere else.

"Good Lord, it's you. What the devil are you doing here? Eh? Speak up!" He sounds irritated; not his usual self at all. I ignore him and keep walking, focussing my stare at a point six feet ahead and slightly to the left, so as not to go cross-eyed. Already the strain of not blinking is becoming serious.

"Hey! Steady on, old man!"

I bump into him, stop moving, go on pushing slightly and slowly swing my right arm upwards. My hand crawls about on the wall, finds the switch and turns out the light. George steps back and holds the folded umbrella across his chest as though warding off evil. From the corner of my eye I can see his flabbergasted look. Flabbergasted is a word specially invented for his kind of face.

"Good grief," he murmurs. "You're sleepwalking." He goes on backing away until he fetches up against the newel post. "Better not touch him. Shouldn't wake him," he whispers to himself. I turn sharp left and head for the front door, so that with my face turned from him I can blink several times and swivel my eyeballs. From behind me he's saying, "Better not do that, old chap. Catch your death out there. Oh, Lord, I'll have to. Here goes!"

Just as I put my hand to the doorknob I feel his fingers on both shoulders as he gently steers me in a tight circle and gets me pointing towards the stairs. As I start to climb, he lets go.

"That's it; well done. Be straight up to see you to the top."

Passing the conservatory on the first-floor landing I shoot a glance sideways but there's only my reflection. Is he checking the library? Have I put the books back in the right order? Does he notice or care about such things?

Then I hear the turning of a heavy key in a lock and I know for certain that he's secured the library against further intrusion and unwittingly imprisoned Fernleaf.

Sleepwalkers in films always look half crazy, all wide staring eyes and clockwork smoothness. Luckily I have more convincing models. Back at Monk's Hill young Allan Hoile was often going walkabout in the middle of the night, and he looked like any normal person wandering round a well-known house with the lights off. So I climb slowly and deliberately up the stairs and reflect on my carefree descent – how many hours ago? Behind me I can hear George's laboured breathing and the shuffle of his slippered feet. He isn't just following me; he's the man who for years has dogged Jackson Armitage; has hovered at his back and poisoned his every hope of service and reward. It makes my neck crawl, as if the Grey Man of Ben Macdhui were stepping in my footprints up a lonely twilight snowfield; and it's with some satisfaction that I turn at last and, looking right through him, close my bedroom door in his face.

But I'm scarcely under the blankets before he comes in. I can hear his breathing subside in the dark until he gives a final grunt, closes the door and leaves me with the sound of his footfalls receding down the stairs. Lock it; I don't want him back in here.

I lie there and my heart pounds with the horror of our situation. Four floors down Fernleaf's locked in the cold library next to a safe that shouldn't be open and that neither of us knows how to close. I know she won't try getting out of the window because she can't refasten it from the outside and anyway there's no way back in if she does. Despite George's words to me at the front door I know all entrances are locked at night and only he and Amelia hold the keys. I hit myself again and again on the chest. "Idiot! Idiot! Idiot! Stupid! Stupid! Stupid!" It takes a while to calm down.

First I must go back down, free her. No idea how, but it's impossible to stay here. Then sort out the business of the combination. Maybe it'll come back. If caught, try the sleepwalker dodge again; Shanks'll get to hear of it anyway. Every damn thing is cocked up. Fubar.

Grand imperial bloody effed up beyond all recognition. The tropical lagoon of our touching hands has turned into breakers that are slamming me onto a beach of stones. And razor shells. And pillows.

My eyes close; and I'm out without so much as a tremor.

When I wake nothing's amiss; for about two seconds. Then I suddenly grab the alarm clock and fumble the bedside lamp into action.

Twenty past five! Sitting on the edge of the bed I feel I have just enough brain to know I'm brainless. There's a trapdoor in the bottom of my abyss and I've just dropped through it.

My second journey down the stairs becomes a little nightmare. Super-sensitive to every creak, every imagined sound, I grope my way in the dark. The chime of the hall clock freezes me gasping in my tracks. But at last I touch bottom and head for the library door.

It's locked all right. A light tapping on the green baize is all I dare. If she comes to the door we can make some sort of plan. But there's no reply. I tap again. Silence.

I go down like one at prayer and hiss through the gap under the door. "Fernleaf! It's me!" Crouching, head to one side, I strain to catch an answer. Has she fallen asleep?

A door opens on one of the lower landings.

I hear it distinctly, but more with disbelief than fear.

Footsteps on the stairs grow closer. Wildly I look for a hiding place; too late for sleepwalking; I'll never get back here in time, whoever I try it on.

Below-stairs toilet? No; might be their destination too. So? No; they'd wait.

Kitchen? Same problem, only over more quickly.

Broom cupboard? Too risky. Stuff might avalanche out, like in Laurel and Hardy. A fine mess, either way. Five seconds later I'm crouched behind the long dining-room table, peering out into the lighted hall and conscious of making all the wrong moves.

A tall figure in black seems to glide past the door and into the kitchen. There's something almost unreal about it. Thank God Fernleaf didn't answer. Sleepwalking is one thing; caught kow-towing to a green baize door is another. I wait. I wait a long time. Whoever it is isn't just after a glass of water; we've got jugs of it in our rooms anyway.

Jesus wept! How long since I was hiding behind a South London tombstone in the drizzle?

Look at me now. That and a punch-up in the East End, plus taking Top Secret wartime papers from a safe. What's my life coming to? Why all this trouble? Why does my fate and Fernleaf's suddenly depend on a stranger hanging about in a kitchen in the dying hours of the night? I could laugh out loud. Maybe I should.

An age passes while I debate with myself.

This can't go on. I peep round the door towards the end of the hall. The figure's sitting at the table, nursing a cup of tea. It's a woman, but her features, though in profile, are hidden by a cascade of black hair. A cloud of cigarette smoke hangs over her. She sits stooped, as though unrefreshed by sleep. Any number of strangers could have turned up to stay over while I was in solitary. Maybe I can show myself after all.

Then the woman sweeps her hair aside and reveals the straight nose and dark eyes of Amelia da Costa. I cringe back. The last person on earth! Why her? Of all people?

The clock answers me. A quarter to six; Amelia is about to start work. About to shed her funeral housecoat, scrape her hair into a bun, straighten her back and put her bloodthirsty past away for another day among the liberals. But first, twenty minutes alone with her humanity. She rises to refill her cup, and I dash soundlessly to the foot of the stairs. If only it had been Miss Maybury.

Connie! Connie knows about us! I slap my forehead; not too hard. Your mind's going; why didn't you just get her up in the first place? She'd have understood; probably. I bound soundlessly up to the landing, then stop.

Which room is hers? Why don't I know?

A sort of maniac determination gets hold of me. I discard Connie and go for something else. It's like the films showing time passing by speeded-up pages dropping off a wall calendar.

The conservatory. Yes! With a squeak the door slides open and shuts again and I slip in among the foliage, invisible from inside or out. Loosening a window catch, I lean out over the pitifully small town garden and a wave of freezing air wraps itself round me.

Along the backs of the neighbouring street of houses a few lights show. Letting my eyes get accustomed to the dark outlines below I brace myself for at least a ten-foot jump. The lessons of a week or so of hiding and deceit now came into play. As my slippered feet crash into dead leaves and I roll over with a thump, I know the sound will reach my sombre jailor in the kitchen. When the light bursts from the opened curtain, I'm already out of sight with a stone in my hand. Flung at low level through the winter undergrowth it makes a satisfactory sound. The shadow of Amelia divides the square of light on the grass for a few seconds, and I picture her haughty face with the bedraggled hair that only her bandit lovers have ever seen, as she dismisses the tomcat in the bushes and draws the curtains shut.

But there are more tracks to cover. The cold air might not penetrate the house but it might disturb the fronds in the conservatory as she goes upstairs again. With a slimy stick I push the casement to. Fernleaf and I will have to get back that way but one thing at a time. At least I can now make contact. The night is deathly cold. I tap on the library window and wait.

Breath clouds round me and I stifle a cough. My fingers are going numb. The long sweep of the backs of these tall Georgian houses loom like a chasm with their festoons of drainpipes. I tap again; no answer.

Come on, I'm not out here for my health.

That small voice which has often spoken to me before now does so again. Its tone is gentle but insistent and it becomes impossible to ignore.

She isn't in there, it's saying. She is safe in her own room and you are an idiot. She got out of the library somehow and now you're stuck outside with no way of getting back. You need rescuing, not her.

This revelation weighs heavily on me.

Still, the remnants of intelligence lurk in the strangest places. Though my hands lack almost all feeling I set about selecting a few small, flat white stones; white so I can watch their flight; and start throwing them at what I'm sure is her window high up under the eaves.

My first efforts miss, bounce off the masonry and dive twinkling through the night where I catch them in my outstretched dressing gown. Those who missed the sight of me prostrated before a green door now have the chance of watching me dancing about on a freezing December night in the back garden of a town house in my pyjamas, holding my outer garments before me like an old woman's apron.

After five minutes I've hit her window twice with no result and stand back, perfectly calm.

The voice is there again. You've had a good run. Now go and knock on the kitchen window and give yourself up before you freeze to death, you half-wit.

But I haven't forgotten all that has passed; not forgotten what we said to each other in that hour many happenings ago. One more try. It's always the third try that does it. The stone flies up and I wait for its tiny white trace to fall back to me. Nothing. I squint up at the target. The window's open! It must have hit her and landed on the floor. Fernleaf's face leans out.

Explanations can wait. Right now the matter of George Shawe-Tritton's wall safe is far from my thoughts. I point at me, then at the conservatory window.

Somewhere a dog should bark. But it doesn't.

Chapter 22

Eleven in the morning and the house is alive. The doorbell rings constantly; people come and go; Damietta Shawe-Tritton and Amelia dash from room to room, rearranging decorations for the New Year bash. Every now and then George pads past, more busy than useful, giving me strange glances that I pretend to ignore. I have other things on my mind.

Only thing is, my mind isn't up to it. When Amelia came to tell me I'd completed my sentence she found a person so deeply asleep that she left me and a cup of ageing tea to discover each other. The kindness of an unforgiving heart.

Breakfast might have happened, might not. Drifting about in a daze I fetch up in the drawing room, slumped in an armchair, trying to shuffle together a few recent memories. There was a spell in a freezing garden waiting for what seemed like twenty minutes and two calls of nature before Fernleaf appeared at the conservatory window. There was a comical interlude involving her making a loop in one end of my dressing gown cord while I tried to warm up my hands, then a lot of hauling and scrambling up brickwork in mortal terror of Amelia repeating her weird appearance at the glazed door. Finally a session that almost made the whole thing worth it as she rubbed and massaged me back to life on my own bed. There was also a conversation.

"What a dill, Mackinnon! When you did your sleepwalking stunt old George had his back turned long enough for me to slip out and hide in the next room. What did you think I'd do?"

"Then why didn't you bloody well come and tell me? Do you know what I've gone through, all for you?"

"I do, actually. But it took a while before the coast was clear and I could risk getting all the way up here. You were asleep, drongo. I didn't think anyone could be so asleep. You wouldn't wake up when I knocked. Why did you lock the door? So I left you to it; set my alarm to go off in half an hour. You were like the dead."

"Brilliant plan. So what went wrong?"

"Slept right through it. Sorry. What can I do to make you feel better?"

"You wouldn't do it. Just tell me the safe's locked itself."

"I think maybe it has."

"Eh? How do you know?"

"I said 'I think'. When I was creeping after you and George, when you started leading him down the hallway – good thinking, by the way; I thought you were doing it for me – I heard these faint clicking noises. Not much to pin your hopes on, really."

But it's better than nothing. "Fernleaf?"

"What?"

"Why was George on his own? If he was expecting trouble – what with his umbrella – he'd have got people up, wouldn't he? And how did he know anyway?"

"Went for a leak maybe. My grandad spends half the night up. What bothers me more is why he doesn't expect some of his guests to be insomniacs or something and feel like a midnight read. Well, it's his house."

When Damietta and Amelia invade the drawing room I retreat to the library. There's someone already in there; a stranger. A short, round little man with Oriental features, dressed almost exactly like me in grey trousers and sleeveless pullover. He's standing by the window with a book open in his hand. As I enter he turns and the morning light flashes in his spectacles. I should have guessed I wouldn't be alone.

"Good morning," he says.

"Good morning. Are you staying here too?"

"Yes."

"Have you been here before?"

"No. My first time. You must be the young person with Doctor Armitage." He pauses, smiling, to give me a chance to remember my manners.

"I'm sorry. Clement Garner."

"I am Mister Lo. Honoured." He gives a little bow, so I do too. We shake hands.

"If you are looking for Miss Maybury and Berenice, I can tell you they have gone out."

"Thanks, I did know. You're good at remembering names."

"It is my job. I am a journalist. And, in a small way, an author and traveller." He says 'in a small way' with no false modesty. I guess he doesn't belong to the League of Supernatural Investigators. Just as well, because this library's haunted. But, courteous and interesting though he is, I need him out of here.

"Bit busy down here at the moment, with all these preparations going on," I remark casually. "They'll be in here soon."

"Very possibly," he replies, closing the book so as not to appear to ignore me.

"There's a little conservatory on the first landing. I don't suppose they'll do anything in there. It's peaceful, if you want to take a book with you. And quite warm and comfortable."

"Thank you; but I shall endure in here. Two months ago I was reading a book in a library in a rich man's house; a most interesting book whose contents induced me to forget my surroundings. Presently a shell from a cannon struck the wall."

"A shell! Who fired it?"

"Difficult to tell. The house was between the lines, but it was probably the Communists."

261

"You were in China?"

"Most perceptive. I was covered in plaster dust. Presently an aged librarian appeared and suggested I move to the cellar, but apologised for the lack of light for reading down there. At that moment another shell fell nearby. Possibly the Nationalists this time. The old man bowed and said, 'but that may not always be the case.'"

He smiles again. "Thank you for your concern, but I shall be quite happy to read in here if the commotion is not too great."

I try a last shot. "Interesting book? Can I see?"

His smile becomes a little more patient. "The publishers must have been in a kindly frame of mind, but the translation is poor." He opens it at the title page. It's one of those long, old-fashioned titles:

> *Conversations with the Warlords Lung Yun and Ch'en Chi-T'ang.*
> *An Account of Travels Through Yunnan and Kwangtung. 1935. By*
> *Euphemius Lo.*

I clear my throat.

"I shall try not to disturb you, Clement," he says.

"Thank you, Mister Lo."

"Not at all." And he continues to stand by the window. I wander to the shelves where the safe's hidden. This isn't going to be easy. At least he's facing away from me. I take down the book without pictures. You can't see a thing in the space. Obvious, really; anyone could choose this book. Without putting it back I crouch a little to get the dark space at eye-level. There's a sound behind me and I jerk my head up. Mister Lo has settled into a chair and is now facing my way.

Heart pounding, I begin to act with that desperate cunning that wouldn't have occurred to me two weeks ago. Pretending to look for a volume on the lower shelves I shuffle round so he can't see my features as I peer into the gap. Ah! You could only recognise the blue steel sheen if you'd seen it before. But is the safe locked? I sense the little Chinese traveller's eyes lifting from his poorly translated words to look at me.

If they have, they'll see me take the first book's neighbour down and appear to be struggling with a choice between *Acts of Parliament Relating to Inland Waterways* and *Russell on Crimes and Misdemeanours 8th Edition; jnt. ed. Judge G B McLure.*

Tough call. I weigh them in each hand, then put one on top of the other, turn them sideways and seem to make a bad job of sliding them together into place, catching the edge of the next book along and pushing it back. With a sigh of impatience I reach behind it to straighten it.

Here goes. The knuckles of my right-hand middle and index fingers grip the handle and waggle it swiftly. It doesn't budge. The other fingers ease the book forward and in a second or two everything's back in place. I rise to my feet.

Euphemius Lo is indeed looking at me.

"Sleepless night. I'm feeling a bit disjointed this morning."

"Then I should go for a stroll. A little exercise will improve matters. A library is no place to tone up one's muscles."

"Good idea. I think I will."

The relief as I pass out of the door makes me lift up mine eyes to the hills, or rather to the – for once – friendly shade of Albert Smallwood. While my attention's distracted I feel a strong hand grab my arm.

It's Shanks. He begins to propel me backwards into the library. Oh, God; he's heard about the sleepwalking. Or something. As usual I've forgotten that other people are in the game. We do what we do and the world turns as it will.

Then he sees the top of Mister Lo's head above the back of the armchair and lets go his grip. "Follow me," he mutters, and starts up the stairs. I begin work on my speech for the defence. But he stops on the second landing and faces me.

"Clement, cast your mind back."

"Yes, sir. Okay."

"Do you recall our visit to that jeweller's premises the evening we arrived in London?"

My mind fumbles to change gear. "Er, well, yes."

"Come on, boy, wake up. You're mumbling."

"Sorry, sir. I'm listening."

"Good. Now think hard. You mentioned something after we left; something you hadn't considered important at the time."

"That's right; something about spiders. There was one, but I didn't see it. It just came to me."

"Precisely. Come in here."

His room is beautifully furnished with strange black chests covered in Chinese pictures. There's a curious, ancient smell as though stale perfume has been polished onto the laquer for a hundred years. Shanks is smoothing out a large map on the bedcover and calling me over.

It's a map of London. I watch him lay a foolscap-size sheet of tissue paper over the central part; a sheet with little inked crosses on it.

"Do you see what these crosses represent?"

"Well; they, er, go round in a circle. Almost."

"They are the locations of Smallwood's supernatural break-ins. There have been five since November. Observe." He takes a pencil and numbers each in turn.

"One: November 27th; Mitre Street, Whitechapel. Two: December 17th; Wapping Lane. That was the incident which led Mr McFee to consult me."

"How did he hear about you?"

"Eh? My name does appear occasionally in the literature, you know. Three: Plympton Street in Marylebone on Christmas Day. Four and five: Coldharbour Lane, Camberwell and Currance Road, barely a mile away; both on the 27th."

I watch silently as he takes what looks like a photo album off a chest and slips it under the map, then lifts off the tissue paper.

"Clement, what do you notice about the sequence there?"

"They follow each other in a clockwise direction. Except the third one."

"Yes. Pity about that one. But its proximity to McFee's flat may be significant. Now, think. If you were expecting a number to be involved in a supernatural event, which would it be?"

"Five. Or seven, I'd say."

"And we have five clues so far. Yes?" He produces a second sheet and puts it where the first one's been. This one has the crosses but he's joined them up to make a pentagon. From the corners lines radiate inwards and meet in a jumble.

"A spider's web," I say, forestalling his question.

"Exactly. See? I bisected the angles at each vertex to produce the co-ordinates. I think we may have the answer here. You sense a message concerning spiders, and here is Smallwood weaving a web around the city. We should find him at its centre!"

There's something that's been eating me for a couple of days. It's been very quiet but insistent; so quiet that I haven't even floated it past Fernleaf. I decide it's time to give it a go. Ignoring his latest brainwave I look straight at him.

"Sir?"

"Yes?" He doesn't often hear me call him that these days, so I've got his attention.

"These break-ins. We've only been to one. No, let me finish. Am I right in thinking nothing has ever been taken from any of the safes?"

"I think that's a given. What are you driving at?"

"And in each case we're left with a safe apparently damaged by explosives."

"Yes." He says this with just enough slowness.

"Okay. And no sign of a break-in."

"Go on."

"Right. The press are being told to keep it dark and so far they've played along. But loads of people must know anyway. They know that safes have been done, that even if there's been stuff in them it hasn't been taken..."

He interrupts me. "Clement, it occurs to me that we don't know if each safe was empty or not."

"What about the Dunkleys?"

He has to think. Finally: "Do you know, I'm not sure about that. I remember that nothing was taken. I have to assume that they would have remarked on it if there had been nothing there in the first place. Could you come to the point?"

"Nearly there. A series of safe jobs close together in time where nothing is nicked and no-one can see how the peterman got in would get people talking, wouldn't it? I mean, ordinary people. People who work in those places. Phantom Safecracker and all that? How wouldn't it get about? Some of these places had workers, surely?"

More thinking. I can see he's having to deal with this. But what I'm not sure about is whether it's stuff he already knows about and it's really me that's the problem. All this is making me uneasy enough to almost wish I hadn't brought it up. But I haven't got to the punchline yet. The one that my Clear Thinking scriptwriter has prepared for me.

His eyebrows go up a little. He's got an answer. "It is possible that even if these jobs, as you call them, have excited local interest, they have been sufficiently separate in location that no one has drawn a connection. We should also remember that the matter of fingerprints remains a closely guarded secret. I know this is a long shot, but the possibility that a series of hoaxes has been perpetrated – admittedly for unknown reasons by a particularly clever operator – may be enough to satisfy the public." He cuts off my answer before I can give it. "Though if that were the case the average citizen might wonder why he reads nothing of in his local newspaper. You will no doubt now tell me what it is you're driving at."

"Yes. What little we know about the break-ins – with the exception of the Dunkleys – is what McFee has told us. Isn't that right?"

Another doubtful, long "Yes?"

"Then how do we know they've happened at all?"

Now he really is on the back foot. And I know I've risked his anger. But he reacts calmly.

"Because, Clement, that would imply that it is he and not Smallwood who has constructed the puzzle that we have been trying to work out, by choosing a series of street names and leaving it to chance whether we make anything of it or not." He lets out a long sigh. "Always assuming that we are remotely on the right track. Leave aside what the point of it all really is if your thinly disguised suspicions are correct."

I look away from him. I know I've deflected him from what should have been his moment.

"No, Uncle, that's all right. I was just wondering." He has to be right. I decide to put my idea away. Not one of my best. And not to bother Fernleaf with it.

There's a knock at the door. Shanks starts up, casts an anxious glance at me and calls out, "Who is it?"

"Amelia, sir. You are wanted on the telephone."

"Not a coincidence," I say, amazed at my own authority.

"Good Lord!" he whispers. "Wait there. I'll be straight back."

With him out of the room I take a closer look at his diagram. The lines make a poor job of meeting at the centre. Those labelled 1, 2 and 4 pass each other so as to form a triangle: a pretty large triangle that seems to contain most of Southwark. The other two cross within the triangle close to one side. Even allowing for a bit of inaccuracy it's hard to tell what it might mean, and the more I look at it the more I know it doesn't mean anything. It doesn't add up. He's barking up the wrong tree.

When he gets back I'll say I have no particular feelings about it; tell him to wait for Smallwood to make it seven. And hope something more believable, less sadly wishful, occurs to him meanwhile.

He's a long time. At last he comes in, pulling a pencil from his pocket.

"You were right. By God, you were right! That was McFee himself on the phone. Upcerne Road, SW10. Off the King's Road near Chelsea Creek." His eyes wander over the map. "There. Chelsea Creek."

He marks a sixth cross, then flings the pencil on the bed. "There! It continues the clockwise trend, see? I shouldn't be surprised to hear of a seventh before long, somewhere round...here; round about Islington. Yes. Where did I put it?"

He picks up a large Army protractor; one of those yellow chinagraph semicircles, and starts measuring angles. I think: Chinaman downstairs, Chinese laquer up here, chinagraph there. Refreshing to have a coincidence with no meaning at all.

As Shanks works his flow of talk slows, then stops. He straightens up with a long sigh.

"It misses by a mile. Completely upsets the co-ordinates. Yet I feel we're on the right track here. What do you think?"

"I think we should wait for a seventh occurrence. I'm sure the picture will be clearer then."

"But what do you think about my hypothesis? The spider's web? You yourself picked up the message." I don't want to argue the toss. This is the brainchild of a man impatient for results. After last night I understand this side of him far better, enough not to want to discourage or disappoint him. I rummage through my stock of mathematical terms.

"Best to wait. Maybe it isn't a matter of simple co-ordinates; maybe more to do with loci, or axes, or even logarithms." Shanks gives this half-baked concoction more house room than it deserves. I press on:

"What kind of place is it, the Chelsea Creek job?"

"Eh? Oh, a small printing works. Doubtful that we can visit it, though."

"Why?"

"Mr McFee's opinion. The owner would be difficult. I didn't pursue the matter."

"No," I say. He looks at me.

"I think we must proceed in a spirit of absolute trust, Clement."

"Okay. So is Smallwood telling us something else, then? Like, keep away from these places? Perhaps we should have seen the hint when Manny Rosenblum's shop went down the hole."

"Possibly, my boy. I could do with a cup of tea; not here, though. Let's go down."

Round mid-afternoon Connie and Berenice get back. The coat looks like new.

"That's invisible mending for you," says Connie. "A little backstreet place in Stepney. So reasonable. They're the places for this kind of thing."

"Stepney? Long way to go."

Finally I get Fernleaf to myself. "Went the day well?"

"Went the Day Well, eh? Great film. I saw it back in New Zealand."

"Do you have electricity in New Zealand?"

"Cut it, drongo."

"Well, did it?"

"Yes it did, thanks. You?"

"No, you first. Go on."

"Well, we got the coat fixed."

"Terrific. Get on with it. You'll notice I'm not sulking in bed."

"No, you're standing up. We had an interesting trip. How about the conservatory?"

"It holds many memories for me. Why not?"

Sitting in wicker chairs, we face the landing.

"We went to the orphanage first."

"Don't tell me. Stepney; near the coatmender."

"Nearer than that. The nuns mended it, in return for a donation. Some of the novices are brilliant seamstresses. They train the orphans. It's very quiet there; all bare and white and crucifixes on the walls. Everyone crept around like they didn't want to be spotted. You hardly saw any kids. Eerie; you wouldn't have liked it."

"Sounds just like Monk's Hill; except for the nuns. And the white walls. And the crucifixes. What did you find out?"

"We spoke to an old Irish sister; well, Connie did. She asked if a girl they called Sally Adamson had been left at their door some time around 1919. Yes, she said – her name was Sister Bridget, by the way – only it was before her time. But she'd known Sal for the last couple of years she was there. So Connie asked about special friends. There was one; a boy; but that was before her time too."

Damietta and Amelia gallop down the stairs past us trailing paper streamers.

"God, don't they ever stop? They look like a flaming tandem. Party's tomorrow night, not in five minutes. Sorry; go on."

"We got hold of a sister who did remember the boy. She described him as about seven years older than Sally; quiet, fairly intelligent and very protective. And built like a tank."

"Are we talking about Horace Pressman?"

"We're talking about Hubert Andrews. Both parents killed in a Zeppelin raid. They dug him out of the rubble."

"But is Hubert our Horace?"

"I'm sure of it. But that isn't where he got his funny voice. He could speak perfectly well all the time he was at the orphanage; and he was no trouble either, apparently."

"Really? They'd better not have any reunions, then."

"I don't know, Mackinnon. Those nuns looked sweet enough but they're bloody hard-boiled. Strict as you like. Hubert – Horace – came unstuck only once, and they gave him the cuts so hard he went over the wall and never came back. And we're talking about a hulking fourteen-year old."

"What did he do?"

"A young man's indiscretion, the sister called it. She didn't elaborate."

"Better not ask then. What were you trying to prove by all this?"

"Just tying up loose ends, like I said."

"Go anywhere else?"

"Yes. Gascoigne, the photographer."

"What! Bit risky, wasn't it? Suppose McFee was at home? No, that's not very likely."

"As you say, but what if he had been? Connie wanted my portrait done and he's the only photographer we know."

"Wouldn't have fooled me. Why would she want a picture of you? She sees your face every day."

"You're such a dill sometimes. It was a cover."

"So you got in?"

"Sat for the great man, then left."

"No loose ends tied up?"

"It wasn't right somehow. But we're going back tomorrow to see the results."

"Be nice to tag along."

"You will."

"Good. They're letting me out, then. I didn't dare ask myself."

"Only if you're truly a reformed character, Mackinnon." This with a confidential smile.

"No character was ever more reformed. Believe me."

"What about your day?"

"Well, I got into the library and checked the safe. It's locked."

She frowns. "I'm glad. It was so important, but I've hardly given it a thought till you mentioned it. Don't you think that's odd?"

"Yes," I say slowly. "I had trouble remembering the whole thing this morning. As if we'd only dreamt it. Didn't dream it, did we? There were some very nice moments."

She bites her lip, still frowning. "What else happened?"

"Shanks showed me this idea of his. He's got this map in his room with all the safe jobs marked on it."

"And?"

"He reckons they go round clockwise in date order. Well, they don't, for a start. Then he reckons...hang on." I draw imaginary lines on the floor.

Fernleaf shakes her head. "Clutching at straws, isn't he?"

"It's bollocks, Fernleaf; a four-year old could work that out. And in the middle of telling me, he gets a phone call from McFee. Remember him? Smallwood again; number six. And number six blows his theory out of the water. But he still thinks there's something in it, just because I sensed a spider without having to look. Well, I'm psychic, aren't I?"

"Old Albert isn't handing it to us. He's not helping at all."

"Is anyone? After everything we've only found out about ourselves."

"That's the point of being on a quest, isn't it? Why us, though? Don't let it get to you, Mackinnon. We'll have a decent day out tomorrow."

Jackson Armitage goes out alone after dinner and I hear no more crazy ideas. At bedtime Fernleaf massages my brow and sends me into a deep untroubled sleep.

The morning of the last day of the year dawns clear and bright and I set out with my two favourite women in the world, one on each arm. It feels modestly heroic.

London in the winter sunshine reflects my mood. Today we'll encounter no dodgy people, get into no trouble and be sure to telephone Shanks at least once.

We see dodgy people everywhere; but they're part of the show. Down Oxford Street spivs with open suitcases negotiate furtively while lookout men lounge around not reading newspapers. Piccadilly Circus teems with young and not so young single women also apparently minding their own business; but it's a hell of a business they're minding. "The Piccadilly Commandos," I say to Connie.

"Oh, really? Anyone you know, Clement?"

"One or two," I murmur, looking around. They both yank my arms at the same time. Pulled apart, I stumble and nearly end up on the pavement, dragging them round me. We stand rocking in a miniature scrum and I burst out laughing. We all do. I haven't laughed so much since the evening of the card game and the discovery that's gripped my life. It leaves me thoughtful for a few minutes as we head back up Regent Street. How would it have turned out with Fernleaf if everything had been normal? Would she have hung on till Christmas, then headed for London? Would Mackinnon ever have found himself suddenly in a dark valley with no exits?

We enter a Post Office and despatch telegrams to Nairobi and Arrowtown, where the old year is just ending in the night, then board a bus to the Tower of London. A lot to see, glancing at centuries from the top deck. On Tower Hill we join a crowd watching a docker stripped to the waist escaping from padlocked chains, gasping and cheering ironically at his non-stop patter as he overdoes his struggles.

For his last trick he takes a length of chain – twenty-two yards, laids 'n' gentlemen! – and swallows it in rasping gulps. Then he walks round inviting us to squeeze the growth that's suddenly bulged out of his side – feel the links, can yer? – before hauling it out with even more alarming spasms. The drink that habitually betrays him at the dock gate dulls his senses enough to perform for more money than he loses in a non-working day. People, not buildings, are the sights for me now. No more 'who built that and what went on there?' but 'who does he go home to after a day like this? Where does that girl take her clients? How long since she turned up at some London station never expecting to see so much of London's pavements? Or ceilings?'

At lunchtime in Lyons Corner House I watch a different set of people. A few uniforms, a couple of assignations and a bunch of middle-agers trying to pretend it's still 1937. We get glances, and for me it's alms for the trick of basking in the company of two attractive women, whose table manners are perfect, whose talk is a mixture of stuff that only our cousins from the Dominions can put together without pretension. I can just see them both in corduroys and check shirts, collars open, riding around on equal terms with whatever they call cowboys, pitching in when extra hands are needed. None of your lady-of-the-manor gentility and forelock-tugging-to-avert-your-lustful-gaze playacting that still goes on in the shires, new Socialist era or not.

Another bus and a stroll across Kensington Gardens, past the Round Pond and nannies with prams sitting and chatting, watching children sailing their model yachts in the light sunny breeze. But the carefree air is dissolving. We're approaching McFee's home ground.

Connie and Fernleaf put together a cover story by which we might introduce McFee into our talk with Mitch Gascoigne, but it worries me. "No cover stories, please. Shanks had one for when we went to that caff to check on the nightwatchman. It was childish. Let's just play it by ear. Trust me."

A little bell tinkles when we enter and we find ourselves in a small lobby formed by heavy curtains that hang to the floor. It darkens and deadens our voices. There's a curious musky smell. No one appears. "Like the entrance to an opium den," I murmur.

"How do you know?" asks Connie in a voice that blends with our surroundings. The atmosphere's close, warm, intimate; her perfume too mingles with the scent of mystery. My back tingles and a distant buzzing fills my head. Upstairs lives the man who's the real reason for us being here; a man we haven't seen for days, up to his own schemes, playing his own game. But I'm glad we've come.

"A film I saw. Peter Lorre's this oriental detective, always in and out of opium dens. Hang on, someone's there."

The curtains part and a small boy and girl appear. They look like twins, both dressed in identical grey coats with bottle-green collars, both with fresh, delightful little faces. As they pass, the girl puts out her tongue at me and crosses her eyes. I sympathise. Having your picture taken at six years old is a trial inflicted by adults who wait fifteen years before reminding you of it in front of an invited audience. I'm about to make a face back when their mother looms up. As my features quick-change to a smile the boy sticks his tongue out too.

"Lovely," I say as they sweep out. The little bell jumps around over the door.

Mitch Gascoigne's tired eyes light up when he sees Constance Maybury. It's been a trying day. It cuts both ways, this portrait business. "Can I help you?" he says in a soft, velvety tone. He has silvery hair that goes back in ripples, and a beaky nose, and he seems quite brown for a man who lives in studios and darkrooms.

"We came yesterday," she says. He knows already. She's impossible to forget.

"Ah, yes. This serious young lady sat for me. I have the prints ready; won't you come through?"

We enter a larger space formed by more hangings and sit on plain bentwood chairs. Gascoigne disappears. "Wait there," I whisper and step back through the fabrics and out onto the street. The bell tinkles again as I look quickly into his window.

I was right. Wilf's picture has gone. I peer more closely. A youth in a herringbone jacket has replaced the airman; Wilfred Gascoigne the younger, in a happier time. I slide back into my seat and meet their puzzled gaze just as the photographer reappears. He says, "Excuse me, won't you?", goes out past us and comes back with an equally puzzled look. It disappears when he shows us Fernleaf's pictures.

"Well, then; here they are. Exquisite, wouldn't you agree?"

I do, out loud. He's got her just right. She's beautiful. Everything I know about you, in the angle and play of light on your face, in your eyes turning away but still speaking to me. This man knows his trade.

"I'd like one, for myself. If that's all right." I'm going to keep it by my bed, or wherever my travels take me.

"Only if I can have one of you," says Fernleaf. It sounds very sweet, but actually part of the game, to keep us in there, to get talking.

"Would that be possible, Mr Gascoigne?" asks Connie.

Mitch is a man and he's still breathing. The next appointment will have to wait.

I'm asked to sit on a bench with a pearly-sky background in front of a half-plate camera next to a side table covered in glove puppets of clowns, jesters, monkeys and big-eyed birds. It's going to take more than him waving a floppy bird to make me smile because I'm going for the distinguished look; but Gascoigne has enough patience to get me meeting him half-way on a sardonic lip-curl borrowed from Clark Gable with a nod towards Robert Taylor. At last we're there and the shutter gives a double-jointed click.

Here goes. "We mustn't forget a copy for Mr McFee, must we?"

Mitch Gascoigne turns with a look of surprise. "Are you acquainted with Mr McFee?"

"Yes," I answer. "He lives upstairs."

Their faces are a picture. Gascoigne's eyebrows rise and I plough on.

"Says he's lived here about eight years. That right?"

"About that, yes."

"Must've been bombed out of somewhere. He said he'd always lived in London."

He looks at Connie and she smiles back. We're not leaving for a while.

"No; the war hadn't started yet. It was a year before there was any real bombing. May, it was. He was quite desperate for lodgings, I remember. If he'd waited a few months he could have had his pick." He pulls a plate out of the camera.

"I suppose so. Good thing he doesn't have a family, eh?" I'm out on my own now. This is better than beating round the bush.

"Oh, he's not entirely alone. You will have to sit for me one day, Miss...?"

"Maybury."

"Ah, yes, of course. Forgive me. Are you in London long?"

"No, Mr Gascoigne. You were saying, Clement?"

"Oh, I do beg your pardon. No, he's a solitary kind of man, I daresay, though you must know that already. He's never mentioned relatives from out of town. You are relatives?"

"Kind of. He's an honorary uncle. We'd love to meet any relatives he does have."

Another plate slides in. "No talking now. Keep that. Good; you're more relaxed. That's it. Let's try the same again. Good. Well done. Actually he does have a cousin who visits quite regularly; ever since he came here, in fact. A young woman. At least he says she's his cousin. Ha, ha."

"Ha, ha, yes. See what you mean. I hope there isn't too much family resemblance. He's no oil painting, is he?"

"How rude. There is, as it happens. But we shouldn't be discussing his affairs, so to speak, should we?" His tone hardens. "I may be his landlord, but as a friend I really ought to be respecting his privacy. They should be ready middle of next week. And an extra copy of your portrait, Miss. And you, Miss Maybury; perhaps we can arrange a sitting? My card. Happy new year to you all."

We hurry to the end of the street.

"Look," I say, "they talk to each other. If he tells McFee we were digging around for facts in a roundabout way it'll look like what it is.

They're not daft. Better he reports a straight-out chat where we didn't try to hide the fact we knew him. Everything we said was normal. It was him filled it in for us. And now we need to get to a phone box."

"I agree," says Fernleaf.

"That will be our second call."

"You've come over all masterful all of a sudden."

"A loose end, that's all."

But I still have to borrow the four pennies from Connie. They watch me dial Whitehall 1212. When we're connected I breathe a sigh of relief and even forget I'm pressed against her.

"Mr Davies? Clement Garner. Remember? Are you alone? Listen, please. I know you said you couldn't help us anymore, but can I ask you one question? Is Mr McFee all right? Only we haven't seen...no, that wasn't the question...oh, right...no, it's this: you mentioned he still uses the same tea mug...uh, huh...got to keep something familiar... yes, I get that. It fell from the filing cabinet...yes...Mr Waterman says...yes...yes...really? And was that when he moved to here... er, Marylebone? Yes...yes...okay. Got that. Thanks, Mr Davies. Nice to hear you speaking normally on the phone. Yes, goodbye." I look at Connie. "Your call."

When we get outside again they wait for me to speak.

"He hasn't seen him in the flesh for days; just phone calls. But listen to this, and tell me what you think. For a long time his mates have thought he was a bit off-beam, right? In May 1939 it seems he was sitting in his office when a wodge of papers, plus his favourite china mug, fell off his file cabinet. Only according to Phil Waterman they actually flew right across the room. Got that? Flew. Next day he leaves perfectly respectable lodgings in Bermondsey. Got that too? Bermondsey is where the Smallwoods lived; and in a great hurry rents a couple of rooms above Gascoigne's shop."

They nod, following every word.

"All this is exactly twenty years after Albert Smallwood volunteered for North Russia and that's almost certainly when McFee started his affair with Alice. We know his daughter comes to see him, and not even Gascoigne knows who she is. I'm betting that's when the joint visits to Alice's grave started. But it's Albert's grave too. D'you see where I'm leading?"

"I think so," says Fernleaf. "He goes to confront Albert, ever since he started to feel him on his back. The spooky bit in his office was the opening shot. But he needs his daughter with him when he's at the grave. He needs her support. He needs to flaunt her to show he doesn't care. But he does care, doesn't he?"

"The safe jobs and the fingerprints made sure of that. After the diversion of the war McFee was in the doldrums. Just the moment for Smallwood to remind him he hadn't gone away; to let him know it's getting serious. It didn't start last month. It started exactly twenty years after McFee got off with Alice. Know what I think?"

"I'd love to know," says Connie, looking around. But no one on the street's paying us any attention. "Because right now I don't know the half of what you're talking about."

"Don't say it," mutters Fernleaf. "It's going to end twenty years from now?"

"God, I hope not. But what about twenty years after he was arrested? Or twenty years after he died in prison?"

"Oh, no. It's not on, Mackinnon. He'll have gone crazy by then!"

"Then I'll be in good company. What if it does take another twenty years?"

They both give me a look that deserves a better moment.

"Come on, Mackinnon," says Connie. "This isn't going to last any longer than our success in sorting it all out. And that's going to be soon."

"Please," I say. "I don't want you to find me in the loony bin on New Year's Eve 1967."

Chapter 23

There is a sound of revelry by night. Outside the portals of the Shawe-Trittons heavily muffled figures hurry along the pavements. The whole of London gravitates towards venues where they will exchange the past for a more hopeful future.

A small band of early arrivals puts down its markers. Amelia strides to the door every few minutes to admit more, to stare at them as they hoot 'Happy New Year!' and answer, 'Yes; you too.'' She's wearing an especially colourful grey comb in her hair.

Dorsey's on the radiogram, then the Hot Club of France; then more variety, more sound as people put their own records on. A second gramophone's brought in and the party splits among the rooms according to listening tastes. At last the pianists get going in the drawing room and the gathering splits again, until the growing throng of arrivals fills the spaces and murmur with music becomes hubbub with laughter. Every now and then Damietta's voice soars above all the chatter like a flock of birds rising from a lake.

I circulate. My hair's parted, just a dab of Brylcreem, and my hand grips a glass of ginger beer. Resplendent in a change of collar and borrowed tie I pick at the cold buffet. To almost everyone here the memory of a priviledged pre-war past gives austerity parties a fascination all their own. But behind the thin punch stand bottles from a cellar whose only lack was not to have been added to in six years. Never mind, says George; this year's vintage throughout wounded Europe is one of the best ever. And Amelia guards the bottles as she guarded me. All in all, I'm happy enough.

Shanks is happy too. He's getting along fine with Constance, and she with him. Anyone who tries to cut in on them soon sees which way the wind's blowing and leaves them to it. I take it on myself to head off the thicker-skinned types by showing them my conversation piece: a hilariously misspelt telegram from my people in Nairobi. They laugh politely and move away. Punch replaces ginger beer in my glass and soon I'm giving Connie big winks behind Shanks's back. She smiles over his shoulder; stolen smiles just for me. Ah.

The voices grow louder. Whiteman, Crosby, Miller can be heard coming up for air. Then I start noticing the people, their groupings and patterns, and suddenly they stand out like one of those pictures hidden among dots. Running like a colour through tartan are the set that used to meet at Inglefield during the war. I recognise them with awful clarity. The scientists, intelligence and propaganda boffs chatting on the lawns; sitting in twos and threes in the sunk garden, met suddenly and going quiet on woodland paths; their laughter echoing down to the kitchen where I ate alone. Playing Indians while they wrestled to wage a secret war.

Now I know I never saw George Shawe-Tritton there, ever. Yet they're all here, all of them, the ones that never visit Jackson Armitage anymore; all here in George's camp.

And I think of Shanks sitting with Connie a few feet from the bundles of papers that have secretly strangled his life's work.

Glasses clink; laughter erupts and dies, and the cigarette smoke gets thicker and thicker. There's one character who insists on reciting chunks of ITMA sketches to anyone who'll listen, but apart from him everyone seems to have found everyone else. Suddenly I'm alone.

I sidle up to the pair in the library.

"Swell party!"

"What's in that glass, Clement?" says Shanks.

"My usual poison. Where's Fernleaf?"

"She's upstairs," says Connie. "Resting, or she'll be dead on her feet come midnight. Would you like her to come down?"

"Oh, whenever you like."

"Fernleaf, eh?" Shanks's eyes narrow. "I think certain aspects of your suavity and nonchalance are somewhat under-rehearsed."

"Really? Which ones?"

"All of them. A little mature company might help."

Connie smiles at us and leaves the room. We both watch her go. A long sigh escapes my lips. Shanks turns to me. He's wearing a dinner jacket, bowtie; the full fig.

"You didn't bring that rig with you, did you?" I say, drawling just a bit.

His eyebrows shoot up. "No, my boy, I did not. Nor is it one of George's, as you might determine from a comparison of our physiques. I keep this rig – as you call it – here permanently. This, for better or worse, is my London base. When you have finished your drink kindly return to ginger ale. By the way, have you given further thought to our conversation earlier today?"

I haven't and I don't want to. "No. I'm sticking with what I said then. Wait for a seventh."

It's time for the first of many visits to the below-stairs toilet. Coming out I meet Connie at the foot of the stairs. "She'll be down in a minute," she breathes. My head swims. I take in a deep draught of the fragrance that enwraps her, reach out to touch her bare elbow and croak, "You've got class, Miss Maybury. Lot of class."

She bestows a smile on me that could cure a blind man and gives me another five seconds of how an elegant woman looks when she's walking away from you. I wait by the newel post, looking up the staircase. My mind's filled with music, mostly from *Gone with the Wind*.

But when Fernleaf appears at the top of the stairs I let out a gasp. She stands there in a long, slim dress that reaches to the ground. It's all black and grey in long twining spiral patterns; strange curves that hint at the figure underneath. Her arms are bare, right up to the shoulders. I've never seen her shoulders, well, not the whole lot. And her hair's up; I don't know how, but it shows all the pale contours of her face. Persephone, I say to myself; Persephone in the antique groves of Sicily.

A fine scarf of electric blue is wound lightly round her neck. Such an outfit could not be found anywhere but in her own desires, or be made by any hand but hers. I hold out my own hand as she descends the stairs, take hers and kiss it. My thoughts come from that strange unfamiliar stock that's been with me since I knew her. My life is running like well-oiled clockwork and I don't care why.

"I've never seen anything or anyone so bewitching. Thank you."

"Do you like it?"

I can only close my eyes and nod slowly. "It's all the things you are. Aren't your arms cold?"

"I don't feel the cold," she whispers. She's ridden, climbed, slept beneath the Southern Cross, fought villains in the slums; and she can look like this. I gaze into her calm grey eyes and draw intoxication from them.

"Will you take my arm?"

Together we walk into the throng.

They're all impressed and they all say so. But after a while the ritual's over and they turn back to their conversations. We are, after all, the youngest people here. So we explore. We move through them, untouched by their indifference, commenting on them and guying them; sipping unattended drinks and discovering couples in dark corners.

The hall clock chimes ten.

"Slow up, Mackinnon. I'm on in half an hour."

"On? On what?"

"On the piano. Got to do my party piece. It's what you get for learning the bloody thing."

"I haven't heard you practise."

"You weren't around. Let's find someone quiet and interesting."

"Right. Pity Mister Lo isn't about."

"The little Chinese bloke? I saw him in the drawing room earlier. He must have gone out for a while. Chinese New Year's all different, anyhow."

But we can't find him in any place. The quest leads us through a human landscape we haven't acknowledged first time round. More and more strangers come through the front door, bearing the scars of political cultures; some red, some black, some brown. There's a fine crop of exiles and adventurers tonight. We shake hands with an Albanian in the retinue of ex-King Zog, a Ukrainian couple who remind us of Alphonse and Ludmilla, an Argentinian anti-Peronist who claims he was a gaucho till Fernleaf starts talking about horses, and one or two characters whose look goes shifty when we mention Amelia's background. She moves silently among the people, taking their empty glasses, eyeing some of them as if she would happily refill the glasses with their blood. But for many already the wine's in and the wit's out. We home in on a loud couple entertaining some poor beggar with amusing tales.

"It's that shiker you had a disagreement with; here, the other night; remember?"

"Yes, perfect."

"Is it?"

"Oh, yes. They've got Mister Lo. Let's listen in."

There's an abuse of conversation that's much smaller than the smallest talk.

"My God, well! By now he was completely plastered! Falling about all over the place!" The traveller and author in a small way stands impassively by the fire, a head shorter than the others. He listens patiently to long accounts concerning the exploits of gilded youth that can't hold its drink, and permits himself short responses:

"Ah, yes. Liquor is a great leveller. All drunks become the same, do they not?"

"Mmh. Quentin, tell him about Lossie Chessell. The time he fell in the Cam when he was pissed!"

Quentin tells Mister Lo about when Lossie Chessell was pissed and fell in the Cam. The firelight dances in the traveller's spectacles:

"Ah, yes. I too recall an incident on a river involving a certain amount of drunken excess. In Sinkiang the warlord Sheng Shih-ts'ai..."

"Shitsy eye? Ha, ha!"

"Not quite. After an evening of carousing one of his officers ordered his men to fire on a ferry-boat on the Kum Darya river. Many hundreds were drowned. For amusement, naturally."

"Well, yes. I used to smuggle the odd bottle into school myself. Kept getting expelled for it."

I catch Mister Lo's eye, then Fernleaf's. She looks straight at Violet.

"How many schools was that?"

"Oh, about fourteen. They couldn't handle me."

"Sounds like it was the other way round. They expelled you? Or did you write to mummy to take you away?"

"No! I was a rebel, that's all."

"Rebel? Anybody who tells you they're a rebel generally isn't. Just a pain in the backside. It's like stupid old bags who say 'I'm quite mad, you know.' They're not."

The wine hasn't equipped our two friends for quick clever answers.

"Mister Lo, hallo again," I say. "Have you been introduced? This is Quentin and Violet. Tell them about some real rebels you've met."

He gives the merest smile. "I would be happy to. But such persons were also, as you put it, pains in the backside. Burning down villages, murdering, raping, extorting. And having the occasional midnight feast, I dare say."

"Right," says Fernleaf, "and I bet they didn't hand their homework in on time, either. See you, Quent. See you, Vi." And she leads Mister Lo by the arm to the library. His struggles are imperceptible. Soon we're standing by the bookshelves, away from most of the crowd, but not so far from the fire. "Thank you," he says, bowing. "You are Berenice. A delightful name. It is in the stars. Our constellations are different, of course. I must say that of all the young women here you are by appearance the most delightful. Are you comfortable here?"

"Let's hunker down," she answers, and her body in its long enchantress dress flows into a kneeling position, where the flames make swirly reflections on the silky material and on her fair skin.

Mister Lo tells us traveller's tales, but only in answers to our questions. He's crossed the Gobi desert in a camel caravan, spied on the Japanese in Manchuria and Korea, and on the Russians while living among the nomads of Mongolia. Both the Communists and the Kuomintang have put a price on his head because of his war reporting. His whole life reeks of adventure.

"I am sorry to say that China is too hot for me at the present time. Who knows what will happen? But fortune led me to the presence of a far greater man. How different he is; he commands no armies, but wins victories all the same."

"Who's that?"

"Gandhi. On my way through India I was able to meet and speak with him."

"You've met Gandhi?"

"Yes, Clement. And Nehru, and Jinnah. But what can I say about this? How can I describe the great things I have witnessed?"

As we talk I realise that Mister Lo would cause a riot in the Monk's Hill staffroom. To most of my teachers Gandhi is a tricky little troublemaking lawyer who's somehow made monkeys out of us in India. A monster in specs. I listened to them. Now I think I might not. "What will happen to India?" I ask.

"It is a time of blood," says Mister Lo after a pause. "And Gandhi himself will not be spared. The Chinese are great gamblers but I am not. If I were, I would not wager on the Mahatma being alive much more than a month from now. One of his own will surely strike him down."

The punch has cleared from my senses. We're both silent; a little enclave of seriousness amid the festivities. I look at my watch. The piano recital's overdue and I want a good place to stand. "Excuse me," I say, and go to take a leak.

Amelia's at the door taking the hat, coat and scarf from a man. I wait to see who would come so late in the evening, and whether they've brought their drink inside them. But their conversation's in low tones and his back's to me. A squat man with a thickish neck accentuated by a short haircut; a man in a dinner jacket. Only Shanks so far is wearing one. As he turns he mutters a word to Amelia, who responds with a tight smile.

It's Hayden McFee.

What's he doing here?

The Shawe-Trittons don't know he exists, and Shanks wouldn't dare have him anywhere near the place. I walk up to him. He certainly looks different, smart almost. The jacket and wing-collar are more formal than Shanks's rig and he isn't at home in them. The haircut too is a long way from his usual style; but he has a certain daft dignity, like those politicians you see in old newsreels.

"Mr McFee! What brings you here?"

"Not so loud, young man. Allow me to introduce myself. Doctor William Haycroft. Chair of Criminology at the University of Toronto, or Medicine Hat, or wherever. Got that? Long lost colleague of your uncle's."

"Do you have an invitation, Doctor?"

"No."

"A gatecrasher! What will certain people think?"

"Doesn't make much difference; I'm here, aren't I?" He sends a frown past me. "Tell me, why is young Berenice wearing fancy dress?"

I turn and watch her come towards me, her mouth open in surprise. My eyes are signalling: don't say anything.

"Fernleaf, allow me to introduce Doctor Haycroft, Professor of Crime at Toronto University. He tells me he's an old friend of your uncle's."

She smiles. "Are you gatecrashing, Doctor? Bit dangerous, isn't it?"

"Purely for my own amusement, young lady, but I shan't stay long. I'm on my way to another function. Just dropped in."

His short haircut makes his eyes look bigger, less friendly. Suddenly I'm afraid. My skin begins to tingle.

He knows.

He's found out we know his secret.

He's come to tell Shanks face to face, in front of his fiercest critics; in front of people who respect no secrets but their own.

As he lingers there a few revellers pass by, giving him odd stares. He doesn't look like a statesman anymore; he looks like a cinema manager. Amelia will tell George or Damietta that an unbidden visitor is here. They'll tell Shanks, and then we'll have an almighty...what?

The last time I saw this man I was hiding from him. I was cowering behind a gravestone. How does he know?

Gascoigne. Mitch Gascoigne's talked to him. He's a detective, for God's sake. Putting two and two together is child's play. I don't want it to be here, not tonight. There'll be remains splattered everywhere; more than enough for Shanks's enemies to feast on.

"I must say I like your fancy dress. Makes you look older, more sophisticated. That design; Maori, is it?" says The Man I Hid From.

"It isn't fancy dress, but you're right otherwise. Have you been in this country long, Doctor?"

Something's telling me we can do without this banter, but McFee's smiling like a large happy cat. "A little while. I find it most interesting." He lifts a glass from the tray of the passing Amelia but their eyes don't meet. Fernleaf has a dangerous little grin on her face.

"Do you have any family, Doctor?"

My bladder spasms. I walk swiftly to the toilet below the stairs, and pray to the tiled wall that she hasn't blown us away. I'm really frightened of him now. Frightened because he's escaped from under our microscope. Why else is he here? I begin to shake and my skin feels cold and clammy. Him hiding secrets? What about me? Am I dealing straight with anyone except Fernleaf? We've committed crimes in the past few days. There's an old lady out there who might have lost her last few marbles completely because of me. There's a solitary, tireless seeker for a new wisdom in here, the guest of those who have betrayed him. The mess in my mind and body come together and I throw up.

For a long time I lean like a flying buttress against the tiles, gasping and gulping. Small framed photos of rich jolly people at Ascot and the Eton v. Harrow cricket match ignore me.

I glower at them. You save or discard your fellow men like toffee papers.

Ah, you villains.

The house has gone quiet. I follow the hum of distant chatter to the drawing room. No chance of a good place now, and the Shawe-Trittons' chairs aren't for standing on. There's only one way. I push politely but firmly through the crowd; "Excuse me. Page-turner."

She's already seated at the grand piano. It feels very exposed. "Would you like me to turn the pages for you?" I say quietly. "I'll know when if you nod."

"I'll be all right, thank you, Caveman." We exchange a smile and I find the perfect spot from where I can see Shanks, McFee and her all at once. There's still a foul taste in my mouth, but as the murmuring dies down a few things sort themselves out in my mind.

A sense of proportion, to begin with. To the rest of them we're children. I'm a schoolboy; she a girl in a dress she's run up herself, about to show how she's profited from her piano lessons. Why should any of them – apart from Connie – think that we even want to delve beneath the surface of things? And as for keeping secrets from others, John Davies and Connie at least are doing just that, for the best of motives. So relax a little. You don't want to miss this.

I watch her as she takes a deep breath. Her serious grey eyes are something I can be sure of. The music might not interest me very much; this kind of music never has. But her face: the compass that steers me through all storms. Fernleaf and Mackinnon. Let 'em all come.

She begins to play. Quiet and slow, single notes and chords. For her, the room might be empty and her listeners have no existence. My gaze drifts from her to the non-existent figures ranged in the soft glow of the wall-lamps. Most of the men are standing, all of the women sitting. Smoke from cigarettes, pipes and cigars hangs in the air. A far-away expression is in their eyes as though the pianist in the enchanting dress has cast a spell over them. I watch Jackson Armitage's features let go their look of annoyed surprise, though he still glances warily across the room to where McFee sits in a wing armchair; the same chair that Fernleaf and I shared that night in the library. Is this chance? Has Albert Smallwood led him here?

I put this thought from my mind. Hayden McFee is resting there, that's all; his eyes half-closed, his hands in his lap clutching a dying pipe. In his formal black he reposes against the colourful, casually dressed backcloth of listeners like an old-time African chief in European clothes sitting for a photograph.

Other faces: Connie Maybury, Amelia, the Shawe-Trittons; Mister Lo. He's used to a different music. He's heard concubines playing their one-string melodies in Chinese pavilions, a world almost too different to imagine.

And again I come up short to ask how I can even think like this and how much a stranger to my old self I've become; to wonder what – or who – is the cause of it. The rest of the room is polite. They listen. But only Mister Lo hears what she's really playing. Increasingly I confine my attention to the girl in the swirling patterns and to the modest explorer, and I almost begin to hear the real music too. It sounds deceptively simple, full of measured silences, and it flows over me like a refreshing stream.

A ripple of applause brings me back. Fernleaf comes over, brushing past hands and words of praise. I want to thank her but she puts her fingers on my lips. "No need to say anything," she whispers. "Satie, by the way."

"Huh?"

"The composer."

Fair enough. Never heard of him. I wouldn't say no to hearing more, though. So long as it's played by her, in a remote pavilion of our own.

We watch the detective cross the room and shake hands with Jackson and Connie.

"Look at that," I murmur. "McFee doesn't know that we know and Shanks doesn't know that we know and neither of them knows about the other and Connie only knows the half of it. A fine tangle."

"What a tangled web we weave."

"Mmm?"

"When first we practise to deceive."

"That's good. Why do you know all the quotes?"

"Can't remember. Let's go and talk to him. You didn't stick around the first time."

"Don't remind me. We'll have to call him whatever he said in front of Connie."

"Oh, I'll be careful."

"No questions about family, I hope."

"I meant to do that. It was you nearly blew it by rushing off."

"Yes, to avoid an embarrassing incident."

"So funny. No, I did it to see his face, but his face did nothing. D'you think I took a risk?"

"No more than I've grown to expect. I was sick as a dog."

She laughs and ruffles my hair, then goes after McFee who is now circulating. In the old days he'd have had his eye on half of this lot, but he's smiling, joking, enjoying himself.

"Swell party, eh, Doctor?"

"Oh, rather," he beams. "But I'm afraid I must be leaving shortly."

"Your other function? You'll need to hurry; it's twenty-five to midnight."

"Ah, it's not a New Year do, you know."

"What else could it be?"

He leans forward and whispers: "My birthday."

"What, today?"

"Tonight. In thirteen minutes' time, according to my dear late mother."

"You're kidding!"

"Then so was she. And now I must say goodbye. Excuse me."

"A good time to be born if you want to fit in anywhere and nowhere," says Fernleaf. I hope we meet again, Doctor Haycroft." She turns to see Damietta waving her over to meet a few admirers, so McFee and I walk to the door alone and I help him on with his coat. He adjusts his white scarf, pulls on his gloves and takes the black fedora from the hallstand. I've never seen him with anything but a bowler hat before.

Outside under the portico the night air is frosting the railings and laying a sheen on the empty pavements. The street is quiet. The whole city waits for the midnight stroke. He starts filling his pipe, clearly in no hurry.

"There's one thing's been intriguing me lately," he says.

My heart misses a beat. "What's that?"

His tone is calm; like when you start questioning a suspect. "When we called in on Manny last Sunday we came through Bethnal Green station."

"Yes, we did." Thank God. Thank God it's not the other thing.

He strikes a match. Clouds of smoke curl upwards, a sharp aroma in the sharp air.

"Did you pick up anything there, at the station? On the stairs?"

"No. Nothing. Why?" Too late, I remember why maybe I should have.

For a few seconds his eyes bore through me out of the veil of blue smoke.

"There was an incident there in '43. An air raid warning. Someone stumbled on the steps as they were rushing down to shelter. People had got a bit slack because the big raids had been over for a while, so there wasn't the usual calm. Over a hundred people were crushed to death. I'm surprised you didn't sense anything, that's all. All those deaths, only a few years ago."

He steps down. "Don't stay out here. Go and be with your girl. She's some girl."

"Yes, she is. Goodnight, Mr McFee. Happy New Year. Happy birthday."

He walks away, the familiar echo of his heelcaps on the deserted pavement.

I have a dream about Hayden McFee that night. In my dream he walks alone from South Kensington, past all the festive houses, past the change of the year, down to Chelsea Creek, and lets himself into the little printing works with a skeleton key. And I dream that he sits in the dark and the silence, his coat open, staring at the safe through the shafts of moonlight while the hours pass; daring his quarry to appear to him; willing the dead peterman to show himself. The dream is so strong and so real that when I wake in the early dawn of the year I believe it to be true. I never find out if he did or not. He's a strange man and we live in a strange time. I wouldn't be surprised.

They're filling glasses when I get back. The wireless is warming up.

No one's sorry to say farewell to 1947. After the storm of war the steady, increasing drizzle of austerity. Bright moments and longer, darker hours. There are millions of children younger than me whose childhood has been shot to ribbons, caught up in struggles that weren't their business. In some ridiculous, trivial way I share that with them. I grip Fernleaf's hand till it nearly hurts. The first chimes of Big Ben ring out and a hush falls over us.

BONG.

We all cheer, drink, kiss. We look into each other's eyes and her lips touch my cheek.

Then we sing *Auld Lang Syne* in eight languages at once, as if it's the anthem of the whole world.

In the Territorial Army drill hall at the Kentish Town end of Prince of Wales Road, Staff-Sergeant Tom Cronin looks for his beer glass. He's left it somewhere, and the lads and their wives and sweethearts are filling up to see the New Year in. Then he remembers, and starts walking down the corridor that smells of paraffin heaters, linoleum and cigarette ash, towards the office. He's got about half a minute. He puts his hand to the doorknob.

There's a deafening bang and crash.

He staggers backwards, then rushes in. The room's full of smoke; smoke and an explosive stench he knows well. The door of the safe is still swinging back from its impact with the wall.

Tom Cronin has the place to himself for a few seconds before his comrades join him. In those few seconds in the billowing fumes, he realises that the other sound he heard was a human scream.

He's a brave man, a man who has done his duty. He takes in the fact of the safe and of the otherwise empty room. What he finds harder to accept is the mess on the opposite wall, under the framed photo of the King, where bits of skin and flesh and embedded teeth are slithering down through gobbets of blood, while a large piece of a man's tongue slowly detaches itself and falls like a fat red slug to the floor.

Chapter 24

The black Lanchester stands at the kerbside as we come round the corner. The rain is hammering down, a strange sudden rain. We close up our umbrellas and get in. No one speaks.

Hayden McFee eases her out and drives north, then east towards Hyde Park Corner where the brooding caped figures on the Artillery Memorial watch us pass. Swinging past Apsley House he again points north, to Marble Arch and Oxford Street.

Nobody mentions last night's strange visit. That too has taken on the quality of a dream. The windscreen streams and the wiper motor whines as the blade squeaks from side to side.

Our breath and our warm wet coats steam up the glass, so Shanks rubs with his gloved hand to produce a decent field of vision. Camden Town slips behind us and after a few minutes McFee brings the car to a halt. The whole journey has passed in silence. He half turns in his seat to speak to us. He looks haggard from too little sleep. We've all had too little sleep.

"Phil Waterman is in charge of this one; nobody else. He's done enough to check that Smallwood's dabs are on it. We're passing it off as high security because it's a military installation, right? The man who made the discovery is at home getting over the shock and we can't see him, more's the pity. Is something the matter, Miss?"

His tone is sharp and cold; a different man from only eight hours ago.

"No, not really," she answers quickly.

"Wondering where John Davies is?"

She nods. I gasp, and bury it in a cough.

He lets out a long breath. "Right. Get this straight. This one is different. Quite apart from what Mr Cronin thinks he saw, the fact is that Smallwood chose to have forty-six witnesses to his latest stunt. Now we can keep the security blanket on and blame a few terrorists. We can do that. But we can't stop ordinary people talking about fresh blood and bits on the wall belonging to someone who wasn't there. This case needs an experienced man; Sergeant Waterman is it and John Davies isn't. Also he's an ex-soldier so he'll get on better with the CO. We're going to play this one straight. No bloody play-acting. Mister Garner here will be introduced as a psychic, which is what he's damn well supposed to be."

Our talk on the steps is still fresh in my mind. If I don't get something out of this there'll be few other chances; maybe none.

Two men greet us in the drill hall. One is straight-backed, with a toothbrush moustache and the sort of regimental tie some of my teachers wear. The other is tall, loose-limbed, clean-shaven and wearing a tweed suit and jumper. The second man steps forward and shakes hands with Shanks and McFee.

"Major Norton. Jolly pleased to see you. This is the medium, is it? They're turning them out young these days. Hope he knows what he's doing. Mind you, I saw some strange goings-on in India from types half his age. I'll be frank with you; I can't make this out. I like an enemy you can see. Come to the Sergeants' Mess and I'll put you in the picture."

We troop into a dismal room with lino and green and cream walls. Even the King and Queen don't seem too happy to have to look at it every day. There's a tiny tiled fireplace and shiny brown armchairs that remind me of McFee's place. It smells of dog-ends and stale beer and it's cold. A few tatty paper chains hang around. I hope the Sergeants are a cheerful lot.

Major Norton acts throughout as though Fernleaf is invisible. She isn't supposed to be there, so she isn't there. But he can't hide the fact that he's a worried man. Before attacking the problem, he lays a smoke-screen.

"Soon as I saw Sergeant Waterman and his tie, I was onto him. 'Rajputana Rifles?' I said. And he answered, quick as you like, 'Hodson's Horse?' just from seeing the knot on mine. That's observation; I like that. So we've been telling each other lies about our Indian Army days while we waited. Great times. Shall I brief them, Phil?"

Phil Waterman nods. He looks like he's been listening all morning. Major Norton rattles on and slowly comes to the point while we sit in silence. Much of the time I don't listen at all. My mind keeps going over recent events.

Why can't I just let things go? Whenever the bouts of clear thinking sweep away the fog it closes in again. The same riddles reappear in different forms.

We're all tired. Even Phil Waterman, serious and professional, is weary from protecting his boss. This isn't his only work. Everyone's worn down. The answer must come soon.

"…By the time I got there poor old Tom was flat on the floor. He couldn't have been the worse for wear because he never is; very moderate drinker. We got onto you chaps straight away of course. I must admit we thought it was a bomb; the Paddies up to their tricks again. We had a few alerts in the '39 scare; tip-offs that they'd have a crack at the armoury. That was my first thought anyway; a bomb. But even I could see there wasn't a scratch anywhere. The window was intact. Glass was cracked, that's all, but it may have been already. It's got bars, by the way. I wasn't here in '39 of course. North-West Frontier."

Suddenly he leans forwards. It startles me. His eyes have grown wide.

"It was when he came round that we realised what had hit him. He started babbling. We had to calm him down. Kept going on about bits of a man's face plastered on the wall. We looked, of course. Nothing there, naturally."

He sinks back. "Tom had a hard time in the war. This may have triggered off a particularly nasty memory. That's all I can think of. I've been on the blower to his wife. She says he's still pretty groggy."

"Did Mr Cronin see much active service?" asks Shanks.

"Oh, rather; the whole lot. Western Desert, Greece, Crete, Italy. Wounded twice."

"And he must have seen people being blown up?"

"I'd be surprised if he didn't."

"Then I'm inclined to agree with your conclusion."

"Seems to be the thing, doesn't it?"

"Tell me, Major, were all those present here last night reliable people?"

"Absolutely. Well, a few girlfriends who aren't following the drum, so to speak. Sergeant Waterman advised me to let no one leave till he got here."

"That's correct, sir," says Phil Waterman. "I took brief statements, then addressed everyone on the need for total secrecy."

"How long do you expect that secrecy to be upheld?" asks McFee.

"Twenty-four hours at most," answers Waterman. "Don't get me wrong, Major. Twenty-four hours argues considerable self-restraint in such a large group."

"Thank you," says McFee, not an entirely happy man, but surely not surprised. "Better let our young fellow here have a look at the room."

"Of course," says the Major, rising. "I'm not squeamish myself, but if there's anything to what Tom said it would leave you thinking, eh?" He does not mention fingerprints because Phil Waterman has not told him, or anyone who was here. "I suppose a medium's the only thing for it. Clear the matter up." He gives the medium an encouraging, puzzled smile.

As we step out into the corridor I become very wary. Through a window to my left I see the rain has stopped. Great lumpy clouds almost cover the sky. Yet the passage is dark. I peer down it, but I can't see the end. It's as though the dark has swallowed the light that we're standing in. The rest of them are behind me, and I know Fernleaf is there; or is she? I have to walk. There's no choice.

I can hear the motley scuffle of footsteps as I move forward. The passage grows longer, the steps louder. They begin to merge into one pace, one measured tread. The sides of the passage crowd in. Seconds pass, and the darkness stretches away from me.

Crash, crash, crash. Behind me the feet mark time and leave me to stumble forward, my hands feeling along the walls. Every inch of my skin is electric with terror. Now I'm no longer moving. The walls slide past me and a door appears to my right, a prison door with bolts and a little square window, gliding like the door of a railway wagon coming to rest. As my hand touches it, almost sticking to the metal with its sweat of fear, the light returns and the men appear at my back. I find myself leaning for support against a plain panelled wooden door, gasping for breath. No one asks how I'm feeling. We've merely gone a few steps and the medium is obviously working himself up into the appropriate state.

Without turning round I say, "Please wait outside. I have to be in here on my own."

I know I don't want to be alone. But I turn the handle and enter, closing the door quietly behind me.

Here at last.

No one but me this time, with the seventh and last visitation that a dead man has made for the purpose of meeting a living one. I don't know how often Albert Smallwood has walked behind Hayden McFee or stood quietly at the foot of his bed. But I know he will leave no further messages.

As I stand there I feel all the strangeness of my recent life drop away. There is a wonderful aura of peace, of silence. This room is higher than it is wide; and so small. A neat little table and chair stand against a wall. A cabinet stands nearby. The paint is glossy bottle green to the dado and cream above. It is covered with tiny crazing.

My memories are falling away, emptying. I turn, slowly, smiling.

There is a sash window, barred and cracked, in the wall next to the safe. Sunlight streams through. The room fills with golden air. Motes of dust float lazily in the beams. I feel like a contented child, standing in that nursery light, and look at the blackened safe with delighted curiosity.

I could stay here forever.

The safe is so beautiful. I run my hand over its steel surface, then turn and brush the backs of my fingers across the opposite wall, across the crazed paint that is so bare, so old; old with the ancientness of the time just before you were born. The shafts of sunlight fall on the wall and warm it and glorify it, then very slowly fade.

And I touch something warm that is on the wall.

The hair on my neck rises. Hot waves crawl up my back and I want to pull my hand away. I begin to cry out because I know what's coming.

My shouts are trapped in me. Only rasping grunts, pain, hatred; mouth hanging loose, slobbering, howling.

Darkness. Peace.

I float without a body. But somewhere in this darkness the silence seems to expand and contract. It disturbs the sweet stillness and grows insistent.

My own heartbeat.

The dark dissoves in a silver mist; a world of light. Within it other lights move. The face of Berenice looks down on me.

"Hallo," I say. My voice sounds like an echo from far away.

She just watches me and I'm content to let her. The pillows are soft and deep and it doesn't smell like a hospital. I'm fine if I don't move.

"I know what happened. Just tell me what you saw."

She doesn't answer. Her eyes travel over my face.

"Please."

"You were just like that time at the church, only worse; louder. They tried to keep me from seeing. I wasn't allowed to hold you. It was bad, Mackinnon. It was horrible."

Her voice is flat. She sounds defeated.

"Jackson saw what was happening. They got you back in the car and back here straight away. Well, to round the corner anyway. That Major found it all very interesting; a medium having a fit. But he thought it would upset good order and discipline if it got out. Pin it on the Cronin bloke having a benny and drop the whole thing. We all thought the same." She takes my hand and squeezes it. It's cold up here in my room under the roof.

"You got me all the way up here? What did you tell them? Do they know how I got like this?"

"You were walking. All they know is you've had a turn. They don't suspect anything."

"But they're ghost experts. They'll have seen, I don't know, psychics taken over by it. They'll recognise the signs."

She strokes my brow. "Don't fret. You've been taken ill. Something you ate or drank last night. Walking in the rain just brought it on – right? Don't forget he's a doctor."

"What about Connie?"

"All sorted. Relax."

"McFee?"

"Pretty lemony, I'd say. It's obvious something happened back there, but there's no talking to him. He just drove off." She bites her lip and frowns.

"Jackson wants to drop the case. He's worried about you."

"Is he? This isn't the first bloody time it's happened. Didn't worry him before when he was all fired up."

"Not fair, Mackinnon. He knows it isn't easy being a psychic. Anyway he feels responsible to your parents."

"Well, I can put his mind at rest there. Least of anyone's bloody worries."

"He wants to give up just the same."

I close my eyes against the whiteness of the ceiling. "Tell him he can't. I want this finished so maybe I can go back to being normal. Let him know what I think. What do you think?"

"I don't like what's happening to you either."

"Thanks, Fernleaf; I mean it. Get him up here, would you? Tell him I want a word."

When he comes he takes my pulse and lifts my eyelids.

"Berenice told me you want to drop it. Is that right?"

He shakes a thermometer and examines it. "Yes, my boy, it is. As your guardian I am responsible for your welfare and conduct. We cannot risk further occurrences."

If he takes my temperature I'll have to keep quiet for at least a minute. Mustn't lose the thread.

"There won't be any more occurrences."

"Even so. Take this."

"Hang on. What exactly did Mr Cronin say he saw last night?"

"He says he saw bits of flesh, bone, blood and part of a tongue on the wall."

"I didn't see those things, but I felt them. Before I, well...Know what I think?"

"No, Clement."

"I think that's what happened to Horace. His face got in the way of a safe job that went wrong. Lost most of his tongue. Left him unable to talk properly."

"Are you saying that this Horace is in some way connected with Albert Smallwood?"

302

"Maybe. Smallwood worked alone, for other people. Suppose Horace was one of a gang watching him blow a safe, only it didn't go off and he got impatient, so he went up to it even though Albert told him not to, and it blew up in his face?"

"And left him unable to speak properly?"

"Why not? And suppose it left him wanting to get back at Albert? The informer who shopped him; why shouldn't it be Horace?"

"An interesting speculation, Clement, but hardly conclusive."

I'm heaving myself up onto my elbows. We're not letting this one go.

"Look. The man on the phone who set Albert up; he was drunk, wasn't he? Or rather, he sounded drunk. See what I mean?"

Shanks does his surprised eyebrows routine. "Did he? Who told you that?"

I freeze. Nobody told me. John Davies told me. Behind the Doctor Fernleaf's eyes widen in alarm. "Nobody. It just came to me then, while we were talking. I sensed it. It came together in my mind. He sounds drunk when he talks, doesn't he?"

"How should I know, my boy? I've never met him."

"No, of course not." I sink back onto the pillows. It's like someone's pulled the plug.

He gives me a long look. "I have a phone call to make. Berenice, Clement needs to rest. Come with me please."

"Are you going to ring McFee?" I ask.

"Yes, if I can get hold of him. He seems rather elusive these days."

Fernleaf puts her hand on his arm. "I'd rather stay, if that's all right."

"As you like." He strides out and I'm filled once again with my own stupidity.

"I'm sorry. I've really blown it this time."

"I don't know. Just rest. It'll happen as it's meant to happen." She takes my hand and I close my eyes but there's too much turmoil there in the dark. So I open them again and we wait in silence. Twenty minutes go by.

He comes in. We both search his face, so as to be prepared.

"That was a very fortuitous piece of psychic observation on your part, Clement." He sounds cynical, almost bitter. Having to go out to a phone box every time hasn't improved his temper. He's contacted McFee. McFee knows about our visit to the cemetery. He had John Davies followed to the meeting at Paddington. John Davies has admitted helping us. It can't get any worse. All this flashes by in an instant.

Shanks has taken a deep breath.

"McFee already knew."

My mouth goes dry. So that's it then. All over. Nothing left to say. Fernleaf speaks.

"How did he know?"

"He said he worked it out as soon as he heard what that Cronin fellow said he saw. It merely confirmed a number of suspicions he already had on the question of the informer. Or so he said."

My mind goes back to those unwitnessed five minutes with Danny Ogden in the Anderson shelter. He knew then; and he said nothing. Why? Does it matter anymore?

No.

No because it means he doesn't suspect me after all. He believes my story about sensing that the informer sounded drunk, because he's seen me having a genuine medium's fit, a psychic trance. And Shanks is ratty with McFee, not us. It's okay; we're in the clear. We're in the clear. I start laughing. I want to say something – any old thing – just to balance up that feeling of relief. Just before I splutter something that'll throw it all away he says:

"Do you feel all right, my boy?"

I'm unstoppable. "Oh, as well as can be expected!" Tears are running down my face.

He may be a doctor – a doctor who does people who are off their chumps – so the fact that I'm laughing at something funny obviously has nothing to do with humour.

"Clearly a hysterical reaction," he mutters. "Not uncommon. I fear his health has been affected more than he realises. George found him sleepwalking the other night."

I have a sudden choking fit. He slaps my back a few times. "What did you say?" I gasp.

"I said it appears you've been sleepwalking, my boy. It simply reinforces my view that for the sake of your wellbeing we should not continue with the case. Hmm?"

"When? I've never done that, ever."

"I would answer better if I could believe the other night's episode was the first."

Talk business. It's worked before. "Did the drill-hall job complete your circle?"

"Eh? Yes, it did, as a matter of fact."

"And the co-ordinates?"

He looks at Fernleaf. "She knows," I say.

"Mmm. No good at all. I'm afraid that theory no longer holds water."

"But do you agree that it was the seventh and last?"

"I hope so, Clement. The circle does seem complete. I trust we aren't about to go round a second time."

He's listening. Keep going.

"I never thought Smallwood would set us a complicated puzzle. But I do think we've been given all the clues we're going to get. Can we go for something more obvious?"

"Such as?"

"Such as your first idea. When we stood at the street corner after visiting the Dunkleys."

"But that was precisely when you referred to spiders."

"Forget spiders. You said it might be a decoding business after all."

"I remember. Street names!" He says, "Wait there!" and rushes out. We hear him galloping down the stairs.

"Well," says Fernleaf. "It does rather appear that we might continue with the case after all, my boy, eh, hmm?"

"Fernleaf, put your hand on mine."

"Like that? Three musketeers?"

"Promise: no more digging up secrets. Just the case. Just solving the puzzle. No more sweating every time we think they've rumbled us. We're all on the same side; okay with you?"

"You know it is. There's no more running around to do, anyway. We just forgot that we weren't alone in this. Kids, eh? We think the groaners are the waxworks and it's only us that move around."

"Deal, then?"

"All apples, Mackinnon. I'm through with it too."

We're sitting; me in bed, Fernleaf on the bed and Shanks in a chair, surrounded by a litter of bits of paper, each with seven names on it. We try alphabetical number codes, series, anagrams, mirror writing, anything that might make sense. Words sometimes emerge, but none of them appear in Shanks's gazetteer of London. After an hour he sighs, looks at his watch. "I have more calls to make," he says. We know his first enthusiasm is slipping away.

"We'll keep on," says Berenice.

"Make sure he rests," he answers.

I'm sure we're on the trail this time; but I'm tiring. Have we lost the skill of simplicity? Each time we try something clever or convoluted

I try to imagine Smallwood talking, reading, thinking. Not a well-educated man. He isn't setting us a Times crossword puzzle.

But then again, not educated in our sense. I ask myself what the final meeting will be all about. Who is it needs justice? Smallwood may have a score to settle with McFee. Horace may have a score to settle with Smallwood. Or is it the other way round? Which way is justice going?

Will understanding a simple man's notion of setting things to rights help us in the search?

Bangbang!

We jump. Like clockwork models out of control we scoop up bits of paper and shove them under my blankets. Heart pounding, I put on the old soldier and croak, "Come in."

It's George Shawe-Tritton with a tray. "Nice cup of tea for the invalid," he says, smiling, and puts a bone china cup and saucer on my bedside table. "And one for the visitor." He rests the tray with its fine teapot and jug and bowl on the tallboy and turns to Berenice. "Will you be mum? How is he?"

This is a nice gesture but I'm alert. I know from the safe downstairs that behind his old duffer's exterior lurks a keen and ruthless mind. What's he really doing in here?

"Where's Amelia?" I'm almost missing her. Crazy, perhaps, but not devious.

"Her half-day off, old boy."

"Right. She's probably got people she needs to bump off."

"Beg pardon?"

"Thought she'd bunked off."

He looks around. Maybe he's surprised at how neat I keep it. He wouldn't be if he saw how much living space Monk's Hill gives me. If it were a wooden three-decker and me the lowest midshipman I'd get more room. No wonder I'm neat. He bends down.

"What's this?"

It's a piece of paper not quite under my bed. Letters, numbers all jumbled; and the names of seven London streets.

It's just one damn thing after the other. For crying out loud.

"Word puzzles, to pass the time," says Fernleaf quickly, reaching for the paper.

He holds it away from her. "Do explain, my dear. I'm quite fond of word games."

"Well, you have to find hidden words, that's all."

"These are names of roads if I'm not mistaken."

"Yes. We picked them out of the gazetteer. Make a street name out of other names."

He looks at it intently. We hold our breath.

"Did Jackson set this one? He's a dab hand at this kind of thing, you know."

"Yes, he did."

"Got anywhere?"

"No, not yet," she says, still politely holding out her hand. But George continues to peer at it. I want him to shove off.

"Tea's getting cold."

He ignores me.

"This reminds me," he says at last, "of a little game we used to play in 1940."

"Oh, yes? What was it called?"

"1940."

"Yes, but what was it called?"

"1940. That's what it was called. Got another piece of paper? And a pencil?"

Fernleaf pretends to hunt around. Finally he sits on the edge of the bed while I pray he doesn't feel or hear the bits under the blanket, and licks the pencil point. He writes something, holds it away from him, grunts and lays it down so we can both see it.

"There. Sort that lot out!"

We look. Four names and two words. The names are those of Allied and Axis leaders in early 1940, during the Phoney War. Above them the title. It looks like this:

```
1 9 4 0
M U S S O L I N I
H I T L E R
C H A M B E R L A I N
D A L A D I E R
W H I C H
W I N S ?
```

It makes no apparent sense. "We'll give it a go," I say. "Let you know how we get on. Thanks." He doesn't move. I can feel my leg going to sleep with the effort of not rustling all the litter that's in there with me. Fernleaf takes her cup and hands me mine.

"Aren't you going to try it?" says George. We both frown and look studious, but it's no good. Brains are worn out with doing stuff like this for half the afternoon.

"I give up."

"Me too."

"Feeble youths! Give me that; and a pencil. Now watch." He draws two lines down through the letters, like this:

```
1 9 4 0
M U S S O L I N I
H I T L E R
C H A M B E R L A I N
D A L A D I E R
W H I C H
W I N S ?
```

309

"There you are! What do you think of that? Stalin! Not far out, eh?" He looks thoughtful for a second. "Yes. We never thought when we sprang that on our friends at cosy little cocktail parties how true it would turn out to be. Uncle Joe certainly rules the roost over there now, eh? Still, not your worry, I suppose. Not yet, anyway. Hmm."

"Thanks," I say. "I'll try it out at school."

"Good. Drink your tea now. I'll see you later."

"Coincidence?" says Fernleaf when he's gone.

Half an hour later we're not so sure. We've tried something like this already. Our first goes with the street names in date order produce nonsense: MWPCCUP, IALOOPR, TPYLRCI, RPMDREN, EIPHARC and the rest.

"Maybe the meeting's supposed to be in Moscow after all," I tell her. "Or Belgrade, or Lhasa." We change the order, level up the letters backwards. Meaningless jumble every time. Outside it grows dark. We struggle on, but the idea that we can contact a dead peterman by means of word games begins to look threadbare. I've even forgotten this morning's horror in all the effort to make sense of it. Scribbling and frowning, we drift out of each other's presence. At last I put it away and yawn.

"Anything?"

"Not really. One last go, then I'm jacking it in."

"Mind if I doze?"

"Be my guest." It's not to be, though. Shanks barges in; we've forgotten him too. He looks none too happy.

"Damn their flapping ears! All this wandering about looking for a phone box that's free. Devil of a job to get hold of him when you manage it. The news gets worse."

"How do you mean?"

Fernleaf's too absorbed to listen.

"That Horace fellow. The one you and McFee had the same idea about. McFee can't have him picked up – you understand that – but all the same it would be useful to know his whereabouts."

"And?"

"He's vanished."

"Don't be too surprised. None of Danny's odd-job men stick around for long."

"Really? Well, it's worse than that. The young woman – Sal – seems to have gone too. Nowhere to be found."

Fernleaf looks up. "How do they know they're together?"

"Because before they left they set about Ogden in his hut and left him in a bad way."

"Both of them?"

"Apparently."

"Then," I say, "they can be picked up, surely. Assault and battery?"

"Not so, it seems. Ogden doesn't want the matter pursued. A private tiff, as he put it."

"You can't stop people going where they like."

"Perhaps, but from your description of them they'd hardly merge into the background."

"No," she says. "Horace would stick out a mile. Sal wouldn't."

"A striking blonde?"

"Suicide blonde."

He sighs. "Meaning what?"

"Meaning she isn't really blonde. Didn't you spot that, Mackinnon?"

"Well, you know… Fact is, they're out of it. So's Danny by all accounts."

"They're all on the drum, I reckon. What else is new, Uncle?"

"What else? Smallwood's sister is out of it too, I'm afraid. A very frail old lady, though not yet seventy. She's in a mental institution."

"Is she a lunatic?" The picture of her cowering as we exploded into her life is before me.

"I find such terms distasteful. Apparently she was recently re-admitted following an intrusion of her flat in broad daylight by a couple of thugs. She was literally frightened out of her wits."

"Poor old lady," I say, with feeling. The feeling's for me; disgust, mostly.

"Hmm. According to witnesses the fracas extended to a fight with two youths who were visiting the flats."

I begin to find breathing difficult. My throat goes dry. "Did they get a description?"

"Oh, yes. Several people got a good view of it. Why do you ask?"

"Um, she's on our list of people to see, if we can. Suppose the thugs were from Horace? Part of his revenge?"

Again he looks at me for a long time. Like someone watching me floundering before he strikes. "How do you know one of them was not Horace himself?"

"I don't, of course."

"Of course."

Fernleaf's been watching each of us like a spectator at tennis.

Say something. Anything.

"Well, that's it! I've tried everything."

"Still no luck?" Keep it going.

"No. I just stuck to the names; left out 'street' and 'road', then made anagrams out of the last letters and then the second to last letters. Not for the first time, by the way. But you never know if you've missed something."

312

Shanks's eyes are on her now; but so what? There's no steam in this little digression.

"And?"

"And nothing. Nearly got one. Been there before; close, but not good enough."

"What was that?"

"Rearrange the second to last letters and you get UNECORN. Frustrating, eh?"

"Yes," says Shanks. "A real pity. It would have been a curiously apt solution. The unicorn: symbolism and mystery. A creature of strange powers."

With a shout of 'Yes!' I throw back the blankets. A shower of bits of paper cascades onto the floor. They both start back in alarm and I grab the sheet from her hand.

"All that stuff about Danny Ogden reminds me. He said something about Smallwood writing letters in prison. And he said he couldn't spell. He was always getting words wrong! It is supposed to be 'unicorn'. Look it up. Go, on; look it up!" I'm trembling now for a different reason. Shanks leafs through the index on the gazetteer.

"There is one; only one: Unicorn Passage. Good Lord, Bermondsey. Wait there!"

"He's gone for the map."

"Yeah. That was close, Fernleaf; thanks. Do you think they know about us being at the flats? And maybe those two ratbags went back and really shook the old dear up, so it wasn't us. Too much to hope?"

"There's one thing he does know."

"What?"

"He knows I call you Mackinnon. Don't worry. If you're right about this it won't matter anymore."

Returning, Shanks unfolds the map on the bed. We all look, but it takes a while to find.

"There," he says." There. A dead-end by the Thames, off Tooley Street, near Tower Bridge. Very small; hard to see at first." Then his finger moves across the river and stops.

"My God. My God, look at this."

We lean closer, searching.

"See? Half a mile away, over the river. Mitre Street. Unicorn Passage points directly towards the place where his fingerprints first appeared."

He straightens up and lets out a long breath.

"So our moment comes. We have him at last."

Chapter 25

Now for the waiting. It isn't going to pass easily or quickly.

The Doctor gives me something to help me sleep, but that doesn't stop the peterman breaking into my dreams. Again I find myself searching alone through the dreadful city, till my loud restless mutterings bring Fernleaf across the landing.

"Hold my hand," I ask her. "Don't let go till you know I'm sleeping. And then stay to see I'm peaceful. Will you do that?" I haven't been like this since those nights of my childhood in the turret room at Inglefield, begging not to be left alone with the things.

But it does no good. The city of millions cowers and leaves the streets empty again. I climb down a stairway covered with staring corpses and walk through tunnels that echo to that distant scouring cough, searching for the last thing on earth I want to find.

Morning fails to deliver reality. I wake into a half-world so confused that the dark seems a better place to be. Unrefreshed by sleep and sedated into semi-idiocy I half-lay, half-sit while Amelia brings me trays of food that has no taste and drink that's nearly all sugar. Rationed sugar for the patient. Four o'clock draws curtains on another darkening evening and while I'm feeling a bit better I'm not looking forward to tonight. I need someone to tell me what's been decided; to know how the thing is going to be.

When they do, I wish they hadn't. I've read that in France they rush the condemned man to the guillotine in a few seconds; no time to think, or notice the ceremonial. But I'm stumbling in slow motion towards my moment, aware of everything. It's not a happy time.

"The first thing," says Jackson Armitage as he and I sit alone in my room, "is that we cannot stay here after tonight."

"Why not?"

"Because we can hardly leave this house, secretly or otherwise, in the dead of night, meet the ghost of a dead convict in the middle of London and return here at who knows what hour without an explanation worthy of our hosts."

"So we pack our bags?"

"Yes. We shall deposit them at Paddington."

"We're leaving London?"

"What do you suggest? Leave the hospitality of the Shawe-Trittons and book into an hotel?"

"Then why not go to someone else you know in town?"

He looks at me critically. "That school of yours has done little to teach you refinement, Clement. It is courteous to inform our present hosts of the names of our future hosts, and courteous to make contact upon our safe arrival. There is no such arrangement. And people talk. We shall be returning home when this is over."

"Right; understood. What will Connie do? She'll be on her own."

"Hardly, my boy. She will accompany Berenice back to Inglefield."

"What, tonight?"

"Of course. What else did you expect?"

My chest feels tight. "I expected her to be with us. I'm not at my best when she isn't around. What's the problem?"

He sighs. I'm sitting up but my body feels ready to slide to the bottom of the bed in a shapeless heap. Listening's difficult.

"Look; I appreciate this will not be easy. It won't be the first time since this started that you've been put through a distressing experience. But it all proves the intensity of your powers, of your gift."

"Gift?"

"Gift, Clement. We don't always ask for what we get. Just consider two things that may not have occurred to you. One: the Shawe-Trittons for a variety of reasons are close to discovering our true purpose here. I've warned you before not to be fooled by their apparently amateur way of going about things. What I should have added is that few of their house guests are what they seem either. Do I need to go on?"

"No. What's the other thing?"

"Just this: it's bizarre enough that two grown men and a school-boy are going to be spending half the night up a dead-end alley for no explicable purpose. For at least part of that time Mr McFee and I will be waiting in a car parked nearby. We may encounter the police on their beat. Now imagine the presence of a fifteen-year old girl in a car with two men at one o'clock in the morning. This is a wicked city, if you only knew."

"Really? But McFee could surely handle that."

"I'm sure he could. But it's just another complication in an already uncertain business. We cannot afford distractions."

"I've had a very strong feeling since we were at Manny Rosenblum's shop – what was left of it – that there'd be four of us." I realise as I say it that it's news to me too.

"Not possible. We cannot always have what we want; least of all in this business, God knows!" End of discussion. I stare straight ahead while he outlines the plan.

Target for Tonight. And my only support gone.

Paddington Station. Twenty Hundred Hours. Her hand feels frozen as I squeeze it. She's been through the same argument with both of them. She smiles and whispers, "It'll be all right. You're in good hands. They're professionals. Think of the excitement of it."

Yup. Heady stuff. It's just that I haven't recovered from the little sunlit room at the drill hall, not in my mind anyway. I'm not ready for a repeat performance. I feel and taste all wrong.

"Good luck," they both say. Why can't they just sit here overnight and we all go off together when it's over? Sounds silly, but no sillier than what we're about to do. Every feeling I've had so far in this thing;

317

fear, power, curiosity, bewilderment; it's all mixed into a brown mud. What's up, soldier? Nothing, sir. Good, good; carry on.

Connie smiles, but it doesn't work. "See you soon, Clement. Be sure to keep warm."

Yup.

The latticed gate squeaks across and they diminish into the steam and smog. I don't want to say goodbye on the platform. The signs now say British Railways. So much change. Except for the mist. It's here again, getting thicker.

Far out beyond the great arch of iron and dirty glass the locomotive exerts its muscles and draws the Oxford train into the night. We leave the station for a long wait in a Kardomah coffee house. There's a lot of time to kill.

For over an hour as we nurse our cups Doctor Jackson Armitage hardly speaks. He's a ghost-hunter and I'm his best hope for a serious professional triumph – fame being another matter – but on the eve of the big event he can find nothing to say to me. That suits me at first, because all I can think of is being without Berenice. Every second the distance is increasing; she's being borne back towards a saner world, real smells, real mist, white and silent. Outside, the smog paws at the glass doors of the Kardomah, slipping in with each new customer, tainting the odour of comfort, of sophistication.

The couples at their tables are only interesting for a while. Their normality is so out of reach I can't even envy it. When they step out again into the pea-soup dark they'll be part of something, part of each other at least. Somewhere in a dark alley off some street among these millions Albert Smallwood will contrive to see we're alone, just like all the other times when he's wanted to show us something. For us the city will empty. No help or comfort anywhere.

Jackson Armitage is reading a succession of newspapers. They're piled on the table next to his coffee and his eyes are swimming through them, forwards and backwards. I watch him. We've been kidding ourselves. The waxworks have been moving too, while Berenice and I were sniffing around, intent on peeling away their secrets. I roamed round

318

the Shawe-Trittons' house while everyone was asleep, but I've done a lot of sleeping myself. And they know about it; about why we're here. Shanks can feel their breath on his neck; that's why he's filleting the columns for any sign that McFee's little problem is in the open. He even looks through those personal small ads for hints of hints, because that's the kind of world it is; great weights balancing on signs and whispers.

"Uncle?"

"Mmmh?"

"Have you ever actually seen a ghost?"

He turns a page without looking up. "No."

"Ah." For some reason this answer alarms me. "Do you know exactly what'll happen tonight?"

"No. The plan rests on certain assumptions. One must be ready for anything."

"Could Mr McFee come to harm?"

"More than he has already? I've no idea. I doubt it. I've generally investigated past events."

His eyes continue to flick across the pages. I know he's worried, but he's doing me no good like this.

"Mind if I go back to the station; watch the trains?"

"Not at all, if you're finding it tedious here. I'll see you at Left Luggage in thirty minutes. Do not be late."

The thickening, freezing fog doesn't smell of coal yet, but it's only a matter of time. I turn my coat collar up and pull my scarf over my chin.

"Bit late for train-spotting ennit, chum?"

I take the platform ticket. "I've got exceptional night vision."

"Please yerself."

More Esperanto over the tannoy as I walk to the sloping end of Platform Four. Ahead of me an array of coloured lights stain the gloom, but the rails have none of that gleam of silver or rainbow glow. There's a point along these tracks where I stood a week ago. On balance it was a week I could have done without. Except that I know I love Berenice. If it means anything, it has to be stronger than what's about to happen, has to be still there when Smallwood has come and gone. That's right. How little I've allowed this great thing to be more important.

Serpents of lighted windows glide sinuously through the murk. Like most of my thoughts they simply follow each other without touching the earth, except for that one earth-touching thought.

The cold seeps into my shoes and I head back. But I'm happier now.

Shanks is picking up his bag of tricks when I meet him. We start off, retracing my first London steps to McFee's lodging. With each corner we turn, the smog closes in.

And some of that courage begins to leak away. At first I shore it up with the hard reflection that whatever we've thought or believed or discovered about anybody will stop mattering very soon. Tonight this thing is going to end, for me anyway. I hope.

Everything after that will include Berenice. Real stuff. But the leaks keep getting bigger, and a slow terror crawls into my clothes. It becomes my shape, inhabiting my stomach, throat, knees, pulling at each root of my hair. Fear squeezes my lungs like bellows, sending quick jets of breath to mingle with the smog.

"Well, here we are."

I'm standing, barely. Gascoigne's window runs with condensation and his photos are blurred.

Thank God. But of course I have to look again. The edges of the portraits are moving; moving with a sort of maggoty crawling, and I'm leaning into the tall figure of Shanks murmuring, "I don't know. I don't know."

"Why are you moaning like that? Pull yourself together. Come on; take deep breaths."

McFee gives me a glass of water when we get upstairs, and suggests I use the toilet. While I'm in there I hear them discussing me; not the words, the tone. He hands me a Thermos when I come out and they both slip hip flasks into their pockets. I do the same with the Thermos but it's a poor fit. McFee looks flabby, out of condition; and his flat feels as cheerless as a cell. But there's something about it, an aroma that doesn't fit. Someone's been here. A woman. I'm getting pretty sensitive to scent what with one thing and another. It's the daughter; I'm sure of it. He needed her here, before tonight's encounter, without telling her why. It looks like fear and his fear is added to mine. But everyone's trying to act businesslike.

"The car's just down the street," he says, putting on his bowler hat.

We crawl through the fog, heading for the Embankment. Stuck in the back I feel cold and alone. Near the river the smog gets so bad that I know McFee is driving by some sort of instinct. Twice Shanks has to get out and walk along the kerb just ahead of us. When I glance at my watch I realise that we've been travelling no faster than if we'd been on foot and, come to that, there haven't been many head or tail lights on our way.

It's starting. We're entering a world with few witnesses.

McFee swings towards the bascules of Tower Bridge but there's little sensation of crossing it before he turns right again. The street lamps give no light; they're just small haloes with a tiny incandescent spot in the centre. He asks Shanks to get out again and we creep forward. My watch says eleven thirty-eight and I'm gripped by the thought that time's become distorted, that in whatever dimension you want we're not on ground of our choosing. If I've got to be the tethered goat it'd be nice to be part of a set-up that we have some control over. Hunched over the wheel in the darkness and unwholesome cold McFee says to no one in particular, "I've never liked this part of town; this street especially."

"Why not? What else is here?"

"Now? Mucky commercial buildings and bombed sites, mostly."

"What's wrong with it, then?"

"Too many bad things happen here; more than they should."

Well, that's a terrific help. My mouth's dry and I'm shaking. The car stops and the lights die with the engine. "We're here," says McFee. Shanks gets back in.

"Over to you, Doctor Armitage." Our voices are flat, deadened. For a few seconds nobody moves. It's as if we've all forgotten our lines.

"We should compose ourselves," says Shanks; "then fix up our equipment. You can stay here till we're finished, Clement." They both pull out their flasks and take a long swig. I tell myself it's to keep out the cold. They're two silhouettes; men in hats with their collars up.

"I'd as soon get out and watch. I can't see any passage; have we gone past?"

"You're right on it," says McFee. "About four yards from your right elbow."

A foghorn wails long and slow from the river. Dull thumps as we close the car doors and stand enveloped in freezing smog. There's an empty, sinister silence. I consciously breathe in the coal-tainted air just to clear the sick feeling in my throat, and try to concentrate on Shanks as he prepares our welcome for a dead man.

In these commonplace surroundings the thoughts that gather round Doctor Armitage's movements only make things a little worse. I know that if we were lurking by a carved staircase in a great Jacobean house waiting for some figure in a ruff to float down it wouldn't bother me any more than it would bother him, first time or not. Nobody from that far back would have any axe to grind with us, even if their own enemies did. But this unimportant little villain knows about us. He's brought us to places and left us there. This is his time; maybe his lost lifetime. No; he was dying already. But he might have used his stolen money to get to a Swiss sanatorium if McFee hadn't nicked him. If he hadn't been sent down. I've seen newsreels of English city kids – orphans with TB – getting free holidays in Switzerland.

I as good as killed him: that's what McFee said.

The entrance to Unicorn Passage is a step away and nothing's going to make me go in there.

But Shanks doesn't hesitate. Walking past me into the grey-green mist with his wooden case he disappears for several seconds, then calls softly, "Give me a hand with this."

No. Let McFee do it.

"Clement? Did you hear me?" He comes and rests a hand on my shoulder. "You must be ready to help me, my boy. I've been waiting all my life for this moment. You aren't alone. If anyone is, it's Mr McFee; not you or me."

"Are you sure there's nothing to be afraid of?"

"No, I'm not. The thought that there is nothing to fear outside ourselves is what frightens me. Take this." He hands me the end of a wire flex. "I've suspended a particularly sensitive thermometer of my own design at the end of the passage. Just by your feet is one of those narrow covered gutters running across the pavement. Push this into the gap and up into the driver's window. Look out! Someone's coming!"

He pulls me into the passage. Steps go past in the direction of Tower Bridge. They're slow and shuffle uncertainly, but real enough. So people are about. The world within a world hasn't begun to form yet. It shows Shanks's senses are sharper than mine, though. I make myself useful.

Back in the car he fiddles with a little dial. "The presence of supernatural manifestations is often attended by a sudden drop in the ambient temperature," he says. "This device has worked for me before."

"But you've never seen a ghost."

"No. But I have recorded sudden temperature falls. This will save you the trouble of signalling should you sense anything. The smog is welcome tonight; it conceals our activities."

"A welcome coincidence?"

He smiles. "When things are steered towards each other, is that coincidence?"

I think of Berenice; getting up that distant morning to take a journey to a seat in a winter garden. McFee's face appears at the window.

Where's he been? Patrolling up and down this street that he doesn't like? Checking out the vicinity? Wouldn't surprise me.

The car has filled up with smog. Shanks's voice becomes extra calm. That means the moment is near. He's decided midnight is as good a time as any to begin.

"Once you start to sense a change, Clement, don't be alarmed by the presence of passers-by. They will pass through unawares, as I've indicated. As for the rest, I'm as intrigued as anyone as to why he should have chosen this spot or why he should have led us such a dance to get here."

"How sure are you about all this?" It's late in the day and bad for morale but I have to ask.

"Theory. Just theory; born of experience and near-misses. As far as possible I know what I'm doing. Imagine a surgeon performing a new procedure; one knows all the elements and hopes they will combine successfully."

We synchronise watches. "Three minutes to twelve. Have some tea from your flask."

Its warmth vanishes down the whirlpool in my stomach. I press down the door lever and change places with McFee. "Good luck," he says. "Let's hope he isn't too long."

I step round the bonnet, leaning on it for support. My hand caresses the curve of the nearside headlamp and I walk about two miles from the car. The freezing stillness has a space the shape of me moving within it, but there's no sense that things will stay that way for long; the cold spikes into me here and there and takes hold. And suddenly an urgent need comes. I step back and tap on the window. It winds down so fast my third knock hits empty air.

"Yes?"

"Nothing. I'm sorry, but I've got to go; be excused. One moment, eh?"

"Bloody hell," says McFee. "Just go against the wall."

It's too far to the wall; too far away to stand exposed. What if he comes, like those people who snatch your briefcase when you're in the public bogs? "I'll just go here by the car, all right?" I don't take my eyes off Unicorn Passage as a cloud of blood-warm vapour wraps round me. That's better. I smile at the misted windscreen and take my place again. But only my bladder's really happy.

Midnight.

A shrill whistle comes out of nowhere. I jump and jerk sideways. There's a faint rumble, growing, off to the left. Relax. London Bridge Station, not far away, and a late train setting off across those endless brick arches that march between the back-to-backs of South London.

Albert Smallwood was born in those streets. The chuffing and clanking die away quickly and the minutes pass.

I take a long step forward, then start shifting from foot to foot to keep the blood flowing. Then something does begin to happen. I can see a little way ahead of me.

The smog's thinning. But it can't, just like that.

I turn to the car, but its occupants don't stir. When I turn back the whole of Unicorn Passage stands revealed as though in the clearest of frosty nights. As I look upwards the last few wisps of fog roll up its high walls and vanish. The way they curl over the parapets is furtive, ugly.

It's as though the smog has upped and skulked away.

I stand paralysed, cold as ice, waiting to sink down and become awful with moaning.

Why don't I hear the thump of the car doors? Why aren't they beside me? Can't they see? The fog rolls away down Tooley Street and I can just glimpse from the corner of my eye the shabby commercial buildings standing like stumps amid the bombed spaces; the lamps' hard light throwing shadows. There are shadows in the Passage, pools and crannies of pure blackness.

I still have the power to cry out, but nothing happens. Any second now that cough will advance on me out of those unlit spaces and I'll wrench myself round to find the car and everyone gone.

Still nothing. I force my eyes to close. For a few seconds the images of the street lamps print themselves in spots on the insides of my eyelids, and a pair of fives of diamonds dance slowly in the rust-tinted dark.

I wish... Yes, I wish.

I wish Fernleaf were here beside me.

Just hold out your right hand and wait.

And when I open my eyes again I'm ready for whatever I see.

The alley's still there, every detail as clear as day. A long tremulous breath billows straight upwards towards an empty sky. There's no breeze. Must be they haven't noticed the disappearance of the smog because their windows are misted up. That doesn't sound right and it doesn't explain what's happened, but what helps is that whatever feeling I've got of some approaching menace is nowhere near as strong as the knowledge that she was there with me just now.

Unicorn Passage is about twelve feet wide, floored with cracked grey flagstones. On the left four storeys of brick rise up, grimy with barred windows, with the remains of weeds growing out of the parapet. On the right a blind wall of cut granite and equally shabby brickwork belongs to a seedy-looking place called the Tooley Hotel; Est. 1893. A pair of iron posts guard the entrance to the alley to stop cars and wagons using it. I don't know how we didn't bump into them. On the left wall there's a padlocked green double door with most of its paint flaking off and a bit further on the Passage's own lamp post stands without a light or mantle. It looks like it's had a long retirement. I take in these details one at a time. Every couple of seconds my senses are called back in, alert for any sound, smell or signs of the presence I know is there.

I'm being allowed to see this.

Twenty paces ahead – it's hard to tell – stands a high steel fence, barred like a cage. No, a cell.

It separates the rest from the last few feet before a wall topped with broken glass closes off the end. Somewhere beyond, the dark river swirls. There's a gate in the fence that adds to the illusion and, just to put the finishing touch, a rickety old table and stool occupy the right-hand corner. The light from behind me that makes such evil shadows picks out a hanging sign on the far side of the wall: John Evitt. est 1818. 145 Tooley Street. Sheet Metal Works. Not anymore. And at the very back, just visible, the Victorian gable-end of All Saints R. C. School. My eyes dwell on the perfect simulacrum of a prison cell in a dead-end alley. He's going to materialise in there, and walk towards me.

My back and neck are a washboard of waves of frozen heat.

Still nothing happens. I let myself look down.

At ground level on the Tooley Hotel side are two small skylights next to a door suited only for guilty comings and goings, their filthy panes held in fans of wrought iron. Up the walls on both sides are windows broken, barred, boarded up; their recesses filled with darkness.

The cage at the end of the alley, the dead lamp, the sign with 'All Saints' on it; here in Bermondsey. He's led us here through his maze, torn away the smog to show me every image and trapping of his wasted days. Unicorn Passage is a parable.

I have ears to hear. But McFee himself would understand this. There must be more. Still I don't turn towards my companions.

A church clock chimes the half hour; an interval bell. And the smog begins to return. I look up to see it curling back over the tops of these enclosing walls, crawling down in a vertical tide. It meets the cloud rolling in off Tooley Street and writhes round my feet a while. The alley disappears once more.

More bad things happen here than they should.

Where? Here? Here in this seedy, silent hotel? A murder? Is all this about a murder? A body under the floorboards? Have we got this totally wrong? This is just like one of those slum courtyards where Jack the Ripper did away with his victims; just off the ways where people walk, seconds from discovery. Is this about the Whitechapel murders?

I've had it. The return of the mist makes what it hides even harder to face. My feet are frozen. I no longer care what or how or why about the emergence of a prison death from that cell at the end of the passage. My hands bang on the roof of the car and in an instant Shanks and McFee are beside me.

Before he can see the state I'm in Shanks whispers loudly, "A distinct drop in temperature; small but unmistakeable. Are you all right, my boy?"

"No, I'm not. Do you have to keep out of the way?"

"We're asking too much," says McFee. "Yes, you bloody are," I reply.

"It has to be like this," mutters Shanks. He's trying not to sound impatient. "I know the risks, more than anyone. It's always like this, dammit. Half of them go hysterical on you. Just hold on. I registered a definite ambience."

"Well, that was probably the smog going, or coming back."

"I beg your pardon?"

Neither of them know about it. Misted windows or not, they should have. They look at each other for a second.

"It only happened for me, then. That it?"

Shanks knows about the lamp-post because his little gadget is hanging from it. McFee has only a hazy memory of the Tooley Hotel. The side alley has never engaged his attention. I describe what I've seen. We all know instinctively that's what it always looks like.

"He's here; in some way," says the Doctor. "We may be very close. No more talking." They give me a reassuring pat on the arm and quietly get back into the car. I don't know if all this makes me feel better or worse. My eyes begin to ache.

If he's taking his time just to make a point, then he's made it.

A rush of water down a drainpipe reminds me life's going on only a few yards away. Walls make us so near and yet so far. I imagine an unshaven, hung-over travelling salesman in striped pyjamas relieving himself and I decide I need to as well. My bladder must be in a right state. For a few seconds I'm wholly occupied.

"Hallo, love. Brass monkeys, eh?"

I twitch. No, I spasm. All I can do is look over my shoulder as my left trouser leg becomes wet and warm. The fact that the voice is female makes me say, "Er, do excuse me. I'm awfully sorry."

She's small, with a lot of make-up. Her head nestles in the collar of some kind of fur coat. She's carrying a little handbag and standing far too close.

"Bit young to be out, aren't you, love?" Her voice is soft and cultured but it's part of the make-up.

"Do you want warming up? A good time?"

She has me at a disadvantage. How did she get so close without me hearing? In high-heels? My trouser leg is now wet and cold and any time sounds better than the one I'm having. As I button up, nervousness makes me smile. So she leans closer. Her make-up looks shiny and greasy in the damp and cold but she has nice eyes.

"Want a woman?" she whispers.

"No, no thanks. I've got one already."

"Oh, get you! The Woo-Woo Kid! How much have you got, love? We could go next door. You can have what you pay for. You don't need coupons."

"More than you can say for a dry pair of trousers." Makes me sound like a complete idiot. Her warm eyes search my face and it doesn't hurt a bit. Still, it's a filthy night and I'm fifteen and obviously not drunk. She looks almost concerned. Then her eyes go shifty for a second as a car door creaks and the bulk of Sergeant McFee looms up.

"Okay, Fanny, on your way."

She turns to him. "Hallo, fat boy. Does your mother know you're out?"

"Goodnight, Miss."

"I'm talking to my young friend here. Wait your turn."

"I'm a police officer and you're ruining the view. Take a walk."

Shanks appears. "Trouble, Mr McFee?"

She looks at the two men, then at me, then purses her lips. "So that's how it is. I don't suppose I'm much good here after all. I'll leave you all to it, then." Pulling her fur collar up she mutters, "Excuse me, I'm sure," and walks off. In a couple of yards she's gone.

McFee lets out a long breath. "Cheeky cow."

"I think she's pretty brave," I say. "Out alone on a night like this. With your car there. She must have seen it. We could have been three, well, dangerous types."

He gives a sardonic laugh. "They're all brave. On duty right through the Blitz. Just for future reference, Doctor, don't use my name like that."

"Do you think she knows you?"

"Could be. Line of duty, of course."

"Why did you call her Fanny?" I ask.

"I call 'em all Fanny." He looks round him. "Well, what d'you think of this, then? Do we carry on?"

I shrug. Somehow the trouser leg and other recent events have robbed us of the moment. I can smell alcohol on Shanks's and McFee's breath. But we were never going to have rattling chains and spooky music. And this is still where all the clues lead.

"Your clairvoyance is a bit hit and miss, isn't it, son? I wouldn't put my last ten bob on it." He sounds almost jovial, as though relieved his doubts were right all along.

"We should go on," I say. "We've come too far not to."

Meaning I've gone through too much for it to mean nothing. They get back in the car.

I stand for fifteen minutes while the smog gets even thicker and the hooting from the river sounds further and further away. My thoughts wander to Fernleaf in her sky-blue pyjamas, her face against a soft white pillow. I stand in the doorway as her eyes open sleepily to meet my brave tired smile. A moment's wide-eyed hesitation before she leaps up to help me out of frozen clothes; and then the sweetest warmth in the world.

Every minute a shiver racks me and destroys the dream. I recover and transfer the scene to Connie's room. Then it's both of them. It just shows the cold's winning, increasing its grip. Physical comfort is all I can imagine.

Suddenly I see a point of light moving from side to side on my right. It's coming down Tooley Street from the direction of Tower Bridge, and for a moment I'm too numb in body and mind to figure it out.

Smallwood. His dark lantern pointing the way.

He's coming towards Unicorn Passage, not from it. Of course.

I dive for safety into the alley, but the irony of this flip-flop's lost on me. Slow steps resound strangely, coming closer. Where's the cough? Maybe there's no more pain where he is now. The steps halt, feet away from me.

And exactly where I've been standing. I begin to sink down the wall, tremulous breathing going out of control.

"Evenin' sir? May I ask what precisely...?"

"It's all right, constable; CID." A pause. McFee's voice, muttering confidentially.

"Very good, sir. It's a mixed crowd puts up here; one or two on the game of course. I'll keep an eye out; much good it'll do in this, though. Goodnight, sir." The light swings towards me. I back towards the iron bars at the end of the alley and grip them while the beam searches and dissolves and the footfalls die.

I help Shanks unhook the thermometer. It had registered a jump as I smothered it with my retreating body. We roll up the flex, each take a swig of tepid tea from the flask and McFee tries to start the engine. The self-starter gets no response but a few turns with the crank does the trick and the car crawls like a snail towards the front of London Bridge Station. We pass the probing beam of the policeman's torch and it swings our way. Maybe it picks out the huddled figure in the back seat — who knows? — of a malefactor returning from his crimes, straight into the arms of the law on the threshold of the Tooley Hotel.

McFee has the cabman's knowledge that gets us back with our nerves intact. In fact our nerves are in surprisingly good shape. In the early morning hours we settle into armchairs at his flat and go over the night's events.

Smallwood was never going to show. We read the signs wrong. Strange how unworried, how little disappointed we feel. I'm content to ride on the opinions of the two men to whom this thing matters most, and if they feel okay then so do I. Still, they let me do the talking.

"The smog clearing away and letting me see the Passage was his doing. It couldn't have happened naturally."

"It didn't happen, if you remember."

"You know what I mean. It happened for me. Smallwood was communicating with me. To show me it was just a scruffy little dead-end. I thought the stuff in the alley was the message, but it was the whole place, the place itself. A dead-end."

"But 'Unicorn' is right?"

"No doubt of it; that much we can be sure of. It's going to need more decoding to pinpoint the true spot."

McFee puffs his pipe. "There's pubs, firms, buildings all over London with that in their name; and that's just London. Who says it's here, anyway?"

"It is. Believe me."

"Maybe," says Shanks, "it relates to an object or a book, possibly in Rosenblum's shop. Either then or now, or until the other day. Was anything preserved?"

"Worth a try. I'll look him up."

Shanks scribbles in a notebook as we talk. Failure breeds more ideas than we allowed ourselves when we thought we were certain. McFee's fire begins to warm up the room and he keeps the tea coming. We're cheerful. We mounted a raid; kicked the door down and found an open window with the curtains fluttering. Next time we'll make contact. They've both been there before, dozens of times. The scent isn't going away; we just keep casting around till we find the true line. The hunt goes on.

The hunt. I've been meaning to say something and now's as good a time as any:

"There's never anyone around, is there?"

"Mm?"

"When I was little an old bloke told me never to be afraid of anything in the woods, even at night."

Shanks just looks up from the fire.

"He said a single human, even a child, cuts a swathe of fear a hundred yards wide through the darkest forest. Every creature runs or hides. This city's got millions of people, but when Smallwood's around you feel the place is empty. That's all."

"Except for you," says McFee. It sends a shiver through me.

"Just me, then?" Their faces are carved, tinted by flames.

"Those creatures smell danger in you," says Shanks. "But you mean them no harm."

I join them in quiet. McFee turns out the light to save the shilling and we sit as the firelight flickers and throws huge twisting shadows over the room. I'm comforted by their confidence; even put aside the things that Fernleaf and I know about them. They no longer appear as weaknesses. Jackson Armitage and Hayden McFee carry loads that we don't carry and they put in the same mileage as we do. Okay, we're slightly burdened, but it's only been for a few weeks. If you consider love a burden.

Of course I'm the discoverer of love. Only tonight I think I see other campfires in the forest I thought was all mine. Shanks and Connie; McFee and Alice. Flames or ashes?

The young passions of the weary man in the armchair. The picture of McFee standing at her grave. Is this what it's all about?

333

"I may go back," says McFee into the firelight.

"Back to work?"

"Yes." He gets up to lean on the mantelpiece. "I've been a case for too long. Tonight's told me I'm free to consider it. And go on looking."

That makes me happy. Normal life returning. But when I get to thinking about it my optimism ebbs away. It's like the cheerful flames. They warm your front but your back stays cold, and behind the armchair lies the darkness where the creatures of your childhood blink and shuffle.

McFee puffs at his pipe and neglects his fire. The room sinks into chill shadows. What welcome after a night on cold streets? The lino and thin hearthrug, the greasy dust on the lampshade, the punctuated solitude; I know I won't ever sit here again.

He walks us to the station and we board the near-empty first morning train. Standing in the steam and smoke and sulphur-yellow of the high-hanging lamps he holds his bowler hat above his head as we start to move, and turns his back long before we're out of sight.

I doze fitfully. At one point the train gives a series of jerks and brings me half awake. The lights flicker and go out. I rub the streaming window with my sleeve. We're gliding round a great curve in the line: ca-clack, ca-clack; ca-clack, ca-clack. As I peer out I see a glow, a huge dome of yellow-grey in the distance.

London wrapped in its shroud of smog. I think of all that's happened and the people I've come across who are sleeping under that lurid, unnatural canopy. Till two weeks ago I believed even the metropolis rested on the earth like the smallest villages. In my first dream – in Fernleaf's dream – the wasp's nest of Albert Smallwood's shadow prowled the surface of his city. I know different now. London pushes its roots below the earth, in sewers and tunnels that writhe over and round each other, beneath the heads of sleepers and under graveyards.

Ca-clack, ca-clack; the long curve seems never to end.

Smallwood is in that hidden city now, still waiting, as Hayden McFee turns the key in the lock and climbs the staircase to his dim refuge.

Slowly the train gathers speed and the lights flicker on and off before giving up again. It reminds me of the war. But the darkness outside the carriage is clean and pure, untroubled by the engine's smoke that floats into the dew of fields. Between the shallow-dipping telegraph wires I see the clean, bright country stars before the window mists over again and my eyes mist into sleep.

Chapter 26

The little train's lamp shrinks away under the arch of the footbridge and its sounds die to nothing as I turn to watch the signalman in the warm light of his box. Grasping a lever with a cloth between his two hands he pushes forwards and the signal clunks down. Then he moves to turn the great wheel like the wheel of a sailing ship and the level crossing gates swing, clash, bounce and crash together. A car and two cyclists pass over and the outside world is shut away.

It's dark again and I'm heavy with the lethargy of doing nothing but trail around all day behind someone else. That and an hour long ago of the kind of sleep you're better off without, courtesy of the new British Railways.

Shanks decided to break the journey by visiting college people in Oxford. Places I'd seen from the outside for years became open to me, but I just wanted to be back here. After everything, this is sacred ground.

Jim Haskins is the porter at Inglefield. He's an old man who was a drummer boy in the Boer War, only he calls it the South Africa War. He's always smart and brisk without being officious; the gatekeeper of the happy country.

"Evening, Doctor; Master Clement. Phone up to the house?"

"Thank you, Jim."

He disappears and I sniff frosty air and night smells and look at the pools of light from the platform lamps; welcoming pale glow that draws travellers towards small towns and villages; that doesn't wash out the stars. The waiting-room fire warms us till Alphonse draws up in the yard and his controlled smile is part of the ceremony of homecoming.

Everything feels better already. On the slow drive back the headlamps search the edges of woods as we follow the meanders of the road. Points of light show from solitary houses across the fields. It awakens the memory of my first journeys through the dark between the station and the lonely house; the beams and pinpoints that took all my attention and left the rest in blackness. Different now; I know the landscape. But the landscape's changed too, touched with the knowledge of things that are alien and far away.

Ludmilla and Fernleaf are sitting at the scrubbed table in the kitchen. I hold them both for a long time.

"Soon supper is ready. London is not so good for eating same as here, huh?"

"Miss Maybury is in the library, sir," says Alphonse. Shanks shoots out of the kitchen and we swap glances.

Oh, yes. We're back. "How long will it be, Ludmilla? Supper, I mean."

"Say fifteen minutes. Is correct, to say: say fifteen minutes?"

"Is correct."

We cross the flagstoned hallway to the billiard room. "Do you play?" I ask before we go in.

"No. Not billiards or snooker; not even a bit."

"Nor me. Thank God. Close the door, quick." Her eyes tell me it isn't the time to hold her again so I take her hands in mine. She looks down at the coloured balls on the table.

"I heard how it went. Are you all right?"

"I am now. How do you know?"

"Connie spoke to Jackson when he phoned from Oxford."

"He told her about Unicorn Passage?"

"No, of course not. She knows the gist anyway. It was his tone, that's all. You can't hide failure."

"Right."

"Was it bad?"

"Bad enough, thanks." The desire to kiss her is taking over everything. She lets go and moves away. But being in the same room and undisturbed is enough.

"Fernleaf; do something for me."

"That depends."

"Come to my bedroom tonight"

Her mouth half-opens for a long time before she answers. "I don't think that's a good idea."

"I want you do that thing with your fingers on my forehead; help me get to sleep. Right now I'm so tired I'm past sleeping."

She nods. "Yes, of course. Sorry." The moment's full. It can't hold more.

At the supper table Jackson Armitage leads all the talk. We've left the era of Hayden McFee and entered the time of Constance Maybury, a human being free of overhanging problems, of strangeness. Her presence is exciting, and all her mysteries attractive. I'm revived.

The people we visited in Oxford all turn out to be rivals and enemies in the world of supernatural investigation; soulmates of the Shawe-Tritton faction. Shanks called in on them to see how they stand before he knocks them down with the success – one of these days – of his theories. He doesn't say this openly to us; just caricatures them in their cosy college foxholes. I was none the wiser myself until the day wore on; got to shake hands with a couple of them before being parked in another room with a few papers and books; and not always that. Over lunch I got round to asking him why I didn't sit in and use my powers to pick up their real feelings, like we tried with McFee's contacts. His answer was that I ought to know better, so I left it. Connie seems to enjoy his tales, though. The dons of Oxford or the drovers of the Canterbury High Country, all the same to a woman of the world. She speaks all languages without words.

My mind goes back to the contents of George's safe. When this all comes out it'll be a great victory; yes, indeed. The prophet will be honoured in his own land. Still it's hard to see how my own performance, as far as he knows it, is going to support his claims. We cracked the clues Smallwood left by using simple deduction; helped on by George himself, no less. Maybe lack of sleep's causing me to miss something. The smog business in Unicorn Passage was me; no question. Was it enough? Couldn't it have happened equally well to McFee if he'd been standing there? What does this have to do with psychic interrogation?

"Are you all right, Clement?"

"Mmh? Yes. Just tired."

Shanks goes on entertaining us with the foibles of unsuspecting professors, but it's almost all for Connie, this traitor wit. Our titbits are the mimicry. There's never been so much laughter at a meal in this house in my time. Whenever we laugh like this it brings back the evening round the card table.

"Are you sure you're all right?"

"Positive, thank you. Like I said, just tired." A month ago if he talked like this; the droll anecdotes, the classical references, I'd politely ignore him. Not my line of country; over my head. Now it's the interplay of looks between him and his newest guest that keeps me in the game. After supper he takes me into his study for a chat.

I sink into an easy chair and he sits behind his desk. A standard lamp in the corner is already on and there's a fire in the grate, crackling with early life.

"You're going to be working tonight? You've had no more sleep than me."

"There are things to attend to. I'm going to write to your headmaster to inform him that you are extending your vacation on my medical advice. You have not been well. Does that suit you?"

I nod. Adult deceit fulfilling a childish desire.

"I believe that in a real sense you are not yet well enough to resume your lessons. Also I want to conduct further tests."

"Suits me fine."

"Good." He leans back in his chair. Time to discuss Unicorn Passage.

"Now tell me what you think of Miss Maybury."

I blink. Then I stand up and put my hands in my pockets, just to gain time. Flattered to be asked, happy to know, or suspect, what's prompted it; but still surprised, on my guard. My mind looks around to see who might be listening.

"If I was older, I'd be in love with her."

He raises his eyebrows. "Were older."

"Yes, sorry. If I were older."

"Or she were younger?"

"No, as she is."

"Then perhaps you are already."

"Okay; a little. It's a crush, that's all." Go on, you bloody shy doctor, then; say something. Say you'd be in love with Fernleaf if you were younger, then say what you really feel about Constance Maybury. Man to man.

He glances down at the desk, his face gone quiet in the amber glow of the lamp, and picks up a corner of a piece of paper as if it requires study.

"Thank you, Clement. Good night."

Soon after twelve Berenice comes into my room. I've lain awake waiting but it hasn't been easy.

"I thought you'd be asleep," she says. "Jackson turned in half an hour ago. Where's that owl calling from?"

"Barn owl, that is; lives in the church roof. Been there for years."

"Right. Lie on top of the bed."

"Why?"

"I'm going to start at the bottom by massaging your feet."

"I'll hit the ceiling if you touch them. Honest."

"Not the way I do it. Just relax."

"Bit cold out here to relax."

She's started anyway. It feels delicious and new and I step into a great room where millions who know this experience already are standing, and they all turn to smile at me. Many, many more millions wait outside and will always wait. As her thumbs work, my whole body becomes warm and content and, like a man under hypnosis, I start to murmur things.

"I love stepping off that train. Just this once I wish it had been in the daytime."

"Why's that?"

"In the daytime with the sun still up. Morning or afternoon; doesn't matter. We failed last night. The whole thing's used me up; like explorers who didn't find anything, or defeat in a war. You shouldn't creep back under cover of darkness then. It's not the time to sink down. You should come in, put down your pack and go out again into your fields or your garden. And before long someone brings you something to refresh you while you walk about under a blue sky with a few clouds in it. And you smell the fields and the mown grass; you follow the wind moving through a line of trees and hear the call of birds. The air breathes better where you lift your head and you walk with slow steps that don't touch the ground."

I feel her eyes on me as she gently lowers one foot and takes up the other.

"You didn't sound defeated when you came back, either of you."

"We were, though. Just trying to make the best of it."

"Well, I'm proud of you, Mackinnon. It's the thought of having to go on that's on your mind."

"You were with me for a while, you know that? I wished for you beside me and I felt you were there."

"That's because I was thinking about you the whole time."

341

"Really? That makes me feel very good; but I think it was more than that. It was like when we had the same dream. We were in the same place at the same time. What you're doing with my foot's making me feel light-headed. Don't stop."

"Just a bit more, then."

I float for another minute, till she says, "Now get under the covers before you feel cold. Not too fast. That's it." She starts to massage the bit between my eyebrows. I close my eyes and groan.

"Fernleaf?"

"Mmh?"

"Do you reckon Shanks is in love?"

"He's a different person when he's with her. Like most men."

"I know what you mean. If you see what I mean."

"Go on, Mackinnon. You're no different from the rest. He put on some Chopin when they were alone in the library. Piano music; Nocturnes."

"Romantic stuff?"

"Yes. If you've got blood in your veins."

"Hope it did the trick, then. I hope she likes him. Think if she lived here. Think if we all lived here."

"Good ending for a film. Real life's a bit harder."

"Doesn't she like him at all?"

Her fingers move more slowly. "Oh, yes. There are good reasons why she should; but not enough. She could never love him, so don't think about it anymore."

"No happy ending, then. Boy finds girl; boy loses girl; girl stays lost. Why?"

"Don't get me wrong. Connie would do wonders for Jackson, but not the other way round. Come on, Mackinnon. You know how he can use people, push them to the brink of real damage. Look at us caught up in all the deceit. Look at you, needing me most of the time to keep you on an even keel. She knows about all that. It's how he is. Does it sound worth swapping for the life she already has?"

"But I'm glad I need you."

"Well, I don't want to be needed. I'm not the nursey type. Relax, will you?"

"You're doing all right for a not-nursey type."

"In small doses, maybe. You being tense isn't helping me, though. Leave them be. It'll work out as it should."

She's right. I ought to be enjoying what I have – with her at least. It takes a long time before she's satisfied I'm resting. Her fingers stroke my forehead one last time and push lightly up into my hair; then she leans over me and touches my brow with her lips. As her silk pyjamas fall loose I catch the lamplight glowing honey on the skin below her shoulders, shading into places I've only dreamed of, places that bring her fragrance nearer. A small part of a long mystery.

"Sleep well," she whispers. Then she's gone, and all her work undone. I lay there a good long time, heart thumping. Even when it comes to rest, the body's repose contends with the turmoil in my mind; the visions and the desire.

The days that follow smell, taste and sound different. They're a mixture of the things that can't be unmixed. We walk in the woods, talk like people who can't remember not knowing each other, who can't forget strange happenings and parts of happenings. Sitting downstream from the weir one morning I say:

"Beginnings are the best part."

"Yes."

"That moment when I first saw you, in the sunk garden." Then I look at her and say, "What do I say next?"

"That if you had one wish it would be to relive it."

"You're right."

"And you're not surprised?"

"No. No, I'm not surprised. The question is, would I rather relive it without knowing all that followed?"

"If it was me I would. The freshness of discovery. D'you know what? Looking up at a new mountain is as good as standing on the top; but you don't realise it till you've stood on the top."

"I've forgotten who, but somebody once said 'I love being on trains that are about to leave.'"

"Same sort of thing."

"What's going to happen about McFee and Smallwood?"

"It's going to have to be played out, Mackinnon. You know when you're playing hide and seek and you've picked a really good spot and they can't find you? In the end you just want to tell them where you are and how clever you've been. So you jump out and surprise them. He wants to be found because he's got unfinished business. My backside's getting damp. Move on?"

In the afternoons Shanks puts me through the old tests and a few more while Connie and Fernleaf are out and about. There aren't many chances to talk but I tell him I need to clear my mind before we start.

"How are you managing to keep all this from Connie? I mean, she's not stupid, is she?"

"Indeed not. She knows what I do and she knows that you are psychic. She also knows that we are conducting various enquiries on behalf of Mr McFee. It would scarcely be worth the trouble of trying to conceal it."

"But she doesn't know why."

"Miss Maybury – Constance – is both discreet and courteous enough to understand the nature of a professional confidence. She doesn't enquire."

"It's quite a feeling, isn't it; holding a secret? Knowing that people will always be looking at you and wondering? People you'd like to impress?"

"I shall take your word for it, Clement. Let's get started."

The sessions aren't so strenuous as the first time. There's no one to take notes. He just scribbles in books. We do the things with cards and blindfolds, touching coloured papers, having bands put on my wrists with wires disappearing into boxes. The events in London are turned over and over, but he doesn't push me and I stay calm. Now and then a piece of equipment plays up and he toils in his braces, looking around slowly when he forgets where he's put his watchmaker's screwdrivers; sending for tea to be left outside the door; cursing quietly when the phone rings. It brings us closer, and I feel more comfortable with the thought that whatever power I'm supposed to have might be measured, studied; maybe not have things all its own way.

There's no word from London.

Fernleaf and I are skirting the deep-furrowed field that surrounds the church. There's a light drizzle being pushed along and our faces are wet. It's a morning for holding hands.

"Will you and Connie stay on till the summer?"

"In England? Probably. Why?"

"I've never dared to ask. What will you do when I'm back in the pen?"

"Travel around. Lots to see. I do want to be back here for summer, though."

I squeeze her hand tight. "This field'll be flat as a carpet come August. They'll have the threshing machine out, a dozen men or so, horses and carts, and the motes'll be drifting everywhere with the sun shining through them."

And you'll be in a summer dress and hat and little white gloves and we'll walk over and talk to them so I can show you off; and then I'll lend a hand while you watch me. And you'll understand it and not tire of it because you're from the land too. There'll be this, and the scent of lavender and dry pine needles in Shanks's garden, and the smell of oak boards heated in the sun when we seek shade in the outhouses. And we'll swim in Hob's Pond in the moonlight; naked. I'll dare you, like you once dared me with dark water. Come August, or sooner.

"Penny for them."

"Summer and freedom, Fernleaf."

"Amen and amen. Soon be lunch." We walk to a fork in the path and I start climbing a stile.

"Where are we going?"

"Just up here. Leads past the church."

"I'd as soon go back the way we came."

I lean on the rail and face her.

"You know the tests Shanks has been doing on me?"

"Only about them, Mackinnon."

"He thinks I'm past my best; over the hill. The power's still there but it's erratic. I thought it was erratic before. Still, he's the expert. It worries him."

She says nothing so I climb back over, watching her face all the time, and put both hands on her shoulders. Her beautiful grey eyes are full of a look that I've come to know.

She whispers, "You're going in there to see if it happens again. Am I right?"

"It's a test I can do for myself. You know we never told him about it. If nothing happens, I won't be sorry."

"And if something does happen?"

"Then you'll be with me."

"No," she whispers. "I'm not going in there. And nor are you." There are tears welling up. I hold her as she rests her head on my shoulder. "Come on. You're the tough one. We're together."

"I can't."

"Then I'll go in by myself. Just wait outside for thirty seconds. If I'm not out, do a raid. Don't shoot, G-men! Old Ma Holland won't give you any trouble. Remember how you sorted out Mutt 'n' Jeff at the Flats? Anyway, she's dead."

"So's Albert Smallwood."

We climb the style. It costs me the emotional strength of a journey of a hundred miles to see how upset she is. Every step we take is a step snatched from the chance of being argued out of it. At last I leave her at the porch and push the door open.

There's more winter inside than outside; a deader season beneath this roof. And no one around, like always. But her fear has given me courage.

It needs only a few steps towards the Holland tomb to remind me of the difference between courage and bravado.

The flagstones are cracked and tuneless. I grip the ends of the pews to propel myself along towards the hidden corruption of Lady Anne Holland, her bemused husband and her six murdered children. For a moment I gaze down at the eyeless effigies. She's almost smiling; a dead, satisfied smile, as she lies crushing the bones of the little skeletons beneath her. Despising her is easy, just as it is for the bland stare of Sir John, who was either stupid or a coward. Or both.

I'd like to wring your bloody necks.

No.

My skin's beginning to crawl. The two figures lie there in that sinister odour of corpse-coloured stone but one of them looks like she's deliberately ignoring me.

She knows I'm here.

The heat runs outwards from my spine like a radiator filling. I reach out my hand to the nearest kneeling infant, then draw it away.

I can't do this.

Hold on; the time! Must be up. Fernleaf's still out there, waiting. She should have come in. I grip the head of the carved child and close

347

my eyes. And count to ten. Ten long seconds in the parish church of St Michael and All Angels, Inglefield, on a gloomy January morning.

There's no triumph or even surprise. What has passed should never have begun.

The sound of rooks in the high trees reaches me before I get to the half-open door. It's the raucous laughter of pagans and unbelievers and I nod agreement as I step into the porch. But she isn't there. Fighting down a cold feeling in my stomach I run up the track towards the road.

Then stop, face about and race the other way. She's leaning on the stile with her back to me.

"It's okay. Nothing happened."

Then she turns. Her face is contorted with weeping. I put my arms round her and kiss her face and hair until she sniffs and says:

"All apples. I'm really glad. Can we go now?"

That night she doesn't come to my room, and because of that I'm reminded of its early strangeness. In the dark and silence the things weigh on me.

Whatever it is that we've brought back from London has become part of the air we breathe. There's a taint in it that never goes away, that makes it harder to feel free. Like the early signs of a respiratory disease. Like a consumption of the mind. It troubles me waking and sleeping and doesn't submit to the possibilities of the morning.

Jackson Armitage and Connie are out again all day and we spend the hours after breakfast in the attic rooms of the house. There are generations of bric-a-brac up there, and the magnified sounds from woods and fields. Three of the lightbulbs are so old they're shaped like radio valves. They start flickering and whistling so we turn them off and wait to get used to the half-dark. Daylight creeps in under gaps in the tiles and small birds flit in and out where wrecks of nests cling to beams with the bark still on them. Bats and spiders and woodworm and mice have peopled this for centuries. To Fernleaf it's a New Kingdom burial. We sit back against a huge oak king-post.

"I just don't know anymore," I say.

"You're getting the Joes again, Mackinnon."

"Yeah? Well, straighten me out then. No, seriously. Remember back in London I'd get those moments of clear thinking? And you know how in the end we said it didn't matter anyway?"

"Yes. Got it about right, I'd say. Just stop worrying and wait for what's got to happen."

"Well, it doesn't look so easy anymore. If my psychic power's getting weaker then what was it all in aid of? It only worked for stuff that we now agree doesn't affect the issue. The bits that help McFee we worked out by normal thinking. Or did we? That's what I mean, Fern-leaf. I can't see my way through it anymore. Did you come from New Zealand by boat?"

"Eh? Of course we did. How else? Watch your step; you're starting to ramble."

"Big ship, was it? Ocean liner?"

She studies my face before going on. "From Australia on it was, yes. The *Orion*. Very big. Very up-to-date. Why?"

"I came from Africa on a big boat. My aunt brought me. I don't remember much about it except one thing. I got to explore most of the decks one way or another; thought I knew the place quite well. Not the layout, just the things that were there to see. When I looked out of a porthole or from the deck all I saw were waves and sky. I had no idea which way we were going."

"Okay; I get your point. You didn't know the big picture."

"Worse than that. One morning I was doing what your average five-year old does on board, same as every day. It was just another day, see? Then my aunt took my hand and we went up to a part of the deck where there was a solid barrier instead of railings. It was taller than me so I looked up and saw the sky. Nothing unusual. A bit later we crossed to the other side. And there was this huge crane sticking up above me."

"You were in port."

349

"That's right. Had been for hours. But for all that morning I'd thought we were still at sea. Seeing that crane was a shock. I remember now how I felt. I didn't say to myself, 'well, we've arrived.' I thought, 'what's a crane doing in the middle of the ocean?' I'd missed the signs. I didn't read them. People acting differently, moving around differently; the bustle. That's how I feel now. Remember whatsisname, Phil Waterman, at the Drill Hall?"

"Mmm."

"What did he say? The gossip'll be out in less than two days. Well, it's out then, isn't it? No point worrying about hiding it, never mind the Shawe-Trittons and their suspicions, or newsmen sniffing too close, or anything. And how do we know Shanks is in the dark about what we saw in George's safe? He might know everything. Might account for the way he feels. How do we know it didn't get back to him? Maybe it was supposed to get back to him. It's like being on that ship. I'd got a picture in my mind and it didn't fit the facts that were all around me."

"Us, then."

"Yes, us." You can hear mooing from a long way off. For a while it's the only other sound.

"Could be Uncle's telling Connie the lot right now, while they're sightseeing," says Berenice.

"She'd have no trouble being a Mata Hari, would she; the way he is about her?"

"She wouldn't do that. But would she tell me if she did? Or repeat everything to me?"

"That's what I mean. Waiting's too difficult; there's too much going on. Or nothing going on. I don't know. I really don't. How do you do it?"

"Do what?"

"Stay normal. What's happening scares me. Being scared scares me. Aren't you ever scared by all this?"

"Come on, Mackinnon; you know I am."

"Yesterday, you mean. But you were frightened for me. You didn't want to see me in a state again; I understand that. What about the rest?"

She's quiet for a long time. It's still and cold. Our breath mingles with the immemorial smell of oak; pegged oak that still remembers the forest.

"Parky isn't it?" I say, to break the silence.

"Is it? I don't feel the cold."

"No. So you said." I snuggle up and put an arm round her shoulder. "Tell me about how you do it. You don't feel all this psychic stuff either. It's the same thing, isn't it?"

It must have gone cloudy outside. The light in the attic is the light that suffuses the best hiding places. Seduction of concealment. I've known that feeling for years in Shanks's woods.

"Connie and I used to ride out together," she says at last. "Go miles and miles, all day. As I got older we'd go further up into the High Country. We weren't supposed to, but there you are. One day we were picking our way over a stony slope. We should have got off the horses and led them. Anyway, I had a bad fall, and it looked grim because we were too far out to get back by nightfall with one crock in the saddle.

"Then out of nowhere popped this Maori woman. I have to tell you Maoris aren't exactly thick on the ground round our way. There's no one at all actually when you get up high, so we were pretty surprised. Anyhow, she had a cabin. She took us there and fixed me up to travel. She was a widow. Lived alone."

"How did she manage?"

"By moving around. She was still quite young. She'd been thick for a while with an old prospector called Arawata Bill over towards Jackson Bay."

"What, like...?"

"Shouldn't think so. I'll tell you about him sometime. Anyway, I liked her and I was grateful to her. Never told my parents, and when I

351

was old enough I paid her secret visits on my own. Connie knew, but she kept quiet."

"What was her name?"

"Doesn't matter. You wouldn't remember it. She taught me a lot about looking after yourself in tough spots. A lot of other stuff too."

"I thought that was Connie's job."

"It's anyone's job. We're not here long enough to choose our teachers."

"You can say that again. Was she a witch-doctor?"

"No, Mackinnon. She was fat and she laughed a lot. Listen. She showed me how to be tough. People are miserable in unhappy bodies, so look after them. Cold, discomfort and little aches and pains can be left behind if you're fit and prepared to take the trouble."

"Fine. But I run long-distance, I box and all the rest, and I've got as nervy as hell about everything. Why?"

"Because deep down you're not convinced. Stay with the physical things. They don't lie."

She looks into my eyes a long time. When she does that it always works.

"You used to be convinced, Mackinnon. You started by being afraid of the dark and being left alone and of noises in the night. And you conquered them when you were still a child by running among the trees and paying attention to the real things. And being psychic has made you forget that. Learn it again and you'll be all right. Believe me."

"There's a few physical things on my mind now."

"You mean lunch?"

"You know what I mean."

"Not now," she whispers; and puts her finger on my lips. I take her wrist and hold it long enough to kiss her finger hard. My eyes are shut and my whole body aching.

She smiles, gets up and says, "What's in that chest?"

"No idea."

Captain Kidd's treasure for all I care. Women. One physical reality you can't ignore, and all the pages in the book glued together.

A big black box with leather straps. It opens easily and out comes a lot of time wrapped in the smell of mothballs. Dark material, not even trying to look opulent. Fernleaf claws some of the stuff out. They're costumes; the ones underneath more colourful and intricate.

"What do you reckon?" she says.

I want to sound uninterested. "I dunno. Amateur dramatics, charades. Must be from before Shanks's time. I've never set eyes on 'em." I leave her to it and pretend to examine cobwebs and bat droppings.

"Look at this."

She's beside me with a photo cut out of a newspaper and stuck to a bit of card. The caption says 'Crowds Cheer Belgium'. On the back someone's written 'Ox & Bucks Gazette. 4 / 8 / 17. Allies Pageant. Inglefield Place.'

It's a wide-angle shot. A bunch of villagers, half of them looking back at the camera, stand behind a line of bunting. Some are waving. In the far background you can see the long gallery side of the house. So this was the ploughed field when it was pasture. A straggly procession of women parades past the spectators in the national costumes of Russia, Italy, France and the United States, the last one dressed as Uncle Sam. I suppose John Bull or whoever had already passed the photographer. They're all smiling and waving back.

Except one. Front centre of the shot is a statuesque woman with bare feet and wearing a long black shift with tattered edges that blow round her ankles. She carries a bouquet of lilies and a brave expression. Her costume's gathered in a kind of hood that goes round her head and makes her look like a heroine out of some Greek tragedy. She's good-looking in the way that Connie's good-looking. The weather seems cold and blustery; August's way of dealing with outdoor events.

Above her head, in her free hand, she holds a placard on a stick. It says BELGIUM.

There it is. Third anniversary of our entry into the war; a bit of a fête, a bit of fundraising by the great and good of Inglefield with the peasantry looking on, and the leading lady of the local opera society dressed as the reason why we joined in.

"Like I said, it was before Shanks's time here."

"He's a man without a history, isn't he?" says Berenice absently.

"How d'you mean?"

"Have you noticed there are no portraits on the walls? No framed photos of, I don't know, family events, big-game shoots, hunt meetings?"

"Like at the Shawe-Trittons? No, you're right. He deals in secrets, invisible stuff. His time hasn't come yet, when your house is also your monument. Do I sound impressive?"

"What's that noise?"

"The gong. Sounds different up here. Put it back, Fernleaf. Lunchtime."

When we get back to ground level I stop and turn. She's two steps above me, her hand on the carved newel post. Ludmilla's been polishing all morning and we stand in a world of smoky beeswaxed wood. "Just come with me a minute," I say.

We walk to the door of the big oak-panelled room. The Christmas tree's gone from the corner and the covers are back on the armchairs. Grey light filters through the cold air. There are no shadows, only echoes. It feels like it always has; a room that keeps things to itself.

"What are you up to, Mackinnon?"

"With me it was the Holland tomb. Let's see."

She isn't happy and I'm not too sure myself. "I'd rather not," she whispers. "I can see why you want me to."

"I'll be with you," I say. We approach the fireplace. For twenty seconds she gazes at the eagle picture while I look at it and at her. Slowly her eyes narrow and her mouth tightens. Then she shakes her head, turns and walks out of the room.

I want to follow her, but even more I want to understand what makes her so worried. I let my eyes wander over the canvas. If she can feel it, then surely I can. I remember how it made me uneasy too, in that first hour that I knew her.

Nothing. Just a picture. It doesn't bother me. Much.

The gong sounds again.

Things under the earth are what frighten me. Unnatural things. Fernleaf looks upwards, to the mountains and the sky; solid reality where nothing can hide for long. So this shouldn't be a problem. But as I stand there I realise I've always disliked it. Pulling it from the wall I turn it round and walk softly out of the room so as not to disturb the echoes.

It's me. Little fears that barely get houseroom in my consciousness affect her too. My dreams become her dreams. She suffered the terrors of the Holland tomb because I suffered them. Maybe it ought to comfort me. But anyway, there's worse to come.

Chapter 27

In the kitchen Alphonse and Ludmilla break from our conversation to mutter to each other in their own language. It seems to be about us. The bread and omelettes are going down a treat but everyone's tense. Ludmilla's persuading her husband to say something and keeps shifting her eyes in our direction. He looks uncomfortable and raises his voice. They begin speaking in quick bursts, interrupting each other, and we watch them in embarrassment.

Finally Alphonse lifts his hand, grunts, and wipes both hands on his pullover.

"We think, a problem, maybe."

"Anything we can do?"

He frowns at Ludmilla. "I do not think so. No." She replies in a flurry of syllables. More silence; then he sighs and looks at me.

"This morning, a man comes. We seen him before, since two days. Suspicious person. Asks many questions. We think maybe from newspapers. This afternoon he comes again for sure."

"Have you told my Uncle this? What name did he give? Did he leave his card?"

They shake their heads to all of it. Their expression says: this is about us, and we want no trouble.

I've expended a lot of logic on the question of what happens when the Smallwood case becomes public knowledge; how it somehow doesn't matter; how it won't affect the outcome. In one heartbeat it all goes out of the window. Present danger takes me in a cold grip.

"How do you know?"

"He say as he leave: back later."

"What did he look like?"

They shrug. "Ordinary; just normal. Tall. Bad shave."

"Clothes?"

"Of course."

"I mean, how was he dressed?"

"Hat, trench, the bands for trousers." He makes an open circle with forefinger and thumb.

"Cycle clips?"

"Ya. He had bike."

"So why are you suspicious?"

Ludmilla gives a smile reserved for those who need it spelled out. "When we first come here, everything all right; when we come to England. The war, huh? Still no trouble for foreign people like us. Then Germans attack towards this way. France, Holland all whoosh! Government think spies here, helping Germans. After long time Alphonse and me taken away by police; ask many, many questions. Because Germans and Russians friends that time, no? We say, not Soviet; Lithuanian. They say our country Soviet now. Alphonse tested by tribunal. Someone bad say against him many things. Very hard for stranger; hard for to understand.

"We did not see each one another for many months. Yes, it is so; even the married people. I hear maybe Alphonse sent to Canada, Australia. Lucky for us, no. Both set free, see each one another again." She puts her hand over Alphonse's. His head is bowed. "Now, many years, if strangers ask questions, we worry; still."

"Now you see?" says Alphonse.

Yes, I see. I see the refugee starting up at the knock on his door in a friendly land. I see the fear that lies like a brand on the soul of every fugitive. And I feel the mark on me that will never go away.

The newspapers – some of them – are on the old witch-hunt trail. It won't matter that the Lithuanians have no love for their Soviet masters; they're part of Joe Stalin's empire, victims of the prophecy in George Shawe-Tritton's amusing little puzzle, and this is the Cold War. After the anti-alien campaign will come the officials from Whitehall. The man in the cycle-clips is the first cloud in a gathering storm.

This is what Alphonse and Ludmilla have never stopped believing might one day happen. Thing is, we'll have to let them go on believing it until we've sorted it out.

"When will Uncle be back?"

"Not know."

It comes from watching too many thrillers, where some well-spoken toff minding his own business ends up uncovering a busload of spies without leaving a ripple on the pond of history.

"Leave this with us."

"What you do?"

"Make sure you won't be bothered again."

In the library I say, "This is it, isn't it? I'd rather do something than nothing. Have we got anything to lose?"

She smiles. "No. This is last-throw time. He came by bike?"

"Yup. Look, we may have no time. He could be on his way now."

"Could mean he's staying close by. I don't think he's local somehow. Who knows everything round here? At the not-very-earth-shattering level, I mean?"

"Jim Haskins; the porter. Stand on Inglefield's platform long enough and you'll see the whole world pass by. He'll know. I'll phone him."

"No; don't. We need to talk face to face. This is too complicated. And we can't let them overhear us. How far is it again?"

"Three miles nearly. Game to run it?"

"Absolutely not, Mackinnon. Any bikes here?"

"Two. Both U.S."

"What about that old motorbike and sidecar?"

"What, the one owned by Alphonse which we are (she spells it out for me) too – young – to – ride, you mean?"

"Well, that's a legality. Wait there."

I stand around trying to think of sensible plans for when she comes back with nothing. A dry chugging noise grows louder in my ears. No, Fernleaf; no go. We can't let him take us. What if matey turns up while we're out and catches Ludmilla on her own? She'll probably half-kill him. I would; snooping ratbag.

From the window I see the old combination circling the box tree. Without Alphonse.

"Okay," I say as I walk out to her and she leans on the handlebars. "I should have known. But you've never taken one out on a public road, have you?"

"No. But roads make it easier. It's what they're for."

"You have asked him, I suppose?"

"Of course. He got it started for me. I said we'd admit to ripping it if this goes belly-up. Okay?"

We get warmer clothes. Berenice puts on some cords. But seeing her with pilot's goggles makes me catch my breath.

"What's up, Mackinnon? You're going slack-mouthed as only a man can."

"Really? You couldn't find some tightly belted white overalls, could you? To go with the goggles?"

"Get in, dill-brain. Men. There isn't a sliver of daylight between any of you."

The beast coughs and splutters when she throttles up and almost dies once during a gear-change, but she has the measure of it. Twenty-five miles an hour! Her slim frame straddles the machine, her fingers unable to reach round the brakes, but more or less in control. We pass one car and one bicycle going the other way. Neither of them conveys the law.

I'm more worried about Shanks and Connie getting back. Fernleaf pulls into the trees before the first houses of the village and we trot to the station on foot.

Jim Haskins answers our questions without asking any of his own. Yes, some chap booked in at the Laughing Angler two days ago. He borrows the bike and goes out and about. He's taking it out again in about an hour. Why's he telling us? Because this bloke don't look right.

"What's the story, Jim?"

"I'm not saying he's a wrong'un; just something about him. Signs himself Archibald W. Maskell. Says he's researching small Tudor manor houses in Oxfordshire."

"Yes, very likely. We reckon he's from the papers. Gutter press getting up a panic about alien workers from Eastern Europe." It feels only half-right spinning him a yarn like this.

"Like your people up at the house? Could be. But he ain't a reporter."

"How do you know?"

"Because he's a private investigator."

"Is he?"

"Ask Nobby Lavarack. He reckons he is."

"Who?"

"Norbert Lavarack, Master Clement, is the proprietor of the Laughing Angler Hotel, thirty yards from where we're stood now. You didn't know that, did you? That's because you've never set foot in there."

"Right. How does he know?"

"Because it's a little country inn with two rooms. Like being in a fishbowl. I tell you, I wouldn't spend my honeymoon there."

"We'll bear that in mind."

He looks at Berenice. "Cheeky young beggar, isn't he? I should keep an eye on him." She smiles patiently. Time's passing.

"Mister Haskins, will you do us a big favour?"

He rubs his chin and gives us a toothy grin. "Never volunteer till you know what for," he says. "Actually, never volunteer."

"Well, if our Mr Maskell sets out this afternoon will you ring us at the house and let one of us know? Us two, I mean."

Jim Haskins, ex-drummer boy, is a railwayman of the old school. Duty is his law. "Now hang on. You want me to use railway facilities for purposes entirely unconnected with the business of the railway?" He looks like he isn't joking.

Good point. Ah, but wait:

"You're nationalised, though. It's the people's railway now. Mine as much as yours." His eyes go sad and his walrus moustache droops. "You're right. Don't I know it. Okay, I'll keep an eye open to see if he goes out. While attending to my numerous other duties of course. It's the best I can do. Here, don't do anything daft, will you? I'm not far off me pension. Know what I mean?"

Fernleaf puts her arms round him and kisses him. "It's the uniform," he mutters, "I get it all the time. Go on, then. Railway won't run itself."

She canters through the passage ahead of me, past the ticket office window, then stumbles backwards. We bump. "Someone on the veran-dah! Could be him."

I take a peep. A tallish man in a tweed jacket is squinting up at the sky; like someone thinking of going out for a spin.

"This way." We run back down the platform, luckily without meet-ing Jim Haskins, get beyond the footbridge, climb over the picket fence and creep along the field hedge behind the pub. This leaves me out of breath; another little worry. "If he leaves now we won't get the warn-ing," I pant.

"No, and he'll see us if we overtake him." We heave the motorbike round. Fernleaf stands on the kickstart and bears down.

"Oh, sod it! I'm not heavy enough!" She umphs as she gives it another try. There's a *sssch* and a bang as it swings down and catapults up again. "Ow!" She's hopping and clutching her ankle. "God, I hate them when they do that!"

"Let me try." Kick after kick gets no result. Any moment now Archie'll stop by on his bike and offer to help. Come on now. "Did Alphonse have some trick for this? What did he do when he started it?"

"Nothing. Rock it backwards and forwards."

"Why?"

"I don't know! We used to do it on the farm. It seemed to make something happen."

It does. After two more kicks the thing roars into life and we leap aboard.

When it falls silent at last in the small barn that serves as a garage we sit silent too amid warm oily smells. "So what's the plan?"

"Get dressed up like a local; gardener's boy or something. Meet him before he gets to the house and tell him Jackson's gone fishing. Then take him down to Hob's Pond, the place you showed me. Okay? On the way down spin him a tale about the place being haunted."

"It is."

"Yes, so you say. Now, about a hundred yards from the pond start calling out for him. And walk slow, as if you're hesitating a bit. Right? Now repeat all that back in a local accent."

I ooh and aarr.

"Forget the accent. Just speak normally with a bit of colour."

"Why? Not good enough?"

"Because he's a private eye, drongo. He'll see through you."

"What are you going to do?"

"Better you don't know, then you won't expect it. Just act terrified when it happens."

362

"What if it doesn't work?"

"Then we'll have tried. Better to die on your feet than live on your knees."

"That's quite good. We'll cross it when we come to it. Come on." We separate at the staircase and I hold both her hands.

"Good luck."

"Thanks. Stay by the phone when you're togged up. Just check with Alphonse there haven't been any messages already. See you later."

I sit in the hall in one of Shanks's old tweed jackets with the cuffs turned back, a jumper turned inside out with a worsted scarf shoved down it and my short back and sides mussed up a little. A few minutes pass and I hear the door to the stable block bang shut. She's on her way.

Clocks clunk in the polished shadows.

We're doing this for Jackson Armitage. They mustn't reach him. Who are they, anyway? I start to re-run the film from the moment we set foot in London. Nothing is what it seems. No one is quite who they seem. Maybe even Mister Lo. It all seems a long time ago.

When the phone rings I jump about a foot in the air.

Gumboots on; step outside. Grey silence. And a mist getting up.

I move off down the long gravel drive between the derelict glass-houses and the deep dark pine plantation. The unease of waiting has infected me. I keep looking sideways as I pretend to stack old sheets of green-slimed glass.

There he is, pedalling bigger and bigger. I hold up my hand.

"Looking for someone, sir?" He'll be alert, on the lookout for any-thing dodgy.

"Yes; the owner." Slightly Scottish accent. And his breath smells of drink.

"Only Doctor lives here, sir; and he ain't in."

"Really?" He looks around him, then at me.

"He's down the Pond. I've just come up; take you to him if you like. You shan't need the bike. Leave it at the house if you like."

"I'll keep it by me. Lead the way." As we walk I notice the mist is gathering fast. The songs of birds, each like a bell on a distant shoal, fall silent one by one. Soon the scrunch of our boots on the gravel is the only sound. Archibald Maskell, or whoever he is, doesn't appear to be in his element. Whatever he's alert for, spooky woods don't provide. It's looking good. Except that every now and then I get a tingle of something too.

Smallwood? Is he here, bringing on the mist, making the birds silent?

The mist. Like Unicorn Passage.

We walk past the house, and Archibald clings to his bike until we enter the first trees of the birch spinney. The fog's patchy here, with clearings of pearly light. And for a few seconds I'm lost in a fleeting memory of childhood: a tall figure in leather gaiters, slouched hat and rough belted jacket, disappearing into a smokescreen with bag and gun. Far behind, my hand in a woman's hand. Whose? When? When forests were still eerie and frightening? In that remote time before the war, between Africa and here?

This rough belted jacket I'm wearing, that's way too long for me. Doctor Jackson Armitage, a lonely man. His woods; his water. On the surface anyway.

"It's Hob's Pond, where he is."

Archibald says nothing. He looks completely ordinary. You could forget him in an hour.

"Hob's the Devil," I say. It worked with Fernleaf.

"Is that so?"

"Ah. I wouldn't be 'ere alone, not now; times like this. Good thing you're about." This not quite making sense is meant to sound like country sense. "Still, you don't know the way, do you? Need me to show you; better here with company. Pond's 'aunted. Not far now."

He slows down, putting up a gloved hand to his face, rubbing his cheek.

"What do they say about it, then?"

"Ah, well. Them that's seen it is a bit 'ard put to describe it, if you get me."

"I see." You can hear him breathing now. What's Fernleaf going to do? Some Hallowe'en carry-on won't work with this character. But I've never known the place so creepy, and she hates creepiness like this. My worry could reach her, alone by that little lake living in its own lost time.

I'm not acting anymore; and Archibald's looking pretty edgy himself. Here's the hundred-yard tree.

"Hallo! Doctor! Doctor, sir!"

"Why are you calling him?"

"Eh? I dunno, sir. Just like to be sure."

"Sure of what? He is here, is he not?"

"Oh, yes, sir. Leastways I left him 'ere. We ain't passed him, 'ave we?" My accent's diving in and out of Oxfordshire like a porpoise. We come to the water's edge and I look around. It's signs of Fernleaf I'm searching for. Still, it looks as if I've turned all unsure.

"Doctor?"

Silence.

"Doctor!"

"Did you say he was here?" His voice has a rising note to it. But before I can answer I see something about sixty yards out on that dark water. I shake my companion's arm and nod my head, open-mouthed and starey-eyed, towards the spot.

The gelid, still mirror is beginning to craze. We stand transfixed.

A black shape the size of a football breaks the surface, so slowly it seems only the water gathering into a mass, a growth, a liquid ball. As it rises it drags after it a ragged pillar, a dark column silently breaching, with hardly a ripple.

The thing reaches its full height and begins to turn. I haven't released my grip on Archibald Maskell's arm and my fingers tighten. I forget, in my horrified fascination, that I'm part of this. This isn't something jumping out from behind a tree. This is the thing that centuries of solitary country folk have witnessed and failed to describe in words.

Its head lifts and there's no face; just a hooded void. A sleeve detaches itself and begins to rise. Towards us. A finger will point; and that'll be it. His voice finds itself, tremulous and hoarse.

"Jesus Christ!"

As the arm continues to unbend in vile slowness the whole apparation starts to rise even higher in the water; water that still registers almost no disturbance. I know the depth of Hob's Pond, and this is going beyond reality. But in that moment I see what it is. My voice cracks and nonsense spills out.

"It's Belgium! It's bloody Belgium! Oh, Lord, help!"

He stares at me. I stare back with eyes that have deserted reason and experience. We turn and run and I keep moaning, "Belgium! Oh, Lord!"

He pushes ahead. "Don't leave me here!" I shout. Catching up, I thrust past him and reach the bike first. It's taken hardly any time. He's just behind me. I make as if fumbling in panic, my feet skidding off the pedals. Dangerous moment; he might stop, catch his breath, go back. But I'm nicking the bike; and it's not even his.

"Get off that!" He shoves me aside, not very roughly, so I take a dramatic dive into the undergrowth and watch him rattle off, dried mud spitting from the back wheel. I run after him until I know he's well on his way back to the road.

Time to ring the station.

"Mr Haskins? Clement here. Mr Maskell may arrive soon in an excited state. Whatever story he tells you, don't give him any support. Yes, yes; I mean Nobby as well. Eh? Well, anyone you know that he talks to. Just get him to doubt himself. Well, no. I don't want his sanity on your conscience, naturally. Just don't stand in his way if he decides to check out. He's halfway to you now. Thanks."

In the kitchen the water-hag's costume steams on the rail above the range. Fernleaf sits at the table in her bathrobe, sipping a mug of hot sweet milk, while Ludmilla shuffles here and there, muttering, stopping only to purse her lips and corkscrew one hand in her direction.

"Foolish, huh? I think, yes. Now you get chill, pneumonia. Maybe you die. What for fancy dress in winter, huh? I think maybe some touched, this girl. Such rags! Only for beggars!"

"Don't be hard on her," I say. "Accidents happen. Those ponds are hard to see." The old stagnant carp ponds; the ones I wouldn't jump into. At least we're believed.

"Did that man come back?"

"No. Never see him."

The phone rings. Shanks and Connie will be back after supper.

We ask to take tea in the library.

"When you shouted I waded out into the pond. There was a hollow I'd found earlier by prodding around with a stick. It didn't figure in the original plan, but it made things go even better."

"So how did you stay under? I have to breathe out to stay under, and then you don't last long."

"Held a couple of big stones."

"How did you know when to come up? Looked brilliant, by the way."

"I heard you. Sound travels through water. When you called out 'Doctor!'"

"Right. Then you stood up slowly, pointed, and shuffled up out of the hollow. It all looked so smooth, though. No waves, hardly any ripples."

"Ballet. Muscle control."

"It's got its uses, then. I was impressed. But it was freezing in there!"

"I don't feel the cold, remember?"

"Yes. You'll have to introduce me to your Maori friend one of these days. I detect her hand in this ignoring-the-cold business."

She goes quiet. "Afraid not, Mackinnon."

"About meeting her, you mean?"

She nods.

"Oh, right." There's an obvious question, but not for now.

"Has it worked?"

"No word from the village yet. I think it worked too well. I've stopped believing in simple plots and happy endings; the good guys patting the dog and laughing as the film fades out. I can't accept that a professional operator'll just vanish over the horizon and everything be forgotten. Come on, reassure me."

"Let's make a call," she says. Alphonse and Ludmilla are in their room listening to the wireless. The phone rings just as we're about to pick it up.

"Hallo, Mr Haskins? Any news?"

There is no news. Archibald has returned and is now reading a newspaper in the saloon bar. He seems completely unperturbed. I put the phone down. "He's not going. We'll have to tell them."

We watch them arrive, smiling, happy, and sit down to a good supper. Then, in Shanks's study, they listen to our tale without a word. When we've finished, Jackson Armitage doesn't reply for a long time. Finally he says:

"I've told Constance everything."

It's good to hear. "Welcome aboard," I say, and Fernleaf hugs her. I open out my arms and she lets me hug her too; worth every penny.

We roll onwards on the crest of his good humour. He finds our little prank amusing. Still, we wait for the backwash.

"Tell me again why you think this man Maskell is a private investigator."

"Jim Haskins reckons the landlord of the Angler had him down for one."

"Ah, yes; Mr Lavarack. A man with a history. Very well, let us accept his premise for a while. Who do you suppose has employed him?"

"I've gone through a whole list of possibles," I answer. "It's endless."

There's a subtle change in his tone. "Did this endless list include say, Miss Lendery?"

"Who?"

"You met her at a dinner party in London. She kept a small dog under her arm."

"Anemone Woman!"

"It seems you remember after all. Petronella Lendery has been a guest here, though not for some time now. I need not enlarge on that matter. She believes that Inglefield Place is stiff with fairies. Suppose our visitor reports to her that he unwittingly conjured up the Queen of the Night or some such drivel while at Hob's Pond? Where shall we be then?"

"Good point. Could it be her?"

"Describe him again."

I do.

"Did he seem like a dipsomaniac to you?"

"Eh?"

"A drunk, dammit!" Things are taking a less good-humoured turn.

"He did smell of drink. And he sounded Scottish; or maybe not. Why?"

"Because your description fits her nephew, the worthless Cecil; who, if you recall, is a journalist."

"Oh, God!" says Fernleaf. "He'll be back, then. We've just whetted his appetite."

It isn't him," I say. I've been here before. "This bloke wasn't a ponce."

"What was his cover story? I assume he had one, though I suppose he would hardly discuss it with a yokel he met on the drive."

"Hang on," says Fernleaf. "We do know that. What was it?"

"Research. Yes, research. What, though?"

"Country houses! Manor houses in Oxfordshire. Very likely, don't you think?"

Shanks goes pale; his eyes blaze.

"Everyone follow me," he mutters. We're led towards the library through Dangerous Calm country. Cheerless, fireless; atmosphere none too good. From a shelf he takes a small blue book and thrusts it into my hand.

Tudor Manor Houses of Lincolnshire. By 'Vitruvius'.

And another. *Tudor Manor Houses of Leicestershire*. By 'Vitruvius'.

There are six in all. With an imperceptible nod he bids me open the first one.

A photograph of a much younger Archibald. 'A.W. Maskell, who as 'Vitruvius' has for many years written his famous articles on rural architecture in *Hill and Dale* magazine.'

At this point it would be nice to pat a dog and laugh a lot.

"I cannot allow a serious author to represent this house and its estate as being haunted. One: because it isn't; and two: because I live here and I prefer not to become a laughing stock."

"We've made a bish of it. I don't know what to say. Sorry."

First meeting is with Alphonse and Ludmilla, who are too relieved to care about anything else. Archibald's status as an architectural historian neither convinces nor impresses them. The affair of the motorbike remains a secret. Sufficient unto the day are the cock-ups thereof.

Second meeting, after a telephone call, involves Mr Maskell himself, chauffeured up to the house by a solemn Alphonse. We've spent a while rehearsing our explanations because while it's easy enough to admit to what happened it's impossible to say why, or who else we've dragged into it.

Berenice opens for the defence. "There's an old Lithuanian superstition about spirits living in lakes."

"They've got lots of lakes round there," I say.

"So we cooked this up to try on Mr and Mrs Stankeivitch. Clement was going to bring them down to the pond and then I'd go through my act. When you came along he thought you'd be good for a dry run. Sheer devilment, I'm afraid. I didn't know who he was bringing, except that it wasn't Alphonse or Ludmilla, but I went through it anyway. So I'm just as guilty."

"Why then were you dressed in odd clothes, young man?" Archibald isn't going to let it go that easily. "And why were you fiddling with panes of glass while your cousin was lurking in even odder attire over half a mile away?"

"Well; there was this mucky job I had to finish first. We thought it'd be better if we'd done all our allotted tasks before, well, going through with it."

"Why aren't these young people at school?" he says to Shanks.

Doctor Armitage remains polite. For the moment he has little choice. We've put him in a bad position.

"I can assure you that their education is well in hand; in the academic sense at least."

"Hmm. Character training is what's needed. I trust you will see that appropriate action is taken?"

"You may depend upon it, Mr Maskell. You two will go to your rooms. Behind you, sir, you will see that I have on my shelves the com-

371

plete set so far of your valuable works. Had these young people made better use of this library they might have been more aware of your identity and purpose; except of course that you did not introduce yourself by name either to Clement here nor, I understand, to my manservant the other day. I may say, though they have not, that your somewhat clandestine manner gave rise to some apprehension on his part."

Good shot. We both know Shanks can't warn Archibald off. He'll have to do the decent thing and co-operate with his researches. His position as a respectable if reclusive pillar of the community would make refusal look suspicious. And it means hiding his activities while the house is scrutinised inside and out for the future curiosity of the public.

Long after midnight Fernleaf and I kneel on my bed and look out of the turret window at the twin poplars swaying in a rising wind. A shared sense of stupidity has a strange way of isolating you. The warmth of mutual admiration is missing. I spend the minutes trying to lessen the distance between us.

"That tangled web you talked about. Remember?"

"When first we practise to deceive. Yup. We never learn."

"We've got used to making things complicated, Fernleaf. We say to ourselves how simple it all is, then something comes up and we forget and rush round like blue-arsed flies. Sometimes I wonder what McFee's up to now. The answer to the unicorn business is all we need to sort his whole problem out. Get that solved. But has Shanks mentioned it recently?"

"He's on another quest at the moment, Mackinnon. More personal."

"And less likely to succeed. Still, fingers crossed."

"If he'd been here today – no, yesterday now – none of this balls-up would have happened."

At last we're able to look at each other as if we like it. She lets me put my hands round her face. The slightest give, and I'll draw that face towards me. But she holds herself. The first rain slashes suddenly against the windowpane.

372

"I still can't get over how you did it this afternoon. It makes me want to warm every bit of you. Have you got any idea how good you look in pilot's goggles?"

"So long as you like it, you sad boy." Her eyes, beautiful naked grey eyes, smile at me.

"And have you got any idea how good you sound sometimes?"

"No. Is there anything else I should know?"

"When will you wear that dress again; the one you made for New Year?"

"Soon. All right?"

"I can't wait. I'm glad we've got Connie with us now. I mean, that she's in."

"She's been in for a long time, Mackinnon."

"Most of it, anyway. Or maybe more than we think we are ourselves."

"Let's make sure we don't lose sight of Mister Smallwood again. Just let it happen; don't do more than you're asked. All right? You're dog-tired and so am I. Sleep well."

But I don't sleep. From that night on it seems as if all the separate fears I've attracted have come together in some place not very far away. Some valley hidden in my thoughts hides this muster of dark things and one day they'll decide my time has come. It begins quietly, robbing me of proper rest, regardless of anything Fernleaf does for me. I want Albert Smallwood to appear soon and have done with it; and I want the whole thing to go away, now.

Fernleaf. A girl who creates all kinds of emotions in me by physical means; by what she is and the things she does. And Clement Garner. Psychic things leave him physically devalued. But what have been separate episodes until now have become joined up. Permanent fear has brought me permanently low; lower than I've ever been.

I know now what my body's been telling me for weeks: that my gift is a sickness.

A boy on a red motorbike breezes up to the door in the morning wind and rain. He brings a telegram. Alphonse in his white jacket carries it to the breakfast table.

```
NIGHTWATCHMAN  TRACED  WALTER  CHINNERY  BARBER
BARTON  VILLAS  CLAYTON  ON  SEA  STOP  REGRET
CANNOT  ACCOMPANY  REGARD  THIS  LEAD  LAST
CHANCE  REPEAT  LAST  CHANCE  MCFEE
```

"Pack for a night's stay," says Shanks. "We'll leave in an hour." Fernleaf and I go into action. He waves us down. "Finish your breakfast and digest it properly. We have a long car journey ahead of us. And I have things to do; put off our Mr Maskell for one. Just relax."

Schoolboys like me have done more packing to travel than you can shake a stick at. I do it automatically, so I have space to think.

The barber is the last living person on our list. If there's a plan, then he may complete our jigsaw and reveal the unicorn. But how? By speaking plainly? By unwittingly saying things we can only now make sense of? Or by me finally using my powers effectively to penetrate what he tries to conceal? I lug my bag downstairs into the hallway.

Shanks's study door is open. I look, expecting to see him putting a few affairs in order, but he isn't there. So I go in.

It's still a strange place to me, this room. This is his desk, his chair. A part of my winter garden that I've never really set foot in.

I lower myself into it, onto the green leather with its rim of brass roundheads. My back presses against green leather. The palms of my hands rest on arms of oak. Outside the leaded window a poor, rain-washed light falls on everything.

The room suddenly seems different.

As though small things have been rearranged. As though: what? I peer at the shelves. It could be the books are less tightly packed, less squashed together by the additions of time. The room feels younger.

And my thoughts emerge from a fog formed from the additions of time. Clearer. Crystal clear.

I become Doctor Jackson Armitage.

My eyes roam the surface of the desk. Blotter in its morocco corners; pen-holders; ink-holder. Clear, classical. No romantic embellishments. No photograph in its frame. No clutter. I too am persuaded, more than ever, of the power of physical things.

I am in love with Constance Maybury. She sees my obsession with the unknown and insubstantial and wishes I could connect with her reality under the sun. But this is my life's sentence. Like young Clement, neither of us chose what we have. His psychic gift; my lot to look helplessly, a young doctor, into the eyes of those unbalanced by cruel promises and lies.

There is a postcard-sized text in a small surround on one corner of the desk. Strange not to have noticed it before. A quotation from Protagoras, twenty-five centuries ago:

> Concerning the gods I am unable to discover
> whether they exist or not, or what they are
> like in form; for there are many hindrances
> to knowledge; the obscurity of the subject and
> the brevity of human life.

A shape passes the doorway. Ludmilla Stankeivitch, her arms filled with folded linen. Her fears for freedom are her ghosts. They never leave her. Sometimes she hears their knock on her door. We're off now to knock on Mr Walter Chinnery's door. Has something told him to expect us?

Chapter 28

We drive south. An easterly gale of rain and sleet buffets the car as we haul across the counties between Inglefield and the sea. Wet leaves cartwheel out of hedgerows and flop in circles on the road like wounded birds. Not till the Sussex border does the sky change, shredding into blue, and branches stop flinging marble-sized drops on our windscreen.

Usually I take note of strange scenery, but the scenery inside is more interesting. The wiper squeegees like a pendulum, the tyres bump rhythmically on the concrete roads, the fragrance of *Tweed* by Lentheric merges with the smell of leather upholstery and petrol. The outline of Connie's face as she half-turns to speak to Doctor Armitage; his eyes in the mirror, flickering towards her when she isn't looking.

We stop at a filling station where a man in overalls cranks a pump and talks to himself. As he wipes our windows with a soft cloth his eyes stay fixed on us. The basic petrol ration has been abolished and hardly anyone now motors for pleasure. The man's weekend trade has become a wilderness. Shanks gets a supplementary allowance because he lives more than two miles from public transport; that and a few cans hoarded by Alphonse, who trusts neither good times nor bad.

The people in this expensive, polished car live in another world. None of us feels easy with the government's poster on the wall behind the pump:

WE WORK OR WANT

For mile after mile I hold Fernleaf's hand until her fingers are just foreign spaces between my fingers and I'm left with myself.

When I got into the car this morning I put away doubts and decided to really give it a try. But it doesn't last. I lift up each episode in the Smallwood search like a holiday snapshot, and it makes a tall pile; only the more I look the more it doesn't interest me anymore. I turn my face to the things outside the window and realise that whatever the nightwatchman-turned-barber Walter Chinnery says or does, I hope it won't amount to anything; that McFee's last throw will roll into the dark corners so we can all go home. If he and the old peterman really want to meet, let them get on with it.

The Langdale Hotel on Clayton's seafront receives us well after midday. We're stiff, tired and hungry and for some reason the restaurant people aren't thrilled to see us. Seems everyone else has finished lunch, so we sit under the gaze of three waiters who stand in a row by the wall, lunging forward impatiently at every stage of the meal.

"Hard to be enraptured, I'm afraid," says Shanks over the menu. "Meat or fish? They recommend whale or snoek. The bread is a separate course, naturally. Take your time. This place is open till two o'clock."

Conversation isn't easy under the waiters' gaze. "Tell us about Arawata Bill," I say to Fernleaf. Connie looks up suddenly; at me, then at her.

"Who?" says Shanks.

Too late. Done it again.

"Some old prospector Fern, er, Berenice knows in New Zealand."

"Heard about," she says.

"Well?"

"He thought there was gold in the streams; spent his whole life looking for it. That's all."

"And did he find any?"

"No. Or if he did he didn't tell anyone. Lived poor, died poor. Last year."

Shanks leans back, napkin in hand. "Because he didn't look in the right places, or because it wasn't there?" We're smothered in a flurry of white sleeves. The subject vanishes with the dishes.

We're in two rooms, the men and the women. As we unpack, Jackson Armitage tells me we should be about our business without delay. "Constance and Berenice will spend the remains of the afternoon enjoying the delights of Clayton-on-Sea, while you and I get a haircut. All set?"

I'm due for one. But:

"Isn't she coming with us?"

"Into a gents' barber shop? Are you serious? Come on, man, think. They'll be company for each other."

Something snaps. Doesn't he remember how I felt about Unicorn Passage? I don't want my first ever stand-up row with him to be here or now, so I snatch up my coat and scarf and head for the door.

"I'll be on the beach."

Scrunching down the steep shingle I hope he's watching from a window. I haven't seen the sea for years and I'm angry that it's this way. He needs me more than I need him. And I need Fernleaf. Why doesn't he get it? Does he think she kept out of sight when some drover was getting a trim under the verandah back home? It's no different from sheep shearing. He's overdone it this time. Let him sort it out.

Breakers curl and crash and film me with spindrift. My nostrils tingle with the smell of the dying storm, of the weed swilling in the long fetch of the sea. Even if you've never heard it before you know this booming voice of the ocean is the oldest music. Not an original thought, but new in each one who meets it. I need to be strong like the sea, to get out from under this weight of fear and dreaming, get back to the world you can smell and hear and feel; a cheerfully imperfect world. I breathe deep and push my feet into the stones.

Connie's beside me. I've heard her stepping over the shingle in her smart shoes, but not acknowledged it till the last second. This makes me feel tough, in possession.

"Is it settled, then?" I say into the wind.

"I just want to say this, young man. Never do that again. Jackson has been through a great deal."

"Is that so? Well, I've got a story of my own."

But the strong pose is coming apart. Thankfully my face is wet and salt enough already. I sit down on the stones and look away. Next moment she's by me, her legs drawn up beneath her; a nylon-snagging business which would compromise the elegance of most women. I take the gesture as a bigger compliment than her closeness. Her elegance remains intact, but still vulnerable. I wriggle my coat off and spread it over our shoulders. Like this we both sit and watch the breakers as their crests smoke in the raw whipping wind.

You can walk to the edge of cliffs, climb rocks and trees, dare lightning; but you can't stand where the waves smash down and not feel the littleness of your life. Our silence while we think the same things prepares us. The way her perfume mingles raggedly with the smell of the sea acts on me and I put my arm round her waist and pull her closer.

"The mask of Gaiges," she says at last.

I raise my eyebrows as if to say: well yes, very true. I've never heard of it.

"In the legends of ancient Greece they believed it made you invisible. Students would be asked an ethical question: what would be your first act if you wore the mask and were hidden from the sight of men? Do you know what most of them answered?"

"No." I want to sit here and listen to her voice. For the moment she's mine and nothing else matters. A dog bounds along the furthest advance of the surf. Behind it a man with a stick leans into the gale. I want him to think we're lovers, to measure my manhood by the rough comfort that a beautiful and sophisticated woman will endure at my bidding.

"Well, they all said they'd do something immoral: spy, eavesdrop, steal things, torment people they didn't like or commit indecency with people they desired. Very few considered doing good. The answer's never changed; it's the same today."

"You think I should be doing good? I thought I was."

"That's just it, Clement; you are. Jackson is what he is because of people who didn't."

"So? Compared with how I was feeling a month ago, I reckon it's about time someone did me some good in return."

"I'd say a month ago you were more privileged than you knew. Life's evening up the score a bit. It's hard to accept."

"Well, you're an expert on being privileged. Has life taken anything back from you yet? Or Fernleaf? Or Shanks? I can't sleep; when I do I have nightmares; and I'm frightened of things that never used to worry me, not since I was little anyway. And I keep having smart, bright little thoughts about people like a bloody lah-de-dah in words I didn't think I knew, and all I ask is to have one person along who makes me feel halfway good about anything that happens. What's the bloody problem? Can't you talk to him?"

"I didn't have to. He was ready to agree when you flounced out."

"I don't feel like apologising, Connie. He started this off."

"You won't have to. He's learning, Clement. We all are."

I want to use this moment to tell her to love him, to help him keep learning; but my thoughts are lost in the booming and surging of the sea. She gets to her feet. "I'm going window-shopping, in an English seaside town on a winter's afternoon; on my own. Wish me luck." Her brown eyes fill me up. I'm standing there with my overcoat over my arm and I'm freezing, but the touch of her gloved hand on my cheek makes me shiver for something else.

"Somebody wrote that the sea was masculine and the air that touched it was feminine. He must have thought that when he was standing on a beach with someone like you."

She cocks her head a little sideways. "You don't talk like most boys of your age."

"I just told you that myself. Maybe I didn't have the right company. Now there's so much. Half the time I wonder if it's me anyway."

I'm ready now.

But finding Walter Chinnery doesn't come easy. Barton Villas is no problem; a straight tree-lined avenue that stretches between the main road and the promenade. We discuss our approach as we walk up it from the sea. The barber was the man who guarded Smallwood in the minute or two of relative freedom that McFee granted him, while he stood round the corner asking himself what was going on and why. Surely he'll have something to tell.

The Villas is precisely that: two rows of detached houses behind hydrangea bushes. Nowhere for a barber's shop. No red and white pole, no sign. Has McFee got it wrong?

We say goodbye to Connie at the junction with the High Street. The buildings at the corner are ornate Victorian apartment blocks sitting on banks and shopfronts. Turning about, we start to walk back towards the promenade, looking more carefully. Suddenly a shout from behind us stops us in our tracks.

"Squad! Preeeee-sent... Arms! Two-three! Two-three! Two-three!"

A gaunt man in a belted trenchcoat with a beret on the back of his head stands bolt upright at the kerbside across the street. His whole body quivers as he presents invisible arms to the few passing cars. "Squad! Squad, slo-hope... wait for it, wait for it... Arms! By the right, quick... march!" He steps smartly into the road, right arm swinging. A woman on a bike with a little petrol motor on the front swerves to avoid him. Her hat comes off and lollops along in the breeze. "You stupid bleeder!" she bellows. A man standing in a shop doorway calls out, "Go easy, Jacko! You've got 'em on the run now!" Here and there people shake their heads and smile.

Jacko, street-character, nutcase, who sought the bubble reputation even in the cannon's mouth and ended up sans anything, marches away from us issuing words of command.

Jackson Armitage doesn't smile. All he says is:

"We could have shortened the war; by years perhaps."

Okay. I'll try. I will try.

Back again down Barton Villas. The wind seems to have dropped. The houses are brick with carved white wood brackets; functionally fussy. A lot of them have conservatories stuck on the side, and little balconies. Pollarded trees flank the empty road. A street for genteel recluses, widows of drowned families. But still no barber shop. On the promenade we're forced to ask for help.

And we run up against an unwritten law of nature. It has many versions. One: given double doors and a choice of pull or push you will only succeed on the fourth and last option; two: the last screw you need to loosen will be rusted solid; three: the caddy will be empty when it's your turn to make the tea. But the one that's carved on granite in letters of fire says that when asking directions in a strange place you will meet, in order: a first-time visitor, a foreigner, a local who thinks he knows and a local who does know but is profoundly deaf. We overturn the law. Everyone we try is local and can hear perfectly well; just that none of them has ever heard of Walter Chinnery, Gents' Hairdresser. At our last attempt we approach a man in a cloth cap. He politely removes it to reveal that he is completely bald.

"Who? Oh, you mean Sailor; it's old Sailor you're after. Not surprised you missed him. He don't advertise. Go back up the Villas and it's under the flats on the corner, this side. Not on the main road. All right? It's in the basement. He never has a sign out. And don't worry. You won't have to wait." He strolls off, whistling.

Beside the spot where we watched Jacko drilling his phantoms there are nine steps that lead down into a narrow area that smells of dustbins. No name on the dirty brown door, no card in the sash window where a curtain sags from a piece of washing line. It's meant to be a shop though, so we go in without knocking.

A coal fire glows in the smallest grate that money can buy. A few feet away a cast-iron paraffin heater joins in to bestow on the room that heavy, unnatural warmth that we in this country call 'cosy'. A collection of bits of carpet and lino almost meet edge to edge like ice floes on a grey shiny sea of sealed concrete. Yellowing newspapers fill some of the gaps. There's a smell of cat.

The cat lies in a low-backed carver chair standing before a wall mirror where the light from the window can catch it sideways. A shelf next to the mirror holds an assortment of bottles, bowls and card prop-ups suggesting things I used to think you rubbed in your hair. But what catches the eye are the photographs; dozens of them, hanging in frames all round the room.

Old dreadnought battleships, groups of officers and ratings seated beneath huge turreted guns, men o'war massed for review in bays from Penzance to Malta. The Edwardian navy in sepia, or black and white becoming sepia. Of Sailor himself there is no sign.

At the back of the room a curtain divides us from whatever else he calls home. Beside us a hatstand and a wide plank resting on two bentwood chairs where the clients must make themselves comfortable while they wait. It's bright January outside, edging towards a colourful sunset, but in here it's all gloom. Whatever Walter Chinnery's life has been, it lies decaying now among these sad accoutrements, unknown except to a loyal few. I see him trimming and shaving amid the sham-bling talk, then wandering down in the evening to breathe the sea air among strangers before descending once more to the fire, the cat, the racing page and mementoes of the Grand Fleet. He must have played his part in some huge dramas on the ocean. And now this.

He's been there all the time, in the shadows. He folds his paper and rises to his feet. A big, tall man; McFee has said as much. Rubbery, veined face, pouched eyes and white toothbrush moustache. What hair he has lies like an atoll on his head. Huge puffy hands. He wears twill trousers, a cricket blazer with the martlets of Sussex on the breast pocket, pullover, tie; and carpet slippers. His expression says we're not regular and maybe we should have knocked. No one who's asking for a barber ever gets sent down here.

And the girl. His eyes narrow and his lips twist as if he's got a lemon instead of an orange. He's reached the age, has Sailor, when you can choose whether to be civil or not.

"The lad and I need a trim," says Shanks. He sounds like a man in a church. I suddenly find myself holding his hat.

"'Ook's behind you." It's half-growl, half-whisper. He shuffles forward, pulling a steel comb from behind the county badge. Wiping it on his sleeve he rests it on the mantelshelf. While Shanks is shrugging off his coat into my hands a white sheet billows out of nowhere and is round his neck almost before he's sat down. The cat, a tortoiseshell tom, transfers to my lap and we look into each other's eyes; and suddenly I understand the reason behind my hit-and-miss performance as a psychic.

It's about atmosphere; atmosphere and character.

In Vic's caff, in Danny Ogden's shelter, I got nothing but what sharp eyes and ears could tell you. Those surroundings were too strange, too exotic. Fifteen-year old public schoolboys who are also woodland-running loners could only be fascinated aliens there. My deeper, rarer senses were swamped, like the canny ploughman fleeced by the three-card trickster at the annual fair. But in the Dunkleys' conventional parlour and the ordinariness of washday in Sal's prefab the power could get to work.

So down here it's going to be a struggle, and knowing the problem will make little difference.

"'Ow d'you want it?"

"Just a trim."

Walter Chinnery isn't just any old barber; you can see that. But he suffers, like they all do, from a peculiar hardness of hearing that comes on whatever the answer to his question. All they hear is 'short back and sides'. Any further refinement sends them completely deaf. They can't all be ex-servicemen so I suppose it's in the blood, this conviction that your neck goes all the way to the top of your head and that air should circulate freely right round your ears. At the first sound of the scissors the cat abandons me for Sailor's slippered feet.

I watch him as he sets about Shanks's greying hair. There's hardly anything barberish about his style, what with his strange front parlour of a shop and the scrofulous animal that rubs up against his legs while he works. None of that quickness of cutting; the few decisive snips, then *snipsnipsnipsnip* in the air and in again. No. Old Sailor does a snip here, a snip there, then looks into the mirror with his watery eyes and lets his scissor hand drop to his side as if reminding himself of what he's meant to be doing. He has no notion of what a later age will term 'throughput'. Because down here is all the time in the world. It's curiously homely, curiously personal, and I almost look forward to my convict cut at the hands of this old man; hands with fingers too big for the scissors jammed onto them.

Now and then his eyes find me in the mirror, then shift to Berenice. A girl. In his shop. He can't know she hails from a more vigorous society. She doesn't give a damn; but he does.

At last Shanks opens the ball.

"I see you're a member of Sussex. Do you get to many of their matches?"

"No."

"Not enchanted with them last season?"

"Wouldn't know. Got the jacket in a pawnshop."

As he speaks, Sailor lets out short impatient sighs. Surely he talks to his customers? Perhaps not to strangers; strangers who bring girls in. Snip. Snip.

"You sound like a Londoner. Did you cut hair there too?"

"No. Only down 'ere."

"Been at it long?"

"Long enough." Snip. Snip.

"Not complaining, you understand, but I get the feeling this wasn't your original trade. Navy man? Couldn't help noticing the pictures."

"Yeah; once."

"First War?"

"Must have been, I suppose." Snip.

"Grand Fleet?"

"Yeah."

"Looks like you were on big ships, from the photos."

No answer. Snip. Snip.

"May I ask what ship you were on?"

Sigh. "*Centurion*."

"Ah, yes. She ended up as a target ship after the war, I believe. Second Battle Squadron at Jutland. Were you there?"

Snip. Snip.

"Yeah."

I'm impressed by Shanks's grasp of naval history. But then boys my age think older people are stuffed with knowledge when all they've done is take an interest. Walter Chinnery isn't impressed. He goes quiet; and after a few more tries so does Jackson Armitage. I look at Fernleaf and she raises her eyebrows. Hard work, this. And I'm getting nothing.

Sailor takes up tongs and puts a couple of lumps of coal on the fire. He unhooks a small square mirror from the mantelpiece, holds it behind Shanks's head, then bends to whisper something in his ear. He murmurs back and the white sheet comes off for him to get to his feet and have his shoulders brushed.

Fixing me with a cold stare the barber stands waiting as I swap places, then vanishes through his curtain to reappear with a cushion. A sharp tap on the shoulder tells me to get up again and he slaps the cushion on the seat. Why? I'm plenty tall enough; taller than some of the wizened old codgers he must get in here. But of course. I'm a child, and all children get a cushion.

The sheet is tied none too gently round my neck and out comes the steel comb again. This time he holds a wax taper to the fire, then runs the flame along the comb, backwards and forwards.

"'Ow d'you want it?"

No point arguing the toss. "Short, please."

Shanks tries again. "The Geddes Axe was a bad business, eh?"

"The what?"

"Cutting down the Navy after the War. Did it affect you?"

Snip, snip. "Yeah."

"Must have been hard. Did you have trouble finding work?"

Silence, then a long sigh. Sailor jerks my head round and starts to lay bare my left ear.

"'Oo didn't?"

The light outside is fading fast. Down in the basement it simply gives up, and little by little parts of the room begin to disappear; vanish in a forever kind of way, as if dying, merging back into some underworld. The old man turns a switch by his curtain and a different kind of gloom fills the place; a sad amber mist. The world beyond the window goes dark. The cat mews a couple of times.

I'm starting to worry. This haircut'll be done in five minutes. The atmosphere that's gripping me is solid and real. Walter Chinnery is real and nothing is coming out of him except that he wants us to go away but a job's a job.

Snip. Snip.

"You're right there. I had the same trouble myself; Army in my case. I wanted to stay in."

I hear him lying his head off, but I know it's not easy. He's winging it and it's not his style. "Fit homes for heroes, remember that? How did you get on?"

"Went under the Red Duster."

Forced laugh. "Ah, well. Then along came the Slump. Hit the Merchant Navy hard, didn't it? Come unstuck again?"

Sailor clears his throat, shoots him a look in the mirror and starts stropping a razor. It's the fastest he's moved since we came in.

"Yeah. For a while."

"Was that when you took this up?"

"No." He wrings out a flannel under the tap and wipes the back of my neck. The razor waves uncertainly and he puts a hand on my head to hold it still. "Nightwatchman."

Contact. Maybe. Careful, now.

"You're a Londoner. I was with the Highways department oh, around nineteen-thirty, thirty-one; the docks. Wapping; Shadwell way. We employed a lot of watchmen."

Now I'm really uneasy; maybe because I know this is all codswallop. The unease makes it even harder to concentrate and I begin to colour up. Luckily the back of my neck is now raw and aflame, so perhaps it looks normal. I want Shanks to leave off, pay up and get us out of here. It's going nowhere. The scissors get to work on top.

Snip, snip...

"Ha, yes. They had one or two adventures, those chaps. Not surprising, really. How about you?"

"Suppose so."

Snip... Snip...

"Yes. How about this? One night one of our chaps found himself guarding a criminal, for the police."

"Yeah?"

Snip.

Snip.

"Mmm. Where was it? Garnet Street, that's it. You know it, I daresay. A chap was caught robbing a pawnshop. Quite a celebrated safebreaker, apparently. Hang on, his name'll come to me."

I close my eyes.

Snip…

Snip…

"Smallwood! That's it."

Snip.

I open them again. Walter Chinnery is standing, stock-still, his great hand sitting on my head like a starfish, his eyes no longer watery, staring over me into the glass.

"You're the Bill."

"Pardon?"

"The Law."

"No, Mister Chinnery; not with these two here. But I believe you know what I'm talking about."

Suddenly everything goes completely black.

"Shilling's gone!" shouts Fernleaf.

"My God, so has he!" There's a scuffling. The cat screeches.

"Through the curtain! There may be a back way!"

I've still got the sheet knotted round my neck and I'm blundering around like a Hallowe'en spook, but we leap into an invisible gap and find ourselves in even deeper darkness. The smells say it's a kitchen. Our groping reveals that three doors lead from it. I just know they don't lead directly to any room and that Sailor Chinnery knows the dark passages and he may be at bay in one of them, an open razor in his hand. Amid the odour of old fat and cat's fish we feel for the handles and, momentarily, we hesitate.

"Does nobody have a light?" Shanks hisses. "We need to see him. He's a big man and probably desperate."

"And probably well away by now," I say, finally throwing the sheet off me.

Just then the lights come on. It's not for a shilling in the meter, because the little black mechanism is here in the kitchen. Just happens. No time now to work it out; we have to find him. The passages are narrow. They lead to two cellars and a coal-hole and he isn't in any of them. Gingerly I try the handle of the last door; it isn't locked. I've always wanted to do this; not like the panic-stricken farce at the Hopetown Flats, but like in the movies. The excitement overrides any thought of our reception, and I throw the door open.

It's a bedroom and it has a sash window that opens onto a twitten. Beneath the window is a cast-iron bath with a wooden lid and on the lid sits the old man, slumped in defeat. The window only opens nine inches and the state of his clothes shows how he's tried to squeeze out. From behind us the cat comes in and joins him.

"Come on, Sailor," says Shanks. "You're in no trouble. You have our word."

We get him back to the front parlour-shop. He sits in the carver chair absently stroking the cat while I poke up the fire and Fernleaf makes everyone tea. Shanks introduces us and tells him why we're here; which he knows anyway. "Here you are, Mr Chinnery, two sugars," says the girl whose presence so upset him, and she hands him his mug. He drinks it off in quick gulps. She smiles warmly right into his eyes and takes one hand in her small fingers.

He'd be a hard old man not to respond.

"Yer a Kiwi, ain't yer? We used to call yer Fernleafs, in the first war."

"That's right," she says.

"Never 'ad a young lady in 'ere before." His face softens like a great melting candle.

"Been 'aving these dreams. No, it started before that. End o' November. I'd be comin' dahn the stairs after me evening walk on the prom, dahn into this basement. It ain't exactly Buck 'Ouse but it's all I could get. It'd be dusk time, not dark yet. Comin' dahn the steps was like, steppin' into a kind o'shadow. Creepy, unwelcomin'. It made yer 'air stand up. None of the regulars ever seemed to notice nuffink. But that was during the day. No, it was when I was on me own, comin' back; every evenin'. So I stopped goin' out."

390

He stares at each of us. "Imagine that. Big bloke like me. Windy abaht, well, nuffink'. Then I started 'aving the dreams."

"Can you describe them?"

"Nah. Just dreams. Yer woke up finkin' they was real. Stayed in yer mind a long time."

"Anything in particular?"

"Nah, just crazy fings. Never made no sense."

I'm standing there with half a haircut, trying to make something come through. I want to read the dreams he won't talk about. Nothing, not a thing. Just this warm homely cave; a human version of Badger's house in the Wild Wood. I'm seduced by its feeling of security underground, away from the gales and the noises of the street.

"Tell us about the night you looked after Albert Smallwood."

He doesn't ask why. "Yeah. Seems very clear now. It was a dirty night, a bad smog. Garnet Street, like yer said; well, rahnd the corner, like. I was watchin' a pile o' wood blocks 'cos they 'ad the road up. People used to nick 'em fer their fires. They burned well 'cos o' the tar. Times was 'ard; you couldn't blame 'em for tryin'. I used to drop the odd one in the brazier meself. You must 'ave 'ad troubles wi' blocks in them days. Oh, no, forgot; you're a doctor."

I watch his eyes, his mouth, the top of his head. I close my eyes to concentrate on the words, trying to recall McFee's account of these events, trying to merge them like in a stereoscope. But it's still not working. And there'll be no more chances like this one.

"First I knew, there was these two men, a broadish bloke and a little skinny geezer in a flat 'at. The big one was the Old Bill; always stands out a mile. Not that I didn't get on wiv 'em. Met 'em all the time on the job. Me and the bobby on the beat 'ad the street to ourselves after midnight. They'd share the fire wi' me and yarn a bit; ex-matelots, one or two of 'em. Anyway, 'e says; would I keep an eye on the little geezer on account of 'e was coughing 'is guts up and needed to sit dahn. 'Wasser game?' I says, but e' says not to worry; 'e won't give no trouble, just for a minute. You could see he wasn't kidding. So I sez, make yerself at 'ome, mate; be my guest."

"That was Detective-Constable McFee. Was he away long?"

"'Bout five minutes."

"That long?"

"He was by the car, thinking," I say. There's something niggling at me again. "Hold on a second, will you?" And I turn out the light. The room doesn't go completely dark. The fire glows and the evening light picks out the shape of the sash window.

It was him. He's been here. For a few seconds I sense the shade that Sailor felt around him as he came down his steps from the street above. I turn the switch and light floods over us again.

"Happy, Clement?"

"Yes, thank you." But we all exchange looks over the old man's head.

"Go on, Mr Chinnery."

"I watched 'im till 'e gave over coughin', then I sez, 'I reckon they forgot you, chum; fancy a cup o' char?' 'E nods, so I says not to do nuffink silly, like, while me back's turned, and I went into me 'ut." He's sounding more London all the time, as though he's coming up for familiar air. "So when I come out 'e's pokin' up the fire, in the brazier, like. I sez, jokin' like, 'You feelin' chilly, mate? Nicked a couple o' them blocks? Ain't you in enough trouble? Never mind me.' Then 'e gives me this look and 'ands me a fiver. Like that. A fiver! I sez, still jokin' like, 'All right chum, I won't breeve a word.' Well, a fiver's a fiver, ennit? Two bloody – pardon my French, Miss – bleedin' weeks' wages. So I took it. So would you. I fought it was bit much, but there you are. Then back comes the law an' takes 'im away. Never saw 'im after that."

"Weren't you called to witness in court?"

"Nah. Only read about it."

"That's it?"

"Yeah. Then years after, I start gettin' these... feelin's. Then the dreams. Then you turn up. Look, I admit it was a sweetener an' I took it. But I didn't know what it was for. I ain't never been in no trouble, not real trouble. Don't need it neither, not now."

We all watch the fire in silence for a while. I want to stay longer; not because I think I can get anything with my wonderful psychic powers; they're a washout, again. But because I like this poor shelter under the street with its warmth and its cat and its difference.

"You needn't worry, Mr Chinnery," says Fernleaf. "No one's after you for anything."

Jackson Armitage takes his coat and hat from the stand. He's tight-lipped, lost in his own thoughts and I don't dare guess at them.

"Hold it there." Fernleaf picks up the scissors and snips a few tufts from the top of my head, then leans and whispers very softly, "Something for the weekend, sir?"

As I put on my coat Shanks pushes a folded five-pound note into Sailor's breast pocket. "For your trouble. This one's clean." The old man doesn't look up. The girl kneels by him and holds his hands between hers. "There won't be any more dreams from now on, Mr Chinnery. Good luck in your work and your life. Do take care of yourself."

It's the thing he wants to hear. Smiling back he murmurs, "Fank you, Miss. Come back any time." So we leave him.

It's surprisingly light outside. The sun declining over the sea suffuses Barton Villas with a pinkish glow. We walk towards it slowly and in silence. The barber's story adds little to McFee's account and nothing that helps us. My failure to connect with any knowledge he might have concealed is obvious from my unwillingness to speak. Shanks asks me anyway and I only shake my head.

A man on a bike squeaks past, in an overcoat and floppy hat, carrying a long slender pole over his shoulder. As we watch him on the wide empty road he cycles up to a lamppost and, without stopping, swings the pole up and pushes an iron rocker switch below the lantern. Magically, the glass fills with soft white light. He pedals across the street and repeats the movement. Zig-zagging down the Villas he causes the lamps to glow one by one, each a separate beacon ready to contend with the night, among the shorn plane trees that lead down to a stupendous winter sunset in bands of lilac, orange and green. Three abreast we walk without a word and see the sun touch the rim of the ocean. The lamplighter is a silhouette now and his bicycle makes no sound.

Behind their curtains the widows of Barton Villas play solitaire.

What have we come away with? The mystery of the sudden darkness in the room can now be added to the incident of the mist in Unicorn Passage and the opening of the safe in the Shawe-Trittons' library. Jackson Armitage doesn't know about the last one. And we've lifted a weight from an old man's mind; or just been around when someone else did. But the riddle of the unicorn is no nearer to a solution; and I don't know whether to feel relief or sorrow. McFee's last throw has rolled into the shadows after all.

The lamplighter touches the farthest lamp and turns out of sight. I look at the Doctor's face and Fernleaf's face and see the last glow of the sun on them as it sinks into the sea. Between us we know all the questions and nearly all the reasons.

But we don't have a single answer. The trail of Albert Smallwood has gone stone cold.

Chapter 29

Chairs squeak and scrape. Bursts of polite laughter punctuate the murmur of voices. I sit at the back near the edge of the room and watch it fill with a company of familiar faces, some of them surprising. This place above the refectory is no longer used as a classroom but it hasn't changed; still the cream-painted matchboard and chamfered panelling, still no curtains in the windows whose shutters haven't worked in my lifetime. You get a superb view over fields and copses from here, and at night the wall-lamps give the room a familiar comfort that just about keeps the dark at bay, making you feel as if you're in an old ship beset in a remote, frozen sea.

Every term the Monk's Hill Literary and Debating Society posts its forthcoming programme and every week it meets to talk to itself in symposia, readings, debates. When I was old enough I went along to a symposium and sat with my mates among a lot of older boys, not knowing what to expect. One after another the Long-hairs stood up and delivered long chunks out of their favourite books; very long chunks. At the end of each one nobody clapped. Nobody ever clapped at symposia, not even out of sheer relief. It was the convention. I didn't go again.

Until tonight. I have a special interest in tonight.

Still, not everbody here belongs to the group who look down on games and never rise above cadet in the Corps. There's Harrison, Vice-Captain of Boxing, talking to Henry Attridge, our one-man rugby pack. I nod, and they raise their eyebrows in surprise.

It's okay being back. I haven't been asked about the kind of holiday I had. That's for day one and I missed it. Anyway. I've got one thing which I'm keeping close because here is not the place. What matters is to be enfolded in the ludicrous normality of school. For a week I've wallowed in it, glad to be out of a world where unreal, bizarre things keep hauling you back by the collar; out of a dream that dived down into nightmare, where you were sure that even worse had happened than you could remember. This place has become home once more.

Fernleaf and Connie are off on tour again and promise to send me cards and letters. I feel secure in both of them. None of this lot have women like mine.

A figure slides into the next chair, his eyes flickering round doing a who's who. Harilal Gosalia, best mate; thank the Lord.

"You lost, old chap? This is the Lit'n'Deb."

"Is that what it is? Well, then the humble shall be exalted, you ratbag."

"No, truly. What does an Outer Barbarian seek in this place?"

Chess and looking at the stars don't call for a lot of chat. To be able to speak is the thing here; speech is power; a good line of talk a beacon against the darkness. They call Harilal 'Swatty'; less to do with habits of study than just sounding Indian. To some he's Harry. It doesn't matter to him. He's a natural; you can listen to him for hours because he speaks better English than most of us and handles it like a juggler.

"I have to tell you, old chap, that we don't shower after doing this."

"Thanks for the tip. I'm here because the debate interests me. Doesn't it you?"

"Of course. But your people are in Africa, aren't they?"

"They could be in bloody Antarctica for all..."

"Order! Order."

Toady Hopwood presiding. "Is he always in the chair?" I whisper.

"Oh, yes. He is the chairman. And he's noticed you. Don't worry; many strangers in tonight. Pretty full house."

"Order. Before opening the one thousand and sixth debate meeting of the Society, here are the announcements."

The four speakers lean back in their chairs behind ancient tilted desks and look like old hands at the game. A strange air of exclusivity wraps itself round me.

"The motion before us tonight is: 'This House Regrets the Passing of the British Raj'. I call upon Gracie Major to propose the motion."

Pete Gracie's all right, blood of the blood of generations of our white servants of Empire; and he shows a good grasp of the history of the thing without sounding too arrogant about it. After ten minutes of gory details about Thuggee, Suttee and Dacoity he sits down to clapping and cheering. Then Frank Musgrave gets up and replies, reeling off a list of the jewels of ancient Indian civilisation, of the monuments of the Mughal Empire, and finishing up with equally gory details of the suppression of the Sepoy Mutiny and of the Massacre of Amritsar. Cries of 'Shame!' accompany his comments on the last incident from boys whose families supported the shooting down of hundreds of civilians less than thirty years ago. I notice Toady Hopwood doesn't call for order.

Swatty utters an occasional 'hear, hear.' He turns and whispers, "It's usually funnier than this. More jokes. India's a very funny place."

Frank Musgrave sits down to thin applause, mostly mine. Then up jumps Herbie Killick to second the motion. His line is to deliver a personal attack on Mahatma Gandhi, blaming him for the huge death toll that's followed Partition and is still going on. He trots out Churchill's jibe about the 'naked fakir' and goes on to regret that Gandhi wasn't locked up and the key thrown away. Our chairman nods vigorously, remembers himself and puts on a straight face. The clapping that follows Killick's five-minute rant is the longest so far. I turn to Harilal Gosalia, whose arms remain firmly folded, like they've been since the start.

"Is clapping against your, er, religion or something?"

"No."

"Killick's talking bollocks."

"Not entirely, old chap, but he does lay it on a bit thick."

Something's taking over my body. It's as if my knees are going to be sick. The upper parts of my legs seem to be connected to my stomach and everything's trembling. The more I want to stand up and answer what I've just heard, the more I'm filled with a fever of fear and excitement. Mr Lo's words echo in my head. I hardly hear Don Cathcart's offering, just see his mouth move; too busy composing my own speech. I don't hear the audience's reaction to Don either, because there isn't any. It looks like this house is ready overwhelmingly to regret the passing of the Raj. Smiling, Toady calls for speakers from the floor.

"Can anyone speak?" I hiss.

"Of course, troglodyte. Free country, you know."

My hand shoots up, but someone's already on his feet, spouting on about the jewel in the Imperial crown. I'm sick with impatience, every limb quivering. The more I put my hand up the more I'm ignored. A couple of sensitive types stick up for the new Republic but it's wishy-washy stuff about self-determination. You need to hit this crowd where it hurts.

"I will take two more from the floor before the concluding speeches."

Not me, then. Attridge, of all people, rises up to blast India as the next stronghold of Communism. People actually stand up to applaud and Toady's lips can be seen going 'Quite right, quite right.' My hand bounces around on the end of my arm. Beside me Harilal Gosalia sits, unmoving, inscrutable. The chairman nods towards me. I leap up, arm still in the air, words crowding my throat in quavering disorder.

"I'd just like to say..."

"Order! Order!" from all sides. "Address the chair!"

"You must speak through the chair."

"Why not?" I whisper. "You've all been talking through your arses."

"Yes. Thank you. Mr Chairman, Killick over there..."

"Order! The seconder! Order!" Toady Hopwood smiles as the audience does his job for him.

"The seconder for the proposition. Observe the rules or give way."

My ignorance gains me time. Somehow I become calm. "Mr Chairman, sir; gentlemen. Wherever the Mahatma, Mr Gandhi, goes there is no trouble. He dispels it by the force of his personality. He doesn't need troops behind him…"

Murmurs of 'rot', 'twaddle.' One or two snorts; some laughter.

"I have to tell you this means his life is in constant danger…"

"Good!"

I raise my voice. "Soon someone'll try to kill him!"

"Hooray!"

"About time!"

"And they will! Don't be surprised if it's tomorrow, or today even, while you're all here – most of you – talking nonsense! One of his own people will shoot him, take my word for it. He's as good as dead. Then you can all celebrate." I sit down, trembling, to a heavy silence.

"Thank you, Garner; most entertaining. I now call upon Musgrave to conclude for the opposers." The rest passes me by. I'm in my own world, desperately going over what I've just said. The Nervousness of the First-Time Speaker racks me worse than before. I've exposed my thoughts – actually the thoughts of a once-met Chinese traveller – and you can't take it back. When it's over Frank Musgrave comes over and thanks me. It's the only time he and I will ever speak to each other. As for Swatty, I still can't tell what he's thinking. He takes me by the arm and steers me round the quad a few times under the winter stars.

"You stuck your neck out, I'd say."

"So would I. They needed telling, Swatty. It's true. He'll be murdered, you wait."

"Inclined to agree, old chap. It's a common fate of political showmen."

"Is that what you think? That why you abstained?"

"Tell you the truth, I don't want to offend the old fellow."

"Your dad? Hot for the British, is he?"

"More complicated than that. Politics is a barrowload of monkeys, apparently."

"Don't tell me; nothing is what it seems."

"Nothing is ever what it seems. Can I say for that matter that you are not the Neolithic Garner of old. Something is on your mind. Not the fate of Mohandas Gandhi, though."

"Like you said, Swatty, nothing is what it seems. If I didn't know it before, I know it now."

Morning dawns to porridge and the smell of toast. I've had a bad night, not much sleep. Footsteps come up behind me on the polished stone floor and a folded newspaper slaps down over my side plate. One big banner headline runs across it:

GANDHI ASSASSINATED

Herbie Killick's voice drawls over my head to the suddenly hushed sitters at the long refectory tables. "Shot by a fanatic, Garner; an Indian. One of his own bloody Hindus. I'm heartbroken. Keep the paper."

A journey of a thousand *li* begins with a single step. I look at the huge black letters, begging them to rearrange themselves into better news. And it starts there, the end of any hope that I can sink back among the things I know. The sky doesn't vanish just because you sit down under a barrel. My half-open eyes now open fully, in the place that claims to open them for you. From that moment I begin to fall out with Monk's Hill School.

Gently at first. The odd remark in conversation. "What am I going to do next, then?" If you have a quick answer we all have a laugh. There are worse things than being thought a prophet. But I've made enemies among a small group in the Lit'n'Deb society. In ones and twos they approach, bowing, hands together, calling out in cod Anglo-Indian, "He Who Knows All, Sees All; who will win the 3:30 at Wincanton?"

The FA Cup, the Ashes, the Boat Race, Wimbledon.

A handful of decent types take it seriously. One lunchtime Norman Grierson asks me if I can give him some advice. I like Norm so I say yes.

"I need to mend a few fences with my pa, Garner. I thought, if I could help him out – with his business dealings – I'd be on the right side of him again, see?"

"So what do you want?"

"He's got shares, in Malaya. Tin, rubber; that sort of thing."

"Good for him. Oh, right."

"See? A bit of good advice, from me. Get it?"

"And why should he listen to you?"

"Because he's desperate. I only have to be right once. I'll say I've got someone on the inside. Well, it's true isn't it? You've got the, er... you're a clairvoyant."

"No go, Grierson. It's not the way it works. You might as well read the stars in *The Mirror*. For Christ's sake, they'd all be bloody millionaires if they could do what you're on about."

I watch him walk away from what Doctor Jackson Armitage regards as the finest psychic he's ever come across. Did I really foresee Gandhi's death? If the debate never happened, would I have sat up somewhere and heard those shots under the Delhi sky?

No, not really; and there are others. I say no to all of them, deny my powers, and see friends turn into armed neutrals.

One night I wake from a rare spell of deep sleep. Loud knocking is echoing through the dormitory. Sitting up, I see every bed's empty. The sounds stop. Suddenly a wailing voice cries out, "Are you there, Garner? Knock twice to answer. Woooh." Two loud knocks follow.

"Yes, I'm here," I say wearily, "and I'd like to sleep."

"Wooooh. Woooh. We knew you were going to say that."

The voice of Rupert Kiddle-Nash. Perfect. Just the kind of reptile who needs his features rearranged. Mister Brain Death himself.

Kiddle-Nash puts foreigners into two categories: wogs and niggers; by which time his intellectual resources are exhausted and good-natured replies from the likes of Harilal Gosalia fall like pats on the head of a gurgling baby.

"There, there, Kiddy," I say. "Run along now. Take your playmates with you and go to bed."

"Cut it, Garner. What's going to happen next, then?"

I swing my feet out. "Well, I'll tell you. I can see your future clearly. You're about to go on a long flight." I advance down the dormitory between rows of beds bought second-hand from Victorian hospitals. Who are these merchants? Are there so few jokes in their lives?

"Don't bother to pack," I call out. The vision of his body twitching on the ground twelve feet under a window is bettered only by the thought of a half-year of terrified respect; respect and silence, from a creep with no evidence and mute witnesses. If I'm going to be Public Enemy Number One I may as well get the most out of it.

Suddenly, as I brace myself to push through the door and grab him, there's a warning hiss from the corridor and a rush of bodies flows round me. I'm not going down just for being out of bed so I tack on and in a few practised seconds all's quiet again.

Whispered insults are going to be a bad idea tonight. We're too long in the tooth to have dormitory bullies, but I know they think I've become slightly dangerous. It isn't the boxing; team members aren't allowed to get into fights and everyone knows it; but the eyes, the eyes that look as if they're reading you, that might be homing through the dark like radar. Only days after the whole thing started, the remarks fall away to be replaced by quick averting of looks. Compared to what the too short, too tall, too fat, too thin types go through every day it doesn't amount to much. On the ginger-nut four-eyes scale it rates low. But it takes me a few degrees off my old course; my old school course, that is. As for the peterman, he begins to grow on my mind again by day as well as by night. To avoid the dreams I take to sitting up by the window near my bed, watching the dark countryside, hearing my colleagues snore and snuffle. If I could only transfer a part of my fear to Kiddle-Nash, bring him sitting upright in a cold sweat every midnight, then justice might be served. What the hell. The toerag will end up prosperous, pompous and stupid, dispensing his refutation of the Sermon on the Mount at Prizegivings and Speech Days in joints just like this.

A group of masters who so far have tolerated my existence now begin to move in on me.

It's not just the Gandhi business, or my outburst at the debate, but their suspicion that they no longer enjoy my respect. People dressed in a little brief authority, who ordinarily wouldn't recognise a Cape buffalo if it settled on their nose, are often very sensitive to unspoken contempt. They're put on the earth to see that rank injustice gets an even break and they give it all they've got. Beware the man of straw when you give him the old Anatolian smile. So those charged with power over me and the duty to show me wisdom set out to prove how much more they enjoy using the first than trying the second.

"Well, Garner, let us depart from the usual order of things."

"Excuse me, sir?"

"Why, you give the answer, then I ask the question!" (Laughter)

The vibrant wit of Tusker Oliphant; how it brightens a dull hour. But I'm a different animal now. I've knocked around with Haydn McFee, faced Horace, crossed swords with Sal. And got a girl. Tusker's a fugitive from real life; a freak with no other harbour than here.

"Hardly, sir. Such powers are beyond me."

"I beg your pardon, Garner?" The slow, practised menacing tone.

"I mean, sir, that I am not a mind reader. If I hear a question I shall endeavour to answer it." Laughter fades. Atmosphere very thick.

"You shall answer not one, Garner, but many. Report to me after supper."

Two hours of trigonometry. He isn't alone.

One by one Tusker Oliphant and his kind rock and tumble from their pedestals. Their pasteboard reputations melt in the cold rain of my experience with the players in the Smallwood saga. And because I can no longer hide it, even in the respectable clothes of courtesy, they empty their life's dustbins over me, every day.

Harilal Gosalia watches over me from afar. More often than usual I find myself sitting on a bench next to him; and as often as not he says nothing. One evening I'm watching a sweeping winter sunset from the library. A few others are passing a muted hour and it's very peaceful. He stands beside me and we gaze out of the high sash window.

"Swatty?"

"Tell me, old chap."

"Do you believe in second sight?"

"Of course."

"Why?"

"Because it exists."

"You don't join in with all these jokes about me being a medium?"

"No. You are hardly Mister Aleister Crowley. In fact you're not nearly colourful enough to indulge in the black arts. I don't feel I'm in the presence of the Great Beast."

"How do you know it exists?"

"I've seen it work."

"Tell me your tale, grandma."

"My father has a palace. It would fit comfortably in an avenue in your stockbroker country, but still it impresses his people and they do him honour as they should. He has retainers. Among these are servants of long standing who cast horoscopes and read signs."

"And they get it right?"

"They are still in his employ. I suppose if they foresaw the sack they would have the sense to resign first and enjoy a suitable pension."

"Not trickery? Not just relying on what they know about his character and what he wants?"

"Partly, I suppose. But what does it matter? My father is not a superstitious old fool. Listen to me, old chap. I am hearing things from your own lips that you are not telling me. Something is up."

"I'm not happy, Swatty. Do you believe in ghosts?"

"Yes. They are everywhere. Demons too."

"Thanks a lot. Doesn't it bother you?"

"They are dispelled by simple acts. Surprisingly easy to deal with, really. Three hundred million Indians get through each day all right. They are like irritating children, yapping dogs."

"Nothing serious, then."

"Depends on how you want to take it, old chap. My father used to say, 'The tree does not bear fruit so that men can pick it, therefore do not pick it unheedingly.'"

"Nice sunset, isn't it?"

"Very nice."

I live for games now; it gets me away from closed rooms and the wit of sad men. Out on the sports field they shout at you all the time, insult everything you thought was good about yourself and it doesn't matter. It's brutality without rancour, like the springtime contests of nature.

Otto Mundy of PE and Games is lord of all he surveys. Year on year he tries to make sportsmen of us; year on year he gives slackers and Long-hairs a rough time and trades grudging respect with those of us who do well in the athletic pursuits. By his own lights he's fair, if uncompromising, and he doesn't mix in the backstage politics of the staffroom. So he only notices something's changed when he spots me doing overtime. We call Otto Mundy 'Hoss' because he bellows 'Gee up! Giddup! Get along!' and 'Whoa there!'" A fortnight after the India debate I'm puffing round the outside of the rugby pitch when I hear his ploughman's command floating over to me. "Whoa, Garner! Easy, now!"

He waves me to a bench on the touchline and gives me his scarf as I sit down. The frost's still on the ground and I'm wheezing.

"How come, lad? What's up?"

"Nothing, sir. Making up lost time. Missed the first week and a half, and we've got the match in ten days."

"I don't buy it. Anyone with any sense is indoors. We're not training Commandos here. What's the matter?"

I'm not about to tell him. Though the Smallwood case is supposed to be closed all the fallout from it is still pattering around me, and I know that letting it out would do me good. But Shanks hasn't released me from our oath of secrecy and, anyhow, Hoss isn't the man to understand the half of it. He'll say Pull Yourself Together and nine times in ten it works just because in our little world there's nowhere else to go. He knows that the likes of Hopwood and Oliphant are down on me and we know he doesn't like them, but the old officer code will be stronger than all that and nothing will happen.

Roy Mulligan, wizard maths master and jazz enthusiast – Jazz Mulligan, The Mad Mullah – is an ex-major from some smart regiment and he expresses it for all of them: officers should never argue in front of the men. I wonder what disagreements have flourished closer to home that Fernleaf and I know nothing about.

"Still with us, Garner?"

"Sir? Yes, sir, sorry."

"So what's eating you? Or is it very, very private?"

"Yes, sir. But there's one thing might help, if you'll allow it."

"Well, go on."

"I'd like to do roadwork, once a week. An eight-mile circuit via the pumping station and Curwen Hill. And the golf course."

"That's an odd one; more like nine miles, I'd say. It means you'll have no other time." He snorts hard. "Is this going to bring you back to the fold?"

"Yes, sir."

"Right. But hear this: if you don't cheer up by Founder's Day we cut it. Clear?"

"Thank you, sir."

"And for God's sake talk to your Housemaster. He doesn't charge for advice either. Leave my scarf in the office."

That night I come in from the washroom and find a noisy group clustered round my locker.

One of them has a photo in his hand; Gascoigne's three-quarter profile of Berenice.

"Who's this then, Garner?"

"My cousin. Give it back and never go in my locker again."

"Cousin, eh? Don't look a thing like you."

"Cousins don't. Well, they do where you come from. Hand over."

"None of us has got a secret picture of our cousin. Who is she?" This is Nevil Messervy; a normally inoffensive type who's worked out a little late in the day that sex is worrying and therefore dirty and therefore funny. We get on reasonably well; the odd game of chess. Except he cried off the last one with some remark about X-ray eyes. He's ready to call it a day but the others are egging him on.

"She your girlfriend? Do you do it with her?" Hooting and whoops follow these gems. Monk's Hill's always been an Academy of Delta Wit. I hold out my hand.

"The picture. Now."

Messervy draws it back. My instinct for footwork stops me lunging forward.

"Last chance, Messy."

"Only if you tell us what you do."

I can't risk damage to the picture. But then he drops it on the floor. Fine. Now I'm really pissed off and at least I'm free to rough him up a little. Patience, Garner; one last try. "Pick it up," I say, quietly.

407

"No, leave it on the floor. Let's see him pick it up." The voice of Kiddle-Nash. Better in every way. Messervy's only an idiot for the duration, and still as high over Brain Death as heaven is over hell. I push through and grab him by the throat.

"Your flight was delayed, Kiddie. It can now proceed."

I feel a presence at my shoulder. Only Kiddle-Nash's eyes register whoever's followed me through the gap in the onlookers. It isn't a master or a prefect or Matron; I can tell. The presence taps me on the arm and I let go.

"What a comedown, Kiddle-Nash, from your previous life as a third-rate cockroach. I am not a member of the boxing team, which frees me to inflict injuries upon you; one for each insult." Harilal Gosalia has never raised a hand against anyone. He's an eldest son and his ancestors were chiefs and hillmen. Now the light in his eyes reflects centuries of fierce justice and necessary cruelty towards the wicked. Kiddle-Nash stands as if paralysed.

"All right," says Messervy, reaching down for the photo. "Sorry, Garner."

"Leave it," Swatty replies. "This creeping thing will pick it up."

There's an hour to go before Lights Out. I find him in the library sitting at his favourite table; the one on which someone seventy years before painstakingly carved SACK CONSTANTINOPLE. "Thanks," I say. "But it's tough having your battles fought for you."

"I have to thank you, old chap. You provided the perfect moment for some unfinished business."

"How did you know? Just passing by?"

"Something like that."

We call his father music-hall names like the Jamjar of Hubble Bubble. One day he himself will be the Jem Sahib of back home and we talk of the time when I'll visit him as an honoured guest in the little palace in the hills. We don't know, as our conversation hangs in that quiet room, that when the time eventually arrives for him to come into his own the Princely States will have passed into history, and he will design bridges instead. Civilisation limps along only because it rests on the willing shoulders of people of all kinds, souls of dignity and incorruption like Harilal Gosalia. His friendship uplifts me.

"I'm keeping her picture close by me from now on."

"Very sensible. But say, may I see it?" He looks at Fernleaf for a long time. "She is very beautiful. Like Greta Garbo – in her earlier films – except for the hair, and the…are those freckles?"

"Yeah. She has a few."

"You are a lucky chap."

"Thanks. How come you get it and they don't? You got a girlfriend too?"

"Mmmh, yes."

"What's she like?"

"No idea, old chap. Never met her."

"Make sense, Swatty."

"Let's say, my family are pretty hot on tradition. It's still very much the way."

"Oh, all arranged, is it? Some poor girl of noble birth has been chosen already. Some unsuspecting pearl of the orient to, er, grace your bed and all that?"

"Afraid so, old chap. Sounds quite acceptable, put like that."

"I'll bet. You're okay about it, then?"

"My father chose mine and it will turn out all right. Fate chose yours and who can say what will happen? Not having to worry about it, I can get on with life easy in my mind. Your way may lead to complications and unnecessary hardships."

"Yeah, but suppose someone else came along, like Berenice?"

"That is her name?"

"Yes. You'd fall for her. Then what?"

"Oh, plenty of rooms in the palace. All above board, you know." He smiles. "The trick, apparently, is to be able to organise harmony; so my father says, anyway."

"I wish you could meet her."

"You've really got it bad, haven't you?"

"Crazy about her, Swatty."

"Is that what is worrying you?"

"No, no. She's what makes it bearable."

A letter comes from her. She and Connie have done Scotland again, visited the glen where Bonnie Prince Charlie rallied the clans, seen Carlisle and Hadrian's Wall, and are on their way south once more. The weather's fine. Was it true that last winter we'd been digging out parsnips with pneumatic drills? She's written down all the places they'll be stopping at before heading off for the West Country and back to Inglefield for Easter. Nothing about us. Maybe Connie checks her letters for spelling.

Shanks writes too; a long note arrives on the same day as the standard perfunctory lines from my parents. I reply to them straight away: a variation on my usual cheery stuff. Received your letter. Am still alive. Thank you for your interest in my continued existence. Love.

According to Shanks the Smallwood case is now closed. There have been no further developments and McFee's back at the Yard. A flurry of stories appeared in the London press some time after the explosion at the Drill Hall – a surprising delay – but they dried up after a few days. The Home Office acted quickly. As I read his lines I know that Shanks must be aware of the Secret Service in the background. Still, all that is now in the past.

I try to believe it, but it can't be done. For me the case remains open.

McFee insisted on conditions before going back. One of them was the transfer of Hartington. The letter closes on a regretful note:

"...You must know, Clement, how much a successful conclusion to this affair would have meant to me; and to the future of this branch of science. We might have co-operated on further cases. Be assured that your own health and welfare never ranked below the object of our efforts. Some day, perhaps, I will render you a full account of the high stakes for which this game was played. As for now, I think we may assume that your considerable powers are well in recession. This brings to a close what you must agree has been an interesting chapter in our lives. Give some thought to your birthday and any small thing you may want..."

I put Fernleaf's photo in the envelope, which it fits perfectly.

Night after night I sit up to avoid the dreams, but they come anyway. Deep in the tunnels under London I'm walking alone. The sewers are dry and the floor of the Tubes covered in a thick layer of fine dust as though five thousand years have passed undisturbed. The peter-man moves along them as footprints that appear in puffs of this dust, in trails that lead from the grave in Deptford and Ladywell to the sites of his barren crimes. He passes beneath Danny Ogden and Charlie Carey and the Shawe-Trittons as they sleep; he pauses under Mitch Gascoigne and the Rosenblums. Only one place he avoids: the spot where the overworld has rudely intruded into his domain, where a pawnshop has fallen into a hole in the earth. Yet that is the place he wants to be. I know it, and it won't go away. The Unicorn is still waiting to be found.

"God, you were making a racket last night, Garner. Something you ate?"

"Yeah, your brain. I was still starving afterwards."

It starts to get around, how I howl and mutter in the night. Matron gives me something for it and asks clumsy Freudian questions. It just gets worse.

I'm daydreaming during lessons now, drifting off into every aspect of the case. If I can only think hard and clearly enough I'll turn up some clue I've ignored, something that points to the Unicorn. Then I'll get in touch with Shanks. Or I can forget it and let Smallwood fade away like they do – apparently – if no one understands what they want. Is this just all within me now? Am I carrying the whole thing? Am I losing my grip on everything else?

One morning the beak himself takes us for Latin. Sydney Oakshott, JP; known and not particularly loved as the Sherriff. He's earning his money the easy way, setting us exercises that some prefect or junior master can mark later. Outside the sky is a clear steel-blue. Even the flies have woken up. He strolls up and down the rows as we scratch away in silence. His shadow falls across me, and does not move on. A hairy hand picks up my exercise book. His voice begins to intone:

"*Per Crispinum stetit quominus castra caperentur*. Sal and Horace hold the key. Pressman and Albert's sister."

(Laughter. Cries of 'What?')

"Stand up, Garner."

As I do so he perches himself on his desk-stool and fixes me with an eagle stare.

Please welcome your Master of Mirth, Syd Oakshott, with his absent-minded stooge, Clem Is-He-All-There? Garner. Another bout of entertainment for all the class.

A star is being born.

"Well, Garner. So it was not Crispinus's fault that the camp was not taken. It appears that Sal..." He rolls his eyes and the room erupts. "... and, er, Horace are responsible. Sal? Salt? And would this Horace be our old friend the poet Quintus Horatius Flaccus, by any chance?"

"Er, no, sir."

"But, boys, there is a subplot. Pressman! Pressman? A journalist? And Albert's sister! Prince Albert? Albert Einstein? Albert eaten by the lion? Burlington Bertie from Bow?"

(Prolonged laughter.)

There's not enough mirth in the world. Who would begrudge a dose of the best medicine? It's worth expulsion to give him the old answer: you should be on the stage, sir; it leaves in half an hour.

412

"What is the meaning of this?"

"It's difficult to explain, sir."

"Indeed? Then have an explanation ready for your Housemaster. Meanwhile, expunge this nonsense by removing the entire double page and recopying." He glances at my book with its crop of crosses. "Correctly."

The man in question, to whom I wouldn't appeal if I was the rope in a crocodiles' tug of war, is Toady Hopwood, no less; Franco supporter and Gandhi-hater. There's nothing I wish to say to him. He's seen the world and gained no wisdom from it. Like the Bourbons of old he has forgotten nothing and learned nothing. But the Sherriff is the law in these here parts, so I have no option.

He makes me wait a long time by his door and once inside he starts on me like a doctor with a malinguerer. He's always like that. You just hang on without being insolent and without looking bored until he gets bored himself and chucks you out. This time he has one or two surprises. In my geography exercise book, in the margin beside a traced map of Tasmania, are the words:

Unicorn? Mythical beast. Place? Why Horace? Why Sal? What if sis. dies?

I don't remember writing any of it.

"Well, Garner, what's this all about? Are you compiling crossword puzzles for the school magazine? Or is this a poem in the modern style to perform at the next meeting of our newly discovered society? Part of a script you're sending to Tommy Handley? Or is it something else?"

"Something else, sir."

"What, pray?"

I have to give some sort of answer. "Dreams, sir."

"Ah, yes; dreams. I hear reports of your filling the night with strange cries. In fact I have heard you myself. I am also aware that your work and your attitude are falling off dramatically. Added to this, you have introduced a quarrelsome atmosphere to your dormitory."

He leans forward, his features thrown into deep relief by the firelight, and delivers his second surprise.

"Woman trouble, Garner? That it?"

The question throws me, but not as much as his sudden gentle tone.

"Er, yes, sir. Sort of."

"You have a girlfriend?"

"Yes, Sir."

"And they're ragging you about it."

"So they are, sir."

"And you miss her?"

"Well, yes. Er, sir."

"Then invite her to Founder's Day. We can all meet her then, which ought to shut them up. Two birds with one stone. You are rather young, I daresay, but a few of the older boys are in the same position." He stops and glares at me. "She is respectable, I take it? One or two of the liaisons I just referred to appear to have been, er, business arrangements. There was an unfortunate incident here some years ago involving a movie actress, the aunt of a younger boy. Great scandal; before your time."

"Nothing like that, sir. I doubt she could make Founder's. Good idea though."

"Are you going to marry her?"

I was just getting comfortable with this. Now he's prying. We're only fifteen, for God's sake. Still, what odds? If the thought could be father to the deed.

"Hope so, sir."

He puts on a sad smile. I've seen that smile before on the face of Jackson Armitage.

"Marriage, my boy, begins with a great 'yes' and soon becomes a procession of little refusals. Indeed it does. That is the way." He turns towards the fire and dismisses me with a wave of his hand.

This little flicker of humanity from Toady Hopwood doesn't last. Maybe it's because he let his guard down, but the purgatory he's able to inflict on me day by day gets even worse. Frantically I check all my books for unconscious writing. All the while, a bunch of teachers who can spot every tiny spelling mistake can't see the desperation taking over a human soul.

Early after midnight in the first morning of March I find myself standing in the light of the moon in the middle of a nearby meadow. The grass is springy beneath my slippered feet and a gale's roaring through the elms. The hedges break the force of the wind and where I stand it feels warm. I stare, trembling with strangeness, at the shadows cast by the moonlight and at the few racing clouds. Not only warm, but comforted. This is my childhood again. Instead of dreams brought to me in sleep I've been brought out of sleep into a dream; a memory. For half an hour I wander until I know for certain this is real.

My dressing-gown flaps and tugs, and I begin, in no hurry, to walk back. This is outside the world. I could live outside the world. Out here in the wild warm night I hear a call to freedom. From everything.

Chapter 30

Running as an Aid to Thought: by C. M. Garner. Written in words of air under the sky.

There's nothing to do but think once you're in your stride; take note of your place in a still landscape and let it start you off. I run the nine-mile circuit away from the public gaze and an idea begins to blossom, born of the freedom of the open road. Not wind or rain can divert me, not even the knowledge that the crest of Curwen Hill sets me on the return to a place where I've begun to walk alone except for a few close friends.

There's one light to steer for before the fruition of the big idea. The inter-House boxing match has been postponed due to an outbreak of 'flu, but now it's on again. I've looked forward to it, trained for it and eaten right for it. My body's in good shape, thanks to roadwork and rationing, and it doesn't take an effort on my part to know why I want to compete. It's physical. For ten minutes in the ring I can just punch my way out of the dread that's closing in on me. My unsuspecting assistant will be Venn Haldane, who's never come within a mile of beating me and is already down on our captain's sheet in terms of an easy win.

The usual tumult meets me as I leave the changing room for the oaken arena with its spectator galleries that a long-ago designer of cockpits decided would make a good gymnasium. My seconds are two of the most retiring boys in the school: Edwin McLaws – 'Crab' – and Mike 'Megaphone' Hogg. Crab never speaks when in our corner and Mike has such a quiet voice that he also answers to Whispering Smith. To offer advice and encouragement he has to appear to be consuming my ear. They know their stuff. We're going to walk the bout and the match.

Sitting on the stool I nod across to Venn. I like him. All the boxing crowd get on with each other; you have to. It's the mob around the ring you hate; the weedy types screaming well-honed pugilistic counsel like 'hit 'im!' and 'knock 'im down!' Venn nods back. Hoss Mundy referees as usual in his cords and cricket pullover and he calls us together for the litany.

The bell clangs. I dance straight out of my corner and put a jab clean through Venn's guard. The crowd start yelling. Okay so far.

Then I start to feel as if I'm going to be sick. Somewhere a memory stirs. I shake my head, rush Venn onto the ropes and give him a quick one-two in the ribs. He locks elbows, Hoss slaps me on the shoulder and automatically I step back. But it's all wrong. The yelling in the gym sounds like an electric bell in my head and the back of my mouth feels like an inflating rubber raft's trying to force its way out. He's coming off the ropes, taking up his stance. Such a nice chap, not a difficult proposition; a bit of clever points-scoring without hurting him too much and I'll be home and dry.

It strikes me just before he does. The Hopetown Flats. I hit the big bloke who was slapping Fernleaf around; and then didn't feel too good. Violence, disgust; the look in the old woman's eyes in the top floor room.

There's a huge roar. Venn Haldane's hit me; hard. I stagger backwards and put my gloves up. Blows rain on my forearms and I manage to stop him doing any damage. But I don't land a punch of my own and at the end of the round I know he's ahead. He looks as surprised as I feel. I flop onto the stool.

Crab's looking away at the nearest spectators as if to say: he's not with me. Mike whispers calmly in my ear, "What's up? You all right?"

I can smell wet sponge, witch-hazel and sick, but I nod, breathing a bit harder than I should. His tone changes a notch. "Then what the hell are you playing at? He's knocking you about and you're taking it. Wake up!"

"I don't want to hit him, that's all."

"Could I hear that again?"

"I don't want to hit him."

"Ah. I see. I'm seconding a boxer who doesn't want to hit people."

"Yup."

"Sweet on him, is that it?"

I wrench round. "You arsehole! Would a smack in the mouth help?"

He smiles a patient smile. "It would help us," he whispers, pointing to Crab and himself and me, "if you tried to smack him over there."

Ding! Ding!

Hoss Mundy's looking at me oddly as I come out for round two. I realise I mustn't let him think I'm ill with late 'flu or something or he'll stop the bout. Hitting or not, a no-match isn't what I'm after. For three minutes I defend and jab as scientifically as Gene Tunney, but all my punches lack conviction. The crowd begin to boo and howl. When I sit down I'm not much in need of attention, but Crab and Mike look embarrassed.

"Don't worry," I puff. The next voice I hear comes from the wrong side. Edwin McLaws mutters, "Hogg and me, we reckon you fancy him. That's why you're stroking him like that." He grabs my upper arm in a grip of iron. "Just don't lose. For us. Then you can bloody well run away together; we don't mind. We just don't want to look stupid, all right? You might think of the House as well."

"You're both bastards," I hiss, nodding again at the bemused Venn Haldane. "It'll be okay."

I do enough to get a draw and after the match is over Hoss Mundy gets me in his office. It's a tiny wooden cubbyhole festooned with bits of sports equipment and the smell of polish, sweat and dry rot, with a cluttered bureau and the atmosphere of a corner in some old Antarctic hut. We have about a square yard to stand on. Our faces are close. "What's the matter?" he shouts. "You got religion or something? Conchy? Vegetarian? What?"

"I want to give it up, sir."

"From what we all saw you just have! What's the idea? Come on!" Hoss is going to be out of his depth. Sure, people go off the noble art; it wouldn't be the first time. But not in the middle of a team event. What hope for the world then? He deserves an explanation, for what good it'll do, if only because he isn't one of the persecutors.

"Sir, during the vac I got mixed up in a brawl. Before I was ill, that is. In London; not of my making. I had to hit someone to protect a friend. The thing was, I might not have needed to. I felt bad afterwards, and it all came back when I landed one on Haldane. It made me feel sick. I don't want to box anymore."

He looks at the ceiling, then pushes past me and sits down in his swivel chair. "You learn boxing for self-defence, to survive in a brawl! Was he bigger than you?"

"Yes, sir."

"Then maybe soft-talking him wasn't the answer. There's other reasons for doing it; you know that. Self-discipline, for a start."

"That's right, sir. That's why I want to leave it and concentrate on the running."

"Is that so? I'll tell you what I think, Garner. I think you're losing your grip. I'm hearing about how you're turning into an oddball. Well, there's running and there's running away. I've done what I can for you. You could have been Captain. Bugger off."

My feeling exactly. There's nothing to keep me here now.

Sitting by the window as the dormitory creaks with snoring I hear the temptation of fields.

Easy, easy to climb out, walk the maze of copses and meadows by hedge and gate, mile after mile till I find myself at the edge of Inglefield's woods. A day or two of wild existence and I could sleep in my turret room as safe as a Border reiver in his castle. Or splash along the streams like a fugitive from hounds till I hear the sounds of the weir whispering through the night. Easy but obvious. They'd be there before I was. I need to be with Fernleaf and Connie, protected by their gaze from all my enemies. They'll make Jackson Armitage listen.

St. Francis throws away his finery, the millionaire leaves his mansion for the beachcomber's life, the lady marries her gypsy; the Honourable runs away to sea. The past thrown over and the future left to look after itself.

I bring together her long letter and a railway timetable and get to work.

On March 14th they'll come from Warwick to change at Didcot. Depending on how they feel they'll be going either to London or Bath. There their plans come to an end. I need to catch them then, before they disappear for who knows how long. No time to hope for more news.

Trains from Warwick to Didcot stop at Banbury and Oxford. Round this knowledge I weave a plan that owes a lot to what we've learned about covering our tracks; full of twists, as though each twist somehow makes it safer. I think I remember McFee telling me that simple unplanned crimes were often the hardest to crack. If so, it's a lesson I've decided to ignore. There's nothing to lose.

Oxford station is out. Everyone who does a runner goes there. Often enough, once they've made their gesture, they hang around and wait to be collared. Didcot's less obvious but I'm not taking any chances. I need actually to catch them in whatever train they change to, and only when it's left the station. East and westbound pull out at roughly the same time and I can't risk missing them. They mustn't see me before boarding or the whole thing will falter in a mush of dismay and common sense.

So I choose Banbury, where I can watch for them through the carriage windows as the train arrives. I have to leave them with no choice but to take me in. All I'll need is a ticket from Banbury to Didcot.

In my locker are two boxing photos, taken down from the inside of the door straight after my meeting with Hoss Mundy. One's a posed shot of Bruce Woodcock, British heavyweight champion, still getting over the famous 'sucker punch' fight with Joe Baksi. The other's of Henry Armstrong, the Punching Preacher; my favourite black fighter. He appeals to me more than Joe Louis or Ezzard Charles or Jersey Joe

Walcott because he says things that ennoble his profession. I've done a forged signature in fountain pen across the corner: 'Best Wishes. Homicide Hank.' I take the photos to Basil Harrison and offer them for his boxing album.

"Say, five bob the pair?"

"I've got pages of Woodcock. The Armstrong one maybe. Half a crown. No, hang on; did you put that autograph on? You crooked sod. Two bob."

"Leave off, Harrison. Half a crown. Look at the condition."

"Two bob, Garner. Just for ducking out."

"I retired, Harrison; like Gene Tunney. Split it; two and threepence. Old times' sake."

I wait for the 14th; a Sunday. The fact it isn't a weekday makes my plan blessed. Three trains for Didcot will call at Banbury: the 8:32, 12:37 and 4:42. They'll be on the 12:37 if what the letter says makes any sense. Morning service will end at ten o'clock. By ten fifteen I'll be leaving the school gates for my usual run, but once out of sight I'll make a wide circuit and head north. It's fifteen miles to Banbury by road. I know I can push myself to twelve before slowing to a walk-trot for the rest. It leaves little room for mistakes or mishaps but I'm not going to accept lifts and turn up too early. For someone doing a runner the best cover's actually running all the way. Turn up in trousers and jumper and slip through like a needle in the moving crowd, into the arms of safety.

A cold morning, with drizzle sifting from a dark sky. The beak overruns his sermon by three minutes and my heart's not in an ideal state of calm as I change alone and tie a folded pair of trousers round my middle with a bit of string before putting on a cricket pullover and tennis shoes. It looks a bit tubby but it'll get by. My shorts pockets hold the money and penknife. All set. A note left for Swatty says 'Meet you one day in the hills. Then I'll explain. Thanks for everything.' My watch says ten twenty-five.

As I canter to the gate a couple of prefects cycle past. During the war they used to wear white scarves in the blackout. They wave and laugh. "Can't stop!" I call back.

I fight the heartbeat down to help me get a regular stride. At the Oxford crossroads I turn left instead of going straight on, and feel at last that long elastic that's bound me to Monk's Hill School for Boys for so many years stretch and break. The open road, the outlaw road. The ends of the earth beckon. I get into rhythm. Step, step, breathe.

The next milepost says 'Banbury 14 miles', but I'm timing myself by other signs. Just a matter of putting away the first eight miles in under fifty minutes. The drizzle gets worse. My bare legs are clammy and my face and hair are running into my mouth. I keep having to blow the moisture off my top lip. Step, step, breathe.

The worst problem is the increasingly soggy pullover next to my skin. That plus a shirt would have been too much, but on its own it has its drawbacks. Like itching. And I can't knot it round my shoulders without revealing the grey bundle tied round my middle. Still, people will think I'm only going for a short run; so long as they don't wonder too hard where I could have started from. No, this is best. I read about a British escaped airman cycling halfway across Germany in his RAF uniform without being challenged. Cheeky enough in a country of varied fancy outfits not to draw a second glance. The drizzle stops, and I go into the discomfort of things drying out on your body. The sweat starts to run. But these are small things.

My fists jog up by my chest but there'll be no shadow-boxing; not this time. Thirty minutes and all well.

A few cars amble by, but I'm living by the new code of relying only on the physical things: my own strength, my own muscle, the co-ordination that lets you survive. The metalled road flies beneath my feet; the hedgerows pass in a blurred skein of sticks. From now on I'll work out my destiny through sheer fitness. My body sings. Banbury seven miles.

Ahead a woman in a brown overcoat and hat is toiling along on a bike, head down and legs pumping slowly like an old mine engine.

Most of us runners keep a bit in reserve for when we pass pretty girls, so I speed up and overtake her. Pretty or not, she's on the road and a sister of Fernleaf and Connie. I'm putting all my faith in women. Ah, fit as a flea. Go on forever.

What'll I say when I find them? When the compartment door slides open and I stand there, smiling, tired, but still strong? Up the pace a bit. Step, step, pant.

Every yard one more yard away from the pit. Rooms filled with the galley slaves of our education system. *Amo, amas, amat*; Glorious Revolution; annual output of the Ayr and Clackmannan coalfield. Sit, sit; listen, listen; scratch, scratch, when there are women to love and roads to fly along. Step, pant. Ease up a bit. You're in good time. Get a cup of tea at the station. I'll have earned it.

A car's tooting behind me. Have to be polite and refuse a lift, or maybe they're just asking the way. It rattles by me and squeals to a halt. I flick sweat from my eyebrows and trot to the driver's side as the window winds down. Don't hold me up too long. Run on the spot.

"Garner, isn't it? Bit out of your way, aren't you?"

Jazz Mulligan. The Mad Mullah. My heart's stream becomes white water. My feet ache with sudden panic. I clutch the roof as the legs buckle. "Really, sir? Don't think so. Just a long one, that's all." I look over the top of the car for a break in the hedge. Nothing.

"Do you know what time it is? Come on, hop in. I'll take you back. Damn nuisance."

He turns in the road and we race back at forty miles an hour while I stare forward, muscles quivering in tension and shock.

"Cold?"

"No, sir. Reaction from running."

He says nothing more, thank God, through the longest ten minutes of my life. It beats anything I've gone through so far for total numbing helplessness. The car judders to a stop by the school gate. Through the steam rising from its bonnet my mind sees a train passing signals, slowing for Banbury, with two beautiful pairs of eyes gazing at magazines.

"Dropping you off here, Garner. I'm in a hurry. You'll make lunch if you're quick."

A hundred-year old schoolboy climbs out. Before I can close the door, the Mad Mullah says, "Just one thing."

"Oh? Oh. Thank you, sir."

"It isn't that. Look here, son. I used to see things on active service. Do you know what I'd be thinking right now?"

"No, sir." Not much.

"I'd be thinking I caught you going over the wall. AWOL, or worse. I can't leave it there, laddie. Report to Mr Hopwood. I'll be speaking to him this evening. Think on it."

I don't know if I see Toady or not, or even if I walk through the gates. The next thing I remember is lying face down in mud with dirt in my nostrils and my fingers digging into the ground. I tingle with cuts and scratches and rain's crashing onto my body. Trunks of trees erupt from the night earth all round me. Darkness and cold, too real for a dream. My trousers lay in a soggy tangle beside me. My running kit weighs a ton. Coughing up vomit, I see my eyeballs spinning in rainbows. Torchbeams and shouts flicker far away.

Jackson Armitage sits hunched by my bed in the sick bay. He's muttering, "My fault. My doing. I should have realised the dangers I was exposing you to." His grammar shows he's in a bad way himself. "I am taking you back to Inglefield to recover."

It isn't the answer to anything. I shake my head, again and again.

"I know, my boy. You are overwrought. Constance and Berenice have been told. They will be there in time for your birthday. Then we shall see."

I'm rested, past the worst, walking slowly up from Hob's Pond with Ludmilla when we see them coming down the track. I fall into their arms. How much better than an awkward encounter on a crowded train, this meeting in a wood preparing for spring. Too soon the talk and the emotion overwhelm me and Connie holds me to her, running her fingers through my hair, murmuring, "It's all right. It's all right."

If only. I'm drowning, and the lifebelt of physical hopes is floating away. One more medium with just enough of the psychic virus left to turn me slowly into a crazy, or a grotesque like Anemone Woman; forbidden knowledge poured down my throat like the molten gold that punished those cursed by the gods with greed.

They know Fernleaf comes to my room in the night. She listens to the history of things since we parted, then says:

"Only think of your birthday tomorrow. There's a present for you. That's why you must sleep now."

"Why?" What I say doesn't matter, if only I can place words to mingle with her words.

"Because you'll be receiving it very early."

"How early?"

"I'll wake you. Don't set your alarm." She stills my questions by turning out the light and running her fingers in spirals above my nose. Through the enjoyment of her touch all sorts of doubts and regrets keep surfacing like bubbles from dark depths until at last there's calm. I hold her hand.

"Will it ever get better?"

"Not by itself, Mackinnon."

"It's down to me?"

"Down to us."

"You're not the nursey type."

"It's not a nurse you need."

"What do I need? Tell me."

She bends to kiss my brow.

"You need what you've always needed. It doesn't change. Now sleep. See you soon."

Goodnight, Fernleaf.

Far, far away in the house's silence a clock chimes to tell me I'm sixteen.

Chapter 31

I'm awake before she arrives; don't know why. Between Shanks's sedatives and my own defeated weariness I could have slept a week. This should be time to reflect, to shuffle the mental diary into order; but now it doesn't matter. How little it all amounts to. What was it like, the Smallwood case, Mr Garner? I can't give an answer. Trivial mishaps are retold second by second; survivors of bigger things keep their silence.

Thinking of her in the sharp silence before dawn. Deliciously real and strange. This little room, curiously shaped, arranged in the unsuspecting years for this one hour. What will happen? These are the five minutes before stepping onto Inglefield's platform on a still December morning. But I was a schoolboy then.

She comes in without knocking. She's wearing her dress with the strange swirly patterns, and her quilted bedspread rolled up under her arm. First she places a finger on my lips, then waves her hand like a Balinese dancer, motioning me to get up. I follow her mimes, put on tennis shoes and dressing gown, gather up my own bedspread and follow her past her room. It's not to be there, then. But so what? I'm swirling along on a current of excitement.

My hand is in hers as we descend the back staircase. It's the one that creaks less, its wide oak treads secure and settled after four hundred years. Then along the dark gallery, past the entrance to the eagle room, through the kitchen and cubbyhole with the piano, until we stand on the flagstones of the hall. She draws the bolts on the front door and we step out onto the gravel that sweeps round the box tree on its little lawn.

Alone on the planet, we taste the pure night. It tingles on our skin and brushes our lips and eyes with the air of the warmest March for over a century. After every few yards we stop moving and stand still, heads thrown back, senses floating.

So with our quilts clutched round us like cloaks we wander hand in hand through the Doctor's garden. We watch the mist lift from the fields to disclose the shapes of cows that quietly munch and gurgle, surrounded by their own breath. The moon is low in the western sky and it gleams along their backs and throws long shadows; but we don't remark on this or describe it to ourselves or disturb it with thoughts. Even the church lets its sheltering yews take a little of the moonlight.

After one circuit of the grounds she takes me along the cinder path flanked by the tussocks of the orchard. During the war sheep were grazed here, penned behind hurdles.

The hencoop stands among the trees. We stay very still, listening to the chickens talking in their sleep; then she goes ahead and opens the squeaky gate of the tennis court. We face each other by the net-post, the one with the brass handle. This spot holds some meaning for me. I wait for her to speak.

But she says nothing, only hangs her cloak over the sagging net and walks to the far end of the court. Her dress is her; slim, bare arms shimmering in moonlight which washes the hard surface into a grey so neutral she seems to be passing over ice or air. Only her shadow betrays her.

It's good not to have spoken, not to have broken the spell. I feel like an understudy in a drama where every move comes right in its moment. She turns, smiles, and leans her head to one side. This language of small gestures. I nod to her.

Slowly at first, moving down the tramlines, she turns, head and arms tracing paths through space, weaving spheres like an old model of the heavens. The moon makes her parti-coloured; dark and light, and she plays tricks with it as she goes. Too soon she reaches the far netpost and places her left hand on it, pausing for a second, perfectly still. She's the only person in my memory who's ever done anything close and sensual for me, and every action of hers is a touch so light and deep I feel levitated. There seems to be two inches between my feet and the

428

ground as we walk towards each other. She stretches her hand out and my heart and breathing tumble over each other; and an image sidesteps into my mind. This girl, with a tennis racket swinging idly in her hand, about to give a show of grace and skill that I must not enjoy. W. C. Fields meets Helen Wills Moody. Now I think I understand. She could have done all this on some open lawn instead of here in this enclosure with the high mesh fence. A shiver passes through me and it feels very, very good.

"Do you dance, Mackinnon?"

They're the first words. My reply's going to be an uncouth trespasser on this moment.

"We had an arrangement with a place in Oxford. I learned the waltz, the foxtrot and the quickstep. Cost me twelve bob altogether. Very rusty now."

"Were there pretty girls?"

"They may have been once; a bunch of old dears over forty. You needed a strong imagination."

She puts my arm round her waist and we set off in slow waltz time in silence. My feet find themselves, down there somewhere, because my eyes are busy with hers. Round the tennis court we glide like skaters. I'm overwhelmed by the ease, by the banishment of awkwardness, by how unlike the rest of life this is. I try a reverse turn without thinking about it, then another. It's like realising you don't have to fall off a bike. I smile, then look hard at her mouth. With the slightest shake of her head she smiles too, then begins to hum a simple tune I've never heard before. The rhythm fits our dance, but it's strange and old, for our little republic under the serene stars. When we stop at last she unwinds from me, looks up and says:

"Do something for me now. Tell me about them."

I look up too. "There's nothing I can say to you that will make them seem more beautiful."

"It's not because of them," she says. Our voices are held by the stillness.

I want to impress her. "There's a poem about this and I've forgotten almost all of it. We have to learn one a week by heart. Now I know the first and last lines of hundreds of poems. This one begins, 'When I heard the learn'd astronomer...'"

"Go on."

"And it ends:

'...'Till rising and gliding out I wander'd off by myself,

In the mystical moist night-air, and from time to time,

Look'd up in perfect silence at the stars.'"

"I know what you mean, Mackinnon. But I want to listen to you, your voice, telling me something I don't know. Will you do that?"

So I speak about Polaris, Cassiopeia and Ursa Major, of kite-shaped Bootes the herdsman with superb yellow Arcturus, fourth brightest star in the heavens; all unknown in her Southern sky.

"Why aren't they twinkling? Don't all stars twinkle?"

"There's a haze tonight. The atmosphere's very steady. And the moonlight's washing them out." I point here, there; leading her by the hand now in a dance of my own, facing every way to catch each point of the setting winter constellations. Then, "See that one? Very bright. A planet. Now move left from Bootes and you've got Vega, in the Lyre; fifth brightest. Next to that a huge cross, much bigger than your Southern Cross; my favourite, Cygnus the Swan. See the shape?"

"Yes. A great swan gliding across the sky."

For a long moment I watch her upturned face.

"The tail star is Deneb," I murmur, so as not to turn her from her thoughts.

"Deneb. Strange names."

"The Arabs named them, mostly."

"Tell me some more. Don't show me them. I just want to hear their sound."

"Alpheratz, Albireo, Achernar, Aldebaran. They had more time to watch in the desert; more to see. The stars there are thick as dust."

"I can see it, Mackinnon. A great tent with carpets and cushions under a night blazing with jewels."

I can see it too; just her and me. Nocturne with Diamonds.

She looks into my eyes. "Do you believe you can tell the future from the stars? Are we influenced by them?"

"Only by the riddles they contain, I hope."

"I'm glad that's your answer. Is my constellation visible tonight? It's almost the first thing you said to me; about my name being in the stars."

"There, halfway between the Plough and the horizon. Coma Berenices; Berenice's Hair. Not very prominent, I'm afraid."

"I don't mind."

I go on telling her, answering her questions, and it feels okay to admit how little I know, that everything remains to be discovered; that I practise a mystery. At one point I stop in our orbit round the court and say, "Even when we stand still, we're turning and spiralling and falling through space. We turn in a day, the galaxy turns in hundreds of millions of years. Everything moving, in circles within circles. I enjoyed our dance."

"You're welcome, Mackinnon. Tell me some more. I enjoy listening."

"Look where the moon is. It'll set soon. That's Leo dipping down after it. In about an hour the next constellation will drop below the horizon; but by then it'll be dawn breaking."

"Which one is that?"

"Virgo."

She puts her arms round me. "You're not cold?" I say.

"Why should I be? Come on. Time to go."

"Where to?"

"To the only place. Come on."

The only place to be is the seat in the sunk garden, overlooking the water meadows. We spread one of the quilts on it and sit with only our heads emerging from the other, like a couple of Tibetan monks. Warmth passes between us from shoulders to feet, and fiercely where our hands touch.

The magic of the night sky is fading. Mixed up with the excitement of the hour is a sadness for first things that are gone. Our first dance; my first telling about the stars. For these things only sequels remain. As the constellations are swallowed by a new darkness that grows up from the horizon the world suddenly seems less friendly; colder, indifferent, filled with a universal doubt as though unsure, this time, that the light will return. The meaning of the dark hour before the dawn.

I let go and put my arm round her, squirreling down till my hand rests on her breast. Her curled fingers hold it there while my heart thumps softly and becomes used to acceptance.

"Fernleaf, I wish I'd never been psychic."

"Me too."

"Only one of my mates at school half understood it. But I could never tell him; about me, that is. Didn't dare write to you about what I was going through."

"I know. So does Connie. She wouldn't have had a derry on it, Mackinnon, even if she did read my letters; which she doesn't."

"You know I think it's not over, don't you?"

"Yes."

"It was you that said it would have to be played out."

"Look on the bright side. Smallwood's a harmless old codger as far as you're concerned. It's not you; it's McFee needs to worry."

"He hasn't put it behind him, has he?"

"No. He wants to make a show of getting back to normal, then see how the chips fall."

"Getting back to normal. How nice for him. It was never any of my business."

"Then something else might have been. Something worse."

"Anything without you would have been worse. Look at me. Three months ago I first set eyes on you here, in this seat, and I was an averagely confident...well, normal, anyway. Now I feel tired; really tired. I don't want anyone else to know how afraid I get, or why."

There are sad pools of shadow round her eyes.

"We're both tired," she murmurs, and guides my hand further over. I let out a long breath and close out the world.

"You'll need to see, Mackinnon. A bit to the left of the poplars. It's starting."

She makes it sound as if she's talking about something she knows well, is part of. Something she can almost make happen. My hand keeps as still and respectful as it can while I settle down to concentrate.

The sky to the south seems no longer black, yet no more than not black. The eye, following this change for a long time in both directions, returns to discover charcoal grey where the non-black has been; then after repeating the journey comes back to find grey. The grey lightens and grows and one by one an army of trees and hedges steps out of the mist. They look strange in this light, like flat stage scenery, or a page in a great pop-up book; and a profound hush reigns over this suddenly unnatural face of the world. This is the moment where people have no place, where to earn a place you need to forget for the time that you are people. This is the world before we came.

And then the stillness breaks.

High up in some unseen place a blackbird sings. One phrase, liquid, like a drop falling into a pool; then a pause; then the phrase repeated. A lone sound, almost unbelievable, an accident.

A whole half-minute passes in complete silence. The tang of dew on grass and stone and wood lives in my nostrils, mixed with the air on Fernleaf's skin.

Then a robin answers: tic, tic, tic, tsit, twee. A hairline crack of song.

The blackbird again; five seconds of mellow music, effortless and sure. And one by one the other voices come in, echoing through the countryside, squeezing the pauses to nothing; thrush, woodpigeon, cockerel and crow. Not the crowded chorus of May but the greetings of survivors of the dark months, those who've kept the outposts of the year. Soon the reliefs will come. Passwords criss-cross the fields: all's well; not long now.

While they sing the light grows into bands of blue, red and gold. Level plumes of cloud, unnoticed before, lie along the sky like the breakers of a shallow sea. How long have we sat here without moving? An hour or more has passed in minutes.

A cone of brightness begins to melt the horizon and dissolve the colours. I can feel the dark that still clings to the twisty chimneys above and behind us lighten and lighten and the birdsong rise to new heights. The air shimmers like a struck cymbal.

Daylight washes everywhere, flooding over us, swelling out the trees, held together by a network of sound. The horizon trembles and parts, and for one moment a bead of molten gold appears. The bead swells to an arc, then a dome, then an oval plucking itself upwards, shedding solid slivers of light as it breaks free. All around it the colours boil away into the pale green, then blue of a clear spring morning.

I've seen all this before, a tiny child taken out by an old servant to watch the breaking of the African dawn; that ancient Africa where the sunrise was born. But this is something bigger. I feel renewed, full of the future; full of the cure; the physic of the physical world.

I hold her tight. This star of ours is the bringer of reality to our world. All the fears that trouble me can only run from it. I'm in love. I make cause with bigger things: earth, ocean, sun, moon and stars. Smallwood and all his shadows are what? No more than the turning over of stones.

The sun rises higher. Visions of summer mingle with this sensual perfection. The air is filled with sounds of life. My life is filled with her. I turn to look into her calm eyes.

"Thank you."

"Happy birthday," she whispers.

My fingers touch her cheek.

"I love you. Very much."

"And I love you."

Her eyelids close, and my fingers press upwards into her hair. I brush her pale open mouth with my lips and we kiss for a long time. The sun's rays warm us after their long journey.

When I wake, her face is peaceful and beautiful, resting on my shoulder, and our coverlet is lumped up to our chins. I caress her brow again and again with my lips. But there's an odd sound weaving in and out of the birdsong. I turn carefully.

Ludmilla's standing there, her arms raised like the Pope on his balcony, keening in her strange tongue, voice rising and falling with her hands.

Better say something.

"Lovely morning, isn't it?"

"Are you mad, maybe, huh? Out here in the cold? What your uncle, he will say? How long you been here? Eh?"

I grin sleepily. Fernleaf's eyes flutter open, without showing surprise, and bestow on Ludmilla a smile that would melt stones. I mouth a question and she nods with that look of greeting after sleep which is to us what sunrise is to the world. Ludmilla's hands are in her apron pockets now, sifting through crumbs of chicken feed. She's no fool. She's seen that look on boys' faces before. Her eyes waver between scolding and smiling and she nods too. Broad, not-so-simple, unglamorous Ludmilla Stankeivitch, who's known love in that slow-burning way of survivors everywhere.

"Will you join us," I say, "out here in this wonderful place, with a nice hot cup of tea?"

Chapter 32

Knight to Queen's Bishop six.

I lean back and let the sun warm my face. All around, this hot surprise of a March is quickening the spring, swelling buds and making the grass grow. Somewhere behind this brick wall where masonry bees come and go I can hear Moffat's lawnmower chugging up and down. Hard on the petrol allowance, but Alex Moffat doesn't grumble. He remembers last March.

Occasionally I'm called upon to play the invalid, so as not to over-exert myself. That's why I'm stuck in this folding garden chair, in thick grey shirtsleeves and a plaid blanket over my knees, while Connie and Fernleaf race round the place with wheelbarrows. They pass across my sight now and then in a good approximation of Land Girl uniform, laughing and working, helping Alex keep upsides of three acres and this early season. And I can't help seeing them differently now.

A hand rests on my shoulder. The fingers squeeze gently and my hand joins it.

"How you doing?"

"It ain't quittin' time yet, is it?"

"Connie's getting us a cup of tea. How's the world, Mackinnon?"

"It's a grand place, Miss Fernleaf. A fine place."

"And this little battlefield here?"

"Ah, well. I think he's off his game. Look."

On the touchline stand a black bishop, knight and three pawns. For them the war is over.

"I see. I love you, by the way. Where is he?"

437

"Phone call. I've never had him on the run like this; and I don't think he's taking a dive either. Things on his mind, you reckon?"

"Doubt it. Life's looking up for him too. Connie came back for you and now she's staying."

"For him?"

"Hmm. Don't get your hopes up. Still, it's getting the garden done. Mr Moffat didn't come back straight after his Christmas because of, well, family stuff. I've never seen him till now. Nice bloke, and Mrs."

"Yup. And the lads. We had great times till they went away. I love you too, Fernleaf. Sit down and tell me what you think of this."

She looks at the pieces a while. "Take me back over his last moves."

I run the game backwards. "See what I mean? All obvious. Is he throwing it?"

"I'd say not, Mackinnon; they're pretty good. Not obvious to me at all. Look at that rook's pawn. I'd call that inspired, myself."

"You probably would. Just kidding; no, saw it coming a mile off. Hallo, here he is."

Casual in pullover and shirtsleeves, he swaps places with Berenice. "Ah, sorry to keep you. Watching the kettle for Constance."

"Sounds like a music-hall number. We thought you were breaking a personal record for speaking on the phone."

"Not so, I'm glad to say. It was that country houses chap, Maskell. He wants another visit, with a photographer."

"Another visit? I suppose he would. He didn't get much out of his last one."

"Ah, I see. You're both a little behindhand. Our Mr Maskell has been here twice already as a matter of fact. I invited him to stay over if it was atmosphere he was after, but he preferred to lodge at the Angler. Quite an amusing chap really; very good on the Hall at Armforth Wolsey. Told me things I'd never noticed in dozens of calls."

"And he's on the level?"

"Mmm? Oh, straight as a die; bit nervous at first. Still, hardly surprising, after the reception you two gave him. He was relieved when I told him you were both a long way away."

Connie appears with a tray of tea, and we're a family. Happinesses pile on top of each other. Fernleaf runs off to bring Alex Moffat over to join us. Another contented man, as easy among people as he is with plants, he chats and looks at Connie with the same appreciation as he would a tree in flower, with unpossessive courtesy. Wounded early in the war, he came back to run the Doctor's domain as a smallholding, keeping a couple of lawns well grazed so the mysterious visitors had something to stand around on so long as they were careful. Did he know about Crewe? Was he part of the set-up?

Don't want to think about it now. By and by Shanks and I are left alone with our game.

And the black pieces one after the other go into touch. Soon I control three parts of the board. "You seem to have the measure of me, Clement. Been practising at school?"

"No. I couldn't get a friendly after the trouble started. Too many people thought I had X-ray eyes."

He brings his gaze up from the board. I know that look.

"I'm going to write down my next move. All right?"

"Fine. But frankly you don't have a lot of choice anymore."

"Nevertheless."

This is worrying, and I haven't been worried for almost a day and a half. Now, that is a personal record. "Okay. What do I do?"

"Write down what you think I will do."

He writes. I look hard at his survivors in defensive disarray. I wish; I wish you would go King to Knight one. It's what you should do. It's what I'd do. But that's obvious. He's testing me, so he'll make a silly move; meaningless, hastening his defeat. Or he might knock the old man down and resign. What?

I don't know. I just don't know.

What the hell. Rook to Rook two. But I don't need this.

"Okay. Done."

He puts down his paper. We've always noted our games for future reference. His hand moves to the King and picks it up. Thank goodness.

"J'adoube."

One little word, the last word on earth, surely. A pair of foreign syllables used in an ancient game of war, to say: I'm only straightening it on its space; an elegant evasion for 'I've changed my mind'.

His remaining Rook moves forward one square.

I show him my paper. He shows me his. The move he's written is King to Knight one. I say, "I don't think that proves a lot. The number of possible moves was too small."

"Clement, I changed my choice of move as you were writing it down. I'd like us to play another game now."

"I'd rather we didn't."

He leans forward. "My boy; if it's returning, I think I'd rather we both knew."

He's right. We play again. I have to write down his future moves. After eighteen he resigns.

I saw six of them coming, but it doesn't matter, because his entire strategy unfolded itself before me like a well-known drama.

"Well, my boy. Perhaps your future lies in other spheres. You may become greater than Capablanca or Alekhine."

"Maybe they had it too. No, forget that. I don't see myself as a Grand Master. It's not the way it works, is it? Is it?"

I'm sitting in his study again, going through the old tests, and I'm worried sick. I don't want anything to work and I try to skew the results by changing the answers. But it doesn't make any difference. The scores are still ridiculously high.

"Why is this happening?"

440

"The only answer that fits the facts and conforms to previous experience, is that you have become emotionally stable."

"But I'm not. I'm still recovering from everything. Was recovering."

"Emotional stability isn't the same as peace of mind, Clement. I know that you found yourself off balance when you came here for Christmas, yet you demonstrated your powers at their fullest extent."

"What does emotional stability mean, then?"

"It means changing with the world; trimming your sails to the wind. Balance. As I said, not necessarily happiness, any more than the man who finds shelter from a storm is happy. But he is safe."

"I've got what I always needed."

"If you like."

Great. So much for yesterday's confidence; so much for the certainty. I'm back. And Shanks's explanation does not fit. There hasn't been any sort of pattern. Sometimes I've smelled things; sometimes felt them; sometimes heard them. I've even made things happen; or maybe that wasn't me. How much of this has been Smallwood himself? There's been no correlation with my emotional state. It's a mess. I'm a mess. Goodbye sunrise.

"Why did Raymond and Victoria leave?"

"You know, that's the first time you've asked about them."

"Just that you didn't mention them going when you wrote."

These words simply pop into my head, but they're not what I mean. Surely I must have asked before? Or if I did, why can't I remember the answer?

"Raymond became ill with nerves; incapable of carrying out his duties properly. I ensured that after a period of convalescence they found a position in a less demanding household."

"Less demanding than this?"

"Working for a man in an obscure occupation is not always easy. Let us close the subject."

And get back to this one.

"I'm not happy about this psychic business coming back," I say carefully. "If I've got this right, I'll suffer from it when I'm doing okay, and only escape from it by being unbalanced. Is that how it is?"

"Until things change again that may be so. Things do change, however."

Do they? Thanks, Doctor, but I wonder if you know any more than I do after all.

"Can we open a window? It's getting warm in here. Listen, Uncle; Berenice and me, we think it isn't..."

"Berenice and I."

"Yes, yes. We think maybe it'll go away when the Smallwood case is solved. We've never believed it was over. It only started for me when McFee came here. What about that?"

He says nothing. In that silence I think I remember a bad night about a month before all this started. Early signs? No, you could go crazy trying to connect everything. Unravel the tangle you're stuck with; you've made enough of your own.

"You're still expecting to hear from him, aren't you? Still waiting for the last bit of the Unicorn puzzle. Is that right?"

"Most perceptive. Yes, Clement, you are right; McFee has been in touch with me."

"And?"

"And he still feels Smallwood's presence. Beyond mere suggestion."

"What's the plan, then?"

"We wait. A poor plan, but there it is. Stay here, will you?"

It's Alphonse and Ludmilla's day off. They're belting round the countryside on their motorbike and sidecar in the glorious weather, so Shanks struggles on alone with prepared meals and self-made drinks. Except that the women are here too. Their complete self-reliance turns them, ironically, into our servants. Do they mind? I don't. But it makes

442

me wonder who's really in charge between those who command and those who sustain. Shanks proposes, but he doesn't always dispose. Still, he's ahead of me, who does neither. I hope he's gone to put the kettle on.

A bare breeze comes in at the window. It feels like velvet. Connie and Berenice haven't gone by, so they won't know Shanks has dragged me in here to confirm my worst fears. Now the nightmares will return. Just when love's become more than a dream.

I get up out of the wall-facing chair to stretch my legs, but they feel like lead.

Once again I notice small differences in the study. After a few seconds I see what they are. He's put up pictures. I bet Connie's made him do that. Mostly eight-by-six prints of photos in art-deco frames and still fresh from lying out of the light for years. I take a closer look at the meagre gallery nestling in odd corners between the bookcases; not exactly up to the Shawe-Trittons' *March of Time* collection; but a small step for humanity.

They're group shots. I'm in one or two myself, in shorts and sun-hat, standing with Victoria to one side or in the background. Group shots of the people who came here during the war to hatch schemes for psychic weapons, all smiling; some squinting into the sun, some looking off-camera. Some hot for the cause, others there to make sure the cause did not prosper. And a little chap allowed into the shot to give it the aura of one big happy family. A little chap who didn't have the faintest idea. I look at the slightly out-of-focus features of Victoria and myself and a thought that's been looming up like a train approaching on a straight track suddenly grows huge as it draws level.

I start to hum a little tune:

Oh, Mister Porter, what shall I do?

And sing the second line, with a minor change:

. . . I wanted to go to Inglefield, but they've taken me on to Crewe. . .

Just as Jackson Armitage walks through the door. He doesn't seem to notice, so the moment passes; because now I'm focusing on another woman in another photo.

"Is that Mrs Shawe-Tritton? On the left, by the sundial?"

"Mmm? Yes, it is. Must have been, oh, 1941. Cup of tea?"

"Thanks. You know, I don't remember any of these others, but I do remember playing tennis with people. Useless, most of them."

"That would have been later, Clement. Moffat was away at the war and the tennis court was out of use."

It's strange to look at this picture and compare it with others as I drink my tea. Faces appear and disappear, but they're always in at least a couple of shots. Apart from one.

"That bloke there; next to Mrs Shawe-Tritton. With the beard. He's only in this '41 picture."

He peers at it closely. "Ah, yes; a Naval officer. Don't recall the name, I'm afraid."

"What was he doing here?"

"Friend of George and Damietta. Interested in psychic matters."

"To help with the war?"

Shanks raises his eyebrows. "He might have thought it useful; I don't know."

"He's only in this one."

He clears his throat; not quite comfortable with this. I'm surprised he's let Connie talk him into putting them up; or maybe I'm not. What wouldn't I do now for Fernleaf?

"He was killed, I believe."

They must have a bonfire going somewhere.

"How?"

"Mm, can't help you there. Missing believed killed, I think. Soon after this was taken."

"My God, what's Alex burning out there? Car tyres?"

"I beg your pardon, Clement?"

"Well; hey, wait a minute. Is someone burning the dinner as well? Can't you smell it? It's coming from both sides." I head for the study door and Shanks grabs me by the shoulder.

"There is nothing burning, I assure you, either in the kitchen or outside. Are you all right?"

"No. No. I'm feeling sick. I'll have to sit down."

Missing believed killed. Like Wilfred Gascoigne in the night sky over Bremen. Burned.

He gives me a sedative and I sleep like the dead until ten in the evening. When I wake, Connie's sitting by the bed reading a book from the shadowy shelves behind her. She puts it down and strokes my forehead.

"Where's Fernleaf?"

"She's asleep too. We worked hard all day."

"Sorry I couldn't help."

"That's all right. You need to get better."

I allow myself a bitter little laugh. "Yeah, I wouldn't argue with that."

Love is a lift that takes you from cloud one to cloud nine. Sometimes it stops and other people get on. I grip Connie's hand. "Me and Fernleaf…"

"I know. Can I call you Mackinnon too? Sometimes?"

Going up.

"Any time. Thank you. I'm never going back to school. Will you be my teacher?"

"Lessons start at nine o'clock."

"Since when? I know someone who's been playing truant, Miss."

"Since tomorrow. School's out at lunchtime; for the rest of the day. Now take this."

"Connie?"

"Yes?"

"Does the name Crewe mean anything to you?"

"It's a railway town; up north somewhere."

"That all?"

"I think so."

"Goodnight."

English and Geography, under a deep oak-post verandah with French windows opening from the dining room. In the warmth of the morning sun we sit at an old table etched and bleached like a washboard, writing, talking. Talking! Education as I've never known it. No wonder Fernleaf's got such a handle on everything. Questions fly in both directions; every fact has a story. I can't wait for the real lowdown on the Ayr and Clackmannan coalfield, Land of Mystery and Romance; or the truth about the Statute of Winchester, or wherever it was.

At breaktime Fernleaf vanishes for twenty minutes.

"Where did you go?"

"Over to Mrs Moffat. They'll lend us their bikes for the afternoon."

"Nice weather for it."

"Actually, Mackinnon, you need the exercise. And you can take that smile off your face."

"Don't know what you mean. Hey, I was looking at the atlas just now. Did you know there's a Mackinnon Pass near where you live?"

"Surely not! I'd have heard."

"Okay, okay. What's the story?"

"There was this bloke called Mackinnon. He discovered a pass."

"But of course; how simple. Is there more?"

"His first name was Quintin. He was Scots — an ex-soldier — they called him Rob Roy, and he found it sixty years ago. Died four years later when he drowned in a lake. That's all."

"Strange, eh? I was born in Mackinnon Road and you were born near Mackinnon Pass."

"I don't know why I never told you."

"No."

For English we do poetry. I ask if I can read *Dover Beach* out loud.

"Any particular reason?" Connie asks in that honey voice that still gives me little spasms behind the knees. "It reminds me of a beach," I say. "With pebbles and breakers."

"But it begins 'The sea is calm tonight', doesn't it?"

I look into her brown eyes. I want to hold her gaze by the power of my own, because my eyes are lover's eyes and must have a special cool, adventurous cast that can't be denied.

Three-quarters of a second.

I start to read, but it's the start of the last bit I really want to do, and do while looking at Fernleaf:

> Ah, love, let us be true
>
> To one another!

And he's right, this poet. His lines end in that old truth that all we have is love, because there's nothing else out there but darkness and uncertainty. Is this the kind of thing they read at the symposia back at Monk's Hill?

Poetry seems to have hit the spot with me lately; like music; and it's down to this girl who magically combines what I thought were opposites. I'm in need of exercise all right.

I emerge after lunch in shirtsleeves and plus-fours, ready to cycle. She appears in shirtsleeves and short white shorts with turn-ups. We collect the bikes from Mrs Moffat.

"Where to?" I say.

"The station for starters. You lead the way."

"Oh, no. After you, Claude."

"Why?"

"The scenery's better."

"Is it, though? I just thought I ought to keep an eye on you in case you weakened and fell off."

"I'm weakened already; and I've fallen. I thought I'd like to keep an eye on you. I'm in love with you. Every bit of you. Come on, I'm sixteen now. Try to make an old man very happy."

A mile down the road, before the bend that takes us past Symond's, I call her to stop. We push our bikes into the trees and I take her in my arms. Our feet scuff in last autumn's dry leaves as we sway, devoured in kissing. All memory drowns as I taste her lips, face, neck, hair. My tongue caresses her eyelids as she searches me all over with hard fingertips. The sun strikes through branches and batters us to the woodland floor.

Sitting with our backs to a tree we get our breath back and agree to move on; a decision that struggles against all the glories of the hour.

Morpeth's General Stores for a bottle of Tizer. Mr Morpeth is an austere man who keeps temperance tracts on his counter and a jaundiced eye on the saloon across the street. He's just about to be reasonably pleasant when he notices bits of twig in Fernleaf's hair and a desiccated beech leaf sticking out under my collar. His gaze dwells on the girl in not-so-white shorts and darkens by the second. It then darkens a bit more as the bell over the door tinkles and a voice calls out louder than the space in the shop, "Afternoon, Ezekiel! And a tin of Mick McQuaid, if you please!"

"The half-ounce?" replies Mr Morpeth, whose name is not Ezekiel, in a refrigerated tone.

"You're the fella," comes the voice. The till clangs. For a second I exchange looks with Mr Breezy Customer. His face says: I know you. My face tries not to say: my God, what happened? Then he's out of the door.

I want to ask old Morpeth who he is, but think better of it. We sit outside on the bench by the entrance and draw in the gravel with our toecaps. Inglefield's a real hamlet without pavements.

"That bloke knows me," I say after a swig of pop.

"He's probably seen you come off the train," says Berenice. "He went over into the Laughing Angler as if he owned it."

"Did you see his face?"

"Yup. He's even worse looking than you."

"I started to have an idea yesterday. Let's sit on the platform and watch the trains."

"You mean the train."

Jim Haskins is thinking about his little flowerbed under the name board. When he sees us his face too turns to a frown.

"What do you two want?"

"Nobody wants to know us today. What is it?"

"I helped you out, didn't I? About that snoopy chap after Christmas?"

"Yes; and we appreciated it. Why?"

"Huge success was it, your little caper?"

"Er, no. Turned out wrong, actually. Sorry."

"Ah. Sorry. Snoopy chap got his apology straight away, didn't he? It's a damn good thing I didn't talk to anyone, show my hand like; just watched out and phoned you; wasn't it? Or I'd have got into serious trouble, wouldn't I?"

"Yes, but it was all right, wasn't it? You didn't, did you?"

"No. But how long did I spend worrying, after I heard what happened? Because nobody told me if you'd mentioned my name when you were rumbled."

"We didn't," says Fernleaf. "And we wouldn't have."

"Well of course. Because as far as you were concerned, I might have asked personally over in the Angler so they knew anyway. Well, at least I've got my apology now. A few weeks late; but then I should be grateful, me being a lowly railway servant. And why aren't you at school?"

"Er, I'm ill."

"Looks it."

"I mean, convalescing; after being ill."

"Really? Can't wait to be ill meself, then. Oh no, I forgot. I need money to live on. Well, that's the working class for you. Excuse me, then. Work to do."

We lean the bikes against the white picket fence and sit down. There's no one else on the platform and birds are singing around us. All it needs to ruin everything is the feeling we've dropped someone in it and deserve what we're getting. Jim Haskins goes about his business and I put my arm round Fernleaf's shoulder. She snuggles into me. Clouds march slowly across the sky, breaking it up into continents and seas.

"And you can cut that out. This is a public place. If that's convalescing, go and do it somewhere else."

She sighs. "Matters unconnected with the business of the railway. I'll be back in a tick."

"It's round by the coalyard."

She's a long time. I spend it piecing together parts of the idea, shaking it around till the edges fit neatly, getting more believable all the time. Clear thinking; it's happening again.

Above my right eye there's a very small niggling pain that comes and goes.

"Welcome back. Did he make you whitewash it as a punishment?"

"No; I grovelled a bit. He's okay really. We got talking and I asked him about the ugly bloke. It's Norbert Lavarack all right. D'you remember Jackson said he had a history?"

450

"Yes. Go on, then I'll tell you what I've been working out."

"Well, he comes from Cornwall. He used to be a secret agent in the war, working with the French Resistance. They used to land him and pick him up in light planes."

"Lysanders."

"Right. One night his plane crashed on landing back in England. He got badly burned. Spent years getting his face fixed by plastic surgery. That's why his skin looks like that."

"And his nose and eyes out of position?"

"That's how it looks because of the way the skin – oh, I don't know. They did their best."

"So how's he get to run a pub? Without frightening the customers?"

"Because he's a war hero."

"Did you think to ask about when he took it over?"

"I did. Two years ago. So, end of mystery. What's your big idea, then?"

"I'll have to take this steady. It started with me wondering about Shanks's manservant and cook before Alphonse and Ludmilla; why they left so suddenly. I only knew about it an hour before I met you. But I didn't ask myself why, because it wasn't my business. I think so many things happened so quickly that it got left behind."

"That seems reasonable. I love you."

"That too seems reasonable; and I love you. When we saw the papers in George's safe I'd begun to wonder if Ray and Victoria were, you know, part of some Secret Service unit keeping watch on Shanks. Yesterday I saw a man in a photo in his study."

"Oh, good; he's put them up, then."

"Yes. And I smelled burning; like when I saw Mitch Gascoigne's brother in his shop window. Exactly the same. Then Shanks told me he'd gone missing in action, presumed dead. Just like Wilf. And I knew straightaway he'd been burned, this bloke in the picture."

"And you think Lavarack is this same bloke?"

"In the picture he had a beard and naval uniform. And he was standing next to Damietta Shawe-Tritton. She'd brought him along to Inglefield Place; alias Crewe."

"Hmm. But Norbert would be a new identity in that case. You can't invent people out of thin air."

"Yes you can. They can; MI5 and that lot. And now he's here, not two miles down the road. I reckon something's going on."

"All right, I'm Lavarack and you hit me with this story. Well, Mr Garner, fact is I liked the area so much when I visited you during the war that when I got out of hospital I thought I'd come and live here, run a pub. What's wrong with that?"

"What's wrong is two people, Miss Fernleaf: Damietta Shawe-Tritton and Raymond the butler. The first gets my suspicions up straight away. The second used to drink at the Laughing Angler and after the new landlord came he started suffering from nerves so much that he finally had to leave Inglefield."

"Maybe he was a drunk."

"Maybe Norbert was trying to get him to spy on Shanks and he wouldn't."

"How could he do that? You can't just pressure people."

"Easy. Blackmail. Threaten to expose some dark personal secret or shop him as someone MI5 had already recruited, someone who'd been a traitor in his house for years."

"That would mean he'd stopped spying on him, or he wouldn't need to make him start again."

"Well, maybe it was Victoria then, I don't know. Maybe at the end of the war he or she or both of them expected not to have to do it any-more. Maybe his nerves were shot already."

"All sounds pretty flimsy to me, Mackinnon."

"I hoped you'd support me."

452

"I am. By keeping you out of making a dill of yourself. We should be doing something better than wondering about all this."

"Just shows how it all gets to me. I'm sorry. I'm crazy about you." We sit close and watch the train come in. A woman and child get off; no one gets on. Jim Haskins slides a crate into the back of the single carriage and walks up to the engine.

"Rabbits," I say. "For his cousin in Fingfield." When it's gone he stands looking at us.

"Do the Stankeivitches ever drop in at the Angler?" I ask.

"Never seen 'em there."

"Alphonse is pretty sensitive about being mistaken for a German; or a Russian. Maybe that's why."

"Maybe it is."

"How can we make it up to you?" I say. He points to the little flowerbed. "Do some bob-a-job. Without the bob. That'll square it."

We dig about with trowels, pulling out unwanted microscopic plant forms.

I do some thinking out loud. "Norbert no longer has eyes and ears at the house. But he needs them now because his paymasters the Shawe-Trittons want to keep tabs on Shanks and the Smallwood case. My God!"

"What's up? Found a Secret Service snail with a camera?"

"No! The Home Office! Why it's keeping the press off McFee and the whole thing! How stupid! There we were sitting in that bloody snakepit hoping they wouldn't find out anything from the papers when it was them – well, their people – who were suppressing it! They've known all along! All they needed was details. They needed somebody at Inglefield Place." Suddenly I turn and stare at her. She stares back.

"Hold on, you! You don't seriously think..."

"Just kidding. What about Connie, though? Mata Hari?"

She shoves me onto the soil. For the next five minutes we feverishly replant the innocent bystanders.

"Which brings me to Archibald Maskell. He can walk into any posh house in the county with a cameraman and be welcome. He prefers to lodge at the Laughing Angler. Voila."

"So he's in MI5 too, is he?"

"Or MI6; one of them. He's been recruited. He's been up at the house already. Soon he'll be taking pictures of all the interesting old windows and hiding places. Reporting back to Pretty-boy Norbert. Casing the joint, Fernleaf. To help some professional break-in artist get in and get the evidence."

"Fine. And how do you propose to prove it?"

"By being there when he comes and using my renewed powers to read his mind."

"Without telling Jackson?"

"He'll have to be told. Without knowing about what we found in George's safe."

"Why not just tell him about that, now it's all got so close to home? Assuming you're right."

"Because if he repeated it he wouldn't be believed. And because he'd be done for knowing official secrets."

"Us too in that case. Can I remind you he might know already?"

"Yup; I thought that once. But he's letting Maskell walk right into the place. He'd share our suspicions if he knew, wouldn't he?"

"Okay. But please, Mackinnon, remember Hob's Pond. No more stunts, eh? Now kiss me."

"Oi, you two!"

That night she massages my forehead and instead of closing my eyes I watch her face every second, trying to read emotions; trying to remember words she's spoken now I know they're more than words. Gathering up every grain behind the harvest as our love swings through the sunlit fields. We'll be together now, whatever happens. The dream that's coming true didn't surface only three months ago; it's the dream that's grown up with both of us.

Every part and particle of this room, every sound and sight and influence from the fields, the weir, the trees, the distant railway; every thought and fear and pleasure in freedom of the last ten years that's moulded me can now step back and be the hinterland; their work is done. The world now is Berenice.

But I can't wish the other things out of existence, which means there are things to do. That and the headache that comes and goes, a little stronger each time.

When she goes to kiss me goodnight I put my hands behind her ears and coax her down beside me.

"You could stay."

"I could. But we have so much time."

"Just say you don't mind my asking."

"I'm honoured by your asking."

"You told me to wait before saying I loved you. You turned my journey from one step into a pilgrimage. I saw all the scenery and felt the earth under my feet. That way I arrived to a better welcome."

"You understood, Mackinnon. That's why I love you."

We speak like this, enjoying the way our words rein in and control the wildness of which we're equally proud, turning it and wheeling it like the wind or the whirlwind.

At last: "About tomorrow. When they come. No plans; just play it by ear."

"Sweet dreams."

A car rolls up the next afternoon. The photographer's in the driving seat and he leaps out immediately. Maskell waits for the white-jacketed Alphonse to open his door. Smiles and introductions all round. For one second I wonder if Mitch Gascoigne isn't paid to spy on McFee, but filling the world with enemies is too easy. I've got to be interested but unobtrusive.

Alphonse serves tea in the library and pleasant small talk ensues. The photographer is a tall, slim man of maybe thirty in a respectable tweed suit. His name is John Adams. I expected him to be called Montmorency Pauncefote and look like Oscar Wilde or something. Don't know why. He doesn't look like a photographer, but then he probably isn't one. He looks at Connie as if he'd like to snap her, though, and before long he asks her if she's ever sat for anyone.

Archibald is dressed for a Sunday stroll; quite relaxed and affable. "Each time I'm here, Doctor, I sense that you don't get many callers."

I butt in. "The usual people drop by, like the vicar. We used to get lots of tramps as well. Not so many, now."

"Quite so, Clement. Well, you are here at any rate. Gentlemen, please feel free to continue your researches. I'm afraid I have work to do. Mr Stankeivitch will attend and assist you."

One day I'd like to be able to get up from a chair so as to say: it's time for you to leave the room. We all stand.

"No need to bother Alphonse," I say. "I know more about this place than he does, probably."

"Very well."

Mr Adams unpacks his equipment. A camera and tripod and a few things slung over his shoulder. A cut above my Vest Pocket Kodak.

"Do you two mind if I take a picture of you at work? You know, famous author? For my album." I'm trying to read their mood. There'd be lots of reasons for not wanting to be snapped by me. Got to get in deeper. Fernleaf joins us. Maskell doesn't refer to our previous meeting, not even jokingly. John Adams walks round the outside of the house, stopping to discuss architectural points. The twisty chimneys seem to interest them both; and the windows.

Maskell starts asking me tricky questions I don't have a clue about, but I know his game. He can't tell us to bugger off exactly, so we both hang back a bit, almost out of earshot.

The tripod is set up and exteriors taken. We offer to carry stuff but they won't let us.

This headache's getting annoying. I'll have to take a powder if it doesn't go.

"No dogs, and the gardener doesn't have one," says Maskell.

"No," I answer. "The Doctor says they'd distract him."

"Pardon?"

"They would distract him. From his work."

"What would?"

A sharp pain hits me under the shoulder blade. "Trees," says Fern-leaf. "Waving by the window. I was just asking my cousin why there are no trees by this side of the house."

"Do you always call him the Doctor?"

"Ha, yes; quite often. Our little joke."

They both look at us; but I definitely got something then. When did it happen like this? Yes! Crossing Hyde Park that day. They were talking one thing and thinking another. And I picked it up. I don't like this. I don't like seeing the enemy so close with all their cameras. Inglefield Place used to be isolated, another world. It's as though unwanted guests have moved in for good.

But I need them to do more. A chance thought about dogs isn't enough. They scrunch along gravel paths looking for good sightlines. "Ground's soft hereabouts. Have to watch that." Maskell's voice, distinct.

"Did you hear that?" I whisper.

"Yes. He said something about the ground."

Oh, right. "Could mean it'd show footprints."

"Could mean watch how you set your tripod."

Suddenly it doesn't seem worth it. I turn to go; another waste of time. The clean break feels strong, decisive, as I walk away by myself.

"Where are you going?"

"Anywhere. It's a washout, Fernleaf. They're probably completely on the level. Anyway, I've got a cracking headache."

She walks beside me. "Sorry about the headache, Mackinnon. But we ought to stay on these two. They're on the lurk; I'm sure of it."

"Really? You're psychic too now, are you? Well, don't be. It's not healthy."

"I know, drongo. That's why I spend a deal of time sat by your bed looking out for you."

I stop and put my arms round her. "Sorry. You're right, as usual. Maybe they are spying. But so what? If we catch up with Smallwood, Shanks will have put it across them. How can they stop him if we're all here on the lookout?"

"I don't know. All I know is the Shawe-Trittons and their weird friends pull a lot of strings and they can bury Jackson just like that when it suits them. They tried before; remember? There's something cronk about these two. Maybe we should tail 'em. They might chat freely if they think we're out of it."

"No thanks; I've played that game too. They're pros, for God's sake. They'd know."

"Right, so they're back on the suspect list, then? That was quick."

We head for the carp ponds. And there they are, looking into the half-overgrown black water.

"How are you getting on?"

They don't answer, so we come nearer. There's a strange sharp smell in the air, an oiled-steel smell like gun barrels; like in the Cadet Corps armoury at school.

"Mind if I look at your camera? It's a bit posher than mine."

The tall one decides to be friendly. "Go ahead. What do you use?"

"VPK. About thirty years old, but it works."

458

"That was my first camera too. Not a Box Brownie like everyone else."

I take a deep breath and pretend to examine the stately contraption pointed at the house. But there's no trace of fine machine oil. This is the smell of, what?

The answer comes up so easily I almost laugh.

Grim, steely purpose.

Him, not Maskell. Maskell's soft; a writer for magazines, recruited because his reputation is his passport. But Adams is a hard case, hard as nails, and trained to a hair. Suddenly I can smell the resolve, the loyalty, the complete lack of doubt that would let him gun down traitors to The King with a silenced pistol as soon as look at them. I hope he can't smell me because I'm frightened to be near him. It's not only his deadly skill; it's the knowledge that he's protected. Even if we could stop him, it would be us ending up in the Tower, or somewhere where soft-spoken men would question us until we just disappeared.

"Thanks. We'll leave you to it, then." Back out of sight, Fernleaf looks anxiously at me. I'm breathing hard and gulping. "Listen, you're right. The photographer bloke is an agent – no, just listen – he's dangerous. If he comes back here and breaks in, and anyone finds him, he'll shoot. I'm certain."

"Hold on, Mackinnon, you've speeded up. How do you know?"

"I smelled it! He smelled of, I don't know, being able to just kill you; checked, oiled, in perfect working order. I can't make it sound like sense. We've got to tell Shanks."

He's not around, though. We follow a sharp thumping sound and find Ludmilla beating carpets. She says he's with the visitors; must have joined them just after we turned our backs. Ten minutes of thinking about it knocks it all out of me too. So I plead the headaches when they finally pack the gear in the car and come in for a spot of tea before leaving. Fernleaf and Connie sit in and they all eat crumpets by the fire and make pleasant talk while I skulk in my room and think of the charade going on downstairs. It gets too much. My body bloats with the feeling that a cancer's taken hold of this little world and whatever we do it'll never go away. Wars and tempests could sweep over Inglefield but after they'd passed we could clear up and return to our former life. Not with these people and their masters and protectors. They'd always know, always have us on their files. We would do all the old things, but only under their microscope. The baker, the new postman, the Jehovah's Witness; even the tramp with his air of independence could be just one more operative sent by the men with clean fingernails sitting in high-ceilinged rooms above the law.

Shanks's house; my house. His gardens, his woods; mine. The silence, the sunsets, the mists and lonely drizzling rain; the stars, Hob's Pond; my territory, my gift among many to Berenice; all harbouring the disease, sick with the intrusion of these people and their villainy. The disturbance I felt when McFee brought his story here is nothing compared to the sense of rottenness that surrounds me from the smiling spies sitting downstairs. The bloating forces its way up my throat, my head pounds and cold sweat rolls down my body like a glaze. Swaying, I head for the door and wrench it open. My limbs are acting on their own, guessing the intentions of my brain. As I reach the top of the stairs one thought keeps station: got to warn Shanks, rid yourself of this. After that, God knows.

My fingers clutching at the bannisters check me as I tumble down the polished cascade of oak. For split-seconds my eyes meet the gaze of china spaniels in their niches before I arrive in a heap at the bottom. Waking from a black instant I find my cheek sliding in vomit as I try to get up; but it's all over. The remnants of the beautiful physical dream collapse. The Tudor floorboards, the rugs, the sunlight shafts through windows separating me from the gentilities in the library; all a wilderness that defies me. My shout is a croak with yellow bubbles.

Alphonse kneels by me, laying his tray aside. My one open eye has a wildness in it that acts on his quick, subtle mind and tells him to keep me a secret for a while longer. The little Lithuanian is remarkably strong. He heaves me up and supports me through the kitchen into his own room, rapping out words to Ludmilla that has her grabbing the kettle from the range. "My wife is to clear the mess," he says. "Lie here."

There are photographs here too, but all I can smell is myself.

A slim girl in a printed cotton dress and a slim man with a good head of black hair, resting against a railing by the sea. A faraway sea. Then war, flight, a harbour in a foreign land. How simple. How lucky they are. How their scarred, battered motorbike and sidecar symbolise the uncomplicated journey. I must get myself one; ride all the roads of the earth with the girl in pilot's goggles in the open cockpit beside me.

They leave, the traitors, covered in good wishes. A complementary copy of the book is promised. Shanks and the others are called into the room where I sit swathed in blankets with an enamel bowl on my knees. Ludmilla fusses a couple of ornaments around and goes out with Fernleaf. They'll sit in the kitchen with Alphonse while she explains away my sickness and they keep their own counsel.

Then I tell my story to Jackson Armitage. I don't expect it to hit the mark, but I'm wrong. You can see the anger rise in him. Something in what I say touches him like fire.

"Are you fit to walk to the study?"

"So long as I can have something for this headache."

They shuffle me through and sit me in an armchair by the hearth while the kindling crackles and a hot-water bottle is laid in my lap. None of this comforts me from the terror. I ask to hold Connie's hand. We've all been here before, the little group on the riverbank studying the next lot of rapids, but at least we were heading somewhere. This time it's the waterfall and we're still in the boat. "What are we going to do?" I keep saying. "They're onto us and they've always been bloody onto us. Those characters are down at the Angler now, reporting to Lavarack. They're here, on our doorstep, and we can't do a bloody thing about it. Can we?"

Shanks's reply surprises me. "Why are you so exercised by all this, Clement?"

"Well, aren't you? You keep saying the Shawe-Trittons and their mates are out to get you. Well, here they are, doing it."

"Doing what?"

I don't get this. He was really angry when I first told him.

"Spying on you, of course."

"To what end?"

"To expose what you're doing! Making it impossible for us to contact Smallwood in peace. Scaring him off! And McFee. So you'll fail. Or am I missing something?"

"I don't know, my boy. I'm merely interested to know how your two spies propose to secure the means necessary to accomplish this."

"Well, by stealing papers, notebooks and things; from here."

"What papers?"

"The stuff you wrote when you put me through all those tests, for a start."

"My boy, I've been conducting such tests for years. Everyone knows it."

"Well, I didn't know it. I mean, I know now. Okay, records of all the times we were on the case, observing people. Excuse me, but why were you so bothered about the newspapers if there was nothing for them to get hold of? I don't get it. Really I don't."

And I smell of sick and disinfectant and embarrassment.

Fernleaf comes in and she and Connie move their eyes to each of us in turn. Is it just me? Jackson Armitage clears his throat. "You may recall that I once said certain differences existed between myself and the majority of the society. During our last visit to London these disagreements came to a head. I have since resigned as Secretary. Now imagine a series of articles in certain popular papers representing me as a crackpot ghost-hunter exploiting young mediums, mentally unbalanced children. A few hints while our investigations were proceeding, then the whole campaign when it was nearly over. My reputation would be ruined."

"With who?"

"Whom."

Sigh. "With whom?"

"With those of the scientific psychic fraternity who are not charlatans."

"Then you could sue them."

"Your ignorance of the world is alive and well, I see. Libel rarely enhances the plaintiff or injures the defendants, Clement; especially if they are newspapers. You are suggesting months of unwelcome scrutiny and exposure."

"So it was ridicule you were afraid of?"

"As much as anything."

"So this is entirely personal – sending the Secret Service to get proof? Which isn't there?"

"Yes."

Tread carefully now. "Don't get me wrong, but why would they bother unless they thought you'd succeed? It's a lot of effort just to scandalise the work of one man. I mean, ghost-hunting isn't exactly taken seriously, is it? And what if you did succeed? Half the people wouldn't believe it anyway. It'd be a nine-days' wonder at most."

"It's about methods, Clement," says Connie. "If Jackson succeeds, with your help, then the way it was done could be applied to other things."

"What, like catching crooks? Like Edgar Cayce in America? Yes, I know about it. The medium they brought in when the Lindbergh baby was kidnapped. But that's not new, Connie."

"No, indeed," says Shanks. "I took quite an interest in that case at the time. March 1932, I believe."

I look hard at him. "Was that when it was? 1932? March? Are you sure?"

"Quite sure. Are you all right?"

"Yes. Yes, thanks."

There's a lapse into silence while I tell myself I'm done with coincidences. It takes a while. Got to get back into my stride. Here goes.

"It's about Crewe, isn't it?"

Fernleaf's eyes widen. Her mouth opens, and I do my best to shrug. "What the hell?"

"Who or what is Crewe?" says Shanks in an even tone.

"He asked me that once," says Connie.

"Tell her, Uncle."

"Apart from a railway town in Cheshire, the term means nothing to me. Unless you are referring to a ship's company."

This damn headache; nothing's shifting it. Now I'm getting irritated.

"For God's sake! Crewe is here! During the war! The codename for this house! Trying out psychological warfare! It was hush-hush, all those people meeting here. What the hell were they doing here, then, when they should have been away fighting? Crewe...was...the...codename!"

Shanks's eyebrows go up a little and he places a hand on my forehead. My gaze is full on him, because he's taking his pretence too far. He knows I know, so what's he playing at?

"I don't understand how you came by this conceit, Clement. The name by which this establishment was known during the war remains a close secret, and I cannot divulge it now even to you. I can assure you, however, that it was not Crewe."

"Then suppose someone else knew it as that?"

"Who, for example?"

"Someone who had their own operation going, even more secret than yours." Fernleaf's hand grips mine so hard the knuckles seem to be grinding together, and I avoid her eyes. Anything that'll stave off whatever's menacing us all is worth a go. "I'm talking about George. He referred to this house as Crewe. Because he was reporting on you to someone in the government and you didn't know. He was blocking your ideas, making sure they got nowhere. And now he's trying to do it again because with me you've got the chance to prove you were right after all."

That's it, then. I've said it. I look at Fernleaf. "He doesn't belong to their damn society anymore. Why shouldn't he know? Does it matter?"

Shanks breaks in. "Why do you think all this?"

"I don't think it. I know. It's true."

"Your psychic powers?"

"If you like, yes. How could I have known without them?"

"How long have you been aware — known — of these matters?"

"When we were in London, in their house. The name Crewe sort of appeared, and things with it. But it seemed too... strange, meaningless. It didn't fit in with trying to solve McFee's case."

"How's the headache?"

"Better, thanks." It is, too. You never notice exactly when they go.

"I thought so."

We're all quiet again, all looking at the fire that's blazing cheerfully and unconcernedly. A thought flashes across my mind as I lift my eyes to study the face of Jackson Armitage, and realise once again how little I know about him. Suppose, just suppose, that the McFee case and my part in it means only one thing to him: not all that noble stuff about new knowledge and a new age, but just the chance to sort out his enemies, to revenge himself. Was Crewe really a surprise? I still can't tell. The rest of us are drifting to the edges of this thing, and all our discoveries about McFee are voices off, muttered by bit-players. And how's he going to do it? If there's nothing here for anyone to find, then where is it? Has he always expected something like this? There has to be some evidence somewhere, or what's he got to throw at the Shawe-Trittons — or anybody else — if we do run Smallwood to earth?

What evidence, anyway? I haven't got a peep out of anyone by direct psychic interrogation since this whole business started.

I don't notice that he's staring back at me. "We shall be leaving here for a while, going to London again; all of us. There's nothing for them to find here and we shall not try to stop them."

"Bit obvious, isn't it? They come one day and the next day we push off?"

"So obvious, Clement, that they will be convinced they are wasting their time looking here."

"I see. You believe me, then?"

"There is little cause to disbelieve you. I have my reasons."

Reasons. How much bigger is all this than we thought? "Will Alphonse and Ludmilla be safe here?"

"Certainly."

"If they did break in they wouldn't turn the place over, would they?" asks Connie.

"No. I assure you there is no danger."

"Even if they did, and got caught," says Fernleaf, "nothing would happen to them, would it?"

"No. It would all be taken care of. It is we who fall under suspicion for attracting such treatment."

"McFee was right, then. There's no justice anywhere."

"As you say, my boy. But the Shawe-Trittons and their friends will not go unscathed. We still have one trump card in our hand, if we can play it quickly enough."

"Smallwood?"

"Sort of," says Fernleaf. "But not at first, anyway. You mean the unicorn."

"That's a card we haven't got," I say. "Correction; a card we haven't found."

"But you, Clement, are adept at finding hidden cards, are you not?"

"Yes. I seem to be." Especially when I'm blindfolded. Like now, when I can't see how we're going to do it. And I'm frightened again. Frightened of change, of decay that can't be stopped; of privacy violated, things taken and not returned; of being watched from cover. But worst of all, of a corner of our existence that I'm not sure even love can penetrate. Not anymore.

Like climbing a sunlit mountain and finding only darkness on the other side.

I kneel on my bed with the window wide open, listening for the owl and the fox and the little one-coach train chuffing across the night. Fernleaf nestles, legs crossed, her back against my chest, her arms covering mine as they wrap round her. Now and again I kiss her neck and her hair, and feel her fingers tighten.

"We won't be coming back here," I whisper.

"I know."

"I mean, it'll never be the same."

"I understand, Mackinnon. I understand what this place means to you. It scared me when I first came, too."

My desire for her is too obvious to ignore. She wriggles and gives a little laugh. I pull her closer. "I was looking at one of my star books last night," I murmur. "Kid's book, really. Thick pages with big circles full of dark blue and the stars with dotted white lines joining them up. The blue isn't dark enough for real night but it makes it more magical. I used to look at them for hours."

"I think I know what you're going to say."

"What?"

"That it wasn't only the stars that fascinated you."

"You amaze me. How did you know?"

"Because I had books like that too."

"You're right. It was the earth. Each picture had the stars shining over a single lonely thatched cottage and a couple of trees. Maybe a low

467

hill in the background, some fences; sometimes a horizon with a sailing ship; and all in silhouette, with a plume of smoke coming out of the cottage chimney like a genie. All stillness and solitude. A landscape in a fairy tale."

It used to mean here, this place; but now she is the landscape in the fairy tale. The invasion of change would destroy the magic that I want to enjoy for a while longer. She's my charm against the darkness of decay.

"Thanks for looking after me. But I know something terrible's going to happen when we're in London to finish this business. Don't ask me how."

"It won't happen to you, Mackinnon. I'll make sure."

"I love you."

She rests her head back on my shoulder. I need what she has, to make myself bigger than the fears that grip me, to shrink them to their true size. When we kiss goodnight in my doorway we release our passion little by little, like an ebbing tide. When we wake it will be full again.

It's all I have left to face what's coming.

Chapter 33

The lobby of the Fairford Hotel is full of normal people. Well-off, a bit overdressed and smoking like chimneys, but normal. Out of the four of us sitting in our leather chairs I know I'm Mister Not Normal. It's been like this since we stole out of the house two nights ago in Shanks's car and turned left to avoid our usual route past the Laughing Angler. What a pantomime. "They're behind you! Where? There!"

The purple and yellow crocuses in the parks don't cheer me up. The crisp sunshine fails to make London look any better. I'm getting on everyone's nerves, even Fernleaf's. And this headache isn't responding to treatment. I've asked if it might not be a brain tumour. You hear of people thinking it's something else till it's too late, but nobody takes this seriously.

We're supposed to be here for two reasons. First, solve the mystery of the Unicorn and McFee's case – God knows how – then hit the Shawe-Tritton gang with it before they can head us off. Presumably exposing their spying campaign comes into it somewhere, but since Shanks isn't sharing his plans with us I'm none the wiser about that part of it.

"Head up, Clement."

"Yup."

"Well," says Connie, "I think London's improved. The streets feel wider; people are stepping along briskly and smiling, and there's a clear blue sky shedding an air of optimism that completely ignores the economic situation; which is what optimism's for." She smiles and I can't help smiling back. Yes, you win. The shop windows sparkle despite what's not in them and the New Look is making headway.

"Froth," says Shanks, "but it adds to the fun. You should have been here twelve months ago. When that ghastly winter finally broke, the country was flooded from the Bristol Channel to the Wash. We felt as though we were cursed."

Suddenly Fernleaf gets up. "Care for a stroll, Miss Maybury?"

Shanks and I stay behind. "Are we waiting for anything in particular?" I ask after a while.

"Hmm. Mr McFee is meeting us here in, um, eight minutes."

"Really? I see. Thanks for mentioning it. To discuss going on with the case?"

"There is no discussion, Clement. He too feels that matters are coming to a head."

"How? Is Smallwood putting the squeeze on him?"

"These American films have much to answer for. Perhaps he will explain how when we see him."

"Did you really believe it was over?"

"As my client, Mr McFee believed we could proceed no further."

"But did you go on trying to work out what the Unicorn meant?"

"No more than you, I imagine. Ah, here he is; a little early. Remember to be discreet."

Hayden McFee looks much older, but otherwise he's the same baggy man in dark mac and bowler. And he raises the same old doubts in me. We shake hands, and as we sit down I have to look round in case anyone's taking too close an interest.

"Relax, laddie. We're alone. You look a bit peeky. How are you?"

"A bit peeky, thanks."

They start talking about nothing in particular, and I drift off. The main reason I'm not happy is that my time alone with Fernleaf has been cut short. Springtime with her would have been perfect; would have kept me the right side of my troubles. Instead of that she and Connie

470

have insisted on dragging me round and taking snaps of me in front of monuments. There's one in the camera of me outside Leicester Square Tube station, pointing to a newsstand with the words: 'Only 37 in UK earn £10,000 After Tax – Cripps'. Appeals to their colonial sense of equality or something. I don't need to share her with so many others. Her interest in her surroundings puts a distance between us.

"Well, Clement?"

"Sir?"

"Daydreaming. We are trying to work out how to go on from here."

"Sorry. Any thoughts?"

"Three heads are better than two. What do you think?"

"I think, why not just let it happen? Keep alert for any sign. It was round this time in March you arrested him, I think. Anyway, either Smallwood's serious or he isn't. We've said before; he wants to contact you, not the other way round. I mean, you've got no message for him, have you?"

His face registers nothing. It strikes me suddenly: he can't ever have believed I could read his thoughts. Or maybe he didn't care. He's still a strange man.

"Remember when you gatecrashed the New Year party? Having my birthday a few days ago reminds me that was your birthday. How did it go? I never asked."

"Fine, thanks. Yes, I enjoyed that little episode. What was their name again?"

"Shawe-Tritton."

But you know that, Sergeant. Wondering what the hell he's really up to isn't improving this headache.

"Lot of people there that night," he murmurs. "Very interesting, very mixed crowd."

471

"They make a profession of taking in the dissidents of the world. Most of them are rather less interesting than their circumstances," says Shanks.

"Hmm, so I saw. A few years ago they might have interested me, just the same. You don't get a bunch like that without a few of them being, shall we say, observant?"

"Too right," I answer. "Loads of them were spying, probably. I remember a couple of them making a quick exit when they saw Amelia."

"Amelia?"

"The maid; Amelia da Costa. She was Portuguese. Scared me to death. When she got worked up she'd start waving kitchen knives around."

Shanks doesn't interrupt. He knows I'm talking more than I've done for a while. He also knows Fernleaf and I are in love. We don't make eyes at each other in public, though, because it embarrasses him. Maybe he's reminded of how he'd like things to be with Connie. The other reason we aren't playing the young lovers is that it isn't going so well. We've all got separate rooms and I fell asleep straight away last night, as soon as I hit the bed. Maybe she did too; she hasn't said. On the surface it's all pleasant enough. I just wish we could be alone.

"Yes, I remember now. Striking woman."

"Wouldn't surprise me if she had blood on her hands."

"No. Well at least she probably stabbed her enemies face to face."

"Why d'you say that?"

"Because she'd have had to make a short speech first, about how they deserved it. The worst killers are in high places. They never see their victims."

"I'm sure you're right. As you say, an interesting bunch, some of them."

I can smell something. What is it? Hard to figure. Not a bad smell, exactly. Could be from round here, but it doesn't fit the lobby of the Fairford Hotel. Maybe it's come in with McFee.

"The Doctor's kept me briefed about your health. Sorry to hear you're not well. Still, lessons with Miss Maybury sound better than that place you were at."

"It's another world, Mr McFee."

"One of many," he replies. "Don't want to be rude, but I haven't got all day. What's the plan?"

My head's turning, a natural reaction to a smell I realise only I can detect.

"You all right?"

"Mmh." It's scent. But why? There could be traces from anyone who's sat here; Connie maybe. But it's not her. There's something mixed in with it. Sharp, and...what? This is coming from knowledge I don't have, but it's trying to suggest something. Something overlaid on what we only imagine. Tobacco. There's tobacco there. But it's foreign. Foreign. Far away.

"The only plan I have is to lunch with the very same Shawe-Trittons tomorrow," says Shanks out of a space somewhere near me. "At their place."

This shakes me out of myself. "Why? Are you still talking to them? After everything?"

"I need to see them," he smiles. "Don't worry. I shall use a long spoon."

Brown cigarettes. Scent. And cheap soap. Luxury and white tiles. Grubby white tiles.

"George is an old duffer, but you have to watch out for him."

"Indeed you do, Clement. How's your head?"

"Fine. Headache's gone." I've forgotten about it. Something else is occupying the territory.

473

The throbbing has turned into ideas and images galloping towards each other from opposite horizons; still too far away. I've never had this so strong before, only it's dealing with things beyond my experience; something I can't grasp.

McFee's getting up. Is he disappointed? He's leaving with very little; except maybe the feeling that Jackson Armitage's medium is still slightly but encouragingly off his head.

"Well, so long as you really think we're close this time. Uncertainty doesn't agree with me; nor you, I daresay."

"Don't worry, Mr McFee. It won't be long now." No, you're right there, sergeant; the trouble is I happen to be dead certain; just don't know what I'm certain of. My eyes meet his and I bring up a few forgotten words.

"Fear not, for I am coming."

The sergeant of detectives becomes still as stone.

"I'll be in touch." Then he's gone.

And it's gone. The headache moves back in.

After lunch I ask Fernleaf if we can walk out together on our own. "Of course," she says. "Only lay off the self-pity. They don't appreciate it. Weep and you weep alone."

Nice warm afternoon; except in the shade. Not a breath of wind or cloud in the sky. The unease in me is a bit harder to satisfy, though. Arm in arm at last with my girlfriend I still find I can't outrun the threat of something heading my way.

A rag-and-bone man and his cart standing in a side street, the horse's head in a nosebag.

The Unicorn. Beers and Spirits.

The Lion and Unicorn. Free House.

The Unicorn Assurance building. At first I nudge her and give a wry smile, but she doesn't smile back. Then a succession of thin, stooping old men in coats and flat hats. We decide to take the Underground, and on a near-empty platform a racking cough echoes into the tunnels.

By half-past three I'm a hollow man with chill trickling into me; turning suddenly at noises like the crash of a wrecking-ball on a bomb site or a pick thudding into the concrete of a last remaining street shelter.

But it's Oxford Street that nearly finishes it. A familiar landscape, only different. I suddenly feel menaced. The same spivs with open suitcases every ten yards; women in headscarves examining the goods while lookout men earn their cut. Gaudy amusements temporarily housed in shopfronts that used to have a name, manned by deserters, lowlife who creep into dim recesses come night. Remorselessly cheerful prostitutes that make me hold Fernleaf closer and wish them something other than what they have, or give. The city of dreary crime, of night and dereliction. The city of Hayden McFee. The city of Albert Gordon Smallwood.

I don't hear her suggestion the first time. When she repeats it, I nearly shout back.

"Tower Bridge! Why? Why there?"

"Why not?" she says calmly. "We got as near as Tower Hill last time we were in London. You okay?"

"Yeah, I'm all right. Sorry. Do you 'specially need to see it?"

She does. There's no obvious reason why she shouldn't. It's the sort of thing you might come twelve thousand miles to see. And she knows all about Unicorn Passage. Still, she squeezes my arm and whispers, "Do you mind? Can you stand it?"

If love conquers all, it isn't without a fight.

Three times the bridge raises its wonderful bascules for us. We walk onto it and look downriver at the world's shipping moored to a part-ruined landscape. The sight of ships and cranes moves me, comforts me. I saw those far shapes, glued to the horizon, from Clayton beach, their smoke searching into the coloured bands of sunset, after leaving Walter Chinnery the barber in his sunken room. They drew time and place together and seemed enchanted, about to enter the silhouette world of the blue skies in my star book.

As we start back, lights appear in windows and street lamps come on. They have a faint halo which makes me look up at chimneys, their smoke rising in the still air. Still, cold evening air making mist of its own. They're joining forces. And night falling.

I'm determined to stay awake. Dinner over, we all go for a stroll. Somehow it's better, the four of us like this, after dark. I feel the safety in numbers now the fog's getting a grip. But the headache keeps thumping away and Fernleaf's gone quiet. After half an hour we decide to call it a day, and ten-thirty sees us in our separate rooms with me still wondering why Shanks has suddenly got so extravagant. Could be he thinks my cries will keep him awake. Could be he has reasons for wanting Connie to be on her own. Or could be I'm making everything more complicated than need be, as usual. This is only the same arrangement we had back at Inglefield. Nothing feels right, though. If only I'd kept quiet about Maskell and Lavarack and the rest, we'd be back there and the world would be a good place after all.

Go on, go on kidding yourself. You keep doing this; one minute it looks hopeless, the next you've worked it out and it's all going to be okay. And here we are; Smallwood, the Unicorn and me. When it happens it isn't going to be pretty. And it's going to happen.

I feel it coming, like that first breeze on your cheek pushed by the speeding Tube train, and no one else can think of anything to do except act normal. Look at this room. There's tramps on the Embankment who'd give their eye teeth to kip on this floor. Hayden McFee sits by a fire in a grim little flat and guards those who can afford these places, when he should be running half of them in. What is he but a night-watchman? The sheets here are clean but cold, the fittings gilt. Where Inglefield has oak from medieval forests this place has Bakelite. The luxury tries to be Hollywood but it's just backlot Hollywood.

And you're a non-paying guest. Most people your age are working. Maybe you should count your blessings; the poor are told to do it and you are not poor. Get into bed.

Fernleaf comes in, still dressed. "In case they decide to come in as well and kiss you goodnight." It's hard to tell if she's joking.

"Well, so long as you tuck me up, that's all right."

"Fine."

"What's up? A few days ago we laughed at anything."

"I'm tired, Mackinnon; that's all."

"D'you think you could do that thing on my forehead? Just for a... no, never mind." I feel leaden, scared. If I rock the boat she'll walk out. "You're not ill or anything? Or is it me?"

"It's everything."

"I love you."

"I know."

"Oh, good."

"Look, I'm sorry too. Connie got a letter from my mother. My dad's up to something; some idea. She doesn't say as much, but now I don't know what's happening and I'm a long way from home."

"Is that what's on your mind?"

"Part of it. Just let me go to bed, eh? We both need to sleep."

"I think I feel better because it's not just me. Fernleaf, I'm not locking my door. You do the same, please."

"Okay. Goodnight."

I dream, and for once it isn't the Dreadful City. Why can't you get used to dreaming the same thing over and over? No, this is worse.

It's a clear, freezing night. I'm walking up a wide, smooth glacier, under a moon that washes the snow and makes the crags and buttresses rearing up around me reflect a silvery, wolfish glare. I don't know where I've come from or what I'm doing there; only feel the mountains watching me as I walk further and further up that curving tongue of ice. My skin is taut with hot prickling. There's no sound. A terrible sense of remoteness weighs on me, as if I'm a castaway on some planet's outermost moon, with only another moon for light; no sun; no stars.

Far ahead, a figure appears, moving away from me and casting a shadow a mile long. Less afraid, almost happy with relief, I stumble after it, calling out. But I'm deaf to my own cries. The shadow touches my feet as I gain painfully on the distant shape, but I can never quite reach it. Sometimes I think I can make out a long coat hung on a gaunt, stooping frame; sometimes the outline of what could be anything or anyone. Whenever I think it's the first my lungs try to squeeze out the name 'Smallwood!', but when it becomes something else, black against the snow, I become empty, crushed by abandonment.

Suddenly this thing I can't catch begins to fade. As far away as ever, it seems to disappear as though sinking into the snow, at the same time half turning towards me. Its face remains invisible; then comes a half-moment when, stopping in my tracks, I see it. But it's the recognition in a dream, leaving no memory. Without a struggle the apparition sinks out of sight and leaves me alone under the clear, starless sky.

I wake, not shaking or sweating, but pinned to my bed by a weight of deadening despair. After minutes of putting together some reality from the dark hotel room I get up with immense effort and rock on my feet while I drag my dressing gown over me. Every movement needs an hour's worth of thought.

I don't want to be alone.

Standing at her door in the unlit corridor I know this isn't how I ever planned it. All the wishing has ended in confusion; the fantasies are frauds.

"That you, Mackinnon?"

"Yes. Mind if I come in?"

"What's up?"

"It would take too long. Can I come in?"

She doesn't say anything or switch on her bedside lamp. I kneel beside her. There's misty moonlight in her room, on this side of the Fairford Hotel. "What is it?" she asks. "Are you okay?"

478

"I've been dreaming. A different dream; a new one, just as bad."

"You want to tell me about it?"

"If you don't mind. Close your eyes while I turn on the lamp."

She only half opens them as I start to tell her, then just lies there staring at the ceiling. When I've finished she says, "I was dreaming too."

"The same?" I want it to be the same.

"No. Can't remember it at all." There are really dark pools round her eyes and her face is so pale she looks like a tragic heroine in some silent film.

"You don't look well, Fernleaf."

"I'm okay."

"You look pretty crook to me, girl." I try to smile her into smiling.

"Don't remind me."

"I don't feel like going back, just yet. Can I get in with you?"

There's a long wait before she turns to look at me.

"Only because you're worried?" she whispers. My face starts to burn. Jesus wept; two in a row. First I bring up her own worries, then I make excuses. Lovers don't need excuses.

"All right," she sighs. "But you must keep still."

My dressing gown drops to the floor and she wriggles sideways to give me room. I lay on my back and stretch my feet out carefully because I know they're cold. Fernleaf rests her head on my shoulder and puts a hand on my chest. For five minutes no one moves or speaks. I don't dare say anything, but occasionally my eyes swivel in case there's a smile of contentment, a wicked little grin or her beautiful grey gaze full on me. But she just stares towards the far wall.

So this is one of the great moments. You spend years imagining it, weaving fantasies round it. But instead all we have is tension and silence.

After a while I relax enough to stroke the hair behind her ear, lightly, almost absently. Nearness and fragrance are conquering hesitation.

"Please don't," she whispers. "Try to keep still."

"I can't help it. I love you. Remember?"

Where was the lift when we sat to watch the sunrise? Cloud eight? Well, someone pressed a button somewhere and cloud nine's doors don't open. We're going down.

I've lost the script. There is no script.

I feel as if the slightest movement will send us crashing down the liftshaft.

"I have to sleep, Mackinnon. I'm not too good. Goodnight." She doesn't take her hand off my chest, so I guess that means I can stay. Soon she's breathing rhythmically, her slim body in blue silk not exactly in contact with mine. And our eyes have never properly met.

It's too late; too late to do anything but lie still and dare not to disturb her. My faint-heartedness depresses me, but this is what I've come to. The fear of losing the one person I depend on. What's going on? She's ill; her physical body and spirit can no longer keep me. I'm on my own.

I get more and more uncomfortable; my arms and legs are in the wrong places and I spend ages easing them into better positions. A word would solve this problem; the problem of lying in bed with the girl I love; to ask her to turn over so I can embrace her protectively like we all dream of doing, of bringing my knees up behind hers, of curling my fingers over her breasts. Instead I lie inert, bewildered, till I fall asleep.

She's curled snugly like a kitten into the curve of my body as I wonder where the leaded panes have gone and who's moved the bed. And not enough birdsong. Holy hotel rooms! Luckily I never took my watch off. Seven o'clock, and there's movement outside the door. Pray it isn't guest movement. Pray it's staff banging up and down.

I kiss the back of Fernleaf's neck and she turns, wriggles; and smiles at me.

"Hallo," she says.

"Hallo. I love you. I thought I'd…lost you; last night." We kiss, legs and arms and hands doing new things by themselves.

"The whole place is up," I gasp. "Got to go. We'll catch it otherwise." Door open a crack. Room maid walking away from me. Dash for it.

Breakfast. Our feet do what eyes mustn't. How quickly miseries fade. Happiness has been like islands in an otherwise cheerless ocean. We never know – or, if we're together, care much – as each island slips astern, how long it'll be to the next one or even if it's there at all. We rise from the table amid the clinking and murmuring, and the ocean closes round me again.

I sit alone in the lobby, flicking through the *London News* while my companions do necessary things. There's an article about gems; garnets, to be precise.

Garnets. Rings a bell. Garnets.

Garnet Street. The ex-pawnshop of ex-pawnbroker Manny Rosenblum. Why hasn't the name of that street ever figured in our calculations? It ought to be important. Is it?

Shanks sits down and picks up a magazine. After a minute we swap, and I wait to see if he spots anything. I'm not that anxious to bring it up, being fairly happy just then, and after a bit I'm browsing through the charity ads on the back page:

We appeal to you to remember kindly THE NATIONAL ASSOCIATION of DISCHARGED PRISONERS' AID SOCIETIES (inc.) Patron: H. M. The King.

Yes, I know a couple of ex-cons. Where are they now?

National – but not nationalised. NATIONAL CHILDREN'S HOME.

The PRINTERS' PENSION, ALMSHOUSE and ORPHAN ASYLUM CORPORATION.

And the odd orphan too. I'm one myself, near enough.

The **POOR CLERGY RELIEF CORPORATION.** Est. 1856. The Committee are guided solely by the **WANT** and **WORTH** of the applicant. More than 72,000 cases of clerical distress have been aided.

That many? Wonder if Inglefield's vicar is doing okay. He always looks comfortable enough. Ask him next time I see him; in about two years' time at this rate.

A **USEFUL LIFE** is the deep longing of the many sufferers from **EPILEPSY.** It **IS** attainable at **CHALFONT COLONY.** Patron: H. M. The King.

A useful life. The useful life. Look at this lot swanning round the lobby. Look at me.

BRITISH SAILORS SOCIETY. Est 1818. It provides, etc., etc., woollen comforts; Sea Training for Boys.

Useful life. Sea training. The ships on the horizon. They call like the ocean in a seashell.

The **SILVER LADY CAFE** is still giving hot tea and food to hungry and homeless men and women. Please help by sending a gift to **MISS BETTY BAXTER.**

A little photogravure of a woman in a cloche hat next to an ancient van with its side down, and a group of unemployed holding mugs and sandwiches. Suddenly I feel like going round these armchairs and little tables and asking for their small change. Send it to 6 Tudor St. London E. C. 4. Hallo: We do not employ collectors and warn the public against...

Never mind. I'll drop in myself. It's seeing a picture that wakes you up.

SOCIETY FOR the **ASSISTANCE** of **LADIES** in **REDUCED CIRCUMSTANCES.** Blah blah helped many poor ladies of gentle birth who, alas, have neither strength nor skill to earn their own living.

Really? Well, tough. Lucky they're not in Russia. They'd be working all right.

Founded by...

Miss Smallwood.

A hand's waving in front of my face. "Anyone at home?" says Connie. I lay the magazine down on my lap.

"Hallo. Just reading; that's all." But it's not all. What's going on? I glance through the ads again. Shanks has stood up, like I should have, and now everyone's comfortable again except me. I feel dizzy, sick; and that smell's back. Conversation flits round me and I know I've got to catch it as it flies.

"We'll meet here for lunch. I'm due at George and Damietta's for seven. Just a small gathering."

"Still on first-name terms?"

"Our association goes back many years, my girl. I may remain till very late. Please dine as you wish and don't wait up. Is that all right?"

"You know what's strange?" says Fernleaf. "It was old George who put us on the trail with his little word puzzle."

"Ah, yes. So it was."

That smell. The images rush together. Men in high-ceilinged rooms above the law; cheap soap and scent. Below, far below, white tiles and blinding lights and dirt.

And blood. And echoes.

Brown cigarettes. Russian. Images from films.

He runs the show over there all right, eh? Out of all of them; victors, vanquished, discredited, dead. Stalin. Uncle Joe.

The Party; single-minded. The Democracies; all over the place.

"Uncle?"

"Yes, my boy?"

"We've got it the wrong way round."

"Got what? You're trembling."

"Just shut up and listen! Sorry; listen. You're going to solve the case, then scupper your enemies with the facts; before they can get at you. Right?"

"Yes." Cautious tone.

"No, Uncle; wrong. Nail the Shawe-Trittons first. Then you'll be free to work out Smallwood. You'll have all the time you need."

"How so? Nail them with what?"

"The Shawe-Trittons are Reds. They're Communist agents. They've been blocking all your researches and ideas about psychic warfare, not because they don't believe them but because they do. They've been sending it to Moscow, for years maybe. Think how they could use it! Millions of Party members. They want you to succeed. Do you see?"

Shanks leans forward. "Are you telling me, Clement, that people I've known for years have been betraying my work, and this country, to the Russians? Are you saying that?"

"Yes. It started when we got talking about them with McFee. I smelled things. You know how I smell things sometimes. It was very, very strong, only I didn't know what it was. It came together just now. Torture and secret police. Stalin! They're working for the Reds. Just for once, believe me. Face them with it. Tell Mr McFee."

No one apart from me seems to know where to put themselves. I realise I'm coming on a trifle strong, but I repeat slowly and quietly:

"They're working for the Reds."

"A heavy imputation, my boy. A grave and unwelcome development." He pauses for a long time. "Constance and I are going out for a while. What you've said is, well, something I need to consider. See you at one. Thank you, Clement." Connie gives us the raised eyebrows as she picks up her gloves and hat and follows him out. I slump back in my chair."

"He doesn't believe me, does he?"

"It's a hell of a pill to swallow, Mackinnon. He doesn't agree with them but what you just said could get them hanged, if it's true. You're threatening his cosy gentlemanly world where all the backstabbing doesn't affect the rest of us. This is playing rough."

"It's true."

"Right. Well, tell that to the judge. A funny smell doesn't amount to proof."

We go out too, for some fresh air, even if it's not particularly fresh. The coal smoke and the mist are here to stay. Already the traffic's moving more slowly and headlamps are coming on.

"Where to?"

"Tudor Street. Number Six. I want to give some money away."

The smog's worse in EC4. We leave the Silver Lady place with me five shillings poorer. "Are you the person in the picture?" I ask the white-haired woman at the table. She just shakes her head. Maybe she's a distressed gentlewoman who's got a job, made good. For a while I gaze into a bookshop window, having little left to spend, before looking up and finding Fernleaf gone. I dive into the shop but she isn't there. Then I hear her voice. She's laughing somewhere.

Next minute I see her emerging from a door twenty yards down the street, her white beret in one hand and a sailor's arm in the other. Bloody hell! She's talking loudly and, as I walk and run towards her, she gives this character a hug and a kiss on the cheek.

"Well, excuse me."

"Mackinnon! This is Tom. Tom, er . . ."

"Maguire. Able Seaman. Pleased to know you, mate." New Zealand accent so strong it makes me realise how much of her own my girl-friend's left behind.

"He's the first fellow Kiwi I've met in this whole bloody town," she says. "Heard him as he was coming down the stairs here."

"Tattoo parlour, eh?"

485

"S'right, mate. Gotter do it, haven't you?"

My smile wouldn't fool a child. She'd better not make us a three-some, that's all.

"Enjoying London, Tom?

"Ah, she's rumpty, mate. Weather's a bit puckerooed, but I forgive you."

"Where's your ship?"

"She's in, well; for a bit of maintenance, you'd call it. Your sister's a beaut."

"Good try, sailor. But you're right; Fernleaf's very nice. We've been going out a while now."

Tom's all right; curly black hair, twenty maybe, but no taller than me. "Fernleaf! Well, you're an old-fashioned bastard. Good luck, mate. Nice meeting you, Fernleaf." For the first few steps down the street I'm expecting him to change his mind and show up on the other side of her, but he doesn't.

"Well, well; thought it was VE Day all over again for a minute there."

"Cheer up, Mackinnon. You'd do the same if you met a fellow coun-tryman so far from home."

"Not if he was a sailor I wouldn't."

"He was just a nice bloke, doing what youth does."

I stop and hold her; then kiss her. "This is what youth does," I say. Good line, only it goes nowhere. She doesn't actually push me away, and I leave it for things even more worrying than wondering what's going wrong with us. She goes quiet again and we ride buses back to the hotel.

Shanks avoids my gaze during lunch. "Have you given more thought to it?" I ask.

"Indeed I have. The whole thing strikes me as too far-fetched. That they are agents of our own government at a level even I failed to grasp is one thing; that they are Communist traitors is quite another. Even if you were right, what could we do? We have no evidence of any kind."

"Doesn't it strike you as wonderful," I say, "that the way I know this is exactly what you're trying to prove to them? That it works? Psychic interrogation! McFee was talking about the Shawe-Trittons but his thoughts went deeper and I read – smelled – them! Get it? If you present your findings, they'll do whatever it takes to make it a state secret or something, then block it, then send a copy to Moscow via one of their colourful visitors. Why can't you take it from me that you have to expose them before cracking the Smallwood business? Or they'll end up passing all your work to the Russians?"

I have to stop when a waiter starts orbiting our table. Shanks declares the subject closed and I decide I don't care anymore. What will happen will happen, and if I'm very, very lucky I'll never have to go through it again.

And Jackson Armitage will dine tonight among those who decided somewhere along their gilded lives that Joe Stalin was the man to go with, the man who stole the homeland of the couple who now wait and cook and wash for him in his peaceful Oxfordshire house. What a charming pair of ratbags his hosts have turned out to be.

Amelia!

If he won't do something, Amelia will. Death to traitors! No, maybe not. She's probably a Red herself.

So why did that safe open? Was it me or Smallwood, and why? I keep asking myself, is this all about something bigger? I'm bloated with worry and foreboding. And here comes the headache again.

"I'm going to lie down," says Fernleaf. "I reckon that's me out of it for this afternoon." Not even a glance of regret in my direction.

"And I'm going out. See you for dinner, Connie. Uncle." Voices calling me back will be ignored. I need time away from all this. A few steps along the road there's a bus heading for a Request stop, and I stick my hand out. Riding away's easier than running away. How was it I was fit enough to run so far, only a couple of weeks ago?

The conductor's jiggling the coins in his leather pouch.

"Er, where's this bus going?"

"Marble Arch, sir."

"That'll do."

"How old are you, sir?" I look up at the grave, fine features.

"Sixteen."

"Tuppence." He pulls the ticket off his board and tings it. Long, slightly trembly fingers.

"Are you an out-of-work actor?" I say, with the confidence of a total stranger. He walks away. "Any more fares, please?" A woman sitting behind me taps me on the shoulder. "Yes, he is," she whispers, "Mind-reader, are yer?"

The further we go along Oxford Street the further I want to go. When I get off this bus I'll jump on another one; keep heading west. Exhiliration of escape. Journey's end turns out be next to Hyde Park and there's a straggly crowd over the road that I'll just have a look at before I go on. I'm feeling better, smog or no smog, just being on my own.

It's an open space bounded by bare trees. The crowd's actually a lot of little groups listening to characters standing on boxes and platforms like library steps with placards. So this is the famous Speakers' Corner. A policeman stands at a discreet distance.

Well, it's different. An educated-sounding man on one of the better-constructed stands waves a gloved hand at an audience of three, above a board asking 'Have You Made Your Peace with God?' They listen peacefully. Next to him a black man on a box is keeping a bigger crowd laughing. He seems to know some of them and there's a bit of banter. His placard stretches above his head: 'Why Do We Have the Colour Bar?'

The crowd aren't arguing with him. Maybe the big photo of Paul Robeson has something to do with it. His use of humour gets me smiling; the way he wields it to make serious points. Maybe I should take part in a school debate. If I'm ever going back. I've given it no thought, or discussed it with Shanks. If I do, though, I'll speak against the colour bar; and have Swatty as my seconder. No, it'd better be the other way round. When will I see him again?

Next along it's a bit more heated. Two Communists on neighbouring pitches are shouting at each other more than at their listeners, who are cheering derisively and adding their three pennyworth.

"The working classes'll always be downtrodden while they don't own and control the means of production!"

"You've never worked in your life!"

"Proclaiming the Marxist message is my work."

"Not exactly a fifty-hour week, is it? Who's paying yer?"

His neighbour's trying to convince his listeners that the Eastern Europeans liberated by the Red Army will be able to choose their future. He's having more luck than the tall bloke in glasses standing alone on his little podium talking to nobody. A Prohibitionist. I stand in front of him for a minute, but he isn't a born orator.

"Did you used to drink?" I ask.

"Yes, young sir. I lost everything to the Demon Rum. But I was saved by the angel of abstinence."

"Does alcohol cause headaches?"

"It attacks every part of your body and mind, young man. Pledge yourself now never to use liquor. I know whereof I speak."

"Thanks. Good luck." This end of the Corner is sadder, more in tune with the thickening pall that's descending everywhere. This is where the grievance men spend their sanity; men who need to tell the world how they were swindled out of an inheritance, wrongfully imprisoned, passed over for preferment or too little rewarded. Nobody cares unless they're entertainingly eccentric, and worth buying a drink for; but these don't look for sympathisers in pubs. Maybe they got caught by their teetotal friend next door.

489

One last speaker actually has quite a little following, but I can't see him through his audience. It turns out to be a woman in a thick coat and boots and many scarves. She's standing on the ground and wears a straw hat with a big label on it. MRS LONDON. ASK ME ANYTHING.

She's also festooned with notebooks on strings and clipboards heavy with sheets of paper.

This is more like it. She's answering questions fourteen to the dozen; sometimes accompanied by applause. I get up close.

"Yes, young fellow?"

"Are you like that memory chap in *The Thirty-Nine Steps*?"

"They all ask that. What's your question?"

"What do you know about Garnet Street?"

"Garnet or Garner?"

"That's my name, Garner." My God. My God; Garnet. Garner. Never thought of that. Why not?

"Well?"

"Er, Garnet."

"It's in Shadwell. Good enough?"

"Anything, er, spooky about Shadwell?"

"Come on, sonny; didn't you learn anything at school? Never learned any poems? 'I am the Ghost of Shadwell Stairs'?"

Ghost? Stairs? I walk away quickly. There's cold sweat on me and I don't know exactly which way I'm going. Suddenly I'm on the edge of one of the crowds. It's the one in front of Mister Free Elections Then the Red Army Will Leave; and it's looking a bit ugly, with shouting and shuffling of feet. A little man beside me starts muttering, then calling out in what sounds like German; or maybe Yiddish, because he's a silver-haired old chap in a dark coat, white scarf and homburg hat. All at once he lunges forward, waving his walking stick above his head. There's a scuffle. And I realise with a shock that I know him, so I pile in. We're all suddenly on the cold ground like a collapsed scrum, a welter

490

of overcoats, caps, hats and grunting and cursing. The policeman runs over, but most of us are up again, leaving the little old man and me still down. I help him to his feet and the policeman goes to talk with the two Red merchants. "Mr Rosenblum?" I gasp.

"Eh? No. No. You are mistaken. Are you one of them?"

"No, sir. I'm not."

"Good. Bolshevik murderers!"

And he's right. Nothing like Manny, really.

It's me; everything I see and hear.

Somehow I know that what's coming has just taken a big step nearer, and I'm on my own at the wrong end of town.

Chapter 34

Sometimes I was with the gardener's kids; sometimes on my own. We'd see and smell the summer storm and plunge as deep into the woods as we dared. In some strange way it was better with no one else. The darkness would infiltrate the trees, the subtle change of wind and temperature give you fair notice. Then race for home ahead of the big fat drops and the certainty of total immersion. Feet running, jumping over roots, thrilling to the chase.

The bus meanders eastwards. Should have taken the Tube, but I need to recognise streets. People with a perfect right to travel keep getting on, and with every halt I work harder to keep calm, heading towards the certainty of something. They all smile, talk, gaze out of the window in some kind of slow motion. I start banging rhythmically with my palms on the handrail of the seat in front and a bloke across the aisle leans over and says, "You should have caught the one before, mate." I nod, and it's half a minute before I realise I'm still nodding.

Poor kid. Still, you can't win 'em all.

Move to the wheel-seat next to the platform so I can catch the conductor's eye. "Will you let me know when we're near the Fairford Hotel?" He pushes his lower lip out. "You're getting further away from it, son." Then he rings the bell.

A lot of walking finally gets me to the hotel and the door of Connie's room. If she's resting too then it's her I'd rather disturb. I've been in that stage of loving where you neglect your friends, and now I think I'm going to get more sense out of her than anybody. She's sitting at a little round table writing letters, in a skirt and cardigan and silk scarf and on her it works, like everything.

"How's Fernleaf?"

"Asleep. Did you enjoy your outing?" The way she lays down her pen, looks up and smiles just turns me inside out.

"I've known worse. Connie, is he still not going to believe me?"

"He didn't show any sign of it when he left."

"He's gone out already?"

"Yes, Mackinnon. He didn't say where, but after that he'll be at the Shawe-Trittons' till late. I think we'll catch up with him at breakfast."

"Oh, God. It's happening, Connie. I'm not joking. It's like an electric charge in the air. We've got to be ready."

"How are you feeling?" she says calmly, and lays her hand on my forehead.

"Shocking headache. Apart from that, terrible."

"We haven't solved the puzzle. Not yet."

"Listen. Have you ever had doubts about any of this? About me being clairvoyant? Have you ever just stood on the outside and thought, it's bollocks, but what the hell?"

"No, I haven't. Jackson and I have had long talks about his work. Believe me, I'm convinced if anyone is."

"Thanks. Then please take this seriously. I am filled with the knowledge that the unicorn business is going to be sorted out very soon. I don't understand how. I also know for certain that those bloody Shawe-Tritton people are only waiting for Shanks to prove his theories and present his findings to their society before flogging the whole lot to the Russians."

"He's not in the society anymore."

"He will be after tonight. They're going to be all matey and patch it up and have him back. They made a mistake in pissing him off so much. That's why they had to set spies on him to get ready to steal his research. Now if we don't expose them he'll end up handing it to them on a plate and they'll swallow their little academic defeat gladly. Wouldn't you?"

"That's the part I don't find easy, Mackinnon. How can you possibly know? He's never discussed what went on at Inglefield during the war; not that part of it anyway. He's very scrupulous about that. So what even makes you think this has any national importance? It sounds like something out of John Buchan."

"Connie, I know whereof I speak."

"Well, you're certainly a stranger sometimes."

Fernleaf walks in. She looks really rough. Before either of us can greet the other Connie says, "We all need to get out of ourselves. Let's go to the pictures. After dinner. There's something with Randolph Scott on round the corner. How's that?"

It sounds good. Does it matter where we are when it starts rolling? So long as I don't fall down and start frothing at the mouth in public. What odds; let's do it.

"I'm game. Fernleaf?"

"Count me in. Someone riding into town to sort out the badmen?" And she looks at me and winks. I love you when you're tired too. Only I don't have a pair of Colt Dragoons, just a nose for funny smells and a wide-open oversensitive frightened mind.

"Yeah. I like B Westerns. Who doesn't?"

The smog's worse when we step out for the Gaumont. It invades the foyer, windmilling in through the revolving doors, but at least we haven't had to queue. The usherette's torch beam pokes into a regular indoor fog of cigarette smoke before waving over three seats in the one and nines. The place is pretty full and already this palace built to separate you from the world and its troubles is working its magic on me. We squeeze by a half-dozen people and settle in. Perfect timing; missed the crowds leaving the last film and caught the interval before the next one.

On comes the Pathé cockerel. Just to prove the genius of the cinema even this reminder of the world doesn't take you back into it. Headache apart, I'm already caught up in the ornateness, the smell of fitted carpet, the uniformed attendants, the comfort and warmth and

494

privacy in the midst of the multitude; just like the false glamour of the Fairford Hotel, only completely different. I even forget I really ought to be alone in the back row with my girlfriend. I forget everything.

Until the item about Russian skullduggery in Czechoslovakia. My head pounds in response to this challenge on my memory, and we get half a minute of Harry S. Truman banging on about the Free World, but seconds later we're watching preparations for the 1948 Olympics, with a little jerky snatch of footage from the London games of forty years ago. Dorando Pietri lopes across the screen with a knotted handkerchief on his head, followed by men in boaters riding bikes. He's heading for a Marathon victory, disqualification and glory. A fellow runner. Then Mr Bevan stumping the country telling us about the new National Health Service. Only a few months away now. We're all going to be healthy; free teeth and specs, from the cradle to the grave. Roll on. Finally a human interest story from the wilds of Norfolk about a girl marrying a German prisoner of war working on her dad's farm. So here's Good Luck and *Gesundheit* to the happy couple! And fade out.

I'm just about to put my arm round Fernleaf's shoulder when she whispers to Connie and they both get up. There's shuffling and seats bumping up; excuse me, thank you; excuse me, thanks. The opening credits are running for the supporting feature as they reappear and go through the performance in reverse. "Okay?" I ask as Randolph Scott, ten-gallon hat and bandana, rides alone through the tumbleweed into town. For the next eighty minutes I'm lost among saloons and sagebrush until he rides out again leaving the Wild West a bit safer for decent folks to live in. Whereupon they get up again. Shuffle, thump, thump, excuse me, thanks; so sorry.

This time I keep my eye on the double doors under the Exit sign by the corner of the stage. What's all this to-ing and fro-ing about? They should have thought about that before we came out. And why both of them? No one's going to bite you in there.

This headache's been kept at bay by the spectacle in black and white that brings colour to our lives, but now it begins thumping away harder than ever. Luckily they come out before the main feature starts.

"What's going on?" I whisper to Fernleaf. "Woman's stuff," she hisses back.

"Which woman? What stuff?"

"Me, drongo. Just leave it."

Woman's stuff. What's that when it's at home?

On the screen an unseen hand turns the pages of a book to inform us that we're about to witness a period drama.

Based on a novel called *Trilby* by George du Maurier. A hat. Okay then.

There's not much action; apart from hand kissing and carriage driving. Closing my eyes against the flickering light and shadow helps the pain, and I doze off. Every now and then I start awake and look sideways to see how Fernleaf's doing. Her face in the semi-dark looks drawn and tired. This woman's stuff can't be a barrel of laughs. Nor's the film, so I drift off again. What a pair of crocks we are; not so much youth at the helm as youth hanging over the rail. I'm used to the idea that we feel things at the same time, and I know it's part of what holds us together, even if it's usually her having to share the fear and strangeness that afflicts me. Still, whatever I've got now, I don't think it's man's stuff particularly.

This film seems to be about opera; a bit like *Pygmalion* with singing. There's this girl with a rotten voice and this mad professor hypnotist type who can make her sound so good that she becomes famous. She's celebrated all over nineteenth-century Europe and he becomes rich, which he doesn't deserve because actually he's a scheming ratbag. Not as good as *Frankenstein*, not by a mile.

I'm brought awake again by Fernleaf whispering loudly and someone behind us going "Sshh!" Then they're on their feet again and it's getting embarrassing. There's an impatience in the thump, thump of the seats, and muttering as they disappear through the double doors with the portholes, with at least half the audience's eyes on them. The swelling of the music says we're in the last few minutes of Doctor

Whatsisname's strange control over the hapless, innocent Trilby. Not before time, for my money.

On the screen a well-dressed crowd's milling into some great Opera House. Rich men doff their hats to the sinister, spade-bearded genius who's trained the finest soprano of the age, as he makes his way to the private box from where he can see the entire stage. Tonight's performance will see his creature become a great diva and set the seal on his triumph.

Hurry up, then. My head's unbearable. I hope they have the grace not to fight their way back to their seats right at the end of the film. I'll tell them later about the Sherriff's advice at school about self-control. If you really can't hold it, if you're caught short in the street, then knock on the door of any respectable house and explain your predicament to the maid. Don't forget to raise your cap, and leave her sixpence when you depart. Simple. Maybe they don't have maids in New Zealand. *What the hell are you on about?* You're rambling. You can't tell them that. I feel sick; cold sweat and trembling.

The girl on the screen is singing, her clear sweet voice floating above the music to a sea of enraptured faces. In the villain's eyes there's a glare of fiendish concentration; his clenched fist grinds into the plush of his box. The camera dwells on his whitened knuckles, then pans across the audience below to a face in the stalls, looking up in puzzled agitation at the evil hypnotist. This is the girl's handsome, upright lover, who's followed her across the Continent despite the fact that she no longer wants to know him.

Where are they? They'll miss the end, and it's more their kind of film than mine. My head's in a vice. I want to sink down on the floor.

The lover stands up, oblivious to the occasion, a fearful look focussed on the woman about to launch into the crescendo, the last top note of her aria. In the box above, Svengali – that's it – Svengali's eyes, which have never left the figure on the stage, blaze like coals. His body contorted in a superhuman effort of will, he too rises to his feet.

497

Out of the corner of my swirling vision I see the doors swing open, momentarily letting in light along with the figures of a girl and a woman.

A cry from the opera audience. Eyes, then fingers, follow the lover's pointing hand as the madman above them sways, clutching his heart, gasping and rattling in his throat. The singer's glorious voice dwindles to a flat, tuneless chant as her controller's power fades with his ebbing life.

The girl and the woman stand unmoving in the side aisle, but it's me gasping now, clutching my chest, rasping, bending over. My mouth hangs open, my eyes stare downwards.

Then I too stand up.

"Sit down!" someone hisses.

No. I'm not sitting down. The nauseous blackness is lifting like a cloud.

Svengali. *Working through the girl.* I shiver convulsively, holding my head between my hands as I turn to look again at the two figures in the aisle.

The man on the screen vaults onto the stage amidst the uproar and takes the bewildered girl in his embrace. All round me people are telling me to sit down as the closing music fills the darkness of the Gaumont cinema.

My mind is full of blinding light.

Working

Through

Another

Person.

My head explodes and I cry out. Hands grab my arm.

"You. You all the time!"

She sees my mouth moving. Connie's put her hand on Berenice's shoulder. She looks worried, frightened. I start to push past the empty seats, stumbling, grabbing for support.

The End. All round me voices are tut-tutting, grumbling. Tough.

"It was you. Not me. You!"

Everyone's standing up because they're playing the King. The coats on their arms block my progress. Can't shove through, but tonight the King'll have to do without me.

Berenice is pulling at her companion, pulling her up the aisle. There's a look of terror on her pale face. I barge into the people whose eyes have turned to the screen despite the ill-mannered lout in their midst. They push back, cursing. The anthem goes on and on; the really slow version. I scramble over the seats in front, dividing strangers in a hail of shouts. She's disappeared in the crowd thronging the aisle, pulling on their coats, impatient to catch buses. The headache's vanished. Utterly. Not even the background buzzing it left behind whenever I seemed free of it. No, my head's clear. Crystal clear.

How well it explains everything.

I rush past Connie – "Clement, what is it?' – and dodge up the aisle, pushing a path through to grab Berenice's coat.

"It was never me, was it? It was you all the bloody time!"

She gasps and breaks free. A large hand yanks my collar from behind. "'Ere, you! Loverboy! You got no manners? Wanna meet the manager?"

I wrench free and turn. "You keep your bloody face out of this!" And of course she's gone. The foyer's full of people but none of them is her. At last the revolving door spills me onto the street and she's not there either.

"That's him!"

I rush over the road and up a side street but there's no need because you can't see five yards in this. When I go back Connie's standing on the pavement next to the film posters. She's on her own. I don't want to talk to anyone, so I make sure she sees me, then head back to the hotel.

I'm sitting in an alcove in the lobby, out of the public gaze, when she walks across and stands over me. I fail to look up.

"Doubtless you're about to explain."

"Why? I think you know."

"You do realise she's out there somewhere, wandering around?"

"Yeah, and well she might. Everything I've been through, it was her all the time! I've been going over every damn thing I said or did or felt and it all makes so much sense now. I was never psychic, ever. I was just the poor sod she worked through. Just like in that film. Bloody hell."

She sits down beside me. "And what do you feel now?"

I'm trembling. The shock of knowing the truth is nothing compared to the deceit, the foolishness, the feeling that Berenice for months has strung me along like a puppet.

"Oh, leave off! How would you feel? D'you remember what I was like when you first met me? Eh? I was well on the way down then, that's what. But I was bloody Charles Atlas compared to what I am now. That's how I feel. But that's just the sodding symptoms. Do you know what really tears me up? It's how I've been treated. Like an idiot. Left to suffer and told nothing. And you knew!"

She throws her handbag down on the table, rips off her gloves and grabs me, pulling me round by the shoulders. Her deep brown eyes narrow and her voice drops to a dangerous calm. "Now you listen to me, young man. Have you any idea what that young woman – not girl – young woman, has gone through herself these last few days? No, of course you don't. Men! Give me strength!"

I'm not going to be browbeaten, even by a goddess. "Okay, so she's been off colour! Needs the toilet every five minutes! I'm sure the chemist's got something for it."

She slaps my face; pretty hard. We look at each other, open-mouthed, then quickly glance round in case of spectators. "Shall we begin again?" she says softly.

"It's serious, then." Cheek stinging like mad.

"Yes, Clement. It's serious."

"Okay. Sorry."

"Me too. Listen; I've got to tell you before she gets back here. Berenice hasn't had a normal sort of life. Her father's, well, back home they reckon he's dingbats."

"Meaning?"

"Strange, eccentric. Full of weird ideas. He's a dreamer, Clement. I should know; he employs me. Lately he's got worse. That's why Berenice's mother angled to get her out of it for a while. She's their only child. Has she told you about her life on the farm?"

"Yes. Sounded great."

"It was. When I first met her she was six; a freckly fair-haired tomboy in bare feet and patched dungarees sitting on the verandah picking her toes. She had that straight grey-eyed look even then. That afternoon we went riding; bareback."

"And what were you like?"

"Very young, just out of Otago; hardly off the boat really. Anyway, we went out riding a lot. When she was about nine she got friendly with a Maori widow who had a shack up in the High Country. Maybe she's told you."

"Yes, she has. Learned a few things from her too, apparently."

"She certainly did. I don't know how to put this in simple language, Mackinnon – is it all right calling you that?"

"I prefer it. Go on."

"Well, this woman claimed she had second sight. Then she told her that when she died, she would pass the gift on. To her."

501

"Fernleaf told you that?"

"Why shouldn't she? I thought it was just a tale, but she took it pretty seriously. The thing was, this woman was barely older than me; so if it meant anything at all it was going to be a long way off. Then just before we left for Europe we heard the news."

"Right. I get it now. Yes, she told me about her all right. So that's why I'd never be able to meet her myself."

"But, you see, nothing happened. It started to look like there was nothing in it after all. Then she turned up at Inglefield and there you were."

"All right. But I wasn't psychic. I was normal."

"Sometimes all it needs is two parts of something – to come together."

The more we talk, the more things fall into place. Our shared dreams, the little fears that seemed to rise up from somewhere I'd forgotten. The eagle picture.

"The Holland tomb. That's when she realised."

"No. It's when she began to wonder. She didn't know what to think. Would you?"

"No. I felt the madness of Lady Holland and it took me over. You're right. I remember the look in her eyes. Then she tried to wish it away by making me play tennis of all things, and a load of other physical stuff. She made me look a complete idiot. I thought I was going bonkers and she set out to make a fool out of me. What was that all for?"

"She thought it would drive it out. The real, solid, physical things. The Maori had talked a lot about how the natural world gave you the power to see how things really were. If she held to that and didn't fill her head with..."

"Horseshit."

"That's right. Then she wouldn't need second sight."

"She never felt the horrors like I did, did she?"

502

"Once or twice, but not what you went through." She leans forward and takes my face in her hands. "You must believe this; it's very important."

"Yes?"

"She never believed that you were carrying the can for her. She wasn't working through you. At first she genuinely thought you were psychic and she'd somehow escaped. Then she thought she'd passed it onto you, like being a carrier and not having it yourself."

"That's not much comfort is it? That really makes it sound like a bloody disease. Which is how I see it, by the way. Would it have happened if we hadn't been so close?"

"I don't know. Then her time started, a few days ago. Very late for a girl, in case you're interested. And now it really is her. I think the Maori woman knew it would prove too strong some day."

"Didn't this woman have a name?"

"She only let us use her nickname; the one the old prospector gave her: Blind Annie."

"Was she blind, then?"

"No. He hoped she'd help him find gold. She didn't. Come on, we're wasting time."

I've begun to tremble, very slightly, like I have a fever. I look at my watch.

"She should be back, Connie."

"Give her time. She'll walk it off."

"So she was called Blind Annie and she wasn't full of horseshit, but it didn't stop her being psychic. Maybe she didn't try hard enough. Or just plain unlucky."

"There's something else I haven't told you. She told Berenice her old man was crazy."

"Bet that helped."

"It left her with the idea that being, well, psychic, was a form of madness too."

"Right. So when she thought I was psychic, it felt pretty close to home. I might be crackers. Pretty much how it is, I'd say."

She sighs. Around us rich people are preparing for a prosperous, self-satisfied evening. If their lives are complicated at all, it can't be like this. I need more answers.

"I'm getting anxious. If she's not back in five minutes we should let Shanks know. Is there anything else I should be told? Like, why didn't you tell him the whole story?"

"She begged me not to. It didn't take long for her to judge what your hit-and-miss performance might mean, but she couldn't be sure. There seemed to be lots of possible reasons. She pushed the true one to the back, all the time. Don't blame her for it."

"Such as, I was too mixed up. Or just not very good at it, full stop."

She smiles. "You're a caveman. When you felt fear it was real, necessary. You didn't have sophisticated emotions. It's why she liked you."

"But I did have them, about almost everyone I met. Cynical, worldly thoughts like I was turning into a right little Long-hair."

"And she knew it bothered you. Didn't change how she felt about you."

"And why she tried to protect me from its effects. Only it didn't always work."

"And everybody thought you were the genuine article. You fooled a lot of people."

"I fooled myself. Remember the night of the memory game? She'd been giving me a hard time, so I wanted to beat her at something. When I got all those pairs I thought her reaction was priceless. I thought that look of surprise was for me winning for a change. But it was because she knew what might – just possibly – have happened. And she was scared. She couldn't really do anything about it either way, could she?"

Wait a minute. Wait a minute.

"Connie, a thought's just hit me."

"Yes?"

"The very first night at Inglefield. She said she could hear them talking in the billiard room. Voices coming up the flue."

"And?"

"And when I tried to as well, they weren't talking about McFee and Smallwood anymore."

"I remember you telling me. So?"

"They weren't talking about it when Fernleaf heard them. They were just having an ordinary conversation. It was like when I heard McFee and Shanks and John Davies talking in Hyde Park that time."

"Was it?" she says. "I don't think I ever knew about that."

But I don't care whether she knows or not. I start to laugh in a silent way and I realise it looks odd, creepy even. "What is it?" says Connie in a whisper.

"Don't you see the bloody irony of it? This all started because of a conversation she picked up psychically; a conversation that was in their thoughts, not their words."

I stop my nodding and twitching, look at her, then lower my eyes again.

"She had no way of knowing what was really happening, and they had no way of knowing because they really had been talking about it earlier and didn't know how long she'd been eavesdropping. The way she repeated what they'd said made them think she'd been up in the empty room for much longer. If either of them had asked her how long she'd actually been there it would have ended up with her and not me getting the psychic test treatment, because Shanks at least would have understood that she'd heard a conversation that had already happened. Like I did in Hyde Park. Oh, yes. And on the radio at Christmas. It's all right; I kept that to myself. That's all. Just makes the whole bloody business even crazier."

"How do you feel now, Mackinnon? Apart from anxious?"

"Part of me's relieved it wasn't me after all. But that only means it's really her. When I worked it out back at the pictures I was so mad I didn't see what she might have been feeling. But she needn't have run off. What did she reckon I was going to do?" I look up at Connie and wonder how much time this beautiful grown-up woman spent thinking about me.

"Towards the end, these last few days, she realised the truth couldn't be doubted anymore. When you shouted at her in that cinema it must have seemed like you were condemning her."

I put my head in my hands. She reaches out and strokes my hair. "She couldn't help you as much as she wanted. Sometimes things got in the way. Like wanting to help her uncle succeed with the case. Her mother had told her about Jackson; how much he deserved some sort of recognition. Yes, I know. She didn't really know the truth about her brother's work, but that didn't matter."

"Wouldn't it have helped him if she'd admitted it might be…not just me? Or not me at all? The end result would have been the same; different name on the scoreboard, that's all. Won't it muck up his research?"

"No. Working through a non-psychic could be even better if it's meant to be hidden, I suppose. I don't know. Your five minutes are up. I'll go and phone."

"Thanks. I'd feel better."

I watch her walk across to the reception desk. I'm still shivering, still tidying away the story I've just heard; breathing long and slow with relief. Reverting to a simple man.

Relief. That's it. I'm not a psychic after all. The weight I've had on me, that increasing feeling something bad's on its way.

Is now with her.

I try to jump up, but my body's stiff with a kind of paralysis. When I do break free I nearly tumble onto the marble floor. "Connie! Connie. Don't ring Shanks; ring McFee. We've all got to go over there, catch him before he leaves!"

506

She smiles at the young chap on the desk. His return smile has a rather-you-than-me glint to it. "All right, hush. What's the matter?"

"The thing I thought I was heading for; the something bad. It's heading for her now."

My God. No wonder she's been feeling rough. No wonder.

"Say it in easy words, Mackinnon." We step away from the counter.

"You know I've had this feeling it's all coming to an end? Well, it is. Fernleaf isn't going to be back."

"Of course she is; just give her time. We're in this together."

"No. She's not coming back here. She's out there, Connie, searching for the Unicorn."

"How do you know? You're not psychic anymore; are you?"

"I don't think so. No, I never was. This is clear thinking. She's out in this city, in this smog; and she either knows where she's going or she's wandering with no idea of what she's actually looking for. But it's the Unicorn whichever way round. Ring McFee. Get him here. Then we go to the Shawe-Trittons and tell Shanks."

"Do you really mean it?"

"Yes! Leave a message for her here if you don't believe me. Can we get on with it?"

"He might not be in."

"If it's going to happen, he'll be in."

It's a dickens of a wait before he approaches quickly across the once-gleaming floor towards us. The lobby's already clearing and the staleness of artificial day winding down clings to everything.

"We should have arranged to meet there."

"We need to talk as we go, Mr McFee."

He looks as if he hasn't been out of his clothes since we last met. The taxi grinds through the fog as I whisper my suspicions about Shanks's host and my fears for Berenice.

"You're looking at an uphill struggle to nail those two," he says.

"So I'm told. Won't it be enough if they know we know?"

He smiles in the half-dark of the creeping car. "The busted flush theory. Yes, it works for the well-connected. They're one-way traffic, assuming you're right; no good for turning. They'd live out their days free of honours, that's all."

"So long as we get them off Shanks's back, it'll do for now. We need to get to Fernleaf — Berenice — but I don't know how."

And I don't. I know she can look after herself against most earthly dangers, but this is a different thing. The Unicorn, whatever it is, or whoever it is, may be beyond reason, beyond the rules.

"Even if it isn't tonight," says McFee, "thanks for thinking of me."

"You know London, even in the smog, especially in the smog. That's why I thought of you. I can't say about the rest because the power isn't with me anymore."

Connie's face is only half-attractive in these greasy shadows. It doesn't have the beauty of sadness in it. Sadness is knowledge, and we know nothing. Nothing that we really want to know.

We stand on the pavement at last. It seems wrong to be entering a house, to be quitting this murky sea even for a minute, when Fernleaf is out there, maybe miles away now. I see her running, ignoring the cold, down dark streets, alleyways slippery with the spew of drunks, round corners patrolled by whores and those who seek them. Standing out in flight, in search, in virtue.

Virtue. Now there's a word. God knows there's enough in this city that will take no account of it: a bus crawling out of the gloom, dark water in a dock, a twisted mind for whom innocence is torment.

I'm not in the mood for pleasantry. A too well-dressed young bloke opens the door.

"Friends and family of Doctor Armitage," I say.

"Please wait here."

When he reaches the door of the drawing room he finds us right behind him, dressed as if we're not thinking of staying but looking as if we might. George looks less than pleased and less than sober. Shanks looks surprised. They're on their own; men talking by the fire. Around us the house feels empty; of visitors, of hospitality, of dignity.

"Where's Amelia?" I ask.

"She, she's no longer with us. Do you mind telling me why you've pushed your way in here like this?"

If anything's going to be enjoyable in the circumstances, it's this.

"Do you remember us? You may not. Wrong set. Uncle, Berenice is missing."

He's out of his seat. "How? Since when? Is she all right?"

"Ask me another."

Connie says, "Jackson, she ran off. She got a bit of a fright this evening. We'll explain as we go."

George nods to the young man, who leaves the room. "Oh, I remember you very well. The girl who's in trouble; she's the one who played for us at New Year. I can see this might be an emergency, Jackson, but your people don't have to be so blunt about it. Do the police know?"

"They know," I say. And I look straight at him, eyes narrowed.

"You're that young medium chappie. That right?"

"So they say."

"Hmm, well; and you, sir, are?"

"Detective-Sergeant McFee, sir. CID."

"As you well know," I add.

"Jackson, I'm not sure I like this young fellow's tone. I don't have to let you remain, young man."

I look round me as if I own the place, then sit down in one of the armchairs.

"Please join me, everyone. Whether I remain or not, *tovarich*, will make little difference."

Just as they've settled in, Damietta enters the room. Shanks, McFee and I stand up.

"Good evening, Mrs Shawe-Tritton. May I call you tovarich too?"

She stands stock-still for a second, then moves across to her husband. McFee leans over to me and whispers, "Not bad. Speak to you about pronunciation."

"Thanks."

"Don't mention it."

"Keep watching."

Shanks has been watching too. Still on his feet he says loudly, "Come on! We shouldn't be lounging round here! We should be out looking for her. Well?"

"Where do you suggest we begin?" I answer. "She could be anywhere. Could be on the train back to Crewe." I shoot the couple a glance. They're looking a little straight-faced. Connie and McFee are giving me all the leg-room I need. This is the moment to put on a show. I go glazy-eyed and start talking in a monotone. My eyes begin to ache and I realise I sound like Peter Lorre.

"Crewe. Ah, yes. Ah, yes. Crewe." I furrow my brow and dilate my nostrils.

"This has gone far enough," says George. "Jackson, order your people to leave or I will."

Connie fixes a beautiful stare on Shanks that says: do that and I'll never speak to you again. This has more effect on him than any of my previous arguments. "Clement," he says in the sort of tone you use for telling the dog a second time, "Clement, are you sensing something?"

I could almost laugh, because I'm walking slowly and deliberately towards the library. The last time I was here, in front of George, pretending to be something I wasn't, I was walking slowly and deliberately out of the library. He suddenly jerks into life and tries to overtake me, head me off; but McFee slides subtely into place like some royal body-guard, and I keep walking.

Damietta's whispering and muttering to George as I go in and leave them all by the double doors. "What the hell are you all playing at?" she says. Her voice is sharp and querulous; the old urbanity and the control is gone.

"I'm going to Crewe," I intone.

"If you're CID, my man, then do something about this!"

"Why, sir; has a crime been committed? I wouldn't like to disturb one of these mediums, sir. Not while they're at it. Could be dangerous."

I walk round the library in its soft light, and a strange slow dance develops around me as one by one the others take up positions in the room. McFee continues to cover me while Connie, with more natural cunning than Shanks, makes sure she can see my face by backing elegantly away as I proceed, flaring my nostrils and staring at a point two feet from my nose. Whenever I can, I blink.

At the spot behind the easy chair where we once sat, I focus on the shelf that conceals the safe. My eyes speak: *there, there*; then: *not now, not now*. She lowers her lids. You magnificent woman. Now I know those book titles again. Slowly I make another halting circuit, then step towards the doors. Is there the merest look of relief on their faces?

I sit down again in the drawing room, the centre of attention. They're all standing there, and I choose that moment to think of Fernleaf. How long has she been gone now? I give two or three great involuntary shudders and moan with suppressed fear, then look up at everyone, shocked at myself.

Shanks has my hand in his. "Are you all right now, my boy?" This terrible anxiety must wait its turn. We've still a little way to go. Has he come on board now? I don't think so; not yet; I need to do more. Let's hope he thinks I'm tuning in to his niece, wherever she is, so I can take this charade to the end. As for the Shawe-Trittons, this is what their supernatural investigator's outfit is for; there's a psychic operating in their house. How can they object?

Another shudder racks me, but this time it's a wave of doubt as I think of all the ragbag of mediums and clairvoyants that must have crept round this place. Didn't they ever worry that someone would sense that safe and its contents? Or did they know they were all fakes and charlatans? Well this one isn't, ha, ha.

"Uncle," I say, putting on the voice of someone waking from a deep sleep, "I need to read something. Connie, would you find me some books on the law..."

Damietta walks swiftly out of the room, but Connie's right behind her. Shanks gives a start and follows them.

"...relating to Inland Waterways, Crimes and Misdemeanours and, what about oh, the Indian Army Act 1911? For starters. What do you think, Mr Shawe-Tritton?"

McFee's impassive gaze fixes on the Blimpish figure standing by the fireplace. Even the fire's going down, as if it too is part of their plot. The three return, along with the young man. Where's he been all this time? Damietta looks at her husband with an old-fashioned tight-lipped I-said-this-would-happen glare which forces him down into a nearby chair. Connie hands me the books with a nod and a smile.

"Thank you, Miss Maybury. What handsome books. We must keep them...*safe*." And I drop them on the floor with a crash. George twitches and begins to colour up.

"You're going red, Mr Shawe-Tritton. It suits you."

Now McFee strides out of the room and presently we hear his voice in the hall. I stand up. "Well, we must be off, just as soon as Sergeant McFee finishes his call. By the way, I tried your cute little puzzle on a few friends. Very good. Mussolini, Hitler and the rest; which wins? Stalin. Dear old Uncle Joe. He certainly rules the roost over there, eh? He'll like the two-edged sword his friends gave him."

They try a last shot. "It's been very entertaining, Jackson. Now suppose you take your friends away and see this poor young man gets the treatment he needs?"

I smile, and give another polish to a phrase I've come to like:

512

"I know whereof I speak. As for the treatment you need; others will see to that."

And Shanks rides in at last. "You are finished. Both of you."

McFee comes in and nods in a restrained but decisive way. The safe will be empty of course; young man's seen to that if it wasn't already. Warrants and all that stuff won't be necessary. We can't prove a thing. The stern sergeant was probably phoning the Speaking Clock. But their cards are marked. It won't end here. They'll buy back a shadow of their public reputation for a few names and the game will go on without them.

We take our leave. Young man escorts us to the door. "Do you work for them?" I say as he holds it open and the fog steps in. He's got a prim look like a prefect in a seminary; if they have them. He thinks a direct stare will do it, but he just doesn't have the balls, not like me right now. A few days into sixteen, I stare back. "You're working for spivs, black marketeers, dealing in stuff that doesn't belong to them. Amateurs."

"You're enjoying this, aren't you?"

"It isn't important enough. I have finer things to worry about."

We can leave now and wish them a restful night, which is more than we're about to get. In the clinging smog we make our way to Shanks's car, and not till we're safely inside its comfortlessness do I ask myself what's just happened. McFee's behind the wheel; driver, navigator and, as far as that goes, entirely on his own.

"Can they make trouble for you?"

"Not as much as they're going to get. String-pulling's a risky business. How long's a piece of string?"

We ease out into the slow sparse current. After the excitement I'm empty, don't even know which way to go. For a while back there on their cream-pillared portico I felt bigger, but it passed quickly enough. Sad satisfaction. Bigger is as bigger does.

So now we're free to look for Fernleaf. I tremble with what we've just had to do and the time it's cost us, and with the absence of ideas for what comes next. The nature of the Unicorn troubles me. That, and knowing how my old fear, which we once shared, is now crouching on her back wherever she is, so far ahead of us, so much nearer to her goal. We must be with her before she finds it. Or it finds her.

Chapter 35

In the back of our little world Connie speaks gently to Jackson Armitage. I like to think she's holding his hand; that her wonderful honey voice which fills our ears fills him with the comfort he needs. He's suffered losses tonight. His oldest associates are traitors; his judgements and hopes have been fastened on an imposter; the desires of his heart continue to elude him and his niece is missing. It's hard to concentrate both on the mystery beyond our bonnet and on his unseen reaction to her words.

At last there's silence, except for an engine in low gear and my sleeve squeaking on the glass.

"Where are we, Mr McFee? Maybe we should stop and put our heads together."

"We're in Birdcage Walk, by St. James's Park." He applies the hand-brake. Apart from the sound, you'd hardly know we were no longer moving.

"Any ideas?"

"It would help if we had the slightest notion about the unicorn. I hope to goodness we're on the right track," says Shanks. "Can anyone see what time it is?"

I squint at my whizzo luminous watch. "Eleven fifty-eight. Tell me there's nothing special about midnight."

"No, you can rest easy on that score. We are, however, dealing with a watershed of sorts."

The other two murmur agreement. "Really?" I say.

"Psychic powers in females appear, in certain cases, to operate powerfully during the transition to womanhood."

"That was the woman's stuff, was it?"

"Posh bloody education," mutters McFee.

"She may be in a state of heightened receptivity. She could already know what she is looking for. That may help us."

"It would have helped us if she hadn't run off, wouldn't it? At least taken us with her? What's the point otherwise?"

"I don't know," says Shanks. "Are we really subject to chance in this?"

"You mean it's going to happen anyway. Well, if it isn't set for tonight, then a lot of drama's going to waste. Are you sure you're not psychic, laddie? Not even a bit? Can't you make some sort of contact?"

"There was a moment," I reply after a second or two, "during our little vigil at Unicorn Passage when I wanted her near me; and I felt she was. When I mentioned it to her she said she'd been thinking about me all through it."

"Can you get her to do it again?"

"Well, hardly. It's up to her, isn't it?"

Connie touches my face with her gloved hand. Her eyes plead. "Try, Mackinnon. Please."

I'm never going to stop falling for this.

"I'll need to be alone. No, don't move; I'll go outside. I may be some time. Anyone got something to drink?"

Two flasks appear, little flat silver ones. I take them both. Shanks clears his throat.

"Thanks. What's in them?"

"You'll find out. Take a decent pull, then wait. Don't sip."

The night's not so thick outside, so I walk along the pavement until I realise it's doing no good; I have to be away from them and from passers-by. Tap, tap. "Look, I'm going into the park a little way, okay? Just

516

be patient and I'll do my best." But the trembling in my legs gives me away to myself.

This is hopeless. There's nothing, nothing.

Two hundred yards or so brings me to a bridge over water. Despite the feeling of isolation in the smog you can hear the low mutter of the city trying to get along all around you; even at this hour. Minute by minute, though, the streets empty and I can see myself still here, sitting on some damp bench at four in the morning, mind blank and sick with terror. No, not a bench; they'll all be occupied. Lean on the parapet of the bridge and stare at black water and use the power that's left to you; pure, straight thinking; just start somewhere.

Start with a drink; one from each flask. Jeez whizz! Cough, splutter. Hmm. Right:

The unicorn, the unicorn.

Are we still in the world without coincidence? If we are, then everything that happens has a meaning. Go back over these last days. If we aren't...no, we must be, or it's all stupid and cruel. Stupid and cruel, like it's been for millions in this world for years? What makes us so different? No, stop; stop. There is a meaning. Have another. Mmm. Not bad.

Can't some reflection appear down there?

There was a bad dream; but it was only me. We went out a few times. I had a headache. She wanted to go to Tower Bridge. I gave five bob to the Silver Lady Café on wheels. She kissed a sailor. Now that was a bit out of the way; I was surprised; no, shocked; felt jealous. Is that why they do it? Not very seemly, anyway, and it got me thinking unseemly things. Then what? Went to the flicks and the headache went, and so did she. Thoughts are flowing well, coming quickly; have to slow down, sort them out; there you go, don't sip; there. Yes.

"Life can be hard to understand at times."

What?

"Life. Not always how we like it."

517

"I beg your pardon?"

There's a tall bloke standing a couple of yards away. No dog. What's he want?

"Would it help to chat?"

"No. I actually need to be on my own."

"That's the danger, old chap. Shouldn't be, at times like this. I know what it's like."

"I doubt it." Hang on. "You one of those types after saving my soul or summink, er, something? Yeah, something?"

"Ah. Very young to be turning to that, you know. Look, I can't say I don't want to interfere, but I'd hate to see you…well, in your state you could come to harm even in the shallow water down there. Your muscles wouldn't co-ordinate, and the shock of the cold…"

"For God's sake! Can't a person just stand here and try to think without some Presbyterian or whatever thinking you're trying to end it all? Just go away. Goodnight, and thank you."

A hand puts a little pamphlet on the parapet beside me. "You might glance over this when you're feeling better. Phone number's on the back. Goodnight to you."

Better look at it or it'll lie there bothering me. MRA? Moral Re-Armament. Wait a minute; old Hopwood was always banging on about this. Buckingham, Buckskin, or somebody. Here he is, Buchman. Stop the Red Menace! S'all right, mate, just done that for you. If old Toady's mixed up in this then it's got to be dodgy. Hallo: world must regain the Four Absolutes. Yeah, why not? Honesty, Purity, Unselfishness, Love. Oh, do me a favour. If Toadface's any example, Reds have got nothing to worry about. Love. Got that or I wouldn't be stuck here. Purity; yup; till she kissed Sailor Sam, right in the street too, I'll have you know.

Purity. Virtue. Hmm. Why are you stood here? This is a complete load of bollocks. We've had three months to work this out and we're still nowhere, so why should I do it all now, on my own? It's ridiculous. Flick. In you go, Mr Bucko; float away and tell the ducks to behave themselves and re-arm. You down there, got any ideas?

No? Nor me. Let the minutes pass. And pass.

Someone like Swatty would be a bit of use here. No woman trouble and relaxed about ghosts and ghoulies; what did his old man used to say? Fruit. Not made for you, so don't think you're entitled, or something. Put some thought in when you eat it. Think before you scoff. Them as thinks, eats. Or summink.

A bit of a problem, old chap. But all the apples are on the tree and you just need to pick the right one. To see it you must stand in the right place.

Footsteps. More interruptions. No, it's a woman.

"Hallo, Mackinnon."

"Hallo, Connie. This is crazy."

"You sound like the Lost Weekend; give me those. I told them it was a mistake, but when you're grabbing at straws then sending a boy into a smogbound park at midnight with more grog than he can handle must seem like solid sense. I came to find you."

"Thanks. Boy, eh? Did you meet a tall creepy bloke on your way?"

"Oh, him; yes. Tried to pick me up."

"Shouldn't think so. He gave me a leaflet. MRA. He was trying to save you from immorality."

"No, he tried to pick me up. What are we going to do?"

"I don't know. Been trying to think it out using first sight instead of second sight, but all I've got is a word; one word. Keeps rattling around."

"And?"

"Virtue."

"Why that?"

"It's what Fernleaf's got. We haven't done anything, I promise; she's still got it, but it can't save her from the things that don't recognise it, like machines, dark places; lunatics. I'm scared she'll have a really

519

ordinary accident. It hardly makes sense and it don't mean a thing. Help me out, will you?"

"Come on, take my arm and we'll go back. They're not in a good mood, marching up and down the pavement. So just take it easy and walk slowly."

Virtue.

"Thinking I saw Manny Rosenblum reminds me of when we went to see him and his wife was all upset. It was the way she looked after her. Then before that we were getting all edgy in McFee's flat, and she calmed us down. That's what I mean, and I thought – yeah, that's right! – I thought, the maid that is matchless taming the dragon of something or other. Virtue, see? Saw it in a book at school; this maiden with a dragon on a gold chain, and it's her virtue that's taming it."

"Unicorns too. Maidens tame unicorns."

Maidens tame unicorns.

"Well, that's it! Her virtue's going to…do something with it, and then it'll happen! That means it's a thing, not a place. Not a street or a pub."

"Something or somebody. Keep talking."

"Connie, that growing up woman business; she still a maid, still matchless?"

"She's matchless all right. Maid's a bit more debatable."

Oh, no.

I stop and sway on the footpath, tearing myself away from her arm, start going in circles, slipping on wet grass, slapping my forehead. "That's the danger she's in. She's losing the power that'll bring it in quietly. We've got to, oh no." And I sit down on the path, head spinning, mind crawling in despair. "All that word means…is how much trouble we're in. Something terrible's going to happen. I feel lousy."

"You sound half-shot. Get up and don't breathe too deep. Come on, and don't stop talking."

They're leaning against the car and it all looks fairly peaceful. The smog's ridiculous now, only the odd lightbeam groping past. "Well? How are we doing?"

"He's getting things, Jackson."

"Like what?" says McFee in a tone I've heard before. His impatience and my alcoholic uselessness panic me into a thought that's mint-new, a word to gain time:

"We need to get to the grave, at the cemetery. Er, or wherever he's buried."

"Right! Pile in. Explain on the way."

I'm in the back now and McFee makes better speed along near-empty roads. There's a different feel inside the car and it isn't the closeness of Connie so much as the presence of McFee himself; not his physical presence but something detached, as though he's in his own world. It's not hard to guess, not for me anyway, what accounts for his hardening away from us as we rumble towards Brockley and Ladywell, far across the river. To a place he knows too well and I shouldn't know about at all.

Fear not, for I am coming. He knows I know something, even if it's only the innocent ramblings of a psychic's stooge. He's remembering a discussion about quests, about how we emerge changed from experiences we don't understand.

"Where are we now?"

"Coming up to the Elephant."

"Where's that?"

"Elephant and Castle. Fair way to go yet. You sound different when you're drunk."

And none too well either. What are we going to do when we get there? Correction; what am I going to do? There's only one consolation in worrying about that, and it's the fact that every minute that passes without feeling stabbed through the heart makes me think she's still safe. It's stupid, but reality and me had better enjoy this break before it comes to an end when we stand by Alice's grave. Compared to me McFee's got nothing to trouble him; only the memory of a youthful indiscretion. It's what youth does.

It's what youth does. A youthful indiscretion.

"Stop the car. Pull up."

"Something else come to you?"

"Maybe. Just pull up."

"Right. What is it?"

"Mr McFee, can you tell us how near we are to Stepney?"

"Stepney! Are we going to the cemetery or not?"

"Er, maybe not after all. Is it far, Stepney?"

"Far enough. All this flitting about's making me suspicious, laddie. What do you think, Doctor?"

"I have to admit this is a little erratic for my liking. You're not ill, are you, Clement?"

"No more than he deserves," says Connie. "What's it about, Mackinnon?"

I take a deep breath, which turns out to be a mistake. When I recover and close the door again I say with as much courage as I can muster, "You must bear with me. It's a hunch, but it's the strongest one yet, and I don't want to tell you until I'm happier about it. Mr McFee, can you drive us to a phone box?"

It glows bravely through the murk. I close my eyes, imagine a deep breath and say, "I only want Connie with me. Please be patient a bit longer."

Being in a phone box with her for this reason is like Dickens. The best of times and the worst of times. "You remember that orphanage you visited with Fernleaf? It was in Stepney, right? I want you to ring them. Ask them, well, ask them what I tell you. Okay?"

"I'm glad you think it's important, young man. Mr McFee's on a knife-edge and Jackson's worried sick…"

"We all are."

"…so this had better lead somewhere; given we're phoning a convent after midnight."

"They're nuns, aren't they? They're always up at ungodly hours, praying. Just find the number, please. I've got three pennies here; what about you?"

"I'm all right. Hmm. Hmm. Got it. Here goes."

I take a look in the direction of the car. Just as well I can't see their faces. At last a woman's voice answers. She sounds pretty ratty, for a nun.

"Hallo, St Joseph's? Good evening, sorry to bother you at this late hour, but I need to speak on a matter of urgency with the sister, er, the one who's been there longest." There's a long pause, then a different voice, marginally less annoyed than the first one. It goes on for a bit.

"Fine, yes, I'm aware she might be quite old, but it concerns a child you once had. Name of Horace – no – Hubert Andrews. Well, yes, it is important. Possibly a criminal matter. No, not you; him. I do have a CID officer with me, but I don't need to involve him if the information I'm after doesn't require it. Yes, a matter of…excuse me." She covers the mouthpiece and rolls her eyes. "What am I asking?"

"A matter of indentification."

"A matter of identification. Most urgent. Thank you." Another long pause. "Connie, ask what his youthful indiscretion was when he was there. He was severely punished for it."

"Do you know what it is?"

"I think so, but I don't want to put ideas into an old woman's head. She might agree to anything, especially this time of night."

"Hallo? Yes, I'll speak up. Thanks for your time. It's about Hubert Andrews; a very large, strong boy you had there during the Twenties. You remember? Wonderful! Do you remember him committing a youthful indiscretion for which you punished him quite severely? Several? Oh."

For God's sake. "Getting himself tattooed," I whisper.

"Getting a tattoo. Yes. Yes, I realise it was against the rules. That's the whole point. Yes? No. Oh, yes. Splendid. No, it's in his favour, I assure you. Can you remember the design? Hmm? Yes, I'll wait." She crosses her gloved fingers and strokes my cheek with them. My spirit's thermometer is rising fast; heart thumping; mouth dry with alcohol and hope.

"Hallo? Mmm. It was a long time ago; yes, of course. Ah! A fish! Are you certain? Definitely a fish. Hold on." She raises her eyebrows to me and nods vigorously: that it?

I've gone cold.

"Ask whether he had a unicorn."

But I don't need to hear more. We stand there in the candyfloss light and I lean against the panes in despair. "He only had the one, and it was a fish. She was adamant. I couldn't argue, Mackinnon. I'm sorry."

I decide to tell them my hunch just because it sounds so right, apart from one minor detail.

McFee sucks in a breath. "He had two when he was in the nick."

"Two! How d'you know?"

"I followed up his file. Wanted to get my hands on him for shopping Smallwood; allegedly of course. Yes, two. Well, no; one really. On the file it says 'lesions consistent with inexpert removal of tattoo'. The one he kept was an eagle."

My head lowers. "No. No!"

"That's becoming a habit, Clement. Please explain."

"The eagle! The eagle is what she's afraid of! The picture back at Inglefield. She's going to run into him and he's going to do something."

"Well, he's not the unicorn, so maybe he's out to stop her finding it." Shanks's voice is anxious; a bad sign. It's all going down the Swannee, and I was so close.

"If you're right, then Horace is back in town – if he ever left – and we should pick him up," says McFee. "He might have headed back to Danny Ogden's yard, but it's a bloody long shot."

"How hard did you try to find him after he sorted Danny out and got away?" I ask. "He seemed a bit difficult to lose. I know you said Danny wanted to drop it, but still…"

McFee doesn't answer.

"Did you ever suspect that he might be connected with the Unicorn?" The question sounds ridiculous, and dangerous. I wish I hadn't asked.

"First thing I thought of when you came up with the word. But it didn't check out, did it? A vanished fish and an eagle don't amount to a unicorn. So there it was."

"Your Mister Smallwood has put us through a lot," says Connie. "Finding out what the Unicorn means is going to be harder than solving his first puzzle."

Mister Smallwood is indeed putting us through it. If he'd only stayed behind his counter and out of the War I'd still have met Fernleaf and Connie; still been at school; missed out on a lot of experience with a high price-tag. Or if he'd only been a bit stronger and followed his own father into the docks. What a world. "Remember that docker swallowing the chain?" I say to Connie. "That's right, I do," she murmurs. This trying to make conversation while Fernleaf remains lost in the night and I'm heading for personal disaster has a surreal feel to it. But we're in surreal times.

"The docks. There used to be opium dens," adds McFee. "You should have heard some of those Chinamen's tales. They used to bring back all sorts of stuff from foreign parts. The pubs round there were like the British Museum; all those anthropology specimens hanging up round the place. They'd pawned them or swapped 'em for whatever. Everybody did it; not only Chinamen."

I try to imagine these places; lifetimes yarning in the pipesmoke. Days ashore and years afloat. Exotic objects nailed to the low beams.

"'Course, your Chinese used a lot of this stuff to make potions. Used to go in their little shops when I was on the beat. Mind you, it was on its way out even then. Limehouse isn't what it was. Steam and the big War changed everything."

"How far now?"

"Don't put your hand to the door yet. Now a unicorn's horn would have made someone's fortune if some sailor had dropped it in one of those shops. Just as well, eh? The stuff people believe in. You couldn't make it up."

Yes, just as well.

Or maybe not. Come on, memory.

"Mr McFee, can you stop by a phone again?" I'm shaking and the rest of me feels like it did when I wanted to speak in the India debate.

"Still going to the cemetery, are we? Or Danny's yard?"

"You may have the answer very soon. Connie, we've got to get the nuns again. Don't look like that."

She has to find the number once more and I watch our breath filling the booth while she dials. This time I've briefed her so she can work her charm uninterrupted. It's a struggle, and at the end of the call she says, "Pray for me."

Yeah, and me too, in case this idea meets its own backside.

"It was a swordfish."

"A swordfish! Good! Thank God."

"A swordfish is still a fish, Clement."

I laugh in a Lordy, lordy! sort of way. "Yep. Or not. Come on."

No one else is excited, but they take a polite interest in why I am.

526

"Let's assume our old nun wasn't a naturalist, and she didn't frequent dockside taverns. Also that she wasn't about to discuss details with young Horace – Hubert – when he was getting done for having a tattoo. Back then I imagined one of your strange objects brought back by sailors."

Shanks has been very quiet. Suddenly he says to himself, "Of course. Of course. Well done, my boy. Not a swordfish. An easy mistake to make. A *narwhal*. Its horn was highly prized; the Unicorn of the Sea."

"Danny's yard, then," says McFee.

And I sit back full of myself; as full as I've ever been. I've discovered Eldorado.

We're there. After all this time.

I babble like a prospector who's struck it rich being plied with drink. They do allow me a celebratory swig from McFee's flask, and I start to retell the whole story from when we knew we were looking for a unicorn; retelling it to its main actors, and they let me go on and on.

Until our driver cuts in with, "Only one or two minutes now." All at once our nearness to an event none of us can decribe crashes in on me, and I begin to tremble all over. Will Fernleaf be there? Will Horace be there? What will he do?

I've absolutely no idea what's supposed to happen.

"Here we are."

The barbed-wire knot holds the high gates shut, but there's a smell of coal smoke. Maybe it's from the engines we think we can hear in the marshalling yard. Running across the uneven ground McFee pulls away the sacking at the entrance to the Anderson shelter.

There's a fire in the grate. We spread out and search the yard, but there's no one, no horse, no cart. The ramshackle stable is completely derelict. The whole place, I know instinctively, has been abandoned; until tonight; until this hour in fact. Horace is about, somewhere close by. We confer by the shelter.

"She's still on her way," I say. I've got no more authority for saying this than anyone else, but the whole idea's been mine so far and it might as well be me. Relief and fear are contending for my soul and only activity can help us now. "I'm going to stay here," says McFee. It's more than just the strain of driving across London; it's the moment when his life separates from our intellectual exercise, the moment when he must bid goodbye to his guides and turn his face to the unknown.

"By all means," says Shanks. "But nothing will happen until the four of us are present. Did you not say so once, Clement?"

"I did, except it wasn't me saying it actually. But which four? There's five of us."

"No doubt it will resolve itself. Constance and I will search up the road, you go down. Turn back in five minutes. We shall continue in that manner until one or the other appears."

"Be careful," I say. "Horace is a tough man. Just be careful."

"You too, my boy. He could be right on you in this smog."

McFee settles on the plank bench by the fire, his bowler hat on his lap. We go our ways. For me, fear is overcoming relief. I still know something bad is coming. One of the five isn't supposed to be around when we keep our appointment with Albert Gordon Smallwood, and I've got a terrible feeling about who it's going to be.

Chapter 36

I reach the end of my beat under a lamppost that wears its canopy of light like a translucent jellyfish. Its fringes undulate in the slow swirling of the smog. For now this has to be the border of our world, the place where monsters appear. Two minutes by my watch before I turn back.

How much did McFee know of what we knew? Sitting back there in the fireglow he looked vulnerable, ready for something to happen that for once is beyond his command. But, like a once-victorious general finally come in to surrender, he fills me with the idea that he was on top of things more than we realised. Suddenly the episode at the Shawe-Trittons seems only a pantomime without his presence. Would he have allowed it unless he knew the score already? He must have had them in his sights for years during the war, watching like a patient spider. Maybe his interest in them went deep but could remain only distant, a hobby, in the days when the Russians were valiant allies.

I know very little about anything now.

Walking back I look behind me and listen for deceptively light footfalls. Naturally there's no one around; no police, no drunks, no insomniacs, no whores. Smallwood's made sure of that. I don't need convincing anymore.

"Well, Clement, no luck then?"

"No, sir. All quiet."

"Isn't it?" says Connie. They don't feel my deeper anxiety about Berenice. To them it's just a matter of everyone turning up for the event. Why are they so calm? Is this something else that's been arranged for us? They look like a couple out for a moonlit stroll.

"Let's wait with Mr McFee", she says. "I think we're doing no good out here."

"Well, I'll stay out then," I say. "Someone ought to."

"As you wish, my boy." I watch them as they merge for a second with the red glow before vanishing out of sight. Whatever weird anaesthetic is affecting them isn't working on me. There must be more for me to do.

So that's three of us present and correct, then. And out of the two remaining there can be only one. Something so wrong calls for a different plan, as if somehow I can surprise fate.

Passing through the shelter's chimney smoke I scramble up the embankment and through a rotten fence. A mile away the great power station by the river is pouring its own exhausts by the ton into this murk, joining the geysers from a herd of locomotives shunting unseen around me. I begin to step over the rails, heading away from our line of search. Some impulse tells me she may be approaching from the other direction, across these tracks. I want the craziness of this to create its own truth.

Finally I reach a boundary of rank grass and weeds and bits of concrete and work my way to the right, listening for a human sound among the invisible noises of the railway. Why she should be within ten miles of here is a question I've abolished. With the confidence of the half-drunk I pick a route over greasy sleepers and smooth damp rails. A couple of times I stumble. Getting to my feet a second time I see a small white object lying on the ballast. I'd never have spotted it standing up.

It's her beret.

Clutching it in both hands, heart breaking into a pounding roar I walk forward, calling her name. Only the distant clanking of trucks answers me. Here no signals or lights illuminate the search. Then I see the heap crumpled on a sleeper, between the wet shining metals.

Speaking her name quietly as if she were only asleep I crouch over her. Her legs are drawn up and both hands are gripped like a vice on the steel next to her head. At first I think it's electricity, but it isn't.

"Fernleaf. Fernleaf!"

I try to loosen her hold on the rail but her fingers are ice-cold and rigid. Her eyes are open but turned up almost out of sight; her mouth agape as if in the act of crying out. Slowly I lean back until I'm sitting on my heels.

I've found you. Before anything else has. You're all right now.

All right now.

I can see my own breath, but not hers. There's no pulse.

I'm here with you, Fernleaf.

But she's dead.

Every particle of my experience leaks away into the ground.

What's left is an animal, nuzzling a lifeless thing because death is only a mistake.

She looks very small, childlike. Born to die here, in this place. So far to come for this.

I struggle upwards but fall into a void. Then the muscles of my face collapse and I crumple down beside her, holding her like I did when she woke in my arms yesterday, a long time ago.

I wriggle to make myself mould into her shape so we can be like one person. I want to sleep too, here on the wood and steel and oily ballast until everything goes away. My hand searches along the sleeve of her coat and closes over her frozen white knuckles, caressing them mechanically while I try to rock us both, gentling us into some kind of togetherness. I bury my face in her hair to drown the slack-jawed moaning that's all that's left of me. Nothing matters anymore.

Nothing is important; nothing to detain senses that have gone numb.

She's dead. Nothing need be anymore. Nothing is anything.

Except the clicking of the rail by my ear.

This time the squeal of axles and the clattering of buffers have an identity of their own.

A brief damp whistle. The rail seems to murmur. This is not right. This makes something matter after all. I'm up on one elbow, then on my knees.

"Come on, Fernleaf. We can't stay here."

I try to coax her lifeless hands from the rail, but her grip is like steel itself; it's as though her hands are welded to it. I tug, wrench, even kick at the bunched fingers. The rail vibrates and hisses. The train will mangle her. I think I can see its lights. They're not loco lights; wrong configuration. My whole generation knows them. I'm looking at the wrong end of a train coming this way.

Her body can't be used like this. She needs sun and space, not a second death in this dirty night under a mindless marching line of wheels.

Breath rasping, I stumble along the track, waving, shouting. This is what happens in films, an unreality I can deal with if I can just get close enough to a points lever. There's always one around. The rumble of trucks drowns me out and I see the first one's shape emerge out of the smog. It's colossal, its wheels huge, turning ignorantly at twice the pace of a walking man. I've watched these coal trains from the footbridge and they're very long. I'll never reach the engine in time. For a moment I stand amazed, useless; then start running back towards Fernleaf. I must be near her, with her if necessary; to be mangled too. Then I'm down, hands and knees gashed by the ballast, as another thirteen-ton wagon rumbles past me, ever so slightly picking up speed.

This is where you spend long milliseconds considering what has been, wasting them on thrusting trivial thoughts aside to make way for those you can't have again. A face looking up at me from a bench in a silent winter garden. Again and again the shutter clicks. It's gone. She's gone. Nothing you did mattered.

Clement Mackinnon Garner: the stars in their courses marched against him.

Away across the tracks, something else catches my eye. A shape, a human shape is approaching, bounding blindly through the fog with an urgency unusual in a railway employee. A huge man, leaping with long, almost graceful, strides.

At first I can't make the word, and it costs two more wagons before I shout, "Horace! Horace! She's on the line!" Waste of time. He can't outrun the train and free her too. The clacking bump of wheels comes faster and faster. Almost jumping over me, he bellows, "Pinnerbrake! Pinnerbrake!" and in the incomprehensible words I forget that Fernleaf's dead. He's not making sense and there's something hypnotic about those slicing, scything wheels: dadoom, dadoom; dadoom, dadoom.

She won't feel it. Nor can I.

He throws himself at the nearest wagon. What's he up to? Trying to wrestle it to a stand? Leave it alone. You've done your work.

Suddenly there's a fearful screeching, so solid and close I jerk my head away. Next I see Horace vanishing into the smog, running with the train. At last I move, chasing after him.

The screeching comes from the wheels of the wagon he was fighting. They're no longer turning.

Yes! He's pinned the brakes! Pushed down the lever that locks them, then rammed the iron pin on its chain into the hole that keeps it there. Now the next truck emits a squeal that pushes a lancet in my ear and loosens the teeth in my head. Of course; he's seen it done a hundred times from his home in the scrapyard; but not on trains that

533

were moving. I turn and run a few steps before an unbraked wagon's upon me.

Where's grief gone? Swept away in action.

I pull out a pin, let it swing and throw my weight on the lever. As the brake shoes touch the wheels they transmit a judder back to me that nearly makes me let go, but I yell with the effort and push the eyebolt into a lower hole. I know Horace is jamming them tighter, but I don't care. The train's slowing, but not enough. The next wagon's easier, with a rachet bar that doesn't need pinning. Buffers are clashing in succession as the free-runners push into the half-dozen leading trucks whose locked wheels are exerting a massive braking force on the whole line. Hands still gripping the rachet bar, I'm suddenly jerked to and fro like a puppet and flung onto the ballast.

Trains like this don't just stop. They set up a mighty shock wave that runs from end to end and back again, then gets out of phase with itself. The result is a series of spasms that sound like the collapse of a bell-tower. The jangling erupts all round me as I lie sprawling. Then a hiss of steam. Then silence.

Nothing left but to remember why; to run and see. I run crouching in dreadful expectation to the front of the first wagon and find Horace, an indistinct shape in the gloom, bending down only thirty feet away. Then a strange thing. He simply stoops and picks her up. Her hands leave the rail and swing for a moment as he turns her over in his arms and, cradling her like a child, runs till he's invisible.

I'm too shot to run; have to lean back against the buffer and let confusion take over. Gulping, gagging, running a hand over the greasy film of sweat and mist and coal dust that covers my face, I think I feel relief. Something like a laugh splutters out, just before a hand grabs my shoulder.

"So you're the comedian. Over 'ere, lads!"

They come puffing up, one from the loco and, from the opposite direction, the shunter who's been waiting by the farther line of trucks to connect the trains.

"Missed 'is mate. 'E was pickin' up whatever 'e put on the line an' run off wiv it. Bleedin' good fing for you, pal. Puttin' obstructions on the railway is not nice."

"It was a person on the line, a body," I gasp. "That's why we were trying to stop the wagons."

"That a fact? 'E was pinnin' the bleedin' brakes, that's all. Like playin' trains, do you, sonny?" They're ordinary middling men, not rough types, but they've got the railwayman's traditional dislike of trespassers. The railroad is a different country. I shake my head to have another go at explaining. It's going to sound stupid. Confusion's just about total.

"Smell 'is breaf," says the shunter putting his face up to mine. "Come on, sunshine. Yer drunk, yer underage an' yer on British Railways property. We got transport police 'oo'd love to 'ear 'ow you do it." The driver grabs my arm and I realise I'm about to be late for an appointment. Come too far to miss it now, but all I want is to see Fernleaf again, alive or dead. An hour under questioning will be too ridiculously ordinary. No time to play responsible citizens with these men. Got to go.

My polite attempts to disengage myself meet with a poor response and it starts to get serious. Suddenly it turns into a blind lashing brawl. Hoss Mundy would be appalled, but I win free and run leaping in the only direction I can, with no idea which way I'm going. There's a bit of shouting behind me, so I dodge under the couplings and run directly across the tracks until I come to the edge of the sidings. Looks like someone's back garden, but it's impossible to see if there are passages between the houses. There should be, with terraces like this. Can't stay on this side of things or they'll find me.

Ah! A semicircle of misty glow where a lamppost stands opposite a covered passageway. Over the fence and into something soft. The sudden smell says it's soot. Good gardening, mate, and your cat; thank God it's not a dog. Down the tunnel and turn right.

It's a matter of half-trotting, half-walking now. The smog and my own exhaustion can't be reasoned with. This must be how far? from

Danny's, no, Horace's shelter. They're all there, waiting. Five of them. What's happened? What happened back there when he just gathered her up without needing to break her grip? Is she really dead? She didn't seem stiff and cold anymore, not like I found her. I try to remember things but one by one all the incidents, people, places of the last months seem to sink away, down, down out of sight into a dark ocean.

A twitten opens up beside me. It must lead somewhere. A lamp shines on criss-crossed metal. A lattice; the footbridge. My pursuers could be waiting; here or on the other side. Ten seconds of hesitation, then I bound, light-footed, up the steps and across. If I can't see them they can't see me. This is not ostrich logic; it's…just keep going. The danger point will be at the bottom of the far side. I've tried not to make the bridge shake, so: and I rush down three at a time, trusting in sheer momentum to overwhelm whoever's there.

This procedure leaves me sprawling alone on the pavement, but it's a fair price for at last knowing where I am. And as I gather up for a race towards the scrapyard I begin to care deeply again about Albert Smallwood. How strangely he's slipped in and out of my consciousness. Now he's growing with every step nearer to whatever it is. I still can't imagine how it's going to be.

An image forms of me meeting them emerging from the shelter. All over! Yes, it was most interesting, my boy.

The barbed-wire gate. I hang on it for support while I bend over and spend a while being as sick as a dog; then walk swiftly, coughing, across the expanse of broken bricks, slabs, stove clinker and weeds, towards the little dwelling in the embankment.

Get ready and sort yourself out. Breathe in a last lungful of coal-tainted air. Close your eyes and wish for one thing above all others. Now pull aside the sacking and go in.

Chapter 37

For an instant I am one with those who, from time to time, have broken into the ancient tombs of kings. All the things I see are things I know and recognise; but they're different, distorted in ways open only to the senses we use in dreams; true yet not quite true; barely within the reach of words.

The fire glows in the salvaged kitchen range at the far end of the dugout. It throws a fantail of quivering red bars up the back wall and across the curved corrugations of the ceiling. They flicker only slightly, like an aurora. There is one other light; a stub of candle fixed in its own wax, burning in a niche above the earth shelf covered in old sacks and rags. As if to remind me that I've entered a place of stillness its long flame stands upright and, for a while, I can't take my eyes from the perfection of that flame because it shouldn't look that way.

Only when I can, do I see the faces of my companions. Jackson Armitage, Constance Maybury and Hayden McFee are sitting on the plank bench, their features thrown into shadow-relief by the fire that glows like a dying star and by the little light that never moves. They sit like stone, facing forward, hands on laps like statues of guardian deities, their eyes fixed and unblinking on the earth shelf opposite, beneath its sacred lamp. They seem already to have passed into another world.

What do they see? After an indefinable time watching their carved faces I turn back to the little candle, and with a start I remember Berenice. My eyes are being opened in stages. Now I'll see her, lying on the frayed sacking, but what state she might be in is a question about which I feel quite calm.

Memories are draining from me again. In the last hour they've advanced and retreated like breakers on a shore, but even that thought is hazy and filled with doubt. Maybe that's how it's been. It's hard to tell.

A space has appeared between the tall man and the good-looking woman. I sit down and immediately feel warm and serene. Nothing remains to concern me now except the candle and its flame and the pool of light it casts on the place opposite. The distance between me and the wall seems to have grown, enough to accommodate shadows beyond the shelf that stretches away like a desolate plain overtaken by night.

A huge man lies at full length, the top of his crewcut head bathed in a red glow, his face lit from above. A rolled-up jacket acts as his pillow and his boots and gaiters reach almost to the entrance. He looks giant-like as the light picks out the folds and contours of his clothing, the shape of his skull beneath raw skin and sunken cheeks. I have a vague sense of surprise as though I expected something or someone else to appear there. This must be the man who owns the fire, but not the perfect flame. The smells of damp earth and iron and coalsmoke and exhausted scent have gone; there are no smells now at all.

He lies there, eyes closed, as if sleeping. His features are as peaceful as a child's.

Berenice is sitting by his head, in the alcove by the fire. As I see her face she gives a little smile and I smile back. It's good to see her. We both ran against the time in our own bodies, not even seeking a safe way. I can't remember why, and it doesn't seem to matter anymore.

Nothing happens for a long time. Here lies the Unicorn, tamed. And here are four of us.

Four because Berenice and I are one person. We're one.

So now we can begin. She lays her fingertips on the big man's forehead, just above the bridge of his nose, and as she does so the whole of his great frame seems to subside and soften. The ridges and valleys of his clothes, etched by the light, begin to melt as though eroding into a patient sea. The contours merge and vanish, fading into nothing. Then everything's gone; the man, the girl, the fire, the candle, the walls, the floor. I look down to find my feet have vanished too. We're surrounded by darkness on every side, above and below, an endless void not made of emptiness but of just nothing. I try to take the woman's hand but find instead a hand I know better. Berenice is beside me.

Hayden McFee has been brought to his rendezvous at last.

Another instant passes, with neither length nor breadth. Our senses accustom to the fact that they have no work to do, and only then do indistinct changes begin to suggest themselves. A square of grey grows out of the blackness, striped with vertical bars; followed by its distorted image on a bare plank floor that rises out of the depths below our feet. The retreat of the dark reveals solidifying shapes: a heavy kneehole desk, a wooden swivel chair, filing cabinet, cupboards against a wall. The window shows itself as the upper half of a door beyond which hangs the old unmistakeable smog, the same old yellow-green-grey murk of a March midnight in another time. There's a door in the inner wall too, with a little tin container screwed to it.

The upstairs office of Emmanuel Rosenblum, pawnbroker, in Garnet Street.

A wave of understanding floods in and I ride it to lean forward and observe McFee on the far side of Jackson Armitage. Shanks is absorbed utterly, innocent of his box of tricks and all his gadgets. The detective's jaw is tightened, his eyes narrowed, while he takes in the details of the room and waits.

From outside the door with the barred window comes a distant cough.

At once I stiffen with fear. Another cough, abruptly stifled, then another. All the nightmares awake at that sound. I grip Fernleaf's hand harder and feel her other hand close over mine. A shadow rises up diagonally across the frosted glass, straightens, then sinks to a shapeless hump. The lock begins to rattle faintly, clicking and squeaking. The hump shifts and the noise begins again, ending in a decisive clack. The shadow grows, the handle turns and I brace myself. I've stopped breathing.

The door opens with the quietest trembling of its window and out of the mist steps the silhouette of a thin, stooping man.

He's wearing a long coat and flat cap. As he closes the door behind him a veil of smog squeezes in and goes searching through the room. There's now a strong smell of dry, wormy furniture. The figure puts his muffler up to his face and stands convulsing silently until the fit passes. He's sporting fingerless mittens and his right hand holds what looks like a doctor's bag. I glance sideways at McFee. His body's angled forward, eyes staring. And as the muffler comes down I look at last upon the face of Albert Gordon Smallwood.

He's exactly as I've always imagined him. Droopy moustache, gaunt, pale, wasted features with large, harmless eyes. The peterman of my better angels; not the terrible desiccated creature that stalked my dreams. The strange specialist, the outcast, standing in this dark, cold, empty room at about the same time that I was being born in a noisy, hot, crowded railway station in a place far away. This draws me to him. My beginning; the start of his slow end.

He looks round, puts his bag on the desk and steps silently to the filing cabinet. With no hesitation at all he grasps the corners. It's too heavy to shift for a man in his condition, yet it moves easily and I hear the bump of castors over the gaps in the floorboards. Behind it, in the wall, is a small safe, about two feet above the skirting. I wonder how he knows.

The smog diffuses the light from a street lamp somewhere nearby, enough to pick out major details. Smallwood is barely three yards from me and much nearer to McFee. I can hear him wheezing as he bends down and runs the back of his mittened hand over the metal door. Then he rises slowly, takes his bag from the desk, lays it on the floor and opens it. From it he lifts a small square lantern; his dark lantern. Soon it's throwing a narrow beam directly onto the lock of the safe, leaving the rest of Manny Rosenblum's office in the same gloom as before.

There's no eerie music, no blue aura, no drop in temperature. It's too cold to notice if there is. Everything feels real except us. We are the ghosts, Albert Smallwood the true presence.

The peterman goes down on one knee and closes his eyes. He seems to be praying. Or maybe working out how to deal with this little door that doesn't look like much of a problem. Either way, he stays like that for half a minute or so and his breathing seems to get louder, less regular, until I'm sure he's going to go down in another fit of coughing. But he recovers himself. There's something curiously inoffensive about his actions; I've seen meter readers behaving with more trespass. If we're witnessing a crime, this hardly looks like one.

But it is. The man in the coat and the flat cap has walked a dozen steps into a room where the first step set him against the King's peace and beyond the law.

Suddenly he stiffens, his head swinging round. His fingers snap the Gladstone bag shut. Rigid with alarm, eyes fixed on the door, he neglects to extinguish the lantern. I feel my heart beating in time with his, my ears straining for the next creak on that wooden staircase out in the smog.

But there is no creak, no shadow on the window.

Horace Pressman has not made his call.

The girl has tamed his desire for revenge so that in this half-world Albert Smallwood can reveal his purposes to the man who arrested him.

The peterman lets out a gasp which becomes a cough, then another. His body bends over as he shakes, muffler to his mouth, for a long time. You want to step over and put an arm round his shoulder, but you can't. You can't move; only watch him racked by the disease that's going to kill him. At last he straightens up, opens his bag again and pulls out a small bunch of L-shaped rods and odd-looking keys. He's not going to blow the safe. Thank goodness; the thought that he might has been at the back of my mind in this too-real encounter.

He rolls something between his fingers then presses some of it onto the safe door next to each of the two locks, before swinging the brass lock covers over and onto it. Then he puts a stethoscope to his ears, places the business end by the upper lock and starts inserting the rods one after the other into the big keyhole, delicately fiddling each one and withdrawing it until he gives a grunt and rests back for a moment on his heels. His hands tremble slightly and he coughs gently once or twice. Now he fishes an oval tin out of his pocket and I take another quick look to see how McFee's doing. His face is registering surprise. Smallwood is a master of his trade, but the tin looks like a departure; some new wrinkle in the process of cracking a simple non-combination safe. Then the distinctive aroma of chest lozenges fills the air; fills it too well; and woven into it is the equally distinctive smell of the breath of decay, of the rottenness that's eating him away from the inside. Reminding me Albert is a dead man.

He puts the tin back in his pocket, always with the same deliberate movements. Selecting a key that looks just like most of the others, the peter delicately feels about in the hidden mechanism and at last gives a half-turn twist. Another rest. He doesn't take his Scrooge mittens off.

The second lock takes much longer, though he deals with it with the correct patience of a surgeon. Grimmer men than me have watched this little old man at his craft, trusted in his methods, his control of lethal materials, his genius for weighing and measuring without visible aid. The one who didn't and suffered for it ensured that he suffered too, and made all this necessary. That and one or two other things.

It's done. Wrapping a cloth round his hand he grasps the brass handle and swings it open. Then with the dark lantern he searches the corners inside.

The safe's empty. No surprise to us who know the story. But to my amazement Albert Smallwood shows no emotion whatever.

What's going on here? Is there some joke embedded in this whole mystery? This is the man who's had us running round the landscape, who's owned our waking hours – most of my sleeping hours too – and put us through mental acrobatics and journeys until; what? This? Is this the quest that McFee thinks we've been sent on? The empty tomb?

Hayden McFee looks like a ghost himself.

Perhaps the real ghost has the benefit of hindsight. But that's not it. Back in 1932 he knew it would be empty. Why?

This time his hand goes to an inside pocket of his coat.

My mind's in turmoil, rolling over and over as if tripped up in full flight. He knew it was empty. He's cracking an empty safe and his wife lies dying. What more is there?

The hand emerges clutching a thin bundle wrapped in newspaper. The size and shape of five-pound notes. He puts it in the safe and closes the door.

The brass lock covers swing back into place. The door gets a wipe with a soft cloth, the stethoscope, lantern and probing instruments disappear into the doctor's bag which snaps softly shut. The filing cabinet rolls back against the wall and gets a wipe too. All this is done in unhurried, careful, almost caring movements. Then Albert Smallwood looks around him to see that all is left in order.

We are a wall in this room. All I know is that the bundle of fivers now resting in Manny Rosenblum's safe comes to exactly one hundred and fifty pounds.

Less five pounds.

And he sees us.

All along he has known about us, more than we ever did about him. He looks at us without surprise, his sad eyes falling on each of us in turn. Once more I stiffen with apprehension. This man has laid a long trail and we've pursued him down it, overturning his past, and the pasts of others, without thinking of anything but the prize. He's here, and we're here, because he felt himself wronged. This is about justice. He holds us and we have nothing.

He puts his bag down, takes two steps forwards, and I hear the scuff of his boots on the bare wood floor.

There's a movement to my left, and Hayden McFee walks out in front of us and stands facing him in the space between the kneehole desk and the filing cabinet. There's no light except the luminous presence of the smog.

"Good evening, Albert," he says.

I'm conditioned to hear a spectral, echoing reply. But it's just a hoarse, deferential voice, the voice of an ordinary man; and after all that's happened I feel curiously privileged to hear it.

"Good evening, Mister McFee. How are you, sir?"

"Fair to middling, Albert. Why didn't you tell us?"

"I didn't need it anymore."

The detective nods as if this answer contains all the answers. But not only that. There's a hint in the peterman's words; an invitation. McFee too takes something from an inside pocket. A slightly wrinkled piece of paper, white on one side, the size of a postcard. He holds it out, and for a moment it's the stooping consumptive who seems to be standing upright and the burly man who shrinks under a burden of imperfection.

The paper floats in the dark, held on each side by a finger and thumb, then vanishes into Smallwood's long coat.

"All right, Mr McFee. All right now. Goodnight, sir."

He picks up his bag and walks to the door, turns, touches his cap, and goes out. A creak on the stairs, a cough or two, and he's gone.

Somewhere round the corner a nightwatchman sits by his brazier, and a policeman waits.

Down in his lonely basement by the sea Sailor Chinnery turns in his bed. Across the fogbound city Jack Sidgwick pauses on his rounds among the silent towering gasholders.

Lost in the time between dreaming and waking, we sit in the Anderson shelter in the waning light of the fire. The candle is out, but no telltale smoke curls up from it. Horace is not among us. No one speaks. Then as one we rise stiffly and climb the steps into the iron-strewn waste ground where we stand, each apart, like strangers.

What has just happened has taken on the quality of a dream, but a dream of something utterly real, where people of flesh and blood saw and spoke with each other.

We have not met a ghost. And now, standing on this uneven ground, a strange air of normality surrounds us. An experience has become a recollection.

It's hard to think about anything. I put my hand in my pocket and touch the rolled-up felt of a white beret. I open it out. It's not so white anymore.

She's looking away from me, here under this sea, on this floor of a sunken realm.

"Are you okay, Fernleaf?" I whisper.

"Yes," she says. "Don't ask about anything. We won't understand it any better."

"I know. I know now." We put our arms round each other, not caring who sees.

"The back of your coat's greasy," she murmurs.

"I leaned against a train. I lay down on a railway. I was tired. Is it over? For you, I mean?"

"Yes. I'm sure it is. I hope so."

"And was that it? After all we went through?"

"People sometimes go through more and find much less."

"I thought you were dead."

We kiss each other's cold faces, again and again.

Shanks approaches Hayden McFee.

"A remarkable event. And all my equipment still in the car. Strangely careless of me."

"You didn't need it," I say. "Do the gods exist now?"

He nods, looking up as though hoping to see the stars.

I'm haunted by loose ends. "Mr McFee, why didn't he just tell you when you picked him up? That he was returning what he stole? You'd have believed him, wouldn't you?"

"The law wouldn't have believed him. I'm not the law, even if I think I am."

"So why didn't he just send the money to Mr Rosenblum, or leave it around for him?"

He's talking in a faraway voice. "He nicked it from under the floorboards in Manny's other shop because he was desperate to help Alice. But that was the act of a common thief. He had to return it the way he did because he was a peterman. It was all he had left. And I stopped him."

"Why did he burn the money in Mr Chinnery's brazier? That's what he did, wasn't it?"

"It's late, laddie, but try. He'd have been done for that robbery too. I don't know. Walking about at night with thirty fivers and a record was bad enough, never mind the rest. We can't know everything."

Almost absently I say: that was the message when we visited the barber. He left him on his own for long enough to destroy the evidence. And we didn't see it.

I'm surprised to find that they all hear me. "Such a little thread and everything hung from it," I go on. "So much needn't have happened if we'd only listened harder."

"Our whole fate hangs on threads," says McFee. "You turn right rather than left, or decide to talk to a stranger in a queue, and ten years later you're a millionaire, or a missionary. Or a murderer. That's how our little lives are."

"Let's remember that Mr Smallwood wouldn't have wanted his secret to be revealed then," says Berenice. "He wanted it to happen like this."

"Are you going to pull Horace in?" I say.

He looks at Fernleaf. "Am I?"

"No."

He grunts and walks a few paces away, merging in and out of the smog.

"Why not?" I say to her.

"What had he done? Apart from save me."

"But he had to do that. Didn't he?"

"I suppose. Think of all the things we had to do; that weren't us."

"There's so much we don't know. Was it all for this? Such a little thing. Needed so little understanding."

"It mattered to Albert. For him it was a big thing. It was about justice, and reputation. It mattered, that's all."

"It was a photo McFee gave him; yes?"

"Probably. It's not for us to worry about anymore."

I think of a young woman we've never seen, not even a picture in McFee's flat.

She holds me again. "Do you remember dancing with me?"

"Yes. Why?"

"We danced to a little tune."

She hums a few bars to remind me. "Do you know it?"

"I'd never heard it before."

She smiles. "It's an old shanty: 'For love is kind to the least of men.'"

"Kind to me, then."

A telegram is growing on the key in an outpost office twelve thousand miles away. The dreamer I've never thought about is calling his daughter home. A few urgent days lie ahead before I stand in the crowd at Southampton, the thinning crowd, as the liner recedes from us. Until only Shanks, Alphonse and I remain to turn and walk in silence between the legs of tall cranes and drab customs sheds through drizzle turning into rain.

McFee is shaking Connie's hand. "Perhaps we'll meet again," he says. "In different circumstances, I hope."

I've missed something. Is he going? Have they said all that needs to be said?

"I hope we do," she replies.

Next, Jackson Armitage. We step over to be closer.

"Thank you, Doctor." He wants to say more. Wants to, but can't.

"It's been an experience, Mr McFee, and an honour to have shared it with you. Good luck."

So he is going. We put out our hands. He takes hers, then mine.

"I owe you both a lot. Thank you."

"It ended well," I reply. It sounds like the thing to say.

Buffers clank out on the sidings. "Just keep believing it," he says.

"I think I will."

"Endings are rare, happy endings more so; in my business."

I nod, wisely. Fernleaf squeezes my hand.

"Mr McFee?"

"Yes?"

"We never knew the half of it, did we?"

"Didn't you? Well, even when we do, there's the next half and we only ever know the half of that. It's what keeps us from endings."

"My car is at your disposal," says Shanks.

"Thanks, but I'll make my own way. I need to walk. Maybe say hallo to Jack Sidgwick at the works. And drop in on the Rosenblums; not tonight, though. Goodbye again, Miss; Doctor; and you two, look after yourselves."

He turns and scrunches over the uneven brick-ends and cobbles, but just before he's swallowed up in the mist he turns again and touches his fingers to the brim of his bowler hat. There's a rusty squeak as he pulls aside the gate, but he's invisible now. We stand and listen to the

548

sound of his heelcaps echoing through the pall of night until they die away to silence.

And we are left alone.

Chapter 38

There was a cry in the night. It was still dying on my lips as I woke and began the short struggle to recognise surroundings. Above my head an expressway of cables and ventilation trunking snaked along the ceiling, ghostly in the dark of the little cabin. I lay listening to the thudding hum of engines and the vibration of steel walls and slowly surfaced into the present.

Not an easy thing. Moments before, I'd been on that lonely glacier again, pursuing the figure with the long, long shadow and watched it sink out of sight. I lay heavy with the reminder of a dead weight of helplessness and despair. It was October of 1955; we were out of Colombo for Fremantle with a general cargo and so far an uneventful voyage; and I hadn't had that nightmare for over seven years. Yet it had come back fresh in every detail and pinned me to the bed with the same crushing emotions without telling me why.

Finally I made it to the bridge; properly dressed because there was no going back to bed now.

All quiet. First Officer and helmsman staring out into the night. A gentle swell and an Indian Ocean of stars.

"Morning, Clem. What's up?"

"Can't sleep. Mind if I stand your watch with you?"

It wasn't a stuffy ship, but he had his own ideas. "Why don't you step along to the galley and get yourself a mug of tea? You might run into Mister Griffiths; he likes to rise early and get a breath of air."

Why not? Sure enough, the boilermaker was standing at the taffrail, cigarette end glowing briefly in the warm following breeze.

"Mister Garner! Don't see you here often. Not your watch, is it?"

"No, Griff. Right on both counts."

It's the fool of the family that goes to sea. My parents never got as far as considering my character or possible mental infirmity, so there was no argument when I announced my ambition to go into the Merchant Service. Maybe it was the smells and bustle of the dock, or those smoke-smudges in the Channel sunset, or some desire to criss-cross the globe until one day I'd meet her again. A useful life.

We kept in touch. Whatever her father had had in mind didn't come to anything and the family and the farm stayed where they were. Our letters were about experiences on land and water, until she went to Otago and I continued at the academy of the sea. Everything we wrote had a sprinkling of the old mystery that still fascinated us; questions and guesses about the actions and motives of others, but really about ourselves. And we never referred to the Smallwood meeting as an exorcism or an encounter with a ghost. Ghosts as we understood them weren't real enough.

Shanks did see McFee again for a while, comparing notes to flesh out his researches, but when that was over they parted for good. For a year or two he wrote me and once I stayed at Inglefield. But it was too lonely. In my pocket throughout the visit was the letter he'd written to me at school, and I waited for him to explain just a little about the high stakes for which the game had been played. But the moment did not come. Worst of all was seeing the heart go out of him. Time dragged on and his work remained hidden away. There was no one left that he wanted to convince, even in a world more and more ready to believe. The Shawe-Trittons carried on, creeping around in the shadows, crippled by rumour and turned backs. And the world of exotic ghost-hunting and psychic fireworks held no charms for him. Maybe the serious doctor had secretly hoped that he would never meet a ghost; that the measurable aspects of extra-sensory perception were as far as we needed to go; that it was ultimately controllable and therefore useful. I never got round to asking him. Meanwhile around him the charlatans went on their merry way, and still do.

He kept up a correspondence with Connie until suddenly everything went quiet from New Zealand for both of us.

551

Weeks, then months and years of silence.

The sea was a good place to be in the Fifties. Each time I put ashore somewhere the world beyond the breakwaters looked better and better. Those mornings when the waves burned like molten gold and the headlands rose up black as we stood out into the open ocean, or when we moved through water so wide that the swell seemed as still as a pewter sculpture; that was where you saw in the professional mask the look in each man that told why we were seeking our living in this way and not in one of a thousand others. We all wanted the wilderness.

On the last day of January 1953 our little coaster shouldered its way up the North Sea into a north-westerly that grew into a gale of exceptional violence. The skipper elected to stay out and not run for shelter. Nine others who did the same went missing without trace before morning. The waves that did for them were joined by a tidal surge that breached the dykes of Holland and drowned whole villages. A bad night that few who were out in it ever forgot.

Soon after midnight our rod-and-chain steering gear gave way, and while we wallowed barely under control a huge sea caught us, smashing the superstructure and pouring into our quarters. By the time we'd achieved the twin miracle of repair and survival we'd spent a half-hour rolling our rails under. Maybe there was a lull; maybe we crept further under the lee shore than we realised. Either way the cargo didn't shift, the boilers weren't extinguished and our little coaster made the nearest haven. But my ditty box with most of my belongings, all of Berenice's letters and her photograph had been washed overboard.

I seemed to remember a time when I'd thought and said things that were uncharacteristic of me. These memories faded. Instead, total immersion in the business of the sea. When I got my second mate's ticket I left the coastwise trade for warmer waters. Although I'd heard nothing from her for many years she kept returning. The waves would divide and swash past and the deck throb quietly beneath my feet and I would wonder how that serious young face with the grey eyes and the blonde hair and hint of freckles looked now.

Then the dream came again.

The wake of the ship gleamed with phosphorescence. "Cocos Islands away to port," said the boilermaker. "They say you can smell the land from miles away in these latitudes."

"And can you?"

"Not me. Lost my sense of smell years ago. Nice night, though. Bit of moon to whiten our pale track."

"Yes. Good, that. My sense of smell was better once."

"I'll be taking a turn. Goodnight, Mister Garner."

"There's no need, Griff. I'm thinking, that's all."

"Just the same. Your tea'll be cold."

"Yes. Goodnight."

The road from apprentice to a master's ticket is a long one. In that time all the landmarks of my life disappeared and left me without a history. Being at sea means you miss funerals.

My parents ended up as victims of a Mau Mau ambush, aided no doubt by the alcohol that steered their car into the ditch. Characteristically, more fuss was made of this incident than attended the hundred or so murders of Africans that month. I made it to Nairobi eventually to enter into an inheritance that was neatly cancelled by outstanding debts. One of the investigating officers turned out to be none other than John Davies. We met, but he preferred to discuss the differences in climate between Kenya and London, and I kept clear of bringing up other matters. He seemed well satisfied to be out of England, Mau Mau or not.

While in Valparaiso I got news of the death of Jackson Armitage. He had been a better parent in every way and I made strenuous efforts to get home, but the company didn't see our relationship as I did. My communications drew a reply from the lawyers as well as a long, rambling letter signed by Alphonse and Ludmilla which painted a picture of decline and silence. I wrote again but heard nothing more.

Twice we docked at Wellington and I took the chance to make enquiries about Berenice's family and about Connie. South America came up. The dreamer had set his heart on rearing creatures more exotic than sheep on the Altiplano of Bolivia, and the whole tribe had shipped for the Andes. So Valparaiso had been close. But the trail seemed to peter out in folklore and avoided questions. I felt uncomfortable and let the matter drop, telling myself that some memories are best left as they are. In the dark watches of the night I could believe that somehow even the reality had vanished, shrunk away under the overlays of experience that we add with each retelling. The pale wake was gone, tumbled in upon by the waves until not even the last shreds remained.

My own ship at last. A vessel from an ancient line and among the last of those still tramping for trade in waters where supertankers ran on invisible rails in the ocean and wooden dhows journeyed by current and monsoon. One May morning under a perfect sky and on a copper-beaten sea between Durban and Bombay a great internal explosion ripped the bottom out of the engine room and she began to settle. The crew took to the boats and I led a party below to search for the missing and see what could be done. The answer was nothing. As we turned to go we felt the groan and shock as her back broke and both ends reared up for the final plunge.

Staying with the ship may have been a tradition; going down with half a ship never crossed my mind. Making an early leap to avoid being sucked under I landed feet first on a piece of wreckage that came weltering up from the depths. The impact broke both legs, and ten days in an open boat before being rescued ensured that much of the damage remained permanent. Captains on two sticks weren't highly prized anywhere, especially since I appeared as chief witness at the inquiry and was declared free of all blame. Innocent but unlucky. Unlucky captains find themselves with plenty of time on their hands. A line operating out of Singapore offered me a desk command and I took it.

It didn't satisfy. It's no good waiting for the excitement to kill you. One day I looked out of the window and thought of the South Seas.

A part-time shipping agent in the Gilberts, bang on the Equator and a few degrees east of the Date Line, had begun to think of the fleshpots of Europe. Contacts were activated and we arranged a switch. I soon discovered that the job was quarter agent, quarter fisherman and half beachcomber. Perfect. I put heart and soul into all three and soon realised that I was among the kings of the earth.

Life in the Islands was good. The world around got smaller and so did people, or at least those who forgot how much we need the wilderness. There was time to travel in the boats that plied between these specks on the ocean, to go unhurriedly here and there and enjoy great things that don't change; the big choices of sky, sea, stars. Because things were changing, and in the widening cornucopia of little choices you could see the growing threat to the few big ones. Beachcombing is an excellent barometer of the mess we make of the world.

I took a trip to the Philippines and ended up at one of those cultural receptions at the Spanish Embassy in Manila. Among the gossiping throng was a group of Meztiza girls in their traditional costume of floor-length skirts and blouses with wide lace collars and sleeves; old Spain in the Pacific. And among these stood a tall slim young woman for whom such an outfit was surely designed: Maria Cristina Enriquez, whose ancestors were Admirals of Castile. She was thirty-two years younger than me and, after the sort of courtship that pleases families whose elders have been around for as long as you have yourself, we were married in the church of San Sebastian. She had many sisters, so they did not need to despair of wealthy marriages. We returned to the speck in the ocean and the rich currency of days and hours of pure living.

Maria Cristina called me *Hermano* – brother – because she said I reminded her of her eldest brother. Meeting him had sealed the compliment. Her English was good and my Spanish grew little by little, because we didn't need to talk a lot. The look in a beautiful woman is so much language. But she sang in a way and in those surroundings that made you believe that singing came before talking in the world.

One day she found me standing on a rock washed by exhausted breakers.

"En que estas pensando, hermano?"

"I was far away."

"Ah."

You can be far away if you want. After a few days she asked me again.

"You know my heart," I said. "Tell me the answer."

"Have you heard of closure? It is a North American word now."

I shook my head. We walked along the beach, one arm in hers, the other heavy on the stick.

"Well. Think of music. What if I kept singing a song and stopped just before the end?"

"Even I would become... *frustrado*. Is that right?"

"I have been to Europe many times, hermano. You last saw England before I was born."

London via the United States. While we sat in a sandwich bar in Regent Street she asked me how much things had changed.

"More colour. The whole world seems to be here. That's good. But there's something about the demeanour of the people."

"It was the same in Manila. Everyone looks like they are late for an appointment with the dentist."

Gascoigne's was an antique shop. The old Shawe-Tritton residence was besieged by double-parked cars. I tried to find the site of Danny Ogden's yard but only got lost among industrial estates and wide snarling roads.

"Maybe I remember it wrong. It's like a different planet."

"It was a different planet, I think."

"I'm glad I came, but I don't want to see any more."

"Just the little passage with no end, hermano? Then we can leave for the country."

Unicorn Passage nestled among cranes and roads muddy with construction and the smell of poured concrete. On a summer's afternoon it ought to have been a long way from my memory of it, but it wasn't. Taking a few steps into the narrow area between high, flaking, overgrown walls I saw all the trappings of fifty years ago as if no one had disturbed them. Maria Cristina joined me in the shadow.

"Strange," I said.

"The big road is called Tooley Street," she replied. "I remember it from your story of this place. Tower Bridge is that way. May we see it?"

I nod. Standing here has partly lifted open a book I'm trying to close.

"Our map says that in this street is the London Dungeon," she continues. "Chambers for torture and many horrible experiences."

"That wouldn't surprise me at all."

On my own I walk slowly and stiffly up a drive lined with young limes full of the murmur of bees. Old people sit in chairs enjoying the sunshine, chatting with women wearing blue overall coats. One of them detaches herself and shows me inside to the sun lounge.

"You'll have to talk slowly to him," she whispers. "Not loud. He isn't deaf but he is rather confused."

I look down at him. His head is completely bald. His skin hangs on his face in folds and his eyes are speckled, staring forwards. Both hands have their fingers curled inwards and tremble ceaselessly. They're all like this. This is a room with statues.

"Hallo, Mister McFee. My name is Clement Garner. Perhaps you remember me."

He just stares forwards. I mention a few names, a few details. To us they wouldn't seem too bizarre, but the nurse's eyes are on me. I straighten up.

"Not much use, really."

She smiles faintly. "I'm afraid not; best to leave it. Thank you for coming, though. You've been his only other visitor."

We hire a car and drive from Oxford. The weather remains fine and warm and reeks of childhood summers, or so I tell Maria Cristina. She laughs and calls it bearable. I want to avoid main roads and bypasses so she steers us down country lanes where I can spend time preparing myself. Every now and then she slows down to glance at me, but I'm all right.

Sunlight dapples through overhanging trees. We're nearly there.

"Stop! Stop. We've gone past. Can you back up?"

The car straddles the entrance between two square pillars. "Okay, hermano?"

"I'll be fine."

She helps me out and hands me my sticks. She doesn't offer to drive right up to the house because she has more imagination. "Say, in two hours by the Laughing Angler? It's a couple of miles further on."

"Are you sure it is still there?"

"It's in the book." She gives me a long kiss and ruffles my hair.

"You will be unfaithful to me for an hour, but I forgive you."

She laughs and kisses me again.

I like her serious humour. "I shall betray you, and then return."

She drives away and I begin my four-legged walk down the wide gravel. They know I'm coming, the people here whose name I don't recognise. I look right and left to see what they've done with the Doctor's domain. Very little. The broken glasshouses are still there, covered with twisting trunks and vines that have pulled the woodwork to pieces. On the other side the gloomy pine plantation stretches away in shadow behind a wrought-iron fence and I watch the straight trunks of the trees pass before each other as if they've all decided at once to make a discreet withdrawal. The birdsong has died away already. It was always quiet along this stretch with its scent of needles and its soughing way of containing the wind. The house should appear round the next bend.

When it does, I stop. Nothing seems to have changed at all. The box tree stands in its circle and the silence carries only the distant cawing of rooks and the croo-croo of a woodpigeon close at hand. Everything stands; all the verticals stand, waiting, as if a moment ago they were in movement and suddenly became still at my approach. They seem to be casting quick looks at each other, eyeing me up; considering the stranger.

I walk across the front of the house to the far side of the box tree and receive a surprise. The ground slopes away sharply in a well-groomed lawn. The grass smells of mowing. Surely this wasn't here then? This was the way to the woods and Hob's Pond. You passed across rough meadow and a thicket to leave sight of the house. I turn round. There are rabbits beside the gravel, moving in short unconcerned hops. The air has become luminous; the silence huge. A golden-green haze softens the edges of everything. I know it's all here; the stagnant ponds, the gardener's cottage, the birch spinney and the twisty chimneys; and that whoever lives here now is still in tune with it. I pull the iron handle of the bell and hear it echo inside. Dogs begin to bark; obviously rabbit-friendly dogs that don't come to the door. A white-haired, thin man with a stoop, wearing a dark jacket and striped trousers, meets my gaze.

"Good afternoon, sir."

"Good afternoon. Captain Garner."

The white-haired man registers a quick description of me. "Would you care to wait here, sir? I shall return presently."

A woman answered my letter in crippled handwriting, but her generous reply gave few details. I suppose from this that she lives alone and would rather be sure of me when I appear at her door. It seems reasonable. The dogs are quiet. I look closely at drainpipes and climbers and old brick round the Tudor-arched porch for the first time in my life. There was once a script prepared for this moment but I put it away. I'm hovering between two worlds while I wait by an entrance that used to be mine.

"This way, sir."

I follow him into a small flagstoned hall where I stand, open-mouthed, as he disappears. When he turns back for me he puts on a patient look and waits.

I can hear clocks clunking in distant passageways.

"Tell me if I'm right. That was the study. That leads to the panelled room and the gallery and the library's at the far end; that way is the kitchen and you were going into the billiard room. Is that right?"

"In a manner of speaking, sir. This way."

The billiard room no longer, but a small drawing room that looks like the headquarters of the house. I see the fireplace from which indistinct voices drifted up over fifty years ago. Then I see the old woman in the wheelchair behind a tray-table surrounded by Scotch terriers. They all look up together. I take her hand with a careful grip, enclosing bunched fingers.

"Good afternoon, Captain. A pleasant trip? All the way from the South Seas! We're honoured. Do sit down."

There's a fly-buzzing stillness about this room that makes me think most of the house stays uninhabited; that the rooms and their sparse furniture go through summer and winter alone. I try to remember the woodsmoke-polish aura of childhood but all I get is smells of old person and dog. Still she seems bright-eyed and interested. Tea is served.

"Might I ask how you earned your sticks? Not arthritis, I hope, or we would share a problem."

A split-second of recollection, and a whole second of summoning a reply.

"An accident; at sea."

"Ah, I see. I remember you, Captain, as a small boy. I used to come to the gatherings here before the war and occasionally during it. You always seemed to be somewhere else. I recall the cook used to know where to find you when Jackson wanted to take his family groups. That's what he called them; his family groups. He had hardly any real family of course."

"Are you family? I couldn't tell from the name."

"Oh, yes. One of the few. He wouldn't have mentioned me to you. Almost too distant to deserve this fine house, but he left it to me. His sister wouldn't have wanted it anyway. So here we are."

"Are you in one of these photographs, here on the wall?"

"Yes. The second one. You're not there. Don't bother to study it, Captain; I lost those looks a very long time ago. Jackson's not in any of them. He never married of course."

"Did he ever have anyone in mind?"

"You know he did."

"I have the feeling you knew all about it."

"If he had achieved his heart's desire, Connie might have been sitting here to receive you. Would you have liked that?"

"I think some memories are best left where they are."

"Is your wife like her?"

Old women and their direct questions. "Yes, she is."

"And a little like Berenice?"

She sees my eyes narrow momentarily but there's no drawing back in her look. I have to remember that I'm sitting here in her house because of all those events half a century ago, so she has a perfect right to press me. Maybe she knows what I'm after better than I do. But I don't answer because it's not the way I want to enter this.

She studies me for a long moment. "As you know, the LSI was breaking up over Jackson's work. There was the Oxford faction and the London faction; a bit like the Civil war, I used to say. But in the end he was practically on his own. Of course there were terrific political undercurrents. I'm sure you weren't unaware of it." Her eyes gleam like the eyes of her dogs. "He became very withdrawn, you know."

There are photographs on the mantelpiece; black and white and not very enlarged. I glanced at them when I came in but the rituals come first. Now I allow myself a longer look.

"Excuse me."

I get out of the chair and take one stick with me. My heart's beating a little. The old woman's eyes are on my back as I search along the ten or so prints. Fourth along is a faded snapshot in a plain leather holder. A

561

girl, in her early twenties; head and shoulders. She wears a check shirt with neckerchief and a pair of snow-goggles sits on her blonde fringe. Her head is tilted back and she smiles a serious smile. A coil of rope is slung across her chest and behind her a jagged mountain rears up clothed in summer snow.

"Mount Aspiring, Captain."

"She said she would climb it; and Mount Cook."

I'm being drawn into the picture. My back tingles. One of the dogs whimpers and a lone fly scrabbles up and down a window in the stillness.

"How did it happen?"

"It was in, let me see…"

"I think I know when."

"Of course. She was with an expedition in the Southern Cordilleras of the Andes. There were peaks which few if any had climbed, so she was in her element. She was traversing a very steep part, alone; I don't know why; a terribly difficult stretch. Halfway across she must have disturbed a hidden nest or something. One of those great birds, an eagle or a condor, swooped down and caused her to lose her footing. She fell."

My heart has become still.

"Where is she buried?"

"Her body was never found, Captain. She must have disappeared into one of those deep crevasses thousands of feet below. She is buried in the depths of the glacier where she fell."

The old woman gives me time.

"I had the picture in the great room taken down," she says quietly. "I never did care for it."

When I came, part of my idea was to look round the house, to stand in the octagonal bedroom and see if it contained…what? Now all such thoughts are gone.

562

"You've been very kind," I say. "I wonder if I might walk around the garden a while?"

She knows I'm going to say this. "I usually take my medication and an hour's rest at this time. So I shall say goodbye now. It has been a pleasure, Captain." She's entitled to lie a little. It's her house, and my need. Again I take her hand.

Hob's Pond ripples clear and sparkling, a shoreline of birches and willows. There are wheelchair tracks in the earth, by this little inland sea in a mysterious country, and birdsong echoes. Far away the distant growl of a bypass comes and goes.

I make a circuit of the garden. The tennis court has vanished under brambles and wild plum trees, but beyond the ha-ha, over the waving barley, stands the dark knot of trees that guard the church from the sun while it sinks tilting into the earth. But after all, these sights are only a preparation.

An arch of ivy leads into the sunken garden. Away to the right the twin poplars stand in the water meadow, more ragged than ever. Their leaves clatter like rain in the tiny breeze. Well-chosen and well-tended bushes of colour overhang the path and fill the bowl of the fountain. The house looms up behind me.

The seat is still there. I approach it and sit down, keeping strictly to one end.

The wood is warm. The air is warm. A blackbird hops along the flagstones. The whispering of the weir reaches me and everything inside my skin is in riot against repose. My heart is unquiet, but closing my heart will leave the book open.

I let it all go. There are things that can't be reduced to words.

As I walk along the drive towards the road I hear tyres on the gravel behind me. The white-haired man draws up in one of those high-roofed cars for wheelchairs.

"Can I drive you somewhere, sir? The road isn't really suitable for walking."

I'm glad to see he drives slowly. A couple of cars queue behind us, late for the dentist.

"Robertson, sir."

"Sorry, Robertson. Have you been here since the Doctor died?"

"No, sir. I didn't meet his staff. Except for Mr Moffat. He was my cousin."

"I might have run into you at some time, then."

"I'm sure I would have remembered, sir."

"We should be coming up to Symond's farm."

Consolidated Feed Mills. The school has become the Community Centre. But few new houses. Litter hanging in the branches provides some of the hedgerow colour.

"Here we are, sir."

He helps me out, this older man. "Goodbye, sir. I hope your visit was satisfactory."

I meant to wait outside the Angler, but the station looks less than derelict. It's in the hands of a conservation society, so I push open the ticket office door and smell new paint; the chocolate and cream of the Great Western. In the cool shadow framed photos hang on the matchboard wall. I look for Jim Haskins. A clean-shaven man wearing medals might be him, standing on the platform before my time. The platform canopy's missing so the sunlight hits me as I step out onto what was once the threshold of adventures.

Two cattle wagons and a tank engine obscure the level crossing. There's no activity except some muffled hammering from the signal box. It has a couple of broken windows and all its bright levers were long ago stripped out for scrap. But the track is still in place, weed-covered and rusty.

I stand for a while, slowly looking around me. My mind has no trouble filling in and refurbishing this once-enchanted place. Once more I feel alive and floating; delivered from the past, each moment filled only with time to come. Day One. Only now I hear not the receding sound of a one-carriage train, but the far-off, rhythmic roar of breakers on the reefs of a distant ocean.

I walk along the platform, under the place where the footbridge was, to the end where it slopes down into a mass of willow-herb sprouting from the ballast, and look towards vanishing-point where the rails disappear among tall trees that seem as old as churches.

Our lives are like bubbles on the tide. We float briefly, jostling and sparkling, on the skin of experience between deep and sky, before we burst and divide our substance among them.

Dark dreams and light dreams. I think of the sleepers and their dreams.

Hayden McFee in his sunlit room; Jackson Armitage and Albert Smallwood in their long home. They moved in a world of ambiguity and distortion and perhaps now it is only the old peterman who sleeps well. He got justice in large measure and asked for the small measure which let him rest at last. He will not come again, and I have said my farewells now to each of them. But not to Fernleaf. She will stay with me because she showed me how beginnings are always the best part. And anyway her journey, like mine, is not over.

Berenice sleeps, borne down from the mountains which one day, ages hence, will lay her at the feet of an unpeopled earth. She understood the real things we are all part of. Her dreams, I know now, are still and white and peaceful.

It's time to go.

When I walk through the ticket office a car will be waiting, with a young woman standing beside the door. She too knows about the journey.

"Master Clement?" she will say with her beckoning smile. "This way please?"

About the Author

Edward Barham was born in 1947,
the eldest child of a much-decorated
Regular soldier and an Italian partisan
who met at the liberation of the little
walled city of Urbino in the Appenine
foothills. His parents decided to bring
him up speaking Italian until he could
learn English at school. This, com-
bined with his lifelong acquaintance
with Urbino, left him with a deep
respect for both languages and for the
ideals of the Renaissance.

He was educated at Brighton, Hove
and Sussex Grammar School, where he excelled at history, art, athletics, chess and the Cadet Corps. At the age of seventeen he was chairman of a religious magazine and had translated the works of Oxford
poet John Heath Stubbs. Following a period of work as a gravedigger
and gardener in a convent he read History specialising in War Studies at
King's College London, where his chairmanship of debates brought him
into contact with some of the prominent figures of the 1960s.

Refusing the offer of an academic career he worked as tutor to a
Brunei prince and then in International and Maritime Telecommuni-
cations before spending some years in primary education. Throughout
the early part of his life he sought adventure, often alone, in a wide
range of remote environments and served in the Royal Naval Reserve.
In 1983 he stood in the General Election for the Green Party in North
Wiltshire. He left teaching before what he saw as the advent of a
prescriptive, mechanistic philosophy of education, but returned some
years later to teach in a Special School for behaviourally disturbed boys.
His message to his pupils was that command of English is the widest
gateway to a more abundant life.

Now retired, he continues his nearly forty years' project of land-scaping an acre of country garden in which he has built a Cotswold-style astronomical observatory. His many interests include astronomy, construction, public speaking and military history. He adheres to the precepts of Stoicism and is happily married to Ursula, a talented musician who fills the house with beautiful sounds. Edward has two children, Kelvin and Eleanor, from his first marriage. Both professionals, they also write.

Apart from *Peterman* in 1986, Edward Barham has written radio and stage plays, short stories and a musical. He is a cheerful sufferer from the 'divine discontent' which spurs us on to further creative efforts and fulfilling days.

Acknowledgements

They say that writers of books tread a lonely path. It's not entirely true. What may set out as a solo journey soon attracts company; some for a part of the way, some who stay by you until the end comes in sight; and a few who guide you into the unknown realms of the scrutiny of strangers. To all these generous supporters I owe a great debt:

Alyson, who at the age of fourteen took the manuscript out of its decade and a half in a dark drawer, read it, understood it and told me her generation was ready for stories told in this way.

Kerensa, who read, analysed and revealed even more complexity than I thought I had put in myself.

Elly, my daughter; welder, fabricator of wonderful objects and a prolific writer herself, whose instinct for written culture and – with much humour at my expense – knowledge of the arcane workings of IT have been characteristically helpful.

Laurence, Ellie and Angela, who convinced me that I was speaking to all ages and backgrounds.

Lis, also a writer among her many accomplishments; the first to hear the story spoken after it lay mute for over thirty years. Her introduction to my publisher helped break another kind of silence.

My wife Ursula. Her love, care and encouragement ensured that the author emerged from self-imposed obscurity as possibly the happiest, most fortunate man who ever tried to write anything.

Vicki Watson, founder, body and spirit of Callisto Green. She took on an old man for his one novel, written a generation before, and showed how the serious business of bringing a book into the light can be full of interest, excitement and humour. Multi-talented, an author in her own right, her sure judgement and exacting standards have made me a better writer. Just imagine your dream publisher. I need say no more.

Lightning Source UK Ltd.
Milton Keynes UK
UKHW020637300721
388036UK00014B/1529